Inventrici

I0593152

Ivana L. Truglio is a book lover. She always has been! Ivana made up her mind to be a writer when she was six years old and never looked back.

Through the years of learning to fly, studying archaeology and ancient history, and finally working in office jobs, she never stopped reading and writing. For 11 years, she worked for multinational publishing companies in the tax team (don't hold that against her!) and learned all the tricks of the trade to start her own publishing company.

Contact Ivana
www.ivanaltruglio.com
Facebook: @ivanatruglio
Instagram: @ivanaltruglioauthor

Also by Ivana L. Truglio

The Paradise Series
Rilla
Illaria
Crystal Dragons
Child of Paradise

Kora's Choice

Inventrici

Guild Series

Ivana L. Truglio

JONQUIL
PRESS

First published in Australia in 2022
by Jonquil Press
ABN: 99871403756

A catalogue record for this
book is available from the
National Library of Australia

ISBN: 978-0-6483416-4-2 (paperback)

Cover illustration by Jane Green

Typeset in Adobe Garamond Pro 10pt/11.5pt

For my son,
the creator of countless Lego wonders and Minecraft worlds.

ACKNOWLEDGEMENTS

My first thanks, dear reader, go to you. Every time someone reviews or rates my books online, it makes me smile so much my cheeks hurt. It's usually the only way I get to find out what you thought. Of course, it's also a great way for other people to decide whether or not they should read my books. The power is in your hands.

Thank you to my wonderful editor, Anicee Dowling. Without her wise and encouraging words, this book would not be the book you have in your hands. She is endlessly patient with me, even when she wants to grab the characters and shake them for being so clueless. Her humour got me through the difficult days of the editing process.

I thank my old writing group who laughed so hard at one particular character sticking his foot in his mouth. Maddy, Sam and Tom, thanks for the late night chats and the time you took reading the very first drafts of every chapter. I appreciate it more than you know!

To my wonderful beta readers, Canela Stockmann, Marisa Truglio, Tori Johnson and Zola. Your thoughts on how to shape and smooth out the storyline was invaluable. Special thanks to Marisa Truglio for making sure I didn't make a complete mess of the Italian sections!

As always, thank you to my family. I spend most of my free time writing, often late into the night. They always support me and offer suggestions, whether helpful or not!

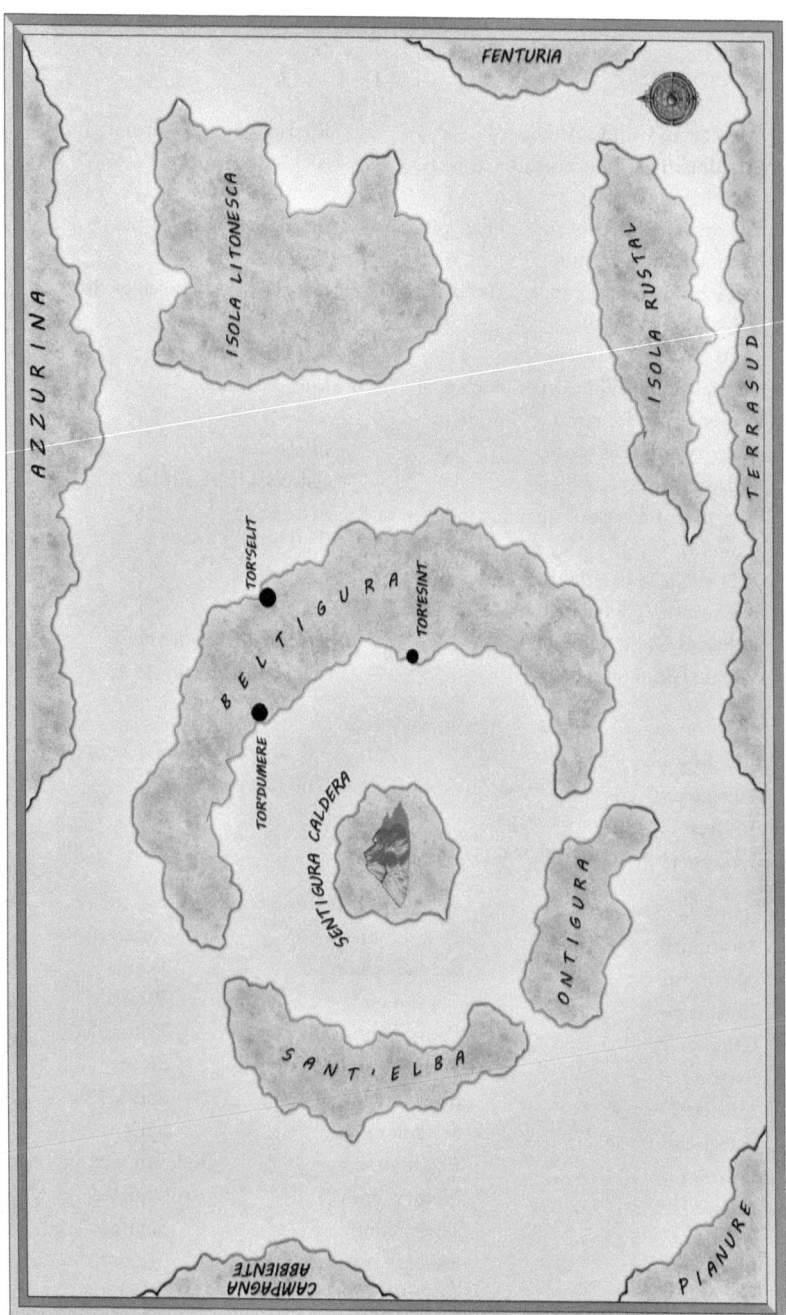

LIST OF TERMS

GUILDS

Mercantili Guild (merchants) — Mercantessa (f.)/Mercante (m.)

Alchimisti Guild (alchemists who also function as doctors) — Alchimista (n.)

Inventrici Guild (inventors of anything mechanical) — Inventrice (f.)/Inventore (m.)

Gioiellieri Guild (jewellers, specialising in gold, silver or coral) — Gioielliera (f.)/Gioielliere (m.)

Sarti Guild (seamstresses and tailors) — Sarta (f.)/Sarto (m.)

Musicisti Guild (musicians, including composers and singers) — Musicista (n.)

Falegnami Guild (carpenters) — Falegname (n.)

Calzolai Guild (cobblers) — Calzolaia (f.)/Calzolaio (m.)

Artiste Guild (artists, including painters and sculptors) — Artista (n.)

Fabbri Guild (smiths, including blacksmiths, goldsmiths and silversmiths) — Fabbro (n.)

Ballerini Guild (dancers) — Ballerina (f.)/Ballerino (m.)

Vetraie Guild (glassblowers) — Vetraia (f.)/Vetraio (M.)

MONEY

1 Gold	3 Electrums	60 Silvers	600 Coppers
1 Electrum	20 Silvers	200 Coppers	
1 Silver	10 Coppers		
1 Copper	smallest unit of money		

CALENDAR

Mercantili	First month	Autumn
Alchimisti	Second month	Winter
Inventrici	Third month	Winter
Gioiellieri	Fourth month	Winter
Sarti	Fifth month	Spring
Musicisti	Sixth month	Spring
Falegnami	Seventh month	Spring
Calzolai	Eighth month	Summer
Artiste	Ninth month	Summer
Fabbri	Tenth month	Summer
Ballerini	Eleventh month	Autumn
Vetraie	Twelfth month	Autumn

DAYS OF THE WEEK

Gildadi	Trading Day (Guild Day)
Ramedi	Trading Day (Copper Day)
Argentodi	Trading Day (Silver Day)
Legaramedi	Trading Day (Electrum Day)
Orodi	Trading Day (Gold Day)
Mercatodi	Market day, every second week for Guilds, every other week for regular vendors
Riposidi	Rest day

GLOSSARY

Amministratore (m.)/Amministratrice (f.)/ Amministratori (pl.)	administrators
Amore	love
Companion	life partners who have had a commitment ceremony
Coppola	flat hat
Corso	course
Funicolare	cablecar
Limoncello	lemon liqueur
Maestra (f.)/Maestro (m.)	Guild Mistress/Master
Mamma	mum
Marinaia (f.)/Marinaio (m.)/Marinai (pl.)	sailors
Miglio/Miglia	mile/miles
Nipotina	granddaughter
Nonna (f.)/Nonno (m.)	grandmother/grandfather
Panettiere	baker
Pastricceria/Pasticcerie	pastry shop/s
Papà	dad
Piazza	square
Piede/Piedi	foot/feet
Pollice/Pollici	inch/inches
Ristorante	restaurant
Signora/Signore	miss/mister
Tesoro	treasure
Trinzale and lenza	decorative headwear
Vecchietta (f.)/Vecchietto (m.)/Vecchietti (pl.)	old people
Via	street
Zona	zone

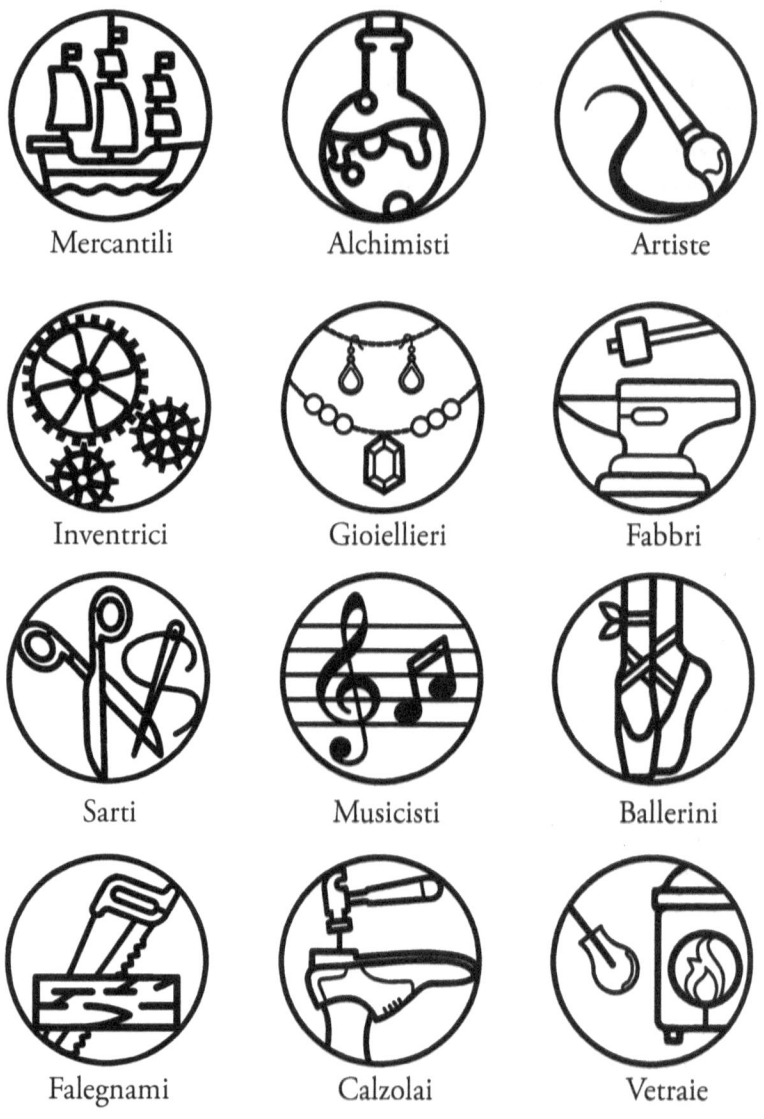

Mercantili

Alchimisti

Artiste

Inventrici

Gioiellieri

Fabbri

Sarti

Musicisti

Ballerini

Falegnami

Calzolai

Vetraie

Author's note: For the sake of having a single version for each Guild name, I alternated between the feminine and masculine for those that weren't gender neutral, completely understanding that this is not how the Italian language works.

Chapter 1 – Gildadi 23 Vetraie 229 Years After Implosion

Riposidi 8 Ballerini
226 Years After Implosion
To Serenita di Albertina, 17 Via Mercantile, Tor'Dumere
From Sebetine di Serenita, 6 Via Corallo, Tor'Esint

Dear mamma,
I've bought my ticket. I'll be arriving on 24 Ballerini on the funicolare. Hopefully, you'll agree to come back with me to finally meet Teresina. I can't believe she's already three years old! She's such a treasure during the day. If only she would sleep through the night. She wakes every few hours and I'm so very tired. She has more dreams than I ever did!
I try to keep her quiet for Telchide. He's working so hard to earn his Silver Guild Mark, and once he does, he'll finally be eligible to get an apprentice to help around the workshop and we'll be able to afford a meal out once in a while. Sometimes I feel like I barely get to see him, even though his workshop is just downstairs.
He asks me questions about his orders, and I can't remember half the things he talks about, I'm so tired. I feel like I'm letting him down.
I need your help, mamma. We both do. I hope you will reconsider coming back to Tor'Esint with me.
Sebetine

Telchide sat at his workbench re-reading his Sebetine's letter for the thousandth time, hoping for some hidden clue but, as usual, he found none. When his beloved companion had failed to arrive in Tor'Dumere as promised, Serenita had set out immediately for Tor'Esint. She'd appeared on his doorstep on 25 Ballerini and handed him the letter, demanding to know where her daughter was.

He knew Serenita couldn't read and would've had to find someone to read it to her. How it must have pained her to let someone else read the tear-stained letter from her daughter, begging for help. He knew she was angry about that, but he didn't know where Sebetine had gone. Three years later, they still didn't know.

A shuffle on the stairs told him Serenita was awake. He folded the letter and placed it back in his shirt pocket, but he wasn't quick enough.

"Telchide Inventore, if you don't stop reading that letter, I'll burn it!" Her anger snuffed out as she put her head in her hands. "None of this would've happened if I'd come the first time she asked me to."

Telchide shook his head. "It wasn't your fault any more than it was mine," he said. "I could've gone with her ... or insisted she stay."

His shoulders slumped. There were no tears anymore. He'd cried them all out in the first few months.

"If we only knew what happened to her, perhaps *then* I could put my mind to rest."

Serenita pulled up a chair beside him. For a moment she sat in silence, her wrinkled and age-spotted hands folded in her lap.

"Chide, you did everything you could. Her likeness in every newssheet in Beltigura. Posters in every marketplace in Tor'Esint and Tor'Dumere. You convinced the Mercantili Guild to help you search the funicolare with a picture of her likeness."

"And all I managed to discover is that she never switched over to the Tor'Dumere funicolare at the waystation. Don't you ever wonder where she is?"

Serenita threw her head back and sighed.

"Caldera's smoke! I love my daughter, Chide, but I can't go on hoping she's still alive. It's been years and my poor heart can't take it anymore. I must assume she's dead. You should do the same."

Telchide stared at her in shock – both at her language and her assumption. Serenita pursed her lips.

"Don't stare at me like that, Chide. You make me feel like a monster. I'm going to make your daughter some breakfast. Do you want any?"

He shook his head firmly. There was so much to be done. He had three orders for music boxes and their owners would not wait indefinitely, even if he was the most acclaimed music box Inventore in Tor'Esint.

Things had been so much easier before the Inter-Guild Edict. He'd been able to work with the Musicisti then, to get every note exactly right. Since the Edict, a little over three years ago, he'd had to do it alone. As he was an Inventore, not a single Musicista would sell him even the sheet music to work from. His clients had to bring that to him themselves or be happy with the selection of music he had already accumulated.

One, in particular, hadn't been happy with Telchide's selection and insisted on a longer tune than Telchide had ever managed before. It required a larger drum, a longer strip of copper and, of course, a larger music box. At least he'd been able to negotiate a higher price for it, but his Silver Guild Mark only helped so much. If he didn't gain his Electrum Guild Mark soon, it would become more difficult to keep both his family comfortable and his workshop fully equipped.

Telchide sighed and went back to work. It was all he could do.

***

The back door slammed back against the wall with a loud bang. Telchide looked up from his work as wind blustered into the room and scattered the screws from his workbench.

"For Caldera's sake, shut the door!" he yelled at Eduardo.

The old Alchimista rolled his eyes and struggled to shut the door. He'd only just closed it when Telchide's six-year-old daughter, Teresina, raced down the stairs and leapt into Eduardo's arms.

"Ardo!"

Telchide couldn't help but smile. Teresina loved the Alchimista like a nonno. They were fortunate their houses backed onto each other. It had made it that much easier when the Inter-Guild Edict had come into effect. They could still see each other without using their front doors and raising suspicion that they might be collaborating.

"Teresina, you get heavier every day!" Eduardo complained as he eased her onto the floor.

Teresina smiled at him proudly. "Well, I *am* six now, after all."

"Six? I don't believe you! Why, only yesterday you were just a babe."

Teresina laughed. "Oh Ardo, that wasn't yesterday. That was *years* ago!"

Eduardo absently rubbed the top of his balding head. "I suppose you're right. How the years fly!"

Telchide sighed. The years seemed to fly by, but the days dragged on.

"Chide, if you don't hurry up, Nestore will have to set off multiple explosions tonight," Eduardo said.

Telchide picked up the fallen screws and placed them carefully in a wooden box on his workbench. He picked up his notebook and tucked it safely away in his waistcoat along with two pencils. As he was putting on his coat, Teresina tugged at his sleeve.

"Papà, are you sure it's safe?" she asked, looking up at him with her big brown eyes, imploring him to stay. How her eyes reminded him of her mother. "I don't want the Mercantili Guild to lock you away."

Telchide shared an anxious look with Eduardo. He knelt on one knee and sat Teresina on the other.

"Resi, we're very careful when we meet. It's a big secret that the Mercantili Guild doesn't know about."

"But what if they find out?" she asked, pouting.

"No Mercantili in their right mind would walk into the Exploding Beakers when Nestore is setting off one of his concoctions." Telchide muttered, "No Inventrici in their right mind would, either."

"But what if?" she insisted.

Telchide heaved a big sigh. "*If* they do, then they would still have to prove that we were working together, rather than simply sharing a meal."

"Papà, I don't want to lose you too," she said, burying her head in his chest.

It almost broke Telchide to hear those words. He swallowed the sudden lump in his throat and hugged her tightly.

"You won't lose me, Resi. They wouldn't lock me away for a meeting. At the most, they might force the Inventrici Guild to lower me back to a Copper Guild Mark or strip me of my Guild status. But I doubt they'd bother. I'm not important enough."

She flung her arms around his neck and hugged him tightly. Telchide hugged her once more, then gently prised open her fingers. With practised ease, Serenita came over and took Teresina's hand.

"Be safe," was all she said before taking his daughter upstairs.

Telchide waited until the two were gone before locking up the workshop. He and Eduardo were known to be old friends. It was the only reason their continued appearances together hadn't been questioned. Yet.

***

The Exploding Beakers wasn't far from Telchide's workshop. Just a few blocks closer to the docks. Telchide and Eduardo walked together in silence most of the way, past the metallic spiders climbing gas lamps to light them, afraid of being overheard by the wrong people. Better to wait until they were within the relative safety of the disreputable Alchimisti tavern.

As they approached the final corner, a loud blast went off accompanied by billowing, enticingly scented blueberry smoke. Telchide and Eduardo rushed the final few pollici to enter under the cover of smoke. They weren't the only ones. Telchide couldn't count how many others might have used the diversionary smoke to hide their entry.

The only reason the tavern hadn't yet been raided during their meetings was because Nestore always had a stash of beakers ready to explode at any minute. The explosions in and of themselves were not uncommon in many parts of Zona Alchimisti, but the abundantly fragrant smoke was a unique touch. Nestore had earned his tavern quite the reputation with his various smokes. He set off at least one a night to keep up appearances and throw off the Mercantili Guild.

Though Ministro Ercolano technically ran the city, independent of every Guild, everyone knew how powerless he was to prevent the consequences of the Trading Edict and the Inter-Guild Edict, or bring an end to them. How the Mercantili Guild had ever convinced him it was in the best interest of Tor'Esint for the Edicts to be proclaimed was anyone's guess. When it became apparent that the Tor'Esint Amministratori were lax in enforcing the Edicts, the Mercantili Guild had taken it upon themselves to ensure it. Few were happy about that, and those who spoke out against their usurpation of power, or ignored the Edicts found out just how dangerous the Mercantili Guild could be.

Telchide hung up his coat alongside everyone else's on the wall. He quickly counted fourteen coats. There should have been seventeen.

With a gnawing anxiety in his stomach, Telchide helped the gathered Inventrici and Alchimisti to drag three heavy wooden tables together against the stone floor, far from the marble-topped bar where Nestore created his flammable concoctions. Eventually, they might break off to discuss individual projects, but first they would hold their general meeting.

Telchide ordered a smoking limoncello from the bar and took a seat between Eduardo and Dania. They were respectively the eldest and youngest Alchimisti in the group. Telchide looked around the tables, trying to figure out who was missing. His eyes met Aveline's for a moment and he smiled.

Aveline was a talented Inventrice, proven by her Electrum Guild Mark. She'd been fortunate enough to submit her most recent Great Work before the Inter-Guild Edict came into effect. He envied her that. Every invention he'd created since the Edict could not be submitted to the Inventrici Guild for fear they'd suspect he'd worked with another Guild to create it. The problem was, they wouldn't be wrong.

His music boxes had earned him his Silver Guild Mark before the Edict, but he couldn't bring himself to submit his message box. The only working one he had was linked between his house and Eduardo's. It allowed them to send messages directly to each other without the need to meet. He didn't have time to create another one to submit to the Inventrici Guild and, even if he did, he was afraid they'd search his house to see if there was one connected to anyone he shouldn't be associating with.

The problem with the message box was that it printed each message on a strip of paper. If those papers weren't discarded properly – ideally burned – then they could easily be used as evidence against both Telchide and Eduardo. Their careers would be over in one fell swoop if a stray message fell into the wrong hands.

Lucrezia banged her tankard against the table, drawing everyone's attention. Telchide looked towards her and suppressed the urge to roll his eyes. Lucrezia was almost twenty years his senior and one of the oldest Alchimisti in their group. He did not have to wonder how she'd seized control of their group in the first place – the force of her personality was reason enough. They hadn't gotten along since the first time they'd met years ago, when he was still on his Copper Guild Mark and excited to try working with Alchimisti. He'd mistakenly brought one of Nestore's exploding concoctions to their table before realising it wasn't his drink. Everyone at his end of the table, including Lucrezia, had been covered in small cuts and stank of oranges the entire evening. Most of them had laughed off the accident, but it had fixed him in Lucrezia's mind as a useless lavalump and she never bothered hiding her opinion of him.

"We're down to fifteen. Ignio and Pietra have been stripped of their Guild status. Caio is missing."

A ripple of anger flowed through the group.

"What do you mean 'missing'?" Eduardo asked. "Dead or in prison?"

Lucrezia looked down at her notes. "Missing. That's all his companion told me. He was taken away by Tor'Esint Authorities last night and she's yet to locate him. Our hope is that he's in prison. At least then, once this ridiculous Edict is revoked, we'll have some chance of getting him out."

"That won't help Ignio and Pietra," Dania muttered beside Telchide.

Lucrezia glared at her. "If you have something to say, Dania, say it loud enough for everyone to hear."

Dania shook her head. Telchide wished he could pat her on the back, but he didn't know her well enough.

"That's five Alchimisti now," Aveline said loudly enough for all to hear.

Telchide looked across the table at her. Her eyes were on Lucrezia. He knew she didn't quite like the Alchimista either, but she usually seemed to tolerate Lucrezia's company better than he did. Lucrezia never hid her views about anyone, no matter how insulting they might be, and Telchide was often a victim of her sharp tongue.

"Do we know if they're targeting Alchimisti in particular? Or if it was related to their association with this group?"

"I doubt it's about this group," Lucrezia said. "Otherwise, all our workshops would've been raided by now. As to the matter of targeting Alchimisti, leaving aside medicines, alchemical solutions are used by all Guilds, so we're easy targets.

"Artiste require our solutions to create certain colours they could never afford otherwise. The Calzolai use our solutions as an alternative to horsehide glue to bind their shoes. And, quite obviously, the Inventrici require our solutions to make some of their inventions work. It makes us particularly vulnerable."

Telchide waved aside the scented smoke rising out of his chilled beaker and sipped the smoking limoncello amongst grumbled agreement, the zesty lemon liqueur making his eyes water. It was unfair and every Guild knew it. The Mercantili, by the very nature of their Guild, were in constant contact and collaboration with every Guild, but they were exempt from the Edict. After all, *they* were the ones who had implemented it.

First, they'd implemented the Trade Edict to force various Guild members to trade through them and not make independent deals. Next, they'd lobbied for the Inter-Guild Edict, ostensibly to put every Guild on the same footing, but realistically to punish those who were collaborating outside their own Guild.

It had forced Guild members within Tor'Esint to deal with each other at arm's length, for fear of breaching the Edict. The newest penalties were too high for most to risk – indefinite imprisonment or being stripped of Guild status. Both were devastating. Even the poorest and most desperate of customers would not condescend to patronise someone who had been stripped of their Guild status. A person couldn't survive like that, especially if they had a family.

"Ignio and Pietra had an apprentice each," Sara Alchimista said. "What happens to them?"

Lucrezia shrugged. Telchide couldn't tell if it was due to apathy or discomfort. He couldn't read expressions as well as most people. It was the main reason Sebetine had always insisted on being the face of the shop. She'd dealt with his customers, flattered them, charmed them, convinced them to pay what he was worth and secured their repeat business.

Since her disappearance, Telchide had run his little workshop alone. His inability to smooth over ruffled feathers had cost him more than a job or two. Those that he managed to keep were often not willing to pay what they should. If he still had a Copper Guild Mark, he'd be one step away from closing his workshop. The Silver Guild Mark was all that had saved him.

In the past three years, he'd learned to say as little as possible. Most of the time, it saved him the embarrassment of insulting a customer without intention. What it didn't do was encourage their repeat business unless they were desperate for the items he was most renowned for making.

That was why he had so many orders for music boxes and pocket watches, but little else. He was one of the few Inventrici who had worked with the Musicisti Guild often enough before the Edict that he could create near flawless melodies in his music boxes. What put him a further notch above the others was that, having lived in a Falegname family and learning some of their skills in his youth, his music boxes were also works of art. He smiled despite the dire discussion around him.

"Can anyone here take the apprentices on?" Lucrezia asked.

Some of the Alchimisti shook their heads. Others avoided Lucrezia's gaze.

"I would, but I'm already at my limit," Eduardo said.

Telchide couldn't understand how Eduardo worked with so many apprentices under his feet. He couldn't bear the thought of a single apprentice – his life was already complicated enough.

Lucrezia shrugged. "Then they'll go back on the apprentice register at the Alchimisti Guild. Now down to business. Who wants to start?"

No one made a move to speak, so Telchide cleared his throat. He saw Lucrezia square her shoulders, but she said nothing as he opened his notebook.

"I want to create a Lightbox. One that doesn't rely on friction or fire. I need a solution that glows. Does anyone have anything like that?"

He saw the Alchimisti exchange glances. Many of those gathered around the table had tried collaborating with him once, but few did it a second time. They were never at their ease with him, and he couldn't for the life of him manage to change his behaviour to suit them.

"I may have something for you," Eduardo said. "It's not a single solution, mind. You'll need to mix two together to create the glow."

Telchide nodded and began sketching out ideas for a Lightbox. It would need glass walls, or the glowing solution would be pointless. A single compartment would be easiest, but movable compartments would create the opportunity to mix solutions multiple times and allow the glow to last for hours. He was so focused on the idea and the possibilities it presented that he didn't pay attention to the meeting continuing around him until a plate of pasta was pushed under his nose. He looked up briefly to see Aveline smiling at him from across the table as she withdrew her hand from his plate.

Scribbling away in his notebook as he ate, it was only when Eduardo nudged him that he looked up once more and he realised most of their party had left. Only Aveline, Dania and Nestore remained. He'd missed all their ideas. Again.

He should know by now to wait for the others to speak before coming forward with his own idea. He always missed everything that came after him.

"I can't give you a ride home today, Dania," Aveline told the young Alchimista as they pulled on their gloves and coats. "My carriage is in for conversion to blazermobile this week."

Telchide took his coat from the wall hanger beside them. He saw Dania look nervously out the window but couldn't understand why. It was dark, but the gas lamps would light her way home adequately.

"I'm sure I can walk home alone," Dania said with a trembling voice.

Aveline looked out herself.

"I'll walk you home. It's not far from your place to mine. I'll be fine. I doubt I'm as fine a temptation as you."

"Are you certain, Aveline?" The hopefulness in Dania's voice was palpable.

"Any man desperate enough to attack me will find himself on the blunt end of this."

Aveline pulled her hand out of her pocket to reveal knuckle dusters already around her fingers.

Telchide suddenly understood what they were talking about.

"Aveline, Dania, would you allow Eduardo and I to escort you home?"

Eduardo choked on the last of his drink.

"Chide, Dania lives even further than Aveline," he called out.

Telchide frowned. "All the more reason for us to walk her home, don't you agree?"

Eduardo shook his head but said nothing.

"That's so kind of you, Telchide," Dania said shyly. She was quite young to have her Copper Guild Mark. Telchide had never seen her Great Work, but it must have been great indeed for the Alchimisti Guild to allow her a Guild Mark immediately after her apprenticeship ended.

"Indeed, Telchide, we don't mean to be an imposition. We're quite capable of handling ourselves," Aveline added.

Telchide waved her protest aside. "I insist. I'd worry for the two of you all night long if we didn't escort you home."

He thought he saw the shadow of a smile pass Aveline's lips, but it was gone so quickly he doubted his eyes.

Out on the cobbled street, they arranged themselves by profession. It wouldn't be appropriate for an Alchimista to walk beside an Inventore. Dania placed her hand on Eduardo's outstretched arm. Telchide glanced at Aveline and belatedly realised she was expecting the same of him.

He held his arm out for her and felt the lightest touch as she placed her hand on his forearm. A sudden longing for intimacy rushed through him, one he hadn't felt in years, until he looked down at her gloved fingers and reminded himself she was not his companion. Telchide squared his shoulders. There was nothing to be embarrassed about. He was simply walking a fellow Inventrice home. He took a deep breath and began walking behind Eduardo and Dania.

A few blocks later, Telchide realised he had no idea where Dania lived or exactly how far away it was. Etiquette dictated he couldn't stay in absolute silence the entire time. Aveline would think it the height of rudeness.

"Are you working on anything interesting at the moment?" he asked her.

Aveline's fingers tightened slightly on his arm as she turned to look at him. He returned her gaze curiously.

"You were quite absorbed in your notebook, weren't you?" she asked.

"Oh, erm, yes," Telchide admitted guiltily. "What did I miss?"

Aveline laughed. "I can't tell you the ideas I need *Alchimista* help with," she whispered, then continued in a louder voice, "but aside from those, I'm working on a contraption to help people up move stairs. I understand the need for people to live above workshops or general trade shops, but it makes life difficult for the elderly, or in fact anyone with trouble walking."

"Why, Aveline, that's a splendid idea!"

She nodded slowly.

"Whatever's the matter? Aren't you excited about it?" he asked in confusion.

"Oh, no. I am," she assured him with a pat on his arm. "It's just more complicated than I'd imagined. It would be nice to work on it with someone, to talk the problems through, but I don't have anyone to help me."

Telchide played with the chain of his pocket watch.

"Can't your apprentice help you?"

"He ... isn't very skilled yet and is taking more time away from my work than I'd expected."

Telchide nodded. "I wish I could help you, but I have three music boxes and no time."

"Do you mean that?" she asked him quietly. "You'd really help me if you had time?"

"Well, of course," Telchide replied easily. "Why wouldn't I?"

They'd first met when Eduardo introduced Telchide to their group of Alchimisti and Inventrici, a few years before the Inter-Guild Edict was pronounced. Aveline was one of the few Inventrici who seemed to understand the way his mind worked, just as Eduardo was one of the few Alchimisti who could stand to work with him. She was patient with him, and listened to his ideas without interrupting.

Her fingers tightened on his arm ever so slightly. Telchide felt a rush of excitement.

"We could work together," Aveline suggested quickly. "I could help you with your music boxes, so you have time to help me with my idea."

Telchide waved his hands in front of him, forcing her to take a step away. "No, no. I cannot pay you for your time and you must have plenty of orders to get on with yourself. You cannot waste your time with me."

Aveline frowned and took his arm again. "It wouldn't be a waste of time, Telchide. And I wouldn't expect payment – it would be a trade. I could come over after the trading day ends to help with your music boxes one night and you could come over the next night to work on my idea. Just think about it."

Telchide did think about it, the rest of the journey. They walked to Dania's house in silence, Telchide barely noticing the ristoranti and cafes bursting with loud diners along the main streets and on the edges of Piazza Mercantile. Eduardo joined them when Dania was safely home and carried on a conversation with Aveline that Telchide heard but did not pay attention to.

Aveline pulled back on his arm and let go. She'd stopped walking. He looked up, surprised to realise they were already at her house.

"Good night, Telchide, Eduardo."

"Good night, Aveline," Telchide returned, along with Eduardo.

She paused before walking up the stairs to her door.

"Think about my offer, Telchide. I'd appreciate it."

He nodded, wondering how she didn't realise he'd already spent so much time thinking about it. He wanted to make it work but didn't think he could. Not really. Discussing projects at the Exploding Beakers for an hour or so was vastly different to working with each other for an extended period. She would undoubtedly find some reason to dislike working with him. She'd only do it because she had no other options.

Telchide tipped his coppola to her and turned to walk home with Eduardo. The Alchimista barely waited until they were halfway across the cobbled piazza before his curiosity burst.

"What was that about? What offer?"

"Nothing, really."

Eduardo pulled on Telchide's coat sleeve to stop him.

"Don't tell me 'nothing'. What did she offer you?"

Telchide sighed. "She offered to help me with my music boxes if I help her with one of her projects, that's all."

"That's *all*?" Eduardo asked in an unusually high-pitched voice. "Telchide, no one has *ever* offered to work with you or asked for your assistance without prompting. This is not 'nothing'. This is *something*. You will march over to her house tomorrow morning, before trading begins, and tell her that you accept her offer before she changes her mind. Do you hear me?"

Telchide stared at him in shock. Eduardo was his best friend and the only one who ever spoke plainly to him. But even *he* wasn't usually so forceful.

The Alchimista looked at him square in the eyes.

"Chide, you need this. An extra distraction from Sebetine's disappearance. A quiet place to work. You'll feel a new man. I guarantee it."

Telchide smiled briefly at the thought. A working night without Teresina. He loved his daughter, but she was a curious and busy child. He'd taught her to read as young as he could just to occupy her with something quiet. It had been a mixed blessing. Now, she insisted on reading every newssheet aloud to him. It kept him appraised of everything happening in Tor'Esint, but it also made it impossible to keep her quiet.

Eduardo left him at their block. Telchide proceeded up the five stone steps to his workshop alone. Cautiously excited for the first time in years. It would be so nice to work on something other than music boxes and pocket watches. And he couldn't deny it would be nice to work with a fellow Inventrice.

Chapter 2 – Ramedi 24 Vetraie 229 Years After Implosion

A series of metallic clinks as Serenita locked the workshop door jarred Telchide from his thoughts. He looked at the time and realised it was already well past four o'clock. Trading in Tor'Esint was from eight in the morning to four in the afternoon. He liked the early closing time. It gave him hours of uninterrupted time in the evening to continue his work. Not that he had so many customers these days, not without Sebetine to greet them and take their orders.

The first year after her disappearance, he'd missed the way she brightened up the room just by sitting and embroidering her latest project while he worked. Now, he was almost ashamed to admit, the main reason he missed her was for her way with customers.

"What time is your Inventore friend coming?" Serenita asked as Teresina snuggled into his lap, disturbing his last attempt to punch a dent into the copper strip of music.

Telchide looked at his pocket watch. "Any minute now. She would've had to close up her shop and walk down here."

"She?" asked Teresina, suddenly pouting. "Why is your friend a *she*?"

Telchide frowned at her. "Can't Inventrici be ladies?"

"Of course, papà," she said in an oddly serious tone for one so young. "I might be an Inventrice when I grow up, or an Alchimista. But why do you have to work with a *lady*?"

"Well, because she's the one who asked me," Telchide spluttered.

There was a rap at the door. Telchide tried to rise to answer it, but Teresina sprawled over his lap, making it impossible. Serenita rolled her eyes and walked back to the door to unlock it.

Aveline walked in, looking resplendent in her dark green coat and matching hat with a leather work satchel over her shoulder. Aveline pulled the hatpins out of her hair and placed them in her coat pocket as she took off the dainty hat and hung it on the coat stand along with her coat. Practical and beautiful, he caught himself admiring her.

He looked away quickly to his daughter and marvelled at the effect Aveline had on Teresina. She went completely still and drank in every detail of the light green work dress, patting the places on her own body where Aveline's dress had pockets. She walked over to Serenita and glared up at her.

"Nonna, why don't you ever sew pockets onto *my* dresses? Papà, can I take Nonna to the markets tomorrow to buy some material for pockets?"

Aveline looked down at her dress as Serenita huffed. It was too much for Telchide. He laughed long and loud. He only stopped when he realised everyone was staring at him.

"What?" He wiped a tear from his eye.

Teresina walked over to where he was sitting and stretched to put a hand to his forehead. "Are you feeling well, papà?"

"Well, of course I am," he said, brushing away her hand. "Why shouldn't I be?"

She looked at him oddly. "You're ... *laughing*."

Telchide's humour dried up. "I'm allowed to laugh."

"I know, papà." Teresina took a step back. "You just never do. You always look like *that*." She gestured to his face, shook her head and walked up the stairs.

Telchide's good humour vanished at the realisation of how his daughter saw him. Serenita bade them good work and followed Teresina up the stairs. Telchide did not respond, nor did he move from his work chair.

"Should I go?" Aveline asked.

He looked up in annoyance. Teresina should not have made her feel uncomfortable here.

"No, we made a deal. You help me, I help you. That doesn't work if you go."

"That's true," Aveline said, taking a single step forward. "But I didn't mean to cause any tension between you and your daughter."

"Do I really not laugh?" he asked her. "Ever?"

"I've never seen you laugh at the Exploding Beakers," Aveline said carefully. "Even a smile is rare."

Telchide frowned. He used to laugh all the time. Sebetine had made him laugh, but so had Teresina. Perhaps too many years had passed for his daughter to remember those times.

"I'll fetch a fresh pot of tea," he told Aveline, recovering his manners. "I'm working on a music box there. You can see the finished ones on that shelf."

He pointed everything out to her and left her in his workshop while he went to brew a pot of tea. By the time he reached the kitchen, Serenita was already preparing dinner. She shooed him away as he tried to put some water on to boil.

"You go back to work. We'll send down with a tray when your tea's ready."

Telchide didn't see Teresina in the kitchen, but knew there was no point arguing with Serenita. It might be his house and his workshop, but the kitchen was Serenita's domain. Sometimes he felt like an intruder in his own home when she bustled him out. Just like now.

He walked back down the stairs with a soft tread. It was a habit he'd learned when Teresina was a baby. Any sound woke her, and the few hours she slept were precious.

Aveline didn't hear him over the sound of the music box she'd wound up and was listening to. He stood on the last step, watching her. She picked up the music box, turning it over to see every angle. It was only when she put it back down that she noticed the push latch. She pressed it gently and was rewarded by the lid opening. He saw the smile spread over her face as she watched the internal mechanism of the music box. She picked it up again with both hands and held it towards the fireplace so she could see everything inside in detail. That was when she saw him.

"Telchide, this is magnificent!" she exclaimed, without preamble.

He smiled at the acknowledgement of his skills. Aveline had a higher Guild status than himself, but they both knew he was just as capable as she was. If he'd had time to create another Great Work, he'd already be at the same level she was.

"They're quite simple, really, once you get the hang of them. That's one of my early ones. The ones I'm working on at the moment are more elaborate."

Aveline placed the now-silent music box back on the display shelf and held her hands behind her back.

"What do you need me to do?"

Telchide looked at her, completely at a loss. He'd never had anyone help him with his inventions before. Not even an apprentice, even though he'd been entitled to one since earning his Silver Guild Mark almost three years ago.

"I could teach you to punch the holes for the music or show you how to put pieces together to make the barrel turn."

Aveline shook her head firmly. "I'll only make a mess of the music. You do that and give me the pieces for the barrel. I'm sure I can muddle through that on my own. It looks like a similar mechanism to the toy dancers I used to make."

Telchide breathed a sigh of relief. In truth, he hadn't wanted her to work on the copper sheet of music. It was a delicate process that was time consuming to fix if many mistakes were made.

He lit several candles to provide better working light at the workbench, pulled up an extra chair and sat beside Aveline, passing her the pieces for the music box itself. She took out her own set of tools from her work satchel, spread them out on a soft cloth and set to work.

Telchide watched her for a minute admiring how quickly she settled into working with his music box mechanism. Only when she shifted slightly and looked over with a smile did he set to work on the copper strip.

He barely noticed when Serenita sent down the dumbwaiter and brought them tea and then later, their dinner. Aveline was the one who poured the tea and made him stop to drink it. Aveline was the one who called a halt to their work so they could eat.

"How much longer will it take you to finish the copper strip?" she asked, between mouthfuls of garlic infused potatoes.

He finished his own potatoes and replaced the plate on its tray. "Another fifteen minutes at the most. Then we can test it."

Aveline glanced surreptitiously at her pocket watch. "Not tonight, Telchide. It's getting late. We both need to open our workshops tomorrow. You can finish it during the day then come to my workshop tomorrow evening."

Telchide found himself nodding before he could stop himself. Then a thought occurred to him. "Will your family mind?"

Aveline laughed. "I don't have a family in my workshop. Just my apprentice, Nevio, but he's visiting his parents in Tor'Selit for his mamma's birthday."

Telchide coughed uncomfortably and sat up straighter. "I, erm, don't think I'll be available tomorrow night."

Aveline put her hands on her hips. "Now fair's fair, Telchide. We made a deal. I helped you tonight, so you'd have time to help me tomorrow night. You can't back out now."

Telchide couldn't fight the blush that was rising from his neck all the way up his cheeks. "I'm not backing out," he spluttered, not knowing how to explain without being too direct. "I *want* to help you, but I don't want tongues to wag."

Aveline stared at him, blinked slowly then started laughing. "You're an odd one, Telchide. Fine, I'll bring my drawings here tomorrow night. But when Nevio returns, I expect you to make the effort to visit my workshop in return."

"Done." Telchide heaved a sigh of relief and held out his hand to shake on it.

Aveline shook his hand firmly, then set about packing up her tools. Telchide walked her to the door and waited as she donned her hat and buttoned her coat. When he opened the door for her, he realised how dark it was outside, even with the gas lamps lining the street.

"I'll walk you home," he decided spontaneously.

He thought he saw Aveline smile before she took his arm. Just like the night before, he felt a rush of pleasure at her gloved hand on his sleeve. It was the oddest sensation. He could not account for it.

It was a pleasant walk. The ristoranti along the streets were full of lively diners, but at least they were keeping close to the buildings. This cooler autumn weather was not conducive to people sitting far from the friction heaters. Telchide preferred it to summer when the tables spread out almost to the cobblestones of the actual roads. He'd never been comfortable around crowds. It was easier for him to speak with one person at a time. It was just that little bit easier to keep his focus on the conversation.

On the corner of his street, he spied a man selling cups of chestnuts. He pulled out a copper coin and paid for a coned newssheet holding a handful of roasted chestnuts. He offered it to Aveline. She carefully plucked one out and tossed it from hand to hand as she walked, cooling it down before she could peel it.

"You're an amazing Inventore, Telchide," she said.

He looked over at Aveline in surprise. "Why do you say that?"

She smiled, causing him to smile also. "I've seen music boxes before, but all of them were simple, rudimentary toys by comparison. You make your music boxes a work of art, fit for the glorious sound you create."

He blushed furiously at the compliment, his stomach flipping at the same time. "I don't write the music. I merely make the copper strips replicate it."

"Yes, but I've never met anyone with the patience to do more than a few bars of music for each box. I saw the one you're working on now. It must be half the song. How do you have the patience for it?" She popped the chestnut into her mouth and looked at him for an answer.

Telchide shrugged. "I find it calming. I know what I'm doing, and I just get on with it. It forces me to concentrate on just one thing. That can sometimes be … difficult for me."

"Yes, I've noticed," Aveline laughed lightly, linking her arm back through his. "Your mind never stops working."

"I can't help it," he replied sourly. "I've always been like that."

Aveline momentarily tightened her grip on his arm. "I didn't mean to insult you. I find it, well, rather endearing. I think it's part of what makes you such a good Inventore. You just need to figure out a way to focus on larger works to gain your Electrum Guild Mark."

"Forgive me, but your zipper was not a *large* work," Telchide pointed out, shaking free of her hand and picking out a chestnut for himself. "The necklace watch for ladies that earned me my Copper Guild Mark was not large, nor was the first of my elaborate music boxes for my Silver Guild Mark. I'm perfectly happy to work on smaller projects to make them works of art, rather than large contraptions that cost a fortune to create in the first place and may not give the same money in return."

Aveline nodded as he spoke.

"That's true. I suppose unless you have a large store of money, you mightn't be able to create larger works in the first place. And not everyone would be able to afford such expensive creations."

"Like your project, for the stairs," Telchide pointed out, suddenly realising that Aveline must have a great deal of money set aside for that project.

"Indeed."

There was a long stretch of silence between them as they ate their chestnuts. Telchide realised he knew very little about Aveline other than the fact that she was a wonderful Inventrice who didn't mind working with him and, apparently, must be quite wealthy.

"Aveline?"

"Hmm?" She turned her head slightly towards him.

"Are we … friends?"

She smiled so widely that dimples popped into her cheeks. "I'd like to think so."

"Then you really must call me Chide."

"Very well, Chide, then I insist you call me Veli. All my friends do."

All my friends.

It was an interesting phrase. Telchide didn't have many friends. Aside from his family, only Eduardo called him Chide. Well, so did Kesida, but she was the Inventrici Guild Amministratrice and knew all the Inventrici intimately, and Filippo Falegname, but they'd known each other since Telchide's apprenticeship. Even Telchide's own maestro had never called him Chide.

His apprenticeship had been an interesting one. Maestro Ugo had spoken little and worked hard. He'd left Telchide to learn simply by watching. Maestro Ugo took on a new apprentice every five years. That meant Telchide had a fifth-year apprentice to learn from in his first two years, then was the sole apprentice for three years before helping to teach the next apprentice in his final two years.

It wasn't a bad way to learn, he reflected, but was the complete opposite to Eduardo's constantly full workshop. He'd rarely seen the Alchimista's workshop with less than three apprentices. Eduardo was one of the few Alchimisti with a Gold Guild Mark, allowing him three. He made full use of that, allowing the older ones to mentor the newer ones. He only ever seemed to teach the older ones more elaborate concoctions. Sometimes the noise in that workshop was so overwhelming Telchide had to depart.

"Chide, did I say something wrong?"

Telchide looked at Aveline in confusion. "No, why?"

She stopped walking. They were at her doorstep now. "You went very quiet. What were you thinking?"

"Just about my apprenticeship. My maestro had very few apprentices – he took a new one every five years – but Eduardo constantly has a workshop full of them. What will you do?"

"I haven't applied for another one yet, even though I could have two," she told him with an air of caution. "I don't want to get myself into the same mess as Greta."

"Greta?"

"Greta Sarta," Aveline said in a low voice. "She rose up through her Guild Marks exceedingly quickly and got a new apprentice every year. She tells me the older one mocks the other two because they don't know things they should. All because Greta doesn't have the time to teach them.

"She regrets her decision but refuses to send any of them back to the Guild for another maestra. I don't think I'd want another apprentice until Nevio can work comfortably on his own tasks, so I have time to spend with the new one."

"That sounds a bit like Maestro Ugo," Telchide told her. "Except he didn't spend time with the new one until their third year. He let the older apprentice teach the younger one for the first two years and then took over for the next three. My last two years, I spent teaching the next apprentice. I suppose it was good practice for when I eventually get an apprentice but I'm not sure how much we helped him."

"My maestro had a full complement of apprentices when I joined," Aveline explained. "He let the older ones work on his smaller orders while he taught the younger ones the basics. But even he didn't have very much time for all of us. Teaching three apprentices by yourself must be difficult. I don't think I'm doing all that well with just the one. I only got him two years ago."

"But you're on your Electrum Guild Mark. Why didn't you get an apprentice as soon as you earned your Silver Guild Mark?"

Telchide noticed a flash of emotion in her eyes but couldn't place it.

"Why don't *you* have an apprentice?" she asked in return. "You've had your Silver Guild Mark for almost three years."

He dropped her arm and took a step away.

"I do not think it fair to ask an apprentice to join a broken household with a child who barely sleeps," he replied quietly. "Good night, Aveline."

"Veli, remember?" she said with a small smile.

"Aveline," he reaffirmed. "I'll see you tomorrow evening with your drawings."

He walked away before she ascended the steps to her front door. He felt comfortable that nothing would happen to her in the short time it took her to open the door and lock it behind her.

Chapter 3 – Argentodi 25 Vetraie 229 Years After Implosion

Telchide used Aveline's absence during the day to carefully check her work, ensuring it was up to his standards. He was suitably impressed. It was true she was an Electrum Inventrice, but he knew some people bribed their way to a higher level.

At the closing of trading, Teresina stood on a chair to lock the door against late customers and sent Serenita up to make a tea tray before following her up to the kitchen. Telchide watched the antics of his child with interest. From her reaction the night before about an Inventrice rather than an Inventore coming to work with him, he'd assumed she didn't want him working with Aveline and could not account for her sudden change in behaviour.

Teresina was just taking the fully laden tea tray from the dumbwaiter when Aveline knocked on the door. Telchide stood to answer it, but Teresina yelled at him.

"No, papà. *I'll* get the door!"

Telchide smiled and nodded in confusion as he took the tea tray from his daughter. At least her voice had been loud enough that Aveline must have heard it and would forgive the tardiness in someone opening the door.

Teresina ran to the door and stood on the chair to unlock it. She quickly jumped down and smoothed her dress before allowing Aveline in.

"Good evening, Aveline Inventrice," she said with an awkward curtsey.

A curtsey! *His* daughter! Telchide had never seen her curtsey in all her life.

"Teresina, what in Caldera's smoke are you doing?" he spluttered, putting the tea tray down on the table behind his workbench.

"Greeting our guest, papà." She glared at him then turned back to Aveline all smiles. "May I take your coat?"

Aveline nodded and unbuttoned the pale blue coat. Telchide thought it had a ridiculous number of buttons but held his tongue. Teresina stood on the chair once more to accept the coat and place it on the coat stand. She stood there for a moment, swishing around in her dress, childishly obvious in her attempt to get Aveline to notice her. Aveline did not seem to mind.

"Oh Teresina, what a lovely dress you have on today! Are those new pockets I see?"

Telchide looked closely at his daughter's dress for the first time that day. It was her old pale-yellow sundress, that she refused to put away for the coming winter. But there were now, indeed, pockets, in exactly the same places as Aveline's work dresses. Aside from the fact that Aveline's dress was a rich navy blue, their dresses were almost identical.

Was Teresina mimicking Aveline? Telchide looked closer at his daughter. She'd even tied back her hair – indoors!

"Thank you, Inventrice," Teresina replied, hopping down from the chair. "Nonna helped me to sew the pockets on today. They're very useful. I can see why you have them."

"It helps that I'm friends with a few Sarti Guild members. They take my complaints about women's clothing and actually *do* something about it. How do you think I came up with the idea of the zipper? It wasn't on my own, I can assure you."

Teresina's mouth gaped open.

"*You* invented the zipper!" She turned to face Telchide. "Papà, why didn't you tell me?"

Telchide raised his eyebrows at her. "Teresina, I've never told you who creates *any* of the latest inventions. Why would I have told you about Aveline's?"

Teresina placed her hands on her hips and glared at him. It was quite the comical sight, but Telchide knew better than to laugh at his daughter when she was attempting to be serious and scold him – it would only make her angrier.

"Forgive me, Teresina. I shall tell you about *all* Aveline's inventions from now onwards. Now, if you don't mind, we have work to do."

Teresina's anger was quickly forgotten. She smiled at Aveline before dashing up the stairs and out of sight.

"I do apologise, Aveline. It appears my daughter has taken quite a liking to you – and your clothing. I fear you'll have to bear her close attentions every time she sees you."

Aveline smiled and looked up at the empty stairs. "She's a wonderful child, Chide. You've no need to apologise for her."

Proud though he was of his daughter, Telchide startled at Aveline's assumption that Teresina was a wonderful child when it was only the second time they'd met. However, it surprised him that he was even more ruffled by her informal use of his name, though he'd given her permission himself. He regretted that – they barely knew each other, but he'd already felt comfortable enough for that familiarity.

Aveline walked over to his workbench and unpacked her satchel. There were many drawings, but not much else. Telchide hadn't yet cleared away his work from the day and saw Aveline's eyes lingering on the music box she'd helped create.

"May I?" she asked, reaching out towards it.

Telchide nodded and handed her the key. Aveline placed the key in the keyhole on the side of the music box. She picked up the delicate creation and turned the key until it would go no further. Telchide was yet to test the timing of it. He hurriedly pulled out his pocket watch and wrote down the exact time, down to the second.

He was not paying attention to the music. He'd listened to it all morning, checking for inconsistencies against the written notes. There had only been two.

He'd made short work of fixing them and had gone straight onto the copper strip for the next music box. He'd needed to distract himself from his thoughts. They'd strayed too often to Aveline and the ease with which they'd spent the evening in each other's company. Though they'd been working together on a project, he couldn't help but feel he was somehow betraying the memory of his companion. She was the only other woman who'd spent an evening with him in the workshop.

"One minute and thirty seconds," Telchide muttered as he wrote it down. "That's less than last time."

Aveline wound it up again and unhinged the lid to look inside as the spiked barrel turned away against the strips of metal, making it possible for the music to sound.

"Have you thought of placing a velvet cushion inside here?" she asked.

Telchide had placed the mechanism in a wooden box and painted the lid with a floral pattern that seemed to be a favourite among the ladies. The small inner wooden section of the box was plain – sanded and varnished, but plain.

"Whatever for?" he asked in confusion.

Aveline smiled. "Jewellery, Chide. A box this size would be just the thing for a lady's favourite selection of earrings. Velvet would make it even more appealing to your customers. I could show you what I mean tomorrow evening, if you like."

"I'd like that very much." Telchide smiled. "Sebetine used to help me with that side of things."

He saw Aveline's smile freeze in place. A moment's awkwardness later, he cleared his throat and moved Aveline's drawings to the largest workbench.

"Show me what you have so far."

Aveline hesitated for only a moment before placing her satchel on the floor and walking over to talk him through her latest idea. She pointed to the drawings as she explained.

"Imagine a chair that can travel up the stairs, removing the need for you to walk. There would need to be a rail of sorts, like this, for the chair to travel along and a device to connect the chair to the rail. I'm undecided on whether to try to source the supercharged magnets they use for the funicolare. They'd probably work magnificently, but I'm hesitant about the cost it would pass on to my customers.

"Then there would need to be a mechanism to force the chair to move up the stairs and back down in a controlled manner. What do you think?"

Telchide looked at the drawings and listened to her description.

"Steam or friction power?"

"I'm not sure."

"Pulley or wheels?"

"I haven't decided."

"Will you connect the chair at the back, or under the seat?"

Aveline hugged herself. "I don't know."

She walked a few paces away and sat down, looking utterly miserable. Telchide frowned. He hadn't meant to upset her. Perhaps tea would help. It had always helped with Sebetine.

He poured two cups of tea from the tray Teresina had brought down. From the aroma wafting up, he could tell it was peppermint. Serenita knew he worked best at night with a dose of peppermint. He hoped Aveline was not averse to it as he carried her cup over. Sebetine had been partial to lavender and chamomile. She had loathed peppermint.

Aveline took it gratefully, finally unwrapping her arms from about herself. Telchide sipped at his tea to give himself time to think. He did not know how Aveline worked, nor how she thought. These seemed very preliminary ideas.

He looked over to see Aveline blowing absently over the tea as she stared at her drawings. She peeked over at him once but averted her gaze as soon as their eyes met.

"Are we assuming the people using these have any help? Or that they need it to function without an extra pair of hands?" he asked, purposely not looking at Aveline but at her drawings instead.

"Presumably they'll have help," Aveline replied. "If they can't move from one level to the other by themselves, they wouldn't be living alone."

Telchide nodded and tapped his finger at the base of the drawing.

"What if there was a handle here that activates a pulley system, and drags the chair up the stairs?"

Aveline drew closer to the drawing. "It would need to be a strong person or an extremely efficient pulley."

"True," Telchide muttered. He took another sip of tea, then placed the cup back on the tea tray. "But if the friction between the chair and the rail is reduced by your magnet idea, it wouldn't be too difficult."

"It would make it more expensive," Aveline replied. Her tea remained untouched as she pursed her lips.

"Perhaps the pulley system is our best option. We could work on one to make it more efficient."

"I think steam power would be more useful here," Telchide said.

"I've don't like steam power," Aveline admitted. "Personally, I prefer hydraulics."

"You've worked with hydraulics?" Telchide asked in surprise. He'd only recently heard of that technology.

"I've had some experience," Aveline replied easily. "It would help most with coming down, to slow the descent. I'm not certain if it would really help to lift the chair, but steam would."

His initial awkwardness forgotten, Telchide dived into the project with Aveline, proposing and discarding a dozen ideas before settling on a short list to work with. Again, he barely noticed when Teresina took away their tea tray to the dumbwaiter and Serenita brought over a dinner tray. He only stopped to eat when Aveline pushed a plate of pasta under his nose.

"Do you think we can get it working?" she asked while they ate. "I mean, actually, not theoretically."

Telchide twirled his pasta, scooping along as much pesto as he could manage on one fork. It was one of his favourite sauces. He couldn't understand how so few ingredients could combine to make such a delicious dish, but he didn't question it. When Serenita had asked if she could plant a herb patch in the back courtyard, she'd used the promise of more pesto dishes to convince him.

"If you can afford the material to create and test it, I don't see why not," he replied easily. "Of course, you could begin with a small-scale version of it to test the theories of lifting the chair upstairs. We might have to talk to a Fabbro for the handrails for those that aren't suitable for the chair lift. I'm afraid my little fireplace won't burn hot enough to forge those.

"I could fashion a small seat from a block of wood by the time the rails are ready. Then we can experiment with different ways of connecting the chair to the rails to see what works best."

Aveline paused with a forkful of pasta halfway to her mouth.

"How could you fashion a seat from wood? You're not a Falegname."

"No, but my parents were, and all my siblings are," Telchide responded. "They taught me, as they did the others, before they realised my true passion lay in inventing. I should think a simple chair would be within the realms of possibility for me to create."

Aveline stared at him, her pasta completely forgotten.

"You have siblings?"

Telchide shrugged uneasily. "Yes, but we were never very close. I haven't spoken to them since I left Tor'Dumere to become an apprentice in Tor'Esint. They sent me a note when my papà and then my mamma passed away. They sent felicitations on my Commitment Day with Sebetine and when Teresina was born, letters of concern when Sebetine went missing. But that's all."

"Better than having no siblings at all I suppose," Aveline said.

Telchide kept his eyes averted as he continued to eat. Eventually he ventured an observation.

"Teresina doesn't appear to mind."

"She mightn't," Aveline admitted. "But I certainly did. It was a lonely childhood for me. My parents had little time for me and gave me no opportunities to play with other children."

"Teresina doesn't play with other children," Telchide said, looking up slowly. "Do you think she's lonely?"

Aveline shrugged. "You don't ignore her like my parents ignored me when I was that young. And she has Serenita. That counts for something."

"Why did your parents ignore you?" Telchide asked before he could stop himself. He knew, from the way she stilled, that it was not the right thing to ask.

Aveline put her empty plate on the dinner tray and folded her hands in her lap before looking up at him with calm eyes.

"They didn't do it on purpose. They were very important, influential people. There were always people begging for their attention in some way or other. They simply didn't have time for a child. They let the household staff raise me until I was old enough to begin studies with a private tutor. Papà tried to put aside at least ten minutes a day to spend with me, to teach me things he thought I ought to know."

She smiled fondly at the memory. "It wasn't much, but I looked forward to those ten minutes. I cherished them. Mamma saw me more as an ornament to be dressed up and paraded around at their dinner parties. It could've been worse."

Telchide didn't know how to respond. His siblings hadn't really cared much for him, but his parents had loved him. Of *that* he was certain. They'd put up with him trying to learn carpentry from them, but instead of getting angry when his carvings turned into inventions instead, they fostered his love of inventing.

It would've been so much easier for everyone if he'd decided to follow in their footsteps, been apprenticed to them like his siblings, but he wouldn't have been happy and would have made a poor Falegname in the end. So, they'd done everything they could to help him get into the Guild he loved so much.

"You said you lived in Tor'Dumere. Why did you leave?" Aveline asked in the silence.

Telchide blinked away the past and looked into her hazel eyes.

"It was too difficult for me to join the Inventrici Guild there. It's not like here, where they have an apprentice registry, and anyone can put their names down. You either join the Guild your parents are a part of, with them as your maestri, or you purchase an apprenticeship with another Guild. It's very expensive."

"That's completely unfair!"

Telchide shrugged. "That's just the way of it. It worked in Tor'Dumere because of how the city is set up. All the Falegnami are in one area, the Inventrici in another and so on. You can never get your own workshop until someone from that Guild dies or sells it to you. In some ways, it's stricter than life here with the Edicts. In other ways, it makes sense."

"Does that mean your siblings took over the workshop when your parents died?"

Telchide shrugged. "I don't know. Like I said, we weren't very close. They told me when my parents died, but not soon enough for me to attend the funeral."

Telchide rose to put his own plate on the dinner tray. He remained standing and began tidying away their work from that evening.

"Were your parents in a Guild then?" he asked.

Aveline rose to help him. "No, they just had a lot of influence. People would come to them for favours of sorts."

Telchide did not understand what she meant, but he didn't bother saying so. Those conversations often just left him feeling more confused.

He helped Aveline put all her drawings back in her satchel and joined her in donning his coat. With fewer buttons than Aveline, he was left playing with his pocket watch as he waited for her. She seemed to be in no hurry. He would never understand why women were so willing to put up with the many intricacies or layers of clothing to keep up with the latest fashions. A simple coat was all he needed.

When she was ready, he opened the door for her and locked it behind them. He offered his arm once they were on the street. Much to his surprise, it was quickly becoming one of his favourite parts of the day.

They walked in silence to her door. It was only a few blocks away, but Telchide knew most people preferred idle chatter to silence. He appreciated the fact that Aveline did not press him to constantly talk or force him to listen to her prattle on about nothing.

"How long until the conversion on your carriage is finished?" he asked.

"Not for another few days at least," Aveline replied, looking uncomfortable. "You needn't walk me home every night, you know."

"I don't mind." Telchide smiled. "I simply feel bad that you need to travel to my workshop every day until then."

"But you'll have to walk to my workshop when my apprentice returns. Perhaps I can return the favour and drive you home of an evening."

Telchide felt the blood drain from his face as he shook his head.

"No need, no need. I like walking. Good night, Veli."

He turned and walked away before Aveline could press him further on the matter. Telchide had found as a teenager that he suffered motion sickness. His family had never required the services of a carriage while he was a child. It was only when he'd first travelled to Tor'Esint in the long carriage ride to the Inventrici Guild Hall, before the funicolare connecting the cities was created, that he realised how ill such travel made him.

The blazermobiles moved much faster than regular carriages. He could only imagine how much worse his stomach would fare with one of those. He was not eager to try it – especially not with Aveline as witness. She was one of the few people who treated him kindly. He couldn't bear the thought of ruining her blazermobile.

Chapter 4 – Riposidi 1 Mercantili 230 Years After Implosion

Every evening that week, Telchide enjoyed Aveline's company at his house. Teresina had grown ever fonder of Aveline, staying longer and longer in the workshop until Serenita had to drag her upstairs. It was an embarrassing display, but Aveline's smile at the antics eased his discomfort over the loud objections from his daughter.

Telchide enjoyed the companionship of working with someone. He finished his music boxes early and had time left over to work on his Lightbox idea. Time was a luxury he was unused to.

Now if only he could get Resi to sleep a whole night through, then he wouldn't be so tired. Her nightmares were not always terrifying, but they were bad enough to lurch her out of sleep which, in turn, made her call out for him. Half the time, he ended up asleep in her bed or woke when she crawled into his bed. It was exhausting, but that was his life.

This had been one of those days. He woke in the early hours of the morning to find Teresina curled up next to him, his blanket wrapped around her, leaving him to shiver. The temperature drop in the early morning was not kind to those without blankets.

Instead of tugging the blanket loose from his daughter to share it with her, he got up and pulled on his well-worn knitted jumper. He would not be able to get back to sleep now, even on Riposidi.

He made himself a pot of tea and sent it down to the workshop in the dumbwaiter. There was no point wasting waking hours. He lit a fire before heading to his workbench.

There was a message waiting for him. Either Eduardo had gone to bed later than he had or the old Alchimista was also already awake.

What do you think of this whole expedition to the Caldera? E

Telchide read it but couldn't make sense of it.

What expedition? T

You need to listen at our meetings. Dania proposed an expedition to the Caldera to look for some sort of special plant. E

The response came through before his tea had a chance to cool down.

Plants are an Alchimista's domain. Nothing to do with me. T

I'm coming over. Make tea. E

Telchide sighed, got to his feet, and burned the messages. At least the tea was already made. All he needed now was an extra cup. He unlocked the back door before heading up to the kitchen.

By the time he returned, Eduardo was already making himself comfortable by the fire. Telchide poured them both a cup of tea before joining his friend. The Alchimista took the cup gratefully and blew over the top of it.

"You've been busy," Eduardo said, nodding towards the workbench. "It usually takes you longer to finish those contraptions."

"Music boxes are *not* contraptions," Telchide replied indignantly.

"How are you finishing them so quickly?"

"Aveline's been helping me. And I've been helping her."

Eduardo nodded. Telchide could see the questions behind his eyes.

"Has she asked you to join the expedition to the Caldera?"

"What? No!" Telchide was so startled, he nearly choked on his tea. "Why would Aveline be going in the first place?"

"Chide, you *really* need to pay more attention," Eduardo huffed, but Telchide could see he wasn't really angry. "Dania has heard rumour of a sparking plant on the Caldera that produces enough energy to badly shock a grown person. Of course, it could have interesting properties for Alchimisti, and who knows what else will be discovered on the Caldera."

"That doesn't explain why Inventrici would go on this trip," Telchide pointed out.

"The plant, Chide, the plant. It could provide an alternate source of energy for Inventrici. Wouldn't you like to be one of the people who discovers it?"

Telchide didn't even consider it before shaking his head. "I couldn't possibly leave Teresina behind and it wouldn't be safe to take her with me. No, Ardo, I think Aveline knew best when she withheld an invitation to me."

Eduardo looked at him sadly. "You were almost there, you know."

"Almost where?" asked Telchide, curious despite himself.

"Almost back to the old Chide. My old quirky friend who was full of life and would've jumped at an opportunity to further his craft. Almost. If Sebetine were still here, would you have gone?"

Telchide almost said no, but he knew that was a lie. "Yes."

"You have Serenita to help you. Doesn't that make it almost the same?" Eduardo asked hopefully.

Telchide shook his head. "I can't expect her to take care of Teresina by herself. I'm certain she only survives living in this house because I'm the one who wakes up every night with Teresina. If she were the one waking up instead of me, she wouldn't have the energy to look after her during the day."

Eduardo nodded thoughtfully and chewed on his lip. The silence stretched for long minutes. Only when Telchide heard someone moving about above did he get to his feet again.

"Ardo, it's a moot point anyway. Aveline hasn't asked me to go. Neither has Dania. It isn't even an option."

Eduardo rose and placed his teacup back on the tea tray. "Pretend it's an option. If Teresina were sleeping the whole way through the night, would you consider it?"

"I don't know." Telchide shrugged. "Probably."

"Probably," Eduardo repeated quietly to himself. "Try to rest, Chide. It's Riposidi after all."

He patted Telchide on the shoulder and made his way out the back door towards his own workshop. Telchide shook his head. What was the point of even thinking about the expedition? Teresina's dreams weren't going to disappear overnight and they both knew it.

Chapter 5 – Gildadi 2 Mercantili 230 Years After Implosion

That afternoon, Telchide prepared to leave after closing. Aveline had sent word that morning that her apprentice had returned, and it was the first time he was going to work in her workshop.

Teresina watched him button his coat with mournful eyes. He hadn't realised quite how fond of Aveline she'd grown until this moment. It made him question whether he should continue this working relationship with the Inventrice. He didn't want Teresina getting too attached to her. She wasn't Teresina's mamma. Teresina shouldn't be looking to her for all the things she'd have looked to her mamma for. She could look to Serenita, though, he knew a nonna would never be quite enough for his little girl.

Already Teresina was mimicking Aveline's dress style and asking Serenita to do up her hair. He knew she was building up the courage to ask Aveline to do her hair in a "pretty" way. She'd been talking about it for days.

"Could you ask Aveline for my permission to visit her one morning? Before trading begins?"

Telchide paused, his coppola halfway to his head.

"I don't think that would be appropriate, Teresina."

"Nonna could take me, papà. I'd be good, I promise."

Telchide squatted down in front of her.

"Teresina, Aveline is busy. She's an Electrum Inventrice with a second-year apprentice. She isn't a friend like Ardo."

Teresina looked him squarely in the eye, her bottom lip trembling. "I've *heard* her call you Chide. And you've called her Veli. That means she's your friend, doesn't it?"

Telchide cursed himself. He knew he shouldn't have given Aveline permission to use his informal name, and he shouldn't be using hers. It led to too many unbidden thoughts and complications in his life, not least of which was this.

"In a manner of speaking," Telchide replied. "But we're not so familiar that my daughter can run to her house for a new hairstyle."

Teresina's eyes widened. Telchide couldn't help but smile.

"You think I don't know why you're asking?"

He cupped her cheek with his hand and kissed her nose. She hugged him tightly. Telchide sent her upstairs and locked the door behind him.

The streets were busier at this time of day. Vendors were to be found at most main intersections, selling honeyed almonds and cashews or roasted chestnuts as shoppers headed home with their final purchases. Apprentices, rejoicing at the end of the day's work, were laughing raucously, presumably on the way to some bar or other. Telchide had never been one of them. The three-year age gap between himself and Maestro Ugo's other apprentices had been significant enough that none of them had ever asked to go out on the town together.

He knew he'd been missing out while others had been forging strong bonds with other apprentices – but he'd been too shy to do anything about it. He hadn't known enough of the other apprentices around Tor'Esint to build such friendships. Perhaps that was another reason none of the Inventrici ever asked to work with him now. Perhaps they'd become friends early on in their careers and were used to working with each other.

It mattered not. Aveline was working with him now and he was grateful for the help.

At her door, he knocked soundly. He'd never been inside her workshop before. It felt odd being there, but at least he knew there was an apprentice this evening.

A young man opened the door. He couldn't have been more than sixteen or seventeen years old. His round face peered out the door suspiciously.

"Telchide Inventore?"

"Indeed," Telchide answered. "You must be Aveline's apprentice."

The boy nodded. "Nevio."

"Good evening, Nevio."

Telchide tipped his hat and waited for the boy to let him in. But Nevio didn't stand aside.

"I believe Aveline is expecting me," Telchide said, pulling out his pocket watch to check the time. "We're to work on her invention together."

Nevio finally let him in. Telchide placed both his hat and coat on the hooks by the door before looking around the workshop. Aveline was nowhere in sight.

"Is Aveline out?" he asked, confused.

Nevio shook his head. "She's upstairs. I'm to tell you she'll be down soon."

Telchide noticed the boy stood as awkwardly as he did himself. This seemed to be unfamiliar territory for both of them.

"Did you enjoy the visit to your family?" Telchide asked, for something to say.

Nevio broke into a smile. "Indeed, I did. Mamma insists all her children return home for one week on her birthday, so we see each other at least once a year. We all complain, but I think we'd all miss each other if we didn't do it."

"Are they in Tor'Esint?"

"No, we're from Tor'Selit but some of us moved away to find apprenticeships. Maestra Aveline is very talented. I'm lucky to learn from her."

Telchide had to agree. She was indeed very talented. "Did you always want to be an Inventore?"

"Papà's a panettiere and mamma works with him," Nevio told him. "They both thought I would take over the pastricceria. So did I, until I realised I was more interested in how their ovens and tools worked than I was in the bread and pastries they made.

"We put my name on the apprentice list in Tor'Selit and Tor'Esint almost four years ago. The waiting list for apprenticeships gets longer every year, especially now that the Edict's in place here. Some apprentices are sent back when their maestri are no longer available, and they're put at the top of the list."

Telchide knew the situation for apprentices was bad, but he hadn't realised it was quite so dire as this. It was no wonder Nevio was older than he'd expected for a second-year apprentice.

He realised after a time that the apprentice was expecting him to say something else, but he had nothing to say. Instead, he walked around the workshop, looking at Aveline's various projects.

The workshop was set up quite differently to his own. Telchide hadn't really thought much of customer comfort when laying out his workshop. It was Sebetine who'd insisted he purchase a small table and chairs for them. She'd always had clever suggestions like that.

Aveline's workshop had an entire shelved area at the front dedicated to her previous inventions. It looked like it housed a sample of every invention she'd ever created, from simple pocket watches to the zipper that had earned her an Electrum Guild Mark.

Telchide was inspecting Aveline's version of a friction light when she came out to greet him. He took in her appearance with some surprise. She wasn't wearing one of the usual work dresses he'd seen her in before. Today, she had on a more functional pair of light brown work pants, with a dark leather overbust corset and a cream-coloured top with detachable sleeves. There was a pocketed apron over the top of it all, with various tools sticking out the main pocket.

"Oh, do you like that one?" she asked.

Telchide tore his gaze away from her outfit and nodded. Aveline unlocked the cabinet with a key from her neck chain and pulled it out to show him. He turned on the light quickly and easily, but it was no more efficient than his own friction light. Until they found a way to store that energy, it would be an exercise in futility.

Perhaps that was what he could work on after his Lightbox – some sort of fuel cell.

"A fuel cell?" Aveline asked.

"Sorry?" Telchide looked up at her in confusion.

"What was that about a fuel cell?" she asked again.

It dawned on him that his last thought must have been out loud. He hadn't meant it to be.

"Oh, erm," he stumbled. "I was thinking how similar your friction light is to my own and how neither of us will get much further without a fuel cell that can store energy."

Aveline looked at him in silence for so long that he began to feel uncomfortable. He hadn't said anything so very radical. He was certain she must've thought the same thing herself, many times. Or perhaps not. In fact, there were enough Inventrici in Beltigura that if someone had thought of it, it would exist by now. It was an idea worthy of not just an Electrum Guild Mark, but a Gold one.

Aveline finally recovered herself and sent Nevio off to make a pot of tea for them. Only when he'd gone did she speak again.

"Chide, did you hear what Dania said at our last dinner?"

Telchide realised that, even in her own house, Aveline was afraid to call their meetings what they really were.

"Ardo told me a little about it this morning," he ventured, hesitantly.

Aveline ensured the front door was locked before continuing.

"She's heard of a plant on the Caldera with enough energy to lethally shock a grown man."

Telchide nodded in stupefied silence. That was not exactly what Eduardo had told him. He'd left out the lethal part.

"My main concern was how to harness the power. But if we do as you suggest and build a fuel cell to contain the power, that could work."

Telchide was still reeling from the supposed power of the plant. It could be enough energy to power an entire house's lights for a week! Imagine not needing candles or friction lights every evening. The thought was so foreign he could barely wrap his head around it.

"A box," he said, coming out of his thoughts. "A box to contain the plant."

"What kind of box would hold it?" Aveline asked, once more checking that Nevio was still upstairs.

"Not metal," Telchide replied. "Metal reacts to friction power – I can only imagine how it would react to the plant. Let me think on it and we'll discuss it tomorrow, at my house."

Aveline's eyes drifted towards Nevio as he entered the room, then back to Telchide. She nodded. Their conversation about the plant was over for the evening. Few Maestri trusted their apprentices implicitly.

The evening passed much as every other evening that week. Telchide remained absorbed in their work, not noticing food or tea until it was put in front of him. He absently wondered if Nevio had made the food while he and Aveline were working so diligently. It was basic fare – warm fresh bread, cheese, sliced cured meats and marinated vegetables – things that Serenita would usually serve for lunch when she didn't want to cook twice in one day.

By the time Aveline signalled it was time for him to leave, they'd finished the main plan for her sliding chair idea. The miniature rails wouldn't be ready until Legaramedi. That would give Telchide time to make the chair.

"Shall I see you tomorrow evening, then?" Aveline asked as she opened the door for him.

"Only if you particularly want to," Telchide replied. "I've finished all of my outstanding orders and am only working on my Lightbox now."

A look of disappointment flashed over Aveline's face. Telchide only caught it as he looked up from his buttons to adjust his hat. He stood still and looked at her closely. Wavy light brown hair tied back to not get caught in her work. Hazel eyes full of emotions that Telchide couldn't read. A pleasing figure, shown up to advantage in the moonlight.

He flinched at the thought and blushed angrily at himself. He was not free to look at other women like that. He was an unavailable man. Telchide coughed to cover his discomfort.

"I thought we were going to discuss the other idea. The box?" Aveline raised her eyebrows.

Telchide shook his head in confusion.

"The non-metal box, remember?" Aveline prompted.

"Ah, yes, very well. We can discuss that tomorrow evening. Will Nevio be accompanying you?"

Aveline huffed. "Chide, has anyone told you how frustrating it can be working with you?"

"Countless times," he replied, before realising it was a rhetorical question. "So..."

"Nevio will stay here and work on whatever I leave him to do."

Telchide nodded, then finally remembered why they were going to discuss the box at *his* place. Her irritation made more sense now. He wished, not for the first time, that he wasn't always so absorbed in his own thoughts.

"Until tomorrow then. Good night, Nevio," he called out.

"Good night, Inventore!" Nevio called from the workshop. "It was nice to meet you."

Telchide almost stumbled on the stairs at the unexpected social nicety. Not many people were ever pleased to meet him, let alone spend an entire evening in his company. Nevio must have added that last bit for Aveline's benefit.

Chapter 6 – Ramedi 3 Mercantili 230 Years After Implosion

"Papà, is Aveline coming over tonight?" Teresina asked between mouthfuls of toast slathered with jam. Telchide nodded, helping himself to two slices of toast. He spread his jam more sparingly than his daughter.

"What will you work on, if all of your orders are finished?"

"Oh, we have another matter to discuss."

Teresina played with her toast, licking the jam off the edges.

"If you're only discussing things, do you think she would do my hair at the same time?"

Telchide laughed. He thought he should be crying instead, but he couldn't help it. This was something Teresina should be asking her own mamma to do, not an Inventrice who was coming over to discuss a work matter. But he had to admire her tenacity.

Since meeting Aveline that first evening, Teresina had taken more care with her appearance – even Telchide could see that. But Serenita could only help her so much. Neither of them was well versed on current hairstyles and how to do them. It only made sense that Teresina would resort to asking Aveline. She was the only other woman Teresina had regular contact with now.

"I really don't think it's the right time for that, Resi, but you may ask her if she doesn't mind doing it another day. If I'm not working, I'll take you myself, otherwise I promise Nonna will take you."

"Take her where?" Serenita asked suspiciously as she walked into the kitchen.

Telchide smiled. "To Aveline's house for a hairstyle. If she agrees to it in the first place and I'm not available to take her myself."

Serenita paused for a moment, but then her shoulders fell, and she nodded. He wondered if the same thoughts were running through her mind as his. Sebetine used to do Teresina's hair in such lovely braids. Her own hair she used to twirl up in such a way Telchide couldn't understand how it didn't fall out. He tried not to think of it. If he thought of Sebetine now, his entire day would be consumed with thoughts of her, and he did not wish to be so distracted when he was just starting to feel like himself once more.

He heard the Guild Hall clocks striking eight and hurried to finish his breakfast. He kissed Serenita's cheek as she took his empty plate from him, then navigated the cluttered stairs to open.

There was a sharp, insistent knocking on the door when he reached the workshop. Telchide quickly unlocked and opened the door to find a short, rotund man with his fist up, ready to knock again. His face was red and beaded with sweat – he must have walked halfway across Tor'Esint to find him – but the most striking thing about his appearance was his purple coat and top hat. They were so bright that Telchide nearly looked away.

"Signore, please do come in. May I offer you a cool drink?"

The man paused, mouth open, seemingly ready to shout. But the offer of a drink must have been too tempting. He nodded and stepped inside.

Telchide took the brief opportunity, while the man unbuttoned his coat and removed his hat, to ring the bell. It had become their code for Teresina to send down refreshments for his customers without the need for Telchide to shout up the stairs.

Before the man was seated in one of the two chairs by the door, Teresina was already working the dumbwaiter. She hastened down the stairs to retrieve the water. The man took the offered glass and smiled genially as Teresina curtseyed at him. She really was her mamma's daughter, with all the same charm.

It was unfortunate that Teresina was not older. Telchide would've taken her on as an apprentice in a trice. As it was, he motioned for her to bring his order pad and a pencil from his workbench. He sat in the empty chair and turned his attention back to the man.

"Signore, what may I do for you?"

The man looked around the workshop before settling his gaze on Telchide. "I understand you make passable pocket watches."

"Indeed, signore," Telchide said, trying not to smart at the insult. His pocket watches were more than just passable. They were works of art, as much as his music boxes.

The man looked around again and coughed. "Do you have any examples of your work?"

Telchide's thoughts went straight back to Aveline's workshop and the cabinet of items on display at the front for customers to peruse. Perhaps he should create his own customer display.

"Of course. Let me fetch them for you."

Telchide walked over to his workbench, opened the left drawer, and retrieved three pocket watches. He paused for a moment, then retrieved one more and brought all four back to the purple clothed man. With the watches displayed on the small table between them, Telchide took his seat once more.

"These three are pocket watches in the standard varieties: open face, hunter and demi-hunter. This other one is sometimes a favourite for the ladies, if they lack pockets in their garments."

He pointed to each of the watches in turn. The open face had glass covering the mechanisms so that one could see the turnings of the cogs and wheels. The hunter's mechanisms were completely covered by the face of the clock. It also included an extra cover that one had to click open. The demi-hunter was like the hunter except that the inner section of the cover was made of glass so that the hands of the clock could still be partially seen without opening the cover. The last was an open-faced watch, hanging like a pendant on a silver necklace. He'd commissioned a small number of these necklaces from his friend Ciro Corallino, specifically to be able to sell these watches more easily.

"Of course, the necklace watch is available in every style. One has only to choose, and I can make it."

The man sniffed loudly and picked up each of the watches in turn. Telchide took the order pad from Teresina and quietly shooed her away. This man looked like he might be difficult and would not appreciate a child writing the order, however competent she might be.

"May I inquire as to who the pocket watch would be for?" Telchide asked, hoping to be able to provide some sort of input.

The man's eyes closed for a brief moment as a smile spread over his face. He sighed heavily before opening his eyes once more.

"My glorious companion," he replied with unabashed affection. "It's her birthday in two weeks. She often complains that she must ask me the time, so I thought it would be a perfect present for her."

Telchide tried to imagine what sort of woman would be happy with a purple-coated man. He wondered if she liked loud colours and had picked his suit out herself. Perhaps she even had garments to match his. The thought almost made him laugh, but he managed to turn the laugh into a large smile instead.

"Ah, such a thoughtful present will be well received indeed," Telchide assured him. "Do you think your companion would like a necklace watch or do her garments sport these pockets I've seen about on dresses recently?"

"Oh, pockets indeed!" the stout man nodded happily. "Only the latest fashions for my amore."

"Very well then, a traditional pocket watch. All that's left is for you to decide which type you think she might like and the design, if any, on the metal."

"Well, she does so love to open my watch, but I'm not certain she'd be happy doing that every time."

Telchide nodded. "The demi-hunter was created for just such a purpose. It allows the owner to catch a glimpse of the time without opening it."

He picked up the appropriate watch and passed it to the man, surprised by the care the man took in handling the watch.

"Such a beauty," the man gushed. "It's no wonder you have a Silver Guild Mark upon your door. I must say I'd have assumed you'd have an Electrum Guild Mark with workmanship such as this."

Telchide couldn't help but blush at the compliment. It wasn't often that his customers gave such praise. Usually, he had to cover up a blunder of sorts from something he'd accidentally said.

"Signore is too kind. Though may I say, if your companion is as glorious as you suggest, she's worthy of only the finest. I'd be happy to create a demi-hunter for her with an etched design on the back and along the metal section of the front."

The man nodded. "Yes, that would please her. And though I know gold is most expensive, I know she secretly loves the colour of silver."

"Then why not an electrum watch?" Telchide asked. "Not quite as expensive as gold, but better quality than silver with a similar colouring."

The man paused. "I've heard electrum is trickier to work with than silver or gold."

Telchide shrugged. "That's true, but it's also more durable. An electrum watch would last much longer than silver. It could be passed down as an heirloom, should you be blessed with children."

Telchide knew it was a blunder as soon as he'd said it. The man's face fell.

"Of course, it will also make your companion the envy of all her friends, especially with the designs I can etch into the metal."

This last comment had the desired effect. It cooled down the man's temper before he lashed out.

"Designs, you say." The man scratched his nose inelegantly. "My companion is partial to birds. Are your etchings precise enough to depict those?"

Telchide pulled his little sketch book out of his back pocket and showed the man his most recent drawings of birds. The man took the book and leafed through the pages with a growing smile.

"Anything you see here can be etched into the back of a pocket watch. However, the more intricate the design, the longer it will take."

The man stopped at a page Telchide had drawn years ago and stared at it. It was a scene of a Tor'Esint street lined with gas lamps.

"This." He pointed to the page. "This is what I want. She was so fascinated by the gas lamps when they installed the mechanical spiders to light them. She will simply adore it."

Telchide cleared his throat. "Signore has a good eye, but I fear I cannot place this entire design on the back of a pocket watch. It simply will not fit. Could we narrow it down to this perhaps?"

He made a circle with his thumbs and index fingers, roughly the size of a pocket watch, and placed it over the drawing, capturing a single gas lamp and the night sky.

The man turned his head this way and that, trying to see it from all angles.

"Can you not create a larger pocket watch to include more of the design?" he asked hopefully.

Telchide tilted his head side to side. "It *would* be possible, but a larger watch may seem cumbersome to one who is used to a regular size. And, if you'll excuse me, the ladies tend to like smaller, more delicate items."

The man nodded knowingly. "Yes, that *is* true. Very well, then. I expect it to be ready next Gildadi. Her birthday will be the day after. And I want an inscription on it."

Telchide wrote the details down on his order pad and read it aloud at the same time to confirm.

"One standard size, demi-hunter pocket watch made from electrum. A gas lamp design etched on the back with your inscription. With the electrum, I would suggest signore choose from the darker watch faces. It will make the time that much easier to see with the lighter coloured watch hands."

The man hesitated, but eventually nodded. "Yes, a darker face could be more elegant. Just ensure that it is. I will not return, nor will I recommend you if I'm unimpressed."

Telchide nodded, writing the extra detail on the order pad. At least this man was implying that he would recommend Telchide and potentially use his services again. It was more than most of his customers did.

"Now as to the price."

The man interrupted him with a cough. "Two electrums if I'm satisfied. One if I'm not."

Telchide swallowed nervously. He was in no position to argue. With his Silver Guild Mark, customers were only obliged to pay him in silver coins, even if they asked for more difficult inventions or more expensive materials. Of course, if it would cost him more money to take the order, Telchide often found himself insisting on a higher price and sometimes lost the order.

"Agreed."

He held out his hand to shake on the deal. The man shook it heartily, donned his purple coat and top hat and left.

Thankfully, Telchide had made the decision years ago to mass order the parts he needed for watches in a variety of materials. He still had stores from that time, though they would run low by the end of the year, and he would be forced to deal with the Mercantili Guild to order more.

This watch would take him a matter of days to complete, even using electrum, then he could spend the rest of the time perfecting the design and inscription. He needed recommendations and repeat business now more than ever.

When Sebetine had still been there, Telchide had made enough to put aside a tidy little sum. But he'd bitten deep into those funds searching for her. There was still some left, but he was not adding to it as much as he would like. If something happened to him, there would not be much left to provide for Teresina and Serenita.

He pushed the thought from his mind. If he continued his working relationship with Aveline, perhaps things would improve. As it was, he'd already completed orders that should've taken him twice as long. It gave him time to work on his extra projects for Great Work submissions. Perhaps the Lightbox would earn him his Electrum Guild Mark and things would start to look up.

***

Aveline arrived early that evening – much earlier than usual. In fact, it was only just after the end of trading hours. Telchide hadn't had time to lock the door and Teresina was still upstairs.

Telchide looked up at her flustered entrance. Her coat was already unbuttoned before she was halfway through the door. She closed and locked the door quickly behind her, shuttered the window and peeked out through the shutters onto the street.

"Aveline, what in Caldera's smoke..."

"Shh!"

She waved him into silence. Telchide closed his mouth firmly and crossed his arms angrily.

After long moments of standing still, she finally turned and glanced around the workshop. She didn't even look at him. Her eyes settled on the back door.

"Is that how Eduardo gets in here?" she asked, pointing to the door.

"Yes, but..."

Before he could finish his question, Aveline dashed to the door and unlocked it. Only then did she look at Telchide. He was standing now, arms still crossed, glaring at her. She didn't appear to notice, or care.

"Is Teresina here?"

"Yes."

"And Serenita?"

"Of course," he replied through clenched teeth.

She bit her lip. "Better tell them to stay upstairs. Just in case."

"In case of what?" Telchide asked, his stomach tightening uncomfortably.

"Chide, please."

Her eyes softened at that moment. Telchide took a breath to steady his nerves, then went upstairs. Teresina was, thankfully, in her room. He did not disturb her but went straight to the kitchen where Serenita was busy with preparations for dinner.

"Serenita, I'm not certain what's going on tonight, but it's best if you keep Teresina upstairs with you."

Serenita was set to argue but then looked at his face closely.

"I'll send down the tea tray."

She placed two teacups on the tray and looked questioningly up at him with a third in her hand.

"I don't know. She unlocked the back door, so I think maybe Eduardo will be joining us."

Serenita frowned and added an extra teacup. "Be careful, Chide."

Telchide wanted to tell her that he was always careful, that whatever was happening tonight was not his doing. Instead, he nodded and returned downstairs.

He found Aveline pacing back and forth at the back of his workshop, near the dying fire. Telchide placed another log on the fire as he waited for Serenita to send down the dumbwaiter. The nights were getting chilly, and he did not relish the thought of catching a cold. Alchimisti were wonderfully clever with all their concoctions, but it didn't mean Telchide had to be happy to take tonics with unpronounceable ingredients.

The fire stoked, Telchide turned back to find Aveline still pacing and glancing at the back door every few steps. He didn't bother talking to her. She was clearly not in a mood to answer his questions. Instead, he poured two cups of tea, handed her one and sat down to enjoy the other one himself. Aveline stopped pacing, looked down at the cup in her hands and blinked at it.

"How's Nevio going with his apprenticeship?" Telchide asked, hoping that the apprentice was a topic she would not shy from.

Aveline glanced nervously at the door and finally took her customary seat beside Telchide. She sipped the tea and drew back with a yelp.

"Smoking Caldera – that's hot!"

"Of course it is. Serenita only just made it." Telchide chuckled. "So, how's Nevio doing?"

Aveline rubbed her lips with the back of her hand. "As well as can be expected I suppose. He tiptoes around the tasks I ask him to perform. He has no confidence in his skills even though he's quite competent. I've never been a teacher before and he's never been a student. I set him the simplest of watches to complete after he returned, and he hasn't even started."

She took out her pocket watch and checked it against the standing clock, fiddled with it and replaced it in her pocket.

"Where are they?" she muttered under her breath.

"Where are who?" Telchide asked, blowing on the hot tea.

Aveline looked at him in confusion. "Dania and Eduardo, of course."

"Of course." Telchide lightly tapped his forehead. "And, erm, *why* are we waiting for them?"

"*Really*, Chide. Think!"

Telchide narrowed his eyes at her tone. Why should he know to expect Dania and Eduardo? He never saw the two of them together except for at their meetings. He didn't know anything about Dania except for the recent mentions of her in connection with the sparking plant. Telchide drew in a sharp breath.

The back door slammed open. Eduardo pushed a heavily cloaked Dania into the room and locked the door behind them.

"Evening," Eduardo said, tipping his hat.

"What took you so long?" Aveline asked tersely.

Eduardo drew himself up to his full height, which was only just above Aveline's. "You may not have noticed, but there have been more and more raids on Guild workshops lately. I trust my apprentices as much as the next mentor, but I'd rather they were all safely away from my home when I come to Chide's house with another Alchimista."

"Have any arrangements been made?" Aveline asked anxiously. Telchide was irritated that *she* was anxious when it was *his* house she'd decided to use for an impromptu Inter-Guild meeting.

"I went down to the docks this morning to enquire about hiring a boat but, well, they're quite expensive and I'm only on my Copper Guild Mark," Dania said in a quiet voice.

Aveline frowned. "But were any of them willing to sail to the Caldera?"

"One. But I didn't like the look of them. I mean, the captain seemed decent enough, but his first mate kept looking me up and down in a lascivious way. Made me feel quite uncomfortable."

"Good thing you went of a morning," Aveline remarked sourly. "Well, what was the price?"

"Five electrum to take us there."

"That's quite reasonable," Aveline pointed out.

"Five to take us there," Dania repeated. "Thirty if we want them to stay until we're ready to come back."

"Oh."

Telchide started forward. That was more than he earned most years. How was such an amount to be paid?

"I could have spared the five, if I had time to save for it, but *thirty*! It's impossible," Dania exclaimed.

Telchide saw the look pass between Eduardo and Aveline.

"I'll fund the expedition," Aveline stated in a matter-of-fact tone. "Chide can help me design a way to collect and store the sparking plants, then we can go together to find them."

Telchide listened mutely. If Aveline was so cavalier about funding such an expensive expedition, she must have a great deal more money than he'd realised. The rest of the conversation sunk in.

"Wait, *I* can't go on the expedition."

Everyone stared at him and Telchide started fiddling with his pocket watch.

"Well, I can't," he repeated. "I won't leave Teresina alone with Serenita. What if something were to happen to one of them? What if something were to happen to *me*? Her mamma has already disappeared. I can't do that to my daughter."

The others exchanged glances with one another, then went on again without him.

"I'll organise the box with Chide when the two of you leave," Aveline said with an air of confidence. "What we really need to discuss is how to get past the Mercantili blockade around the city. They can't do anything when we come back in, especially if we have no imported goods. But they'll do all they can to prevent us leaving if they think we're collaborating."

Eduardo raised a hand. "Leave that to me. I have a friend on the inside. He'll be able to tell me when the best time is to leave. Best be prepared as soon as possible so you can leave whenever our window of opportunity opens."

"We'll need to organise the box first, buy supplies," Aveline pointed out. "We won't be ready for at least a week. What do you think, Nia?"

The young Alchimista looked up at her name. "You heard me say I can't fund the expedition, didn't you?"

"That doesn't mean you can't come along," Aveline insisted, clasping her hands. "We wouldn't even know about this plant if it weren't for you."

Dania glanced sideways at Eduardo, a little smile on her face. "Can I?"

Telchide wondered why she was asking his permission.

Eduardo shrugged. "I don't see why not. Best pass it by the Guild first, to be on the safe side."

Aveline's eyes grew wide. "No. No Guilds involved."

"They're bound to find out, Aveline," Telchide pointed out. "You know we're required to register any absence to them so people can find us if we leave the city."

Aveline pursed her lips. "Fine. We tell our Guilds, but we don't tell them who else is going on the expedition. I'll tell mine which Inventrici are going, and you tell yours which Alchimisti are going. They don't need to know that we're going on the same boat."

"Oh yes, and what happens when they discover you returning on the same boat?" Eduardo asked with a twisted smile.

"We feed them a story about a wrecked boat and a rescue," Aveline replied easily. "The return trip is easier to explain."

Dania nodded excitedly. "We're meeting up at the Exploding Beakers next week. Ardo, will you be able to speak to your friend before then?"

Eduardo nodded. "We're old friends. It won't seem odd that I speak to him, especially if I order a few imported items from him."

"Nia, what's the name of the ship? Or the captain?" Aveline asked. "I'll see what I can organise with them."

"It's the *Avanti*, Dock 34. The captain's name is Corrado. Didn't catch the name of his mate." She sniffed loudly. "Didn't care to."

Aveline straightened her spine. "Right, well I'll deal with that tomorrow if I can. Next day otherwise. You two head back now. No use staying any longer than you need to. We'll see you at Nestore's next week."

Telchide shook hands with Ardo and nodded awkwardly to Dania. She smiled shyly and held out her hand to shake his. It wasn't a new custom to shake hands with a woman, but it still made Telchide blush when he did. A touch was such an intimate thing. Though he distractedly noticed that he didn't feel that same rush of excitement he had with Aveline. Perhaps he was getting used to dealing with women.

Then Aveline's fingers brushed against his arm as she moved to hug Dania in farewell and the rush of excitement returned. Not used to it, he reflected. He quickly pulled away from the situation and opened the door to the crisp night air.

Eduardo preceded Dania and helped her down the dark pathway. He knew it well from all too frequent use.

Telchide locked the door behind them and turned to find Aveline staring at him with crossed arms. He held her gaze firmly.

"You need to come," she told him flatly. "One Inventrice won't be enough on this trip."

"I'll help design the box, but I'm not coming," Telchide asserted.

Aveline raised her eyes and took a deep breath.

"Very well. I'll have to find someone else to come. But I'd rather the person responsible for the idea of a fuel cell has a hand in creating it. I can't very well include you if you won't come."

Telchide grew very still. The fuel cell was *his* idea. She had no right to steal it from him just because he wouldn't go on her smoking expedition!

"Forgive me, but if no one else has invented one yet, I assume no one has thought of a fuel cell before me. If that's the case, you'd be obliged to share credit for the invention with me."

Aveline placed a hand on his shoulder. His stomach lurched.

"Chide, I *want* to work on this with you, but you refuse to make yourself available for me. You say you can't leave Teresina with Serenita, but have you even spoken to them about it? Perhaps they won't be as against the idea as you assume."

Telchide opened his mouth to protest, but Aveline was right – he hadn't spoken to his family before making this decision. Well, he couldn't do that tonight. Aveline sighed and took her hand from his shoulder. She walked over to the coat stand, finally took the hatpin out of her hat and let her hair fall loose around her shoulders.

"Let's just work on the plan for the box for now. Whether you come or not, I'll need it."

Telchide was glad for the project. It gave him something to focus on and he needed that right now. His mind was awhirl with the possibility of going to the Caldera, finding the sparking plant and using it to create a fuel cell to earn his Electrum Guild Mark. It would be the pinnacle of his career. His products would be in high demand, and he would never need worry about supporting his family again.

Chapter 7 – Mercatodi 7 Mercantili 230 Years After Implosion

Telchide sighed heavily as he lay in bed staring at the ceiling. He didn't enjoy setting up his stall every fortnight in Piazza Mercantile, vying for a prominent position and socialising with the crowd to try to get enough orders to keep him busy for the next two weeks. Thankfully, Teresina loved it. She knew his favourite spot to set up and had already dragged Serenita out of the house to reserve it for him. She'd made such a ruckus trying to find her "dress with pockets like Aveline Inventrice" that Telchide had given up all hope of sleeping more.

Now they were gone, he could get ready in peace and quiet. Mercatodi was the only time he meticulously groomed himself. No matter how good his inventions, no one would approach his stall if he did not look presentable. It would also not do to have his daughter looking more presentable than him.

Down in the workshop, Telchide uncovered his own version of Maestro Ugo's Spiderseat. The original invention was a chair with eight mechanical legs which used a sensor to follow the person in front of it. It was mostly for his mechanical limb clients to help them home while waiting for their limbs to be ready. Telchide's modification allowed him to bring the wooden boxes holdings his wares for the Mercatodi stall to Piazza Mercantile and back again. Not only did it give him a way to transport all his goods, but it doubled as a table for him. Though all stall holders paid a price to the Mercantili Guild for the privilege of erecting a stall, they were not provided anything other than a licence.

Years ago, Serenita had insisted on an easier way to transport everything after he'd asked her to help bring his goods to the piazza. Now, he couldn't imagine facing Mercatodi without it.

He filled the box with his display pocket watches, a few music boxes, and a box of spare parts in case people needed urgent repairs. In fact, he generally spent as much of Mercatodi fixing items as acquiring new orders. Telchide closed the lid, securing the box to the Spiderseat, belted on his tool pouch and led the mechanical contraption out the door, taking care to lock it securely afterward.

Telchide led the Spiderseat after him towards Via dell'Oro. As he rounded the corner, he saw Teresina hopping from one foot to the other glancing down from Piazza Mercantile. He waved to her, and she ran towards him, leaving Serenita to reserve the spot herself.

"Oh papà! You'll never believe it!" she yelled at him as she ran.

He smiled at her inability to contain her excitement.

"Your spot was already taken, but Aveline Inventrice said we could set up next to her stall instead! Isn't that fabulous news?"

Telchide paused briefly. He didn't want Teresina to see his disappointment. Aveline always set up on the opposite side of Piazza Mercantile, where it intersected with Via del Corallo, just outside her workshop. If she were allowing them a spot next to hers, it wouldn't be on the corner. Fewer people would notice his stall, especially if it were next to hers. Aveline's stall always had a crush of people around it. He shook his head, trying to get the thought of so many people out of it.

It didn't help that he was still annoyed, mostly with himself, that he would not be going on the trip to the Caldera in search of the sparking plant. He couldn't help but wonder if Aveline had already found another Inventore to accompany her.

Telchide plastered a false smile to his face and followed his chattering daughter up the block to Piazza Mercantile. She did not stop talking the entire time. Telchide was used to it. He'd learned to let her words run past him, not really listening unless something caught his attention.

"...and she said she'd be delighted to do my hair for me if you'd bring me to her place tomorrow morning. Will you, papà?"

Teresina tugged at his sleeve and stared up at him pleadingly. He looked down and let her question register.

"Teresina, you should not have asked her such a thing!" he reprimanded in a quiet voice. They'd reached the piazza and he did not want Aveline to hear him.

"But, she *offered*," Teresina protested. "I only complained that Nonna doesn't know the latest fashions and Aveline Inventrice invited me to her place so she could do something pretty. Please say you'll take me, papà ... please."

Telchide stroked her cheek affectionately. "I suppose so. It's Riposidi tomorrow after all."

Teresina hugged him and ran across the piazza to Aveline, presumably to tell her the news. Aveline caught his eye and smiled brightly at him. Telchide felt a warm glow in his chest. If he weren't so thankful that she'd taken the time to be kind to his daughter, he might still be annoyed that she had a corner stall and he did not.

"Good morning Serenita, Aveline. Thank you for reserving me a spot."

Serenita grunted in reply. "Now that you're finally awake, I'm going home to rest. I'll come and take Teresina off your hands later."

Telchide kissed her cheek affectionately and bid her farewell.

He began to set up his stall next to Aveline's. She watched him quietly, but he kept his attention focused on what he was doing. He took the inner section out of the box and put it carefully to one side. That done, Teresina helped him turn the outer section upside down next to the Spiderseat, covering both with a cloth to keep the mechanical contraption from moving during the day. Teresina insisted on being the one to place his display items on it. He passed them to her one by one, not taking much notice of how she was placing them.

"Are you using that box?" Aveline asked, pointing to the inner section Telchide had placed on the ground.

He shrugged. "We usually take turns using it as a chair."

"If you'll permit me?" she asked and reached out for it without giving Telchide a chance to reply. "Teresina, be a dear and move everything to that side of the table, there's a good girl. Now, we'll place this here and it will display your music boxes more prominently. They deserve more attention than you give them down there."

Aveline didn't bother asking permission before moving his wares around. Telchide watched in stunned silence as she rearranged his entire stall. The end result however was, well, quite magnificent really.

"Now, Teresina, run inside and let Nevio know that we'll require an extra chair today. You can help him bring them out if you like."

Telchide toyed with his pocket watch as Teresina disappeared inside Aveline's workshop. There was a thoroughly uncomfortable moment of silence. Telchide coughed and cleared his throat.

"Erm, Teresina tells me you've offered to do her hair tomorrow."

Aveline glanced over at him with raised eyebrows. "Was that remiss of me? She looks so forlornly at my hair every time she sees me and then touches her own as though she's ashamed of it."

Telchide nodded knowingly. "In truth, she's been pestering me to ask you to do her hair since that first day she met you. I did not think it was proper. Or that you'd have time," he added quickly, seeing a cold flicker cross her face. "You have so many orders and projects you're working on. I didn't want her to bother you."

"I can take back my offer, if you prefer," she stated a little too calmly.

Telchide shook his head firmly. "No, no. If you do that, I'll never hear the end of it. Truly, Aveline, it was very kind of you. I simply didn't want to be an imposition in your life. You've already been such a great help to me, and I can't imagine I've repaid the favour very well."

Aveline's features smoothed out into a smile. "You've been more help than you realise. In fact, if you think Teresina won't mind watching us work, the mock rails for the chair lift project have arrived and I hoped we might put it together tomorrow."

"But's it's Riposodi," Telchide said without thinking about it.

Aveline hesitated. "Well, yes, of course if you have other plans, we could continue it after closing next week."

"Oh. No, I didn't mean that," Telchide fumbled for words. "I thought *you'd* have other plans. I'm more than happy to work on it tomorrow. I've finished carving a miniature chair and was starting on your box. Will dovetail joints be adequate?"

"Dovetail joints?" Aveline stared at him blankly.

"Yes, I thought they might be best as they won't require nails, which might react badly to the plants if they're so powerful as have been suggested."

Aveline laughed lightly. "Oh Chide, I don't know anything about carpentry. If you think dovetail joints are best, then I trust you. But are you certain you won't change your mind and come with me?"

"Come where?" Teresina asked, holding the door open for Nevio as he brought out two chairs.

Aveline went silent and glanced at Telchide. He shook his head quickly.

"To ... the Inventrici Convention next week. I don't want to have to go by myself."

"Of course he will, then," Teresina answered. "Won't you, papà?"

Telchide bowed his head slightly. "I'd be honoured to accompany you to the Inventrici Convention."

Aveline's eyes lit up. Which brought an unexpected flush to Telchide's cheeks. He quickly busied himself making minor adjustments t0 his stall. It simply would not do to have Teresina or Aveline notice.

The Guild Hall clocks struck eight o'clock and the streets began to fill with customers. Telchide watched with envy how quickly Aveline negotiated her first, second and third transactions. By the fourth one, he was beginning to lose hope that any customers would come to his stall over hers.

"I know just the thing for you, Signora Angela," Aveline said loudly. "Have you met my fellow Inventore, Telchide? He makes the most magnificent music boxes! Just look at these. This type would be perfect for your son."

Telchide nearly fell off his chair in surprise when the voluminous lady and her portly young son moved over to his stall. Aveline moved closer to Telchide, and he suddenly felt like there were too many people near him. She turned the handle of the simplest music box and music burst forth from it. The boy's eyes widened. Telchide could see his hands twitching in excitement.

"Would you like a turn, young man?" Telchide asked, moving the music box closer to him.

The boy looked up at his mamma who sighed dramatically.

"Oh, very well then Angelo, but mind you don't break it."

Angelo eagerly reached for the music box. Telchide showed him how to hold it down securely while he turned the handle to get the best sound. After he'd played the tune three times over, Teresina squeezed between Telchide and Aveline and produced another music box from her pocket.

"Try this one," she suggested. "It's my favourite, but papà can do any tune you like if you bring him the sheet music."

Angelo took the proffered music box, placed it firmly on the upturned wooden box and turned the handle. He grinned at the sound.

"Mamma, please may I have one? I won't ask for anything else today if you say yes."

Telchide watched his mamma carefully. She raised an eyebrow at her son and glanced at Aveline, who had returned to her stall. Telchide looked over just in time to see her nod to the lady.

"How much for this one?" the lady asked, pointing to the one Teresina had allowed the boy to try.

Teresina snatched it back. "This one's *mine*," she said firmly. "Papà can make a new one for your son. He wouldn't want this old one anyway."

Telchide glared quickly at Teresina, who had the good sense to hide behind him. He turned back to the affronted lady and attempted to smooth over his daughter's blunder.

"Signora, I can make your son a brand-new copper music box for ten silvers. It can be the same tune as my daughter's own or any other short tune of your choosing."

"*Ten* silvers?" the lady's voice rose to an almost unbearable pitch.

"Ten silvers is half of what it's worth, Signora Angela," Aveline chipped in from her stall. "Believe me! I've recently had the opportunity to work with Telchide Inventore on two of his music boxes and was amazed by the technicality and precision of such a small device. I can assure you no other Inventore in all Tor'Esint could make one better. Young Angelo will be the envy of his friends when they see it."

Signora Angela's face softened instantly into a proud glow. "Well, it *is* your birthday in two weeks. We could call it an early birthday present, and you can show it off to your friends at your celebration. What tune would you like?"

Telchide got his order pad out and wrote down the details. They agreed Signora Angela would bring him Angelo's favourite tune and the music box would be ready three days afterwards. Telchide still had enough pieces to make twenty of these simple music boxes. It wouldn't take more than an hour for him to put it together. The most time-consuming task would be punching out the bumps for the music.

As soon as they were out of earshot, he turned to his daughter.

"Teresina, what have I told you about the Mercatodi stall? It's the same as any other time I have a customer in the workshop."

"If I am to be seen, I am not to be heard," she mumbled. "I'm sorry papà, but I didn't want him to think he could have *my* music box!"

"Then you shouldn't have offered it to him to play with," he countered. "It's getting a little busier now, so why don't you run back home to Nonna? Perhaps you can convince her to take you for a walk through the market if you promise to behave yourself."

"Yes, papà," she answered, chin almost touching her chest.

Teresina made to walk behind Aveline to get to the street, but Aveline held her arm out stopping her.

"Chide, you're not going to let your daughter walk home alone, are you?"

"It's only two blocks away. She knows the way well," Telchide answered offhand.

Aveline rolled her eyes at him. "Nevio, would you mind escorting Teresina home? It seems her papà doesn't realise how dangerous it can be for young girls to go out walking by themselves."

"Of course, Maestra. Come Teresina, you can show me your other favourite inventions while we're there."

Teresina happily placed her hand in Nevio's and walked down the street with him.

"It's broad daylight, Veli," Telchide opined when they were out of sight. "What could possibly happen to her?"

"Chide, your daughter is clearly very independent, which is possibly why you treat her as though she's older than she is. But's she's *six*. Imagine what a nefarious person would do to a lone child, a girl at that, walking down an isolated street. How well do you think she'd defend herself?"

Telchide felt faint and put a hand out to grip the box table before he fell. Aveline's face softened.

"Perhaps nothing would've happened. I think though, that you'll feel safer now knowing Nevio is escorting her home?"

"Indeed," Telchide said, swallowing the bile in his mouth. "Thank you. Perhaps I'm not such a good papà after all."

"You're a very loving papà, Chide. Perhaps you've just never seen the darker side of Tor'Esint. It's nice that you protect your daughter's innocence like that."

Telchide forced a smile. He wasn't certain he liked what Aveline was implying but could say nothing about it as he was accosted by a customer needing repairs. Telchide took down the man's details and promised a working pocket watch in a few hours.

***

By the end of Mercatodi, Telchide had secured orders for three simple music boxes, two elaborate music boxes and four pocket watches. He'd repaired five pocket watches and returned them to their owners. It was, in fact, the most successful Mercatodi he'd ever had. He would certainly be run off his feet now, especially if he intended to make the box he'd promised for Aveline.

Aveline packed up her stall quickly with Nevio's help but kept Telchide company while he packed his own stall into the wooden box and secured it to the Spiderseat. Once done, Telchide shuffled his feet and looked around the piazza. Only the final few stall holders were still there, negotiating last minute deals with their customers.

"Aveline, would you be open to perhaps continuing our previous arrangement of helping each other after hours?" he asked hesitantly. "I think

I've taken on more work than I possibly should have if I'm to finish your box for you quickly."

"Of course, Chide," she replied. "I may not be free *every* evening, but we can certainly try for most. Let's discuss it tomorrow, when you bring Teresina over to get her hair done."

"Agreed." Telchide smiled.

Aveline struck out her hand to shake his. He took it firmly in his own, noticing immediately how cool her hand was to the touch. It was a pleasant contrast, until she held his hand just a little longer than politeness dictated. Telchide cleared his throat.

"Erm, well, yes then. Until tomorrow morning."

"Until tomorrow, Telchide Inventore," Aveline said with a small smile as she walked up the stairs to her workshop.

Chapter 8 – Riposidi 8 Mercantili 230 Years After Implosion

Teresina tugged on Telchide's hand the entire walk to Aveline's workshop. She'd insisted they leave as early as society would allow on Riposidi. Serenita had held firm to the idea that no one would dare be seen on the streets earlier than nine o'clock on the only rest day of the week. So, here they were, trotting along indecently early, just as the Guild Hall clocks struck nine.

"Can we do this every week, papà?" Teresina asked as she tugged, yet again, at his hand.

Telchide tried to pull her back, but she was too excited to slow down.

"No, Resi, not *every* week," he replied. "Aveline was very kind to offer, but one must not take advantage of one's friends or they will cease to be friends."

Teresina stopped dead in her tracks forcing Telchide to sidestep to avoid hitting her. She looked up at him closely.

"How should I know that? I don't have any friends," she stated accusingly.

Telchide stared at her in surprise. "Well, of course you do. You're friends with all of Eduardo's apprentices."

"Well, yes, but papà, apprentices don't count," she remonstrated, tugging him along again. "They're all so much older than me."

Telchide had no chance to say anything further. They'd reached Aveline's workshop. Teresina had knocked loudly on the door and was now busy smoothing down her dress. Telchide noticed that she'd chosen one without pockets today. It was, however, one of her favourite dresses – a dark green velvet bodice with detachable cream sleeves. The cream sleeves were well-worn, as the colour went with most of her dresses. She would need new ones soon and Serenita's failing eyesight would not allow her to sew such complicated garments much longer. Perhaps one of Aveline's Sarta friends could be of service to them.

"What was her name?" Telchide mumbled to himself.

"Whose name?" Teresina asked as Aveline opened the door.

Aveline looked bemused. "Whose name?"

Telchide gestured uselessly with his hands. "The Sarta you said had too many apprentices."

Aveline's eyes went wide. She looked up and down the street, then ushered them quickly inside.

"Telchide, a little tact, if you please!" Aveline reprimanded him. "Greta is one of my oldest friends. She would not like to know that I said she had too many apprentices to someone she's never met before."

Teresina narrowed her eyes at him. "Papà, perhaps this is why *you* don't have many friends."

Telchide felt the blood rush up the back of his neck and into his cheeks. It didn't help that Teresina was probably right. The only people he could truly call his friends were Eduardo and, only recently, Aveline. Filippo Falegname had been a friend of sorts, but they hadn't seen much of each other since Filippo had become a Maestro of his Guild. There was also Ciro Corallino, but he was technically Telchide's papà's friend rather than a friend in his own right.

"Why were you thinking of Greta?" Aveline asked, openly curious.

Telchide pointed to Teresina's sleeves. "These are practically worn through. Teresina will need new sleeves soon and I don't know how much longer Serenita will be able to sew them. I thought maybe your friend, Greta Sarta, might be open to making some."

Aveline choked back a laugh. "Chide, she's a *Gold* Sarta. Wouldn't you rather a Copper Sarta for such a simple job?"

He took off his coppola and turned it round and round by the rim. "I don't know any Sarti. Sebetine used to make our clothes and then when Serenita came to stay, she did the same. The last time I went to a Sarta was for my coat and that was years ago."

"I see," Aveline said slowly. "I'll have a word with Greta and see who she might recommend for the job. Though if those are Teresina's only cream sleeves, you might think about getting two sets."

"Never mind that now," Teresina said with a wave of her hand. "What about my hair? What can we do with it today?"

Telchide stood aside as Aveline led Teresina through a door and presumably up to her living quarters. The workshop felt oddly empty. It was only then he realised that Nevio wasn't there.

With nothing else to do, Telchide pulled out the model wooden chair from his pocket and sat down at Aveline's workbench. He'd seen her put the design for the chair lift in one of her drawers and debated searching for them, but eventually decided it would not be proper. He spotted the metal rails over on the workbench. Without a second thought, he picked them up and began working away at the puzzle.

By the time Teresina and Aveline returned, he'd rigged up a rudimentary pulley system, just to see if it were best to attach the chair from the back or the bottom.

"Look, papà, look!"

Telchide swivelled around in his chair and rose involuntarily when he saw his daughter twirling in front of him. The back of her head was covered with a beaded net, which was fastened around her forehead with a lightly jewelled band. Her long chestnut waves remained loose down her back, though brushed to a sheen.

"Where is my daughter? What have you done with her?" he finally asked, lifting Teresina's long hair to look under it.

She broke into giggles and swiped his hand away.

"Do you like it?" she asked excitedly.

"It's ... exquisite," Telchide breathed. "Is this how all the young ladies are wearing their hair these days?"

Aveline laughed lightly. "Good gracious, no! Something like this would only be used on special occasions. Mamma made me wear this very same trinzale and lenza for her dinner parties, when she would parade me around for her friends to admire before sending me to bed."

Telchide paused and looked down at Teresina again. The beads were no ordinary beads – they were *gems*. He reached his hand out to touch her head but drew his hand back before he made contact.

"Teresina, I think you should take that off now and give it back to Aveline." He noticed how cold his voice sounded but couldn't seem to soften it. Teresina's face fell.

"But ... papà, we only *just* put it on," Teresina said, her voice trembling. A tear was already sliding down her cheek.

"Chide, I really don't mind Teresina borrowing it for a few days," Aveline said quickly. "Or even just around my workshop for today if you don't want her to take it home."

Telchide hesitated. "I don't think that would be a good idea. What if she breaks it?"

Aveline frowned as Teresina's tears continued to flow. "If I didn't manage to break it in all the times I wore it, I doubt she will in one sitting. Telchide, *really*, I insist. At least while we work on the chair lift."

He looked between Aveline and his teary daughter and sighed heavily. "Very well. Just while we work on the chair lift, then."

"Oh, thank you, papà!" cried Teresina. She leapt forward to hug him tightly and Telchide couldn't help but stare at the glimmering jewels all over her head. They really were stunning and must have cost a small fortune. How could her parents justify spending that on a *child*? He could never hope to give Teresina anything so precious. Any hairpiece he bought for her would pale in comparison.

"Papà?" Teresina's voice brought him out of his thoughts. He let go of her and knelt so he was looking directly in her face. "Thank you, papà. I know it's very expensive and I promise I'll look after it. Maybe a Copper Sarta could make me one without the jewels on it when they make my sleeves. Would that work?"

Telchide almost cried in relief for how his daughter's mind worked. "Yes, Resi, I think that would work *quite* well. I'll see if we can't visit one tomorrow to ask. Now, why don't you twirl around and enjoy yourself while we get to work."

She lightly touched the trinzale and broke into a smile as she twirled her way across the workshop floor.

***

Telchide and Aveline worked on the chair lift the rest of the morning. By the time Nevio returned with a basket of food, they had a working model with both magnets and a hydraulic pulley system.

"I think the magnet works best," Aveline said. She smiled as she made the chair go up the rails with the help of a small magnet.

"The pulley system will be cheaper," Telchide pointed out. "You'd need supercharged magnets to make this work on a larger scale and your clients may not be happy to have that cost passed on to them."

Aveline sat back in her chair, crossed her arms, and stared at him. "But this works better."

Telchide held her gaze. "It does," he conceded. "But if your target market is vecchietti living above workshops, only the richest of the rich will be able to afford this mechanism. If you use the hydraulic pulley, you'll reach a wider market."

Nevio came over to have a look. Telchide demonstrated the two different systems to the apprentice and asked his opinion. Nevio looked startled but then took a closer look.

"The magnets are smoother," he admitted. Aveline clapped triumphantly, but Nevio continued. "But how much would they actually cost?"

Telchide looked at Aveline for an answer. She bit her lip.

"I don't know yet. I'll need to ask the Alchimisti. They're the ones who create the supercharged magnets after all. Maybe I can make a deal with them."

Nevio gasped. "Maestra, the Authorities will punish you for that!"

Aveline rolled her eyes. "I won't work with them. I'll simply purchase the first pair of magnets from them for testing."

Teresina joined in the conversation from her spot by the fireplace. "I could ask Ardo to let me play with some."

Telchide coughed to cover her words, but Nevio clearly heard them from the look on his face.

"Ardo? As in, *Eduardo* Alchimista?" he asked incredulously. "You're brave to be such good friends with an Alchimista at this time."

"He was my best friend before the edict, Nevio," Telchide replied evenly. "I couldn't very well just stop talking to him because of the Mercantili Guild now, could I?"

"Of course you could!" Nevio almost shouted. "Maestra, I know it's not my place to say such things, but please don't follow *his* example. If you get imprisoned or have your Guild Status stripped, I'll lose my position as an apprentice."

Aveline's eyebrows shot straight up. "Thank you, Nevio, for expressing your views so very candidly. But as you rightly pointed out, it's not *your* place to say anything about how I conduct my business. You forget I will lose much more than you, should the Mercantili Guild choose to prosecute me for any of my actions. And should the fancy strike me, I could send you back to Kesida at a moment's notice."

Telchide stared in horror at the situation caused, in part, by his daughter's careless words.

"Come, Teresina, I think we have overstayed our welcome."

Teresina wisely rose silently to join him. There would be time enough to reprimand her away from here.

"Take your hairpieces off now and give them back to Aveline."

Teresina did as she was told and held out the precious jewels to Aveline with a whispered word of thanks. Aveline took them carelessly and rose to let them out of her workshop.

"I'll come tomorrow after trading to help you with your orders, Chide." She lowered her voice to a whisper. "We can walk to the Exploding Beakers together and if you can find out if Eduardo has any magnets I can borrow, I'll be forever in your debt."

Telchide smiled tightly and nodded. He knew Aveline was in more danger by going to their meetings with the Alchimisti, but this talk of magnets somehow felt worse because of Nevio's reaction.

"I'm sorry, papà," Teresina said as they walked down across Piazza Mercantile to Via dell'Oro.

"Not here, Teresina. We'll talk at home."

Teresina remained silent the rest of the way, not even asking if she was allowed to visit Eduardo's shop for the afternoon as was her favourite pastime on Riposidi. Once they were in the house and had hung up their coats, Telchide knelt to be face to face with his daughter.

"You know how dangerous this Inter-Guild Edict is, Teresina. I'm careful with how I interact with the Alchimisti. None of it is out in the open unless I am purchasing something from them. And even then, I usually send you around the back. I know it's not fair and that you're just a child, but you need to learn not to let your mouth run away with you, especially when you're around people you barely know."

Teresina frowned at him petulantly. "I *know* papà. But we know Aveline."

"You don't know her apprentice," Telchide pointed out. "You don't know how much she trusts him. You don't know what they speak of in private. Even *you* don't know the names of the other Alchimisti and Inventrici we meet at the Exploding Beakers. And why do you think that is?"

Teresina lowered her eyes and took a deep breath. "So I can't get you, or any of the others, in trouble by what I say. But *everyone* knows that Ardo is your best friend!"

"Clearly not *everyone*. Nevio didn't and look at the mess you made when you spoke so familiarly of him."

"I'm *sorry*, papà," Teresina said again, in a loud voice, before running up the stairs and slamming the door to her room.

Telchide tried not to be upset with her. It was unfair to expect such a young child to understand the severity of consequences imposed by the Inter-Guild Edit, but she really had made a mess of things. If she'd caused trouble for Aveline, he didn't know how he'd live with himself.

With a deep sigh, Telchide walked over to the message box. He'd been reprimanded enough lately by Eduardo for coming to see him.

Supercharged magnets? T, he wrote.

He settled down to begin work on the first pocket watch. He'd rather be working on one of the music boxes, but until his clients provided the sheet music, he couldn't begin.

***

"Papà!" Teresina's scream ripped through the calm night.

Telchide leapt out of bed, heart racing. He ran down the cluttered hallway towards his daughter's room, stubbing his toes.

"Clouds of fire!" he cursed, hopping in place.

"Papà! I had a bad dream!"

"I'm coming, Teresina," he called out, rubbing his toes. "I'm coming!"

By the time he knelt by her bed, Teresina was shaking uncontrollably. Telchide wrapped his arms around her and rocked her gently.

"It's alright, Resi," he whispered, kissing her head. "I'm here. Nothing can hurt you while I'm here. Do you want to tell me your dream?"

He felt her head shake against his chest.

"Can I come to your bed?" Teresina asked in a trembling voice.

"Of course, Teresina. Of course, you can."

Telchide scooped her up in his arms and exhaled sharply. She was getting too heavy. This used to be so much easier when she was a toddler. He put her down gently and moved his hands to her shoulders instead, guiding her to his room. There was a dull thud.

"Ow! Papà, you need to clear the hallway," she mumbled tiredly.

"Tomorrow, Teresina. We'll talk about it tomorrow. I need to sleep now and so do you."

Together, they climbed into his bed. He wrapped his arms around his daughter and kissed her head softly. It wasn't the most comfortable position, but he was too tired to care. This was the sixth night in a row now. The lavender under her pillow and chamomile tea before bed had stopped working days ago. He needed to find a solution before he became too exhausted to complete the orders that were waiting for him. There was one due tomorrow that he would be hard pressed to complete in time.

Chapter 9 – Gildadi 9 Mercantili 230 Years After Implosion

Telchide woke with a start and smashed his hand down on his clockwork alarm. The bells rang loud enough to wake the dead. He usually objected to the volume but, lately, he'd needed it. Teresina's bad dreams were getting out of control. They were both exhausted and nothing short of these bells could rouse him of a morning.

He carefully unentangled his other arm from Teresina, who'd somehow slept through the noise, and got out of bed. He padded down the hall to the kitchen where he could smell Serenita cooking breakfast. She nodded genially as he walked through the door.

"Another nightmare?"

He nodded.

"Does she ever tell you what they're about?"

Telchide shrugged. "Sometimes. I don't push her to tell me because she's always so scared when she has them."

He sat at the table and took a ricotta pancake from the heaped plate. Serenita chewed her food slowly and paused before taking another bite.

"Do you think they're about her mamma?"

Telchide stopped with the fork halfway to his mouth and stared at Serenita.

"You know she had nightmares even before then," he told her.

"I know," replied Serenita quietly.

They continued to eat in silence. Telchide glanced towards his bedroom every so often, waiting for Teresina to emerge. He eyed the clock on the wall. Half-past seven.

"Go to your work," Serenita told him. "I'll send her down to say good morning when she's ready."

Telchide smiled sadly. He didn't know what he'd do without Serenita to help him. He kissed her cheek in thanks before walking down to his workshop.

The workshop was darker than a moonless night sky. The wooden shutters did a surprisingly marvellous job of keeping the workshop secure. He was not the richest of Inventrici, but his fame had grown to the point where knew his music boxes would fetch a decent price on the streets.

Telchide ran his hands along the wall until he came to the shopfront window. There he felt around until his fingers touched the pulley system he'd rigged up for the shutters. He pulled down on one side of the rope and the shutters began to lift away to the top of the window. Sunlight streaked into the room, flooding it with a bright, yellow gleam. He quickly opened the last two shutters then walked over to his workbench.

An unfinished pocket watch and three music boxes were lying on the workbench. Thanks to Aveline, the music boxes were complete. There were still another four pocket watches and five music boxes left to complete from Mercatodi.

Telchide rubbed his tired eyes with the tips of his fingers, trying to moisten them. It was no use. They were dry and scratchy. Nothing but Eduardo's drops would work. He couldn't wait until that night to get them.

Telchide put the unfinished pocket watch to one side and reached for the message box. He typed hurriedly a message to Eduardo into it.

Eye drops. I'll send Resi.

Without waiting for a response, he pushed the metal box back towards the wall, careful not to pinch the wires. Rubbing his eyes, yet again, Telchide pulled the pocket watch closer and unpacked his tools.

An hour later, he heard footsteps on the stairs.

"Good morning, my little Teresina," he said without turning.

"Good morning, papà," Teresina replied quietly.

Telchide paused and put his tools down. He knew what that tone meant.

"Teresina, it's not your fault."

"*You* don't have nightmares," she retorted with a touch of her usual fiery spirit.

"No," he conceded with a small smile, "but your mamma did. In fact, whether it was nightmares or not, your mamma dreamt every night, just like you."

"So, it's mamma's fault, then?"

Teresina crossed her arms and glared at him. There was little he could say to appease her when she was in such a mood, so he didn't bother.

"I've asked Ardo to put aside some eye drops for me. He won't mind if you go through the back fence." Telchide held out two copper coins. "Give these to him. If he asks for more, tell him I'll give them to him tonight."

"Tonight?" Teresina perked up. "Are we going out?"

"No, Resi, *we* are not going out. *I* am going out with Aveline, Eduardo and a few other others."

Teresina frowned. "Papà, I don't like you going to those meetings. I always think the Mercantili Guild will take you away from me."

Telchide laughed. His daughter was quite a clever one.

"*This* is not a meeting. It's dinner, that's all."

"Papà, promise you'll be home before I go to bed."

"That, I cannot do," he said, kissing her on the head. "Serenita will stay with you. I'm sure you'll even be able to twist her fingers to sing you a song before bed."

Before she could argue with him, Telchide pressed the coins into her hand and gently nudged her towards the back door.

***

The bell tinkled softly as the door to his workshop opened. Telchide quickly looked up at the pendulum clock. It was almost the end of trading. He turned his attention to the man at the door. Yes, he'd been expecting this one. His distinct purple top hat was not one Telchide would soon forget. He couldn't decide whether it forced the man to wear a purple coat to compliment it, or the other way around. Either way it was a *striking* colour.

Suppressing the urge to shake his head at the absurd ensemble, Telchide retrieved the wooden box which housed the finished pocket watch from his workbench.

"Your order, signore." Telchide bowed his head slightly as he passed the box to its new owner. He was always sorry to sell his works of art but was realistic enough to know that there was no other way to put food on the table. There was also the niggling thought that his house was already too cluttered with unfinished projects that no longer fit in the workshop.

The man opened the box and took out the electrum watch. Telchide's chest swelled with pride as he caught a glimpse of it. This had been one of his favourites. The demi-hunter was decorated with clouds around the glass on the front, which continued onto the back with a gas lamp in the centre, leaving just enough room for an inscription.

Seemingly satisfied, the man placed a single electrum coin onto the workbench. Telchide choked on a cough. The material alone had cost half of that. A moment later, another electrum coin was added to the workbench.

"This is indeed splendid, Inventore," the customer said with a glow of pride. "My companion will be very pleased. She may well recommend you to her friends when they see this."

Telchide beamed. "Indeed, signore, this watch is of the highest quality. A few turns each day should do the trick or you'll overwind it. If the gears lock up, bring it back and I'll fix it in a trice."

The man glowered at the caution. Telchide realised his mistake too late and hastily tried to smooth the man's ruffled feathers.

"I have inscribed it, as you requested. *Tesoro. Forever yours.*"

Despite his apparent anger, the man couldn't help but smile. Telchide returned the smile broadly.

"She must be one shining gem to deserve such a gift." Telchide stopped himself from asking if the "shining gem" was the one who chose that ridiculous outfit for him.

"That she is, Inventore." The man nodded and turned to walk out the door, now talking to himself. "That she is."

Telchide heard a muffled laugh coming from the stairs but waited until the door closed before rounding on it.

"Teresina, what have I told you about listening at the stairs when I have customers?"

The girl jumped down the bottom few stairs, her laughter flooding the workshop.

"I'm sorry, papà, but did you hear his *voice*?"

She giggled until he thought she would wet herself.

"One day, Resi, you might find yourself in love and *then* what will you say?" Telchide wagged a finger at her.

"No, papà," she said in a serious tone. "I will never fall in love. That would only give someone the chance to leave me." She paused. "Like mamma."

Telchide drew a sharp breath.

"Teresina, she didn't *leave* us. She was taken."

His heart broke as his daughter pursed her lips.

"You don't know that papà. No one else was taken from the funicolare and mamma wasn't particularly special. She must have left us."

"Resi, really, think about it. If she'd left, why would she have written to Nonna saying she was coming and begging her to come back here to meet you? If she'd gone to another town, someone there would've found her and supplied that information for our reward."

Teresina didn't reply. She just stood there, arms crossed, eyes brimming with angry tears. Telchide bent to kiss her forehead. He knew his daughter well enough to understand he couldn't change her mind with one conversation.

"Aveline will be here soon to test the chair lift with magnets. Can you run to Eduardo's workshop to pick them up for me?"

Teresina stared mutely at him.

"I love you," he told her.

"I love you too," she muttered between gritted teeth.

Telchide sighed at her anger as she stomped out the back door. He would have to deal with that sooner or later. He did not want Teresina hating her mother.

Aveline walked in the door a moment later, carrying a small, covered basket.

"Good evening, Chide," she said as she took off her hat and coat. She hung them up and then began setting up their latest experiment on his workbench.

Telchide, stomach tightening momentarily, marvelled at how comfortable she now was in his workshop. Aside from his household, only Eduardo was so familiar with him.

"Teresina's just stepped out to get your magnets from Eduardo. I truly am sorry for the disturbance she caused between you and Nevio. I would never dream of causing you grief."

Aveline's hands stilled on her project. She glanced over at him and straightened. "Never mind Nevio. You're causing me more grief by refusing to come to the Caldera."

"Aveline, please." He wrung his hands together in exasperation. "I cannot discuss this further. My daughter's nightmares prevent me from leaving. It would be unfair to burden Serenita with her sole care in my absence."

It looked like Aveline was about to protest further when Teresina burst through the back door, holding up the precious magnets as though they were her very own Gold Guild Marks.

"Ardo said he can spare these for testing but will need them back soon unless you can pay for them."

Aveline smiled prettily as she took the expensive goods from Teresina. "We'd better get to work with testing then. Thank you, Teresina."

"Can I watch?" Teresina asked excitedly.

"No," Serenita called out from the top of the stairs. "It's been a long day, Teresina. Come have dinner then wash up for bed."

Telchide kissed Teresina good night and sent her upstairs.

"Let's see if we can't rig up something on your staircase," Aveline suggested.

Telchide scratched the two-day stubble on his chin. "I think I may have some spare pieces of metal upstairs. Just a moment."

He took the stairs two at a time and rummaged around his unfinished projects until he found what he was looking for. They weren't rails, but the thin sheets of metal should work just as well for testing.

At the bottom of the stairs, he paused and wrapped one of the sheets around the banister. He took a magnet from Aveline and moved it carefully towards the sheet. The magnet flew out of his hand and almost ripped a hole in it.

"Careful, Chide! Those magnets are powerful," Aveline told him, rather redundantly.

He passed Aveline the other sheet in annoyance. "You can do this one, then."

She took the proffered sheet, wrapped it around Telchide's wooden toolbox and went to place the other supercharged magnet on it. The magnet flew out of her hand and punched a hole straight through the side of the toolbox.

"Whoops!" she cried, reaching out belatedly to catch the magnet. She turned to Telchide, cheeks bright red. "I'm so sorry, Chide. I'll buy you a new toolbox – I promise!"

Telchide waved her concern aside, his mind awhirl with thoughts.

"We don't need two magnets!" he exclaimed. "Just the one. Look!"

He unravelled the torn sheet of metal from his broken toolbox and brought it over to the stairs. As carefully as he could, he brought the sheet to the magnet that was already attached to the handrail. It stuck firmly, just as he expected.

With great care, he dragged the sheet up and the magnet dragged the other sheet along with it. Telchide excitedly walked up and down the stairs, trailing the metal sheets and magnet with him.

"If you can rig up a pulley system to control the magnet itself, then it will negate the need for a second magnet. Actually, if you can rig it up to the sheet of metal around the banister instead, you won't need your metal rails either. It will be much cheaper and easier to fit to any stair situation!"

By the end, he was almost shouting his thoughts. Aveline quickly crossed the floor and placed two fingers on his lips, immediately silencing him.

"If you get so worked up, Teresina will want to come back down and Serenita will never get her to bed."

Telchide froze and stared at Aveline. Her fingers were still on his lips, warm and so gentle they were barely touching him. His heart beat so wildly he thought she must be able to hear it. She returned his gaze and withdrew her hand ever so slowly.

Telchide swallowed and took a big step back. "Yes, well, I can see how it would be affordable with this model. If you manage to submit it to Kesida before you leave, you may have a Gold Guild Mark waiting for you on your return."

Aveline took a small step forward. "We could submit it together," she suggested. "After all, you helped me work out the finer details of it. I only had the idea itself."

"No, that wouldn't work." He walked over to his workbench, unable to cope with the thought of standing so close to her for another moment. "If we submit it together, they won't advance either one of us. It isn't great enough for a combined submission – not for a Gold Guild Mark in any case."

Aveline frowned and began to take apart the experiment. The clock struck a quarter to five, startling Telchide into action. It was almost time for their meeting at the Exploding Beakers.

"Ardo will meet us on the corner," he told Aveline, hurriedly walking to the door and away from her. "We can walk to the Exploding Beakers together."

"Of course." She smiled tightly, putting the broken sheets of metal on the workbench and joining him at the door. "Thank you for your help with this project. I can't come tomorrow night, but I'll be back the night after to help you with your orders, as promised."

Telchide noticed the cool tone but couldn't understand it. He donned his hat and coat and waited for her to do likewise.

Locking the door behind them, Telchide touched his coin pouch reassuringly, walked down the street with Aveline and waited on the corner for Eduardo to join them. The Alchimista was getting on in years, but still had more than enough energy to spare.

"Good evening, Aveline," Eduardo called out as he approached. "Would you please help me convince Chide that he needs to find a solution to his daughter's nightmares? Sure, she looked spritely enough when she came to get Chide's eye drops this morning, but *she's* not the one putting food on the table."

Aveline raised an eyebrow at him. Telchide sighed.

"Ardo, you know I can't stop her from dreaming. I don't really want to. I just wish the dreams weren't so often nightmarish."

Eduardo winked and handed him a small parcel wrapped in paper. Telchide opened it curiously and saw a glass bottle of purple pills.

"What are these for?"

"Give one to your daughter before she goes to sleep tonight. It will calm her mind and should diminish the nightmares," Eduardo said.

Telchide hesitated. "They won't hurt her, will they?"

"Chide, would I *ever* hurt Resi?" Eduardo looked at him reproachfully. Telchide glanced down at the bottle, still doubtful. "Give them to Serenita. I'll negotiate a price for the magnets with Aveline while we wait for you."

***

Five minutes later, Telchide was back with Eduardo and Aveline. They walked together towards the bar. As they approached the Exploding Beakers, they heard a loud explosion and a cloud of orange smoke billowed out of the windows. Telchide rolled his eyes and covered his mouth with his sleeve as they ducked into the doorway during the commotion.

"Do they have to be quite so dramatic?" he asked Eduardo.

"You don't like the orange aroma?" Eduardo asked in an injured tone. "I asked Nestore to brew that one especially for you."

Telchide shot his friend a murderous look. Eduardo knew he hated the scent of oranges. The Alchimista only laughed and pointed to a corner table where their friends were waiting for them.

"What took you so long?" asked Lucrezia. "Nestore had to use two explosions to cover our tracks."

Telchide glanced at Eduardo as the three of them took their seats.

"Resi is having nightmares again. I brewed up a little something to help her sleep better."

Telchide remained silent. He wasn't certain about giving his daughter something that he hadn't tried first himself, but he trusted Eduardo.

"Down to business then," Lucrezia said as she signalled Nestore. The Alchimista barkeep walked over to them, dustpan in hand. He was still busy cleaning the mess his explosions had made.

"How did you like that orange one, Chide?" he asked with a wink. Telchide looked between Nestore and Eduardo and simply shook his head. He was no match for two Alchimisti.

"Our usual, Nestore," Lucrezia ordered for the table. "If anyone does dare come in after that ruckus, this had better look like a nice quiet dinner."

Nestore nodded and went back to finish cleaning the mess. Telchide drew his attention back to the table. There were even fewer of them than last time.

They'd initially come together to share ideas of how alchemy could be used with certain inventions to improve them. It hadn't been a forbidden practice when they started, but some of the other Guilds had frowned upon the apparent ease of relations between the Alchimisti and Inventrici. They'd gained a lot of power working together. It had been hotly debated whether the two Guilds together were more powerful than the Mercantili Guild.

"Where's Eleonora?" Telchide asked as he sat.

"She decided this is too dangerous for her. Her mamma depends on her for everything." Lucrezia pulled out a notebook. They'd agreed it should be written in code in case it ever fell into the wrong hands. "Chide, you and Ardo were working on a lighting project. How's that going?"

Telchide nodded. "I've prepared the box to Ardo's specifications. All I need now is the alchemical solution to test it."

"I've been working on that." Eduardo leaned forward, excitedly. "Different colours seem to last different lengths of time. If you want customers coming back for refills, yellow glows for only five minutes. I don't know why – it's not any less expensive to make, but there you have it."

"Five minutes is ridiculous," pointed out Dania. "Who in their right mind would prefer that to a candle?"

"Ach." Eduardo waved a hand impatiently at her. "I was experimenting. I can't help how the different colours work. The longest one glows for four hours – that's the blue one."

"Four hours," Telchide mused. "That would still mean I'd have to wake up in the middle of the night to create the next glow."

The table fell silent and everyone but Eduardo stared at him.

"Teresina? *Again?*" Lucrezia asked incredulously. "Are *all* your inventions because of her?"

"Of course not," Telchide replied stiffly. "Just some of the more recent ones. Besides, if I could get a good night's sleep, I might have more energy to work on other projects. As it is, I'm only finishing my orders on time because Aveline's helping me."

"We're helping each other," Aveline explained when every set of eyes turned to her. "Chide's helping me with some of my larger projects."

There was a long, awkward moment of silence. Telchide fiddled with his buttons, confused by everyone's reaction.

"We'll test the Lightbox before our next meeting," Ardo diverted their attention. "And if my pills work for Resi, Chide will have more energy and new ideas by then as well."

"He'd better have," Lucrezia grumbled. "It's hardly worth the risk having these meetings if our Inventrici don't bother inventing useful things."

Telchide found a breadcrumb on the table and threw it at her. She swatted it away effortlessly and glowered at him.

Consulting her notebook, Lucrezia continued. "Dania, you were looking into the sparking plants on the Caldera. Have you made any progress on this?"

Dania cleared her throat. "I found a boat and Aveline has agreed to fund the expedition. Eduardo was looking into how to get around the Mercantili Blockade."

Telchide nodded along as she spoke. He'd heard it all a week ago.

"I spoke to Captain Corrado and secured his services," Aveline told them. "He's on standby until we're ready to leave."

Dania bit her lip and glanced at Aveline. "That must be awfully expensive. Are you certain you don't mind funding the expedition?"

"I'm certain, Nia" Aveline replied firmly.

"Well, Ardo, what of the blockade?" Lucrezia asked.

"My, erm, *friend*, will let me know when it's safe to go. It may be a few days' notice; it may be a few hours. Aveline and Dania will need to be ready as soon as possible to give them more chance."

"I don't mean to be imprudent," Telchide raised his hand, "but I believe a male should escort them. The first mate sounds a scoundrel, and I wouldn't trust him with Aveline and Dania."

Aveline stared at him from across the table. "*You* were already invited."

Telchide brushed her comment aside. "What about Zaccario or Claudio?"

"I'm not going. I've heard it's impossible to land there safely." Zaccario pointed out unhelpfully. "And even if you do manage it, the shores are so small, they can't provide any shelter."

Claudio nodded in agreement. "There's a reason no one ventures to the Caldera."

"My marinaio will get us there," Aveline said firmly. "And I don't intend to stay on the shore. My plan is to explore the Caldera and bring back as many specimens as possible. Hopefully, they can survive here."

Telchide's mind was already swirling with possibilities. The argument between the three Inventrici faded into the background. He pulled out his notebook – he never left home without it – and started scribbling away. Distractedly, he noticed Nestore coming and going, bringing out their meals. Eventually, he realised the conversation around him had stopped. He looked up to find everyone staring at him.

"Rubber," he said, pointing his pencil at the paper.

"What about rubber?" Lucrezia asked in an exasperated tone.

Telchide looked at her blankly.

"The box needs to be rubber," he explained.

"What box?" Lucrezia's tone was harsh.

He hated it when she spoke to him like that. It made him feel an incompetent child.

"The box for Aveline – it needs to be a rubber box, or at least a rubber-lined one," Telchide explained. Aveline clapped her hands at the suggestion. "Gloves too, if she can get a Sarta to make them for her."

"Will someone please tell me what he's talking about?" Lucrezia slammed her notebook shut. Telchide looked at her in some surprise. He'd been perfectly clear about Aveline's requirements.

"If this plant really does everything I hope it does, the rubber will insulate me against harm." Aveline turned to Telchide. "It's a brilliant plan, Chide. Are you certain you won't reconsider? I could definitely use your help on Sentigura Caldera."

Telchide was already shaking his head. "I can't leave Resi. She would never forgive me if I didn't return."

"I don't plan to stay there forever, Chide," Aveline pointed out gently. "It'll be a few weeks at the most."

"Things don't always go according to plan, Aveline." Telchide closed his notebook, putting an end to the discussion. Aveline continued to look at him, her eyebrows raised and knitted together in an imploring manner. Refusing to entertain the thought, Telchide picked up a spoon and dug into his soupy pasta.

He listened to the others reporting on the progress of their various projects, including Aveline's chair lift, without comment. Aveline's offer to go on the expedition was terrifying, but so tempting. He allowed himself a moment to wonder if Teresina didn't exist or if Sebetine had never disappeared, would he have agreed.

**

Telchide walked home with Eduardo after the meeting.

"You could go, you know," Eduardo said after a few minutes of silence. Telchide jerked his head sharply towards the Alchimista. "Don't look at me like that, Chide. Serenita would look after Resi, and she could always leave the girl with me if she had to go out alone."

"Resi would never allow me to do that." Telchide said.

Eduardo did not reply immediately but Telchide could feel his restlessness.

"Forgive me, Chide, but Resi is not your mamma, nor your companion. She is your *daughter*. *You* are in charge of *her*. Not the other way around."

Telchide raised his hand to object, but Eduardo ploughed on.

"I know things have been difficult since Sebetine disappeared, but you cannot pause your life until Resi is old enough to look after herself just because you're afraid she'll be angry with you. She's six! Are you going to wait ten years before you do *anything?*"

Telchide drew a sharp breath. "Ardo, you would understand if you had a child."

It was a cruel thing to say, and he knew it. But just now, in this moment, Telchide didn't care that Eduardo's companion had died in childbirth, taking their son with her.

Eduardo's wide and watery eyes hurt Telchide more than he cared to admit. Without apologising, he strode on ahead to his house, unlocked the door and closed it behind him so he wouldn't have to deal with what had just happened.

Chapter 10 – Ramedi 10 Mercantili 230 Years After Implosion

The clockwork alarm rang at seven o'clock. Telchide slammed a hand down on it reflexively. For one blissful moment, the memory of last night evaded him. Then it crashed over him like a tidal wave. He'd no right to say such a terrible thing to Eduardo. In truth, he'd been angry with himself for feeling so trapped in his life, for allowing Resi to make his home a prison. Ardo had simply pointed out what everyone else could see.

Telchide rolled over in bed, careful not to squash Resi. His bed was empty. Heart beating rapidly, Telchide jumped out of bed and walked quickly down the hall. He pushed open the door to Teresina's room and saw her lying peacefully in bed. He stared at her uncomprehendingly.

He couldn't remember her sleep talking. He couldn't remember her screaming. The purple pills! Ardo had promised they wouldn't hurt Resi, but Telchide couldn't help checking that his daughter was still breathing. It was so uncommon for her to sleep an entire night in her bed, without waking and screaming for a light or begging to sleep in his bed instead.

Shaking his head, Telchide walked into the kitchen. Serenita looked up as he walked through the door.

"You must thank Eduardo for those pills, Chide," she said with a smile. "I can't remember the last time she slept through the night."

Telchide grimaced. That was not the only thing he had to talk to Ardo about. Serenita frowned.

"Out with it."

Telchide walked to the stove deciding what to say. How could she read him so well?

"Aveline asked me to go to Sentigura Caldera with her."

Serenita nodded and pursed her lips. "And you want to go, but you won't let yourself. Is that it?"

Telchide held back an urgent longing and shook his head. "Of course not. I don't want to go."

"Chide, I've known you a long time now," Serenita reminded him. "Sometimes, I think I know you better than you know yourself."

"Well, you're wrong about this," Telchide told her firmly.

"When is she leaving?"

Telchide scooped a serving of onion frittata onto his plate and shrugged. "Whenever there's a break in the Mercantili blockade. She needs to gather the equipment she requires and I need to make a rubber-lined box for her. That will take a few days at the most, then any time after that."

Serenita nodded thoughtfully. "How long will she be away?"

"I don't know," Telchide said between mouthfuls.

With her continuous questions, Serenita teased out the details of Aveline's plans. Talking them through, Telchide realised that he was making mental notes for himself – what equipment was needed, how long the boat ride and the expedition itself would take, whether he could finish five music boxes and four pocket watches, as well as Aveline's box before the expedition set out.

It was with that last thought that he realised how much he wanted to go. When he looked up from his plate, he saw Serenita smiling at him and realised the cunning old lady had played him like a fiddle.

"I suggest you have a little chat with Aveline today. If she can't leave for at least a few days, as you presume, it will give us time to see if these pills keep working. If they do, I see no reason why you shouldn't go."

Telchide didn't reply. He was too afraid how loud his excited voice might be if he spoke, and he did not want to wake Resi. He didn't want her to think that he was excited to get away from her.

***

The beautifully decorated dancers atop the music box moved silently along their tracks. If he didn't have the sheet music yet, at least he could create the box itself. He'd already put together two of the simple music boxes, as their patrons had chosen from the selection of tunes Telchide already had available. Signora Angela had dropped off the sheet music for Angelo's music box as soon as trading opened that morning. That order would be ready in a few days.

Teresina came into the workshop and played with the finished music boxes, smiling at the sound. Telchide watched her fondly. Could he really leave her?

"I need to go out for a bit this afternoon," he told her. "Do you want to stay here with Serenita, or shall I take you to visit Ardo?"

Teresina pouted. "That will make two nights in a row, papà."

"No." Telchide said. "I'll be back before bed. I promise."

"I'll visit Ardo," Teresina said as she ran to the door.

"Shoes, Resi!" Telchide called out before she got there. "I may not be a man of fashion, but I do know a young girl cannot go about town without her shoes on. Even the daughter of a lowly Inventore."

Resi groaned loudly and ran back up the stairs. Telchide busied himself putting away his tools and cleaning his workbench until she returned. When she finally did, not only was she wearing shoes, but her long wavy locks had been brushed out and woven into a plait, and she was wearing a fresh dress. Serenita followed her into the room.

"She's only going to Ardo's, you know," Telchide pointed out.

"Ardo has customers coming in and out of his workshop all day, Chide," Serenita reminded him. "Enough of his customers will recognise this little scamp that it was worth tidying her up a bit. Goodness knows she'll never fit in with the fashion of society, but she can at least look presentable."

Telchide held his hands up in mock defeat. He didn't bother closing the wooden shutters before they left. Any thief would be mad to rob them in broad daylight, but that didn't stop him from double locking the door behind the three of them.

"I'm off to the food markets." Serenita kissed Teresina's head. "Be a good girl for Ardo, or next time he'll refuse to take you."

Telchide hid a smile when Teresina stuck out her tongue at her nonna's retreating figure. Instead, he took her by the shoulders and turned her back up the street towards Ardo's workshop. Resi grabbed his hand from her shoulder and held it loosely. The familiar gesture made him hesitate. Was it really for Resi's sake that he was uncertain about the trip or because he knew how much he would miss her?

"Papà, you're hurting me," Resi complained, shaking her hand. Telchide quickly loosened his grip. He hadn't noticed how tightly he'd been squeezing her hand.

They rounded the corner. There was Ardo's door, with the gold Alchimista Guild Mark, an encircled flask, displayed proudly in the centre. Telchide still remembered his chest swelling with pride when he'd replaced his own copper Inventrici Guild Mark, three cogs fitted together, for a silver one. Based on their skill level, the Guild Marks were also a tactful guide for customers to know what price to expect.

Telchide hesitated at the door. It was cowardly of him to bring Teresina today. Any apology he made would be brief. Eduardo would not reprimand him in front of his daughter. Teresina, clearly not noticing his reticence, pushed open the door and ran inside. Telchide followed more slowly.

He patiently waited for Eduardo's customers to leave before making his way up to the counter. Teresina had already gone into the back of the workshop to harass Eduardo's apprentices. When the last customer had left, Eduardo closed the door behind them. Telchide watched his face for any sign of anger, but the Alchimista's face was blank.

"I'm sorry, Ardo," he began.

Eduardo walked straight past him into the back of the workshop. He returned a minute or two later, carrying a number of vials.

"These are for your Lightbox," he said.

Telchide tried again. "Ardo, it was cruel of me to say ... what I did. You were right. I was angry with myself. I had no right."

"Put the clear liquid on the main side and the coloured ones on the slotted side," Eduardo said, completely ignoring him.

"Ardo, *please*." Telchide placed a hand on the Alchimista's shoulder.

Eduardo looked at the hand, then up at Telchide.

"I'm going to see Aveline," Telchide told him. "If she hasn't found another Inventore, I'll go with her."

"Good." Eduardo broke into a grin. "She was in here this morning lamenting the fact that she wouldn't have any Inventrici for company. I'll watch Resi. Go now, before you change your mind."

Telchide smiled back at his friend and ran out of the door.

***

Aveline lived on the outskirts of Zona Sarti. There were fewer Inventrici in this area of Tor'Esint. In Tor'Dumere, where he'd grown up, there were strict laws about the minimum distance required between workshops from the same Guild, which resulted in lower member numbers. Tor'Esint was quite the opposite, with most Guild workshops located in the same district. Depending on the Guild, they held weekly, fortnightly, or monthly meetings in their Guild Hall. For those who had workshops a long distance from Corso delle Gilde, it was a nuisance to travel so far.

Aveline's advantage in being away from the majority of the Inventrici was that she had a dedicated clientele amongst the Sarti and had been able to collaborate with them before the Inter-Guild Edict.

Telchide walked up the stone steps. With a sudden flush of envy for her Electrum Guild Mark, he knocked on the workshop door. Without the heavy tread of footsteps announcing someone on the other side, the door opened. As he stepped in, Telchide studied the door, following the mechanism behind it to a switch on the wall beside the workbench.

"Inventive!"

Aveline looked up at him with a smile. "They didn't give me the Electrum for nothing, Chide."

Her apprentice choked back a laugh. Telchide waved aside the boy's apologetic gesture as Aveline glowered at him.

"What brings you to my workshop?"

Telchide took his coppola off. He couldn't stop his fingers from fiddling with the rim. "I was wondering if you've found a Sarta to make those gloves for you. The rubber ones," he hastily added.

"In a manner of speaking," Aveline said. "Greta Sarta, down the street, said I wouldn't find any Sarta willing to work with sheets of rubber, so we settled on leather gloves instead. I believe they'll have a similar dampening effect; don't you agree?"

Telchide nodded, still turning his hat around and around. "Good, good. Erm, do you know when you're leaving?"

Aveline shook her head. "The gloves will take Greta at least three days. The marinai are on standby for whenever we're ready." She looked up at the pendulum clock on her wall. "I'll be on my way to get the rubber sheets for the box soon. Unfortunately, they won't sell me a single sheet. They requested I purchase three as a minimum, each three square piedi."

"That should do perfectly," said Telchide. "Any extra can be used to insulate an area of your workshop. I think a wooden box will work best. Then, at the very least, it will only scorch rather than shock anyone if the rubber sheets don't work as well as I ... you hope."

He looked down at his hat and realised his fingers had stilled. His love for inventions always soothed his nervous ticks.

"All the falegnami are busy at such short notice." Aveline shrugged. "I'll just use a metal box. I'm sure I've got a spare one somewhere."

"But a metal one simply won't do," Telchide pointed out. "I could make one for you, if you tell me the dimensions you require."

Aveline sat back and crossed her arms. "You're an Inventore, Chide, not a Falegname. Besides, what would I pay you?"

"Let me come with you," he blurted out. "My parents taught me to make fine boxes before I came here. I'll make you a box and pay for my own leather gloves. In return, if you could find it in you to forgive my stupidity in refusing your offer in the first place, I'll come with you."

Aveline's eyes opened wide. "Oh, Chide!"

Telchide couldn't understand her tone. From what Eduardo had told him, he thought she'd be happy.

"You ... don't want me to come anymore," he mumbled, shuffling towards the door. "I should never have presumed. Forgive me."

"Chide, wait," Aveline said, springing up from her chair. "I *do* want you to come, it's just I don't know if you'll still want to come when you find out who's replacing Dania."

"Dania." Telchide looked at his feet in confusion. "Erm, who's replacing Dania?"

"Well, Lucrezia insisted that Dania was too young and inexperienced to be of any use. You know how she can be. So Lucrezia insisted on coming herself."

"Lucrezia?" Telchide asked in disbelief. "But, but she can't, she wouldn't ... what use would she be? She'll only complain the entire time."

Telchide only stopped babbling when he heard the apprentice choke back another laugh. Aveline silenced him with a harsh word, but Telchide barely heard it as he backed away towards the door, head down.

"Chide, I'm sorry," Aveline said, suddenly standing in front of him. "I'll talk to her. Surely she can't forbid you from joining us, after all, *I'm* funding the expedition. However, I simply cannot promise you anything until I've spoken to her."

Telchide looked up at her, his chest so tight it hurt. Now that he'd set his mind on the expedition, he could hardly bear the thought that he might be denied.

"I understand," he said softly. "You'll need the box whether I come with you or not, so I'll still make it if you want me to."

"And we can get a pair of those leather gloves made for you too," Aveline insisted. "Even if you can't come, I'll be asking for your help to study the plant upon my return."

Telchide huffed, trying to cover the desperate hope he felt inside him.

"Agreed."

Aveline bloomed into a smile.

"Agreed."

She held out her hand. Telchide shook it firmly, ignoring the stifled laughter of the apprentice.

"Nevio, I'm going to run a few errands. Mind the shop for me and for Caldera's sake, don't touch anything on my workbench. All finished items are on the front counter."

"Yes, Maestra Aveline," Nevio said, moving his hand to his forehead as if to tip his hat to her.

Aveline chose a rather colourful hat from her collection on the hat stand, though not as tasteless as the purple top hat his customer had worn the day before. Telchide wondered why she would ever need so many hats. He used his flat coppola for every day and his top hat for the rare times he attended a formal function.

Aveline looked up and caught his expression before he had time to change it.

"Greta gave me this hat as a gift for one of the inventions I made her. She was particularly pleased with it. Wearing it might remind her of that, which in turn might lower the price of the gloves when I ask her to make three pairs instead of two."

Telchide grinned at her ingenuity. Perhaps living amongst people other than Inventrici had taught her different, and quite useful, life skills.

Out on the street, Aveline opened the door to her blazermobile. It was one of the newer models with glass windows and a roof – more like an expensive carriage than anything else. Telchide looked at it hesitantly. Aveline rolled her eyes.

"Chide, the rubber sheets are on the outskirts of town and the tannery in the zona next to it. Greta will not appreciate the stench I bring in with me after walking all that way and back again. I had Dania personally create the blazer solution for me. There is very little chance it will explode."

Those Alchimisti and their desire to work with unstable liquids confounded Telchide. Trying not to think of Aveline's last sentence, he climbed up into the blazermobile. Aveline ascended after him. He watched curiously as she poured the blazer solution into the power block and stoppered the opening. The blazermobile rumbled to life. Telchide held tightly to the side rail and couldn't unclench his grip as Aveline manoeuvred the vehicle through the cobbled streets.

***

By the time they reached the rubber factory, Telchide's stomach felt so tightly clenched he wondered if he would ever be able to eat again. He stumbled down from the blazermobile and swallowed the bile which suddenly flooded his mouth. He took deep breaths to calm his racing heart.

"Chide, are you certain you'll survive a trip to Sentigura Caldera?"

Telchide struggled to stand upright. "Is the boat blazer-powered?"

"I don't think so." She bit her lip. "I didn't think to ask. I do know the trip will be longer than this one, even if it *is* blazer-powered."

"If I'm willing to leave Resi, I won't let a little motion sickness get in my way."

Somehow, Aveline's sympathetic smile made Telchide feel worse. He wiped a clammy hand across his sweaty brow.

"Let's go get those rubber sheets," he told her, taking a shaky step forward.

Together, they walked up the stairs to the factory office. Telchide followed Aveline to the counter behind which sat a sharp-edged lady.

"My name is Aveline Inventrice. I've come to collect my order for three sheets of rubber."

The lady glared at her with beady eyes then ran a finger down her ledger, presumably looking for the order.

"That's ten silvers," the woman said in a haughty voice.

Telchide balked at the price. Aveline peered over the counter.

"I believe that says *seven* silvers, not ten."

The woman behind the counter showed no signs of embarrassment. "Seven it is. Hand it over then."

Aveline shot her a brittle smile. "I think I might just wait until you have someone bring the sheets out before I pay you. You don't mind, do you? It's just I've had a little trouble recently with people who think they can hoodwink an Inventrice as easily as they can a beggar."

The beady eyes narrowed. It seemed the woman was thinking of arguing, but instead she reached out for a copper cone connected to a long tube on the wall beside her.

"Boy, bring out three sheets of rubber. Three square piedi each."

They were forced to wait a good few minutes for the boy to arrive. Telchide spent the time studying the room. Aside from the copper cone the woman had used to call the apprentice, there were three other copper cones spiralling out of the wall beside her. Each of them had a copper plaque with a location or name engraved on it. Through these cones came faint whisperings of conversations.

"Do they know you can hear them when they speak to each other?" he asked without meaning to. The woman turned towards him sharply.

"They have just as many cones in their own offices," she told him. "If they're too stupid to realise the sounds travel further than intended, that's their own problem."

Telchide found himself admiring the woman's gall. She had a point, but he would never act as she did. He was saved from making any other remarks by the arrival of the boy carrying three sheets of rubber. Telchide ran to help the boy as the sheets began to tumble out of his awkward grip.

"Thank you, Inventore," the boy said shyly.

"No talking to the customers, boy," the sharp lady shouted. "Be off with you!"

Telchide bit his tongue. He stood impatiently as Aveline paid the woman, then walked quickly out of the office. Aveline rushed down the steps to open the door to her blazermobile. Still angry with the sharp lady, Telchide roughly shoved the bendy rubber sheets into the back of the blazermobile and hopped in.

"You would never treat your apprentice like that," Telchide snapped suddenly.

Aveline risked a quick glance at him as she sped through the streets. "Nevio has never had cause to complain about me. What about your apprentice?"

"My ... what?" spluttered Telchide as the shock fizzled his anger away. "I don't have an apprentice."

"I know, but why ever not?" asked Aveline with open curiosity. "And don't feed me that rubbish about your daughter not sleeping. You've had your Silver Guild Mark for years now. I found an apprentice the day after they gave me mine. I know I'm entitled to two now, with an Electrum Guild Mark, but I want Nevio to progress a bit further before I think about that. *You* don't have that problem."

Telchide stared at her, baffled. Why hadn't he found an apprentice yet? The Guild had lists of people waiting to be signed up with any Guild member willing to take them on.

"Sebetine."

Aveline didn't reply for a moment.

"You don't want an apprentice because your companion is gone?"

Telchide didn't want to think about it, but she gave him no choice.

"They gave me my Silver Guild Mark just after Sebetine disappeared. I spent all my spare time and energy, and money, on trying to find her. I didn't think it was right to bring an apprentice into that environment."

"But that was years ago, Chide." Aveline said with a tenderness he'd never heard from her. "You really should get one. It would make trips like this one much easier to plan for. Your apprentice could continue certain works in your absence or, at the very least, take orders and sell completed works for you."

"What if they live with me like most apprentices? I barely get enough sleep myself with Resi's nightmares waking me up every other night. It would be unfair of me to bring someone else into that kind of life."

"Ardo's pills didn't work, then?"

Telchide smiled briefly.

"Actually, they *did* work last night."

"If they're still working in a few days, you really should find an apprentice," Aveline told him bluntly. "Otherwise, there's no way you'll ever have the time to spare inventing the kind of masterpiece you need for the Electrum Guild Mark. Trust me, I should know."

Telchide nodded knowingly. The thought of an Electrum Guild Mark was often on his mind. Perhaps Aveline was right. It couldn't hurt to take a look at the apprentice list at the Inventrici Guild Hall.

***

Dark clouds rolled in off the seas as they drove to Greta Sarta's workshop. In the time it took Aveline to negotiate a reasonable price for a third pair of gloves, thunder was rumbling. Telchide looked out of the Sarta workshop at the sudden downpour miserably.

"Chide, Greta's offered to make Teresina some new sleeves in exchange for a music box – one of the simpler ones that turn with a handle."

Telchide turned at the sound of his name and let Aveline's statement sink in. He stared at Greta in some surprise. This was the first trade of goods he'd ever been offered.

"That would be most appreciated, Signora Sarta," he said with a bow of his head. "My little Teresina will be overjoyed to have new sleeves, from a *Gold* Sarta no less! Would you like to choose a tune, or shall I ask Aveline to pick one for you out of my current list?"

Greta looked to Aveline who laid a hand on her arm. "I'll choose one, Greta. Telchide has quite a few beautiful pieces of music in his repertoire. Chide, send Teresina here with Serenita tomorrow to be measured and you can pick the sleeves up when you finish the music box. Agreed?"

"Agreed," said Telchide and Greta at the same time.

"Good, now Chide, it's pouring outside. I'll give you a ride home if your stomach can handle it," Aveline offered.

Telchide grimaced at the recent memory. His anger at the rubber factory lady had only amplified his motion sickness. Twice, Aveline had stopped the vehicle so he could be sick in the gutter.

"It's only a short trip, Chide," she said patiently. "I'll drive slowly."

Telchide took a deep breath to brace himself, both for the ride and the rain. He ran from Greta's workshop to the blazermobile. Once he was settled in the infernal machine, Aveline laid a hand lightly on his arm to calm him. He looked down at her hand and found himself smiling at the touch.

Sebetine.

He clenched his fist in anger. Aveline jerked her hand away and quickly busied herself pouring a few drops of blazer solution into the power block. True to her word, she drove slowly. So slowly that they might as well have been walking. At that moment, Telchide would almost rather have been walking. He could see the bright red flush on Aveline's cheek, the way she pressed her lips into a narrow line.

"Aveline?"

"What?" she snapped. Then in a softer voice, she repeated herself. "What is it?"

"Forgive me."

Aveline sighed heavily. "There's nothing to forgive. I should not have been so familiar. You were right to be angry."

"No, I wasn't angry," he said quickly. "Leastways, not with you. I cherish your friendship and appreciate the opportunity to go on such an exciting expedition, if Lucrezia also agrees. I just ... need to remember I have a family."

Aveline looked at him oddly for a moment but said nothing. Telchide wished he could read that look.

They drove in silence the rest of the way to his workshop. Aveline halted the blazermobile outside his door. He could feel the vehicle burning to keep moving.

"I'll start working on the wooden box tomorrow – not too big, with compartments for the plants. I should have it done by the time the gloves are ready."

Aveline nodded but remained silent. Telchide wished he knew what was going on behind those mesmerising hazel eyes. He almost apologised again but thought better of it and got out of the blazermobile instead. The steady rain slapped his face as he struggled to unlock his door. Aveline had already driven around the corner before he got it open.

***

The smell of fried potatoes and garlic wafted through the air. Serenita was home, which meant so was Teresina. Telchide felt a guilty pang of relief that he would not need to tramp through the rain to bring his daughter home from Eduardo's workshop.

He placed three logs in the fireplace and lit it with the help of his tinderbox. Eduardo had once offered him the use of his own special lighter fluid but, when the Alchimista had singed his bushy eyebrows in demonstration, Telchide had politely declined. For a minute or two, Telchide warmed his hands by the fire. It was going to be a long evening. He would need to focus on Signora Angela's music box before he started working on the wooden box.

There wouldn't be much time left to finish his orders. *If* there was room for him. He felt unreasonably angry with himself for having been so adamant about not going in the first place, but there was nothing he could do about that now. All that was left was to prepare himself in case Lucrezia agreed to allow him to join them.

Before he had a chance to pull out his tools and the new sheet music, Teresina came rushing down the stairs. He turned just in time for her to launch herself into his arms.

"Resi," he grunted, laughingly, "you're getting too heavy for this."

"I missed you, papà." She hugged him fiercely. "Nonna said to call you up for dinner."

Telchide looked at his workbench then back at Teresina.

"You promised you'd be home for dinner. You must eat with us."

He put his daughter down gently. "A quick bite only, Resi. I must finish these orders quickly."

"Papà, you have plenty of time," she said with a pout.

He hadn't told her yet. He hadn't even formally told Serenita yet.

"I have some news," Telchide told her. "I'll tell you over dinner. Let's go up."

Resi flew up the stairs two at a time and bolted down the hallway. He wished she wouldn't do that. The hallway was so cluttered that a stubbed toe might easily turn into a broken foot.

He walked over the unfinished projects with greater care than his daughter. She was right – he really did need to tidy up a bit. Perhaps when he had an apprentice, he might find the time to do just that. The thought took him by surprise. He hadn't realised that his talk with Aveline had convinced him so thoroughly of his need for one.

"Did you have a successful outing?" Serenita asked.

Telchide saw Teresina's eyes dart between him and Serenita.

"Is that what your news is about, papà?"

"Yes."

Telchide sat down at the table. His nose hadn't deceived him – there were indeed fried potatoes with garlic. There was also a pot of pasta with pesto, but that scent was not quite as strong. Serenita handed him a bowl. His stomach growled impatiently, but he waited until they were all served before he began to eat.

"So, what's the news?" Teresina asked, chewing her food messily.

"Don't talk with your mouth full, Resi," he scolded her after finishing his bite.

She rolled her eyes and swallowed her food hurriedly. "What's the news?"

He carefully laid his cutlery down and took a sip of water.

"Well, first of all, if Nonna agrees to take you to Greta Sarta's workshop tomorrow, she'll measure you up for some new sleeves."

"Oh papà!" Teresina gasped. "Isn't she a *Gold* Sarta? How can we afford that?"

Telchide laughed inwardly at his fiscally responsible child. "I'm trading her a music box for the sleeves. Aveline negotiated the deal for me."

Serenita raised her eyebrows. "Aveline is becoming a rather useful contact to have, isn't she?"

Telchide ignored her comment. There was nothing he could think to say to that.

"The other part of the news is that I may be taking part in a truly wonderful expedition. There's a plant which is rumoured to produce energy and can shock a person with considerable force if they touch it. With a plant like this, the Inventrici Guild might be able to rival the Alchimisti Guild to power blazermobiles and other such vehicles."

Teresina went very quiet and very pale.

"Where's this plant, papà?"

Telchide hesitated. "Sentigura Caldera."

"The *actual* Caldera?" Resi's voice rose to a squeal. "Can I come?"

Telchide blinked uncomprehendingly as Serenita laughed.

"No, Resi, you can't come," he told her. "It isn't even my expedition."

"Whose is it then? I'll ask them myself."

"Resi, you're not listening," Telchide tried to reason with her. "It could be a dangerous journey, not to mention a dangerous destination. I cannot bring my six-year-old daughter, even if I'm allowed to join the expedition."

Her eyes filled with tears. "So ... you're leaving me?"

"Possibly. Just for a little while."

Telchide looked to Serenita for help. She moved her chair slightly and held her hands out to Teresina. His little girl crawled up onto her nonna's lap and buried her head in her shoulder.

"Your papà needs to do this, Teresina," Serenita said as she stroked Teresina's hair. "Eduardo has already agreed to help me look after you whenever we need him to. You'll have so much fun playing in his workshop that you'll barely have time to miss your papà."

Telchide found his appetite had disappeared, but he forced himself to continue eating. No matter how Resi took the news, he still had a long evening of work ahead of him.

Eventually, he heard a little sniff and looked over to see Resi wipe her eyes.

"When will you know for certain?"

"Aveline will hopefully let me know once she speaks with Lucrezia."

"When would you be leaving?"

"Four days from today at the earliest."

"How long would you be gone?"

"I don't know," Telchide answered honestly. "Part of it depends on if we can find a place to land the boat and part depends on how quickly the plant is found."

Teresina stared at him.

"A few weeks at the most," he guessed. "I cannot see a reason for the trip to last longer than that."

"Who are you going with?"

Telchide shrugged. "Aveline and Lucrezia."

"But they're *girls*," spluttered Teresina.

"So are you," Telchide pointed out automatically.

Teresina threw up her hands in the air, jumped off Serenita's lap and stomped off to her room. Telchide looked down the hall in shock.

"What was all that about?" he asked Serenita.

She glared at him. "Mull it over while you work on your music boxes – perhaps you'll figure it out."

Bewildered and hurt by both Teresina and Serenita, Telchide hurriedly ate the rest of his dinner before going back down to his workshop. He was so distracted by their behaviour that it took him almost an hour to settle into working on with Signora Angela's music box. He was absorbed in it until it was finished, and only then realised that the fire had almost burned out. Rubbing his tired eyes, he packed away his tools for the night.

Telchide turned the handle until the entire tune had played. He simply wanted to hear the music to make sure everything was in working order. The tune was one of his least favourites, but Sebetine had adored it.

His thoughts drifted to his companion. Teresina had grown so much since she'd disappeared, he doubted Sebetine would recognise her. Would she even recognise *him*? He turned to look at his reflection in the glass of the pendulum clock.

There were dark rings under his eyes from all the sleepless nights with Resi. His dark brown hair, shot through with slivers of grey, was a mess of tangles. He noticed a smudge of oil on his cheek and wiped it with his kerchief. Without Sebetine to remind him, his grooming was often ignored until he needed to go out somewhere people did not know him well.

Serenita rarely chided him about his appearance anymore. In fact, Serenita rarely used any *tone* with him. Which brought him back to their conversation that evening. What had he said which had caused both Serenita and Teresina to react so badly?

It wasn't the expedition itself. Of *that*, he was certain. Serenita had encouraged him to go, and Teresina had been excited enough to ask to come. It was only when he'd mentioned going with Aveline and Lucrezia that Resi had changed her view.

But they're girls, she'd said.

He tossed the phrase around in his mind until something clicked.

"No," he said aloud to himself. "Lucrezia is barely tolerable."

But Aveline is quite *tolerable.*

He smiled at the thought. Aveline was more than tolerable. She had a great mind for inventions, proven by her Electrum Guild Mark. She never interrupted him or got frustrated when he was scribbling in his notebook. She'd asked him to go on this expedition with her.

Well, what a mess he'd made of that! If only he'd agreed in the first place, there wouldn't be this problem.

His mind went back to Resi. She didn't even know about that mess. *What in Caldera's smoke was she concerned about?* He stopped turning the handle of the music box and the sudden silence of the music box drew his attention.

Sebetine.

Aveline and Lucrezia. *They're girls!*

Aveline.

He smiled again at the thought of her, then his mouth fell open.

"Smoking Caldera," he whispered. "They're girls indeed!"

Chapter 11 – Argentodi 11 Mercantili 230 Years After Implosion

Telchide was nearing the kitchen when he heard Serenita's calm and steady voice. Careful to keep quiet, he lingered just far enough down the hall to hear them without being seen.

"Your papà won't forget her as easily as you think, Teresina."

"Why not? I have."

There was a pause before Serenita spoke in a strained voice. "She had dreams, just like you."

"I know!" Teresina shouted. "That's all you and papà ever say about her!"

There was a deafening silence.

"Perhaps it's for the best you can't remember her well," Serenita finally said. "After all, we never did find a trace of her."

Telchide let out a breath he didn't realise he'd been holding. It made sense that Teresina had all but forgotten her mamma. She'd only been three when Sebetine disappeared.

He'd lost hope that she would ever return. They didn't even know if she was still alive. He tried to banish that treacherous thought, but it often entered his mind. Everyone else believed she'd either run off, been kidnapped, or was dead somewhere. She'd have returned by now otherwise. That knowledge made it difficult for Telchide to put on a brave face for Teresina, but he had to try.

Pretending he hadn't heard their conversation, Telchide ran a hand through his hair and walked into the kitchen.

"Good morning, Teresina, Serenita." He selected a slice of toasted bread and took a bite. "I thought I might take a walk down to the Inventrici Guild Hall this morning and look at the list of hopeful apprentices."

His comment had the desired effect. Teresina instantly brightened.

"Can I come?"

"Absolutely," he said, stroking her cheek with the back of his fingers. "As long as you let Serenita make you look presentable. I can't have my own daughter looking like a tramp if I expect to attract any apprentices."

Teresina frowned. "Papà," she said slowly, "where will the apprentice sleep?"

"In the spare room," Telchide replied without hesitation.

He saw the look Teresina shared with Serenita.

"You mean the one stuffed full of your old inventions, papà?"

Telchide hesitated. "Yes, well, of course I'll have to tidy up a bit before we take anyone on. I'm sure I could shuffle some of those inventions into the workshop or my own room. Perhaps the hallway..."

Serenita laughed. "Leave it to us, Chide. By the time your arrangements are made, the room will be ready. Go find someone who will be willing to start in a month."

He was deftly shuffled out of the kitchen and down into his workshop. Telchide had to admire Serenita's patience with Teresina. He could hear her squeals of protest, her foot stamping on the floorboards above him. But when Teresina finally descended the stairs, she wore a pale green knee-length smock with dark green trimmings and her old cream sleeves. There was a green ribbon in her loose hair.

"Why, Teresina, you look so..."

"Grown up?" she offered.

"Proper," Telchide replied. "I'll never know how Serenita manages to do it."

Teresina stuck her tongue out at him. He wagged a finger at her and smiled.

"Serenita, will you watch the shop while we're out? We won't be gone long," he called out up the stairs.

He waited until she appeared, then held out his hand for Teresina and they walked out together. Other than the regular Guild meetings, Telchide rarely had occasion to visit his Guild Hall. Teresina had only accompanied him a handful of times, which explained her constant tugging of his hand, urging him to walk faster.

He greeted several other Inventrici as they approached the Guild Hall, but none who took part in the Exploding Beakers meetings. It was just as well. Telchide did not want to accidentally give away anything. He'd never been good at minding his own tongue.

"Smoking Caldera!" Teresina exclaimed loudly. "Look at that!"

Telchide looked up to and his jaw dropped. It was a new addition to the building. An Inventrici Guild Mark, easily as tall as a child, hung above the entrance with a cog each in copper, silver and electrum, encircled by a large gold ring. It would've cost a small fortune if those materials were solid. He noticed a similarly lavish symbol hanging over the Alchimisti Guild Hall entrance next door.

Perhaps *this* was the reason for the Inter-Guild Edict. It must have been clear to everyone that both Guilds benefitted from the collaboration with other Guilds. Telchide swallowed the temptation to step back across Corso delle Gilde to catch a glimpse of the entrance to the Mercantili Guild Hall to see if they too were boasting of their recent successes.

"Let's go in, papà," Resi said as she tugged at his hand. Telchide allowed his daughter to lead him inside, smiling at her enthusiasm. He idly wondered if she would join his Guild when she grew up – if he would ever become her maestro like his parents had tried to be for him.

The purpose of Guild Halls wasn't to strike an imposing image on the public, but that didn't stop them from trying. As Telchide led his daughter through the antechamber, he had to keep her from stopping every few steps. Every submission of a Great Work was kept by the Guild for the express purpose of displaying the variety along the walls. His own two submissions, for his Copper and Silver Guild Marks, were here somewhere – if only he could find them to show Teresina.

He sighed. Perhaps another day when he had more time. Shepherding Teresina with a hand on her shoulder, Telchide finally reached the large wooden desk where Kesida, the Inventrici Guild Amministratrice, sat.

"Good morning, Kesida," he said, doffing his hat.

"Ah, Telchide!" Kesida rose from her chair and peered down at Teresina. "And who do we have here? This cannot possibly be your little Teresina, can it?"

Telchide hid a smile as Teresina puffed out her chest and stuck her proud little chin in the air.

"That she is, Kesida, just not quite so little anymore."

Telchide absently patted Teresina's head, which earned him a scowl as his daughter tried to neaten her hair.

"So, I see." Kesida choked back a laugh. "Tell me, Telchide, what brings you here today?"

"Papà's looking for an apprentice," Teresina said primly before Telchide could answer.

Kesida looked sharply at Teresina, then over to Telchide. He gave her a hesitant smile.

"Well, it's about time," Kesida said, clapping her hands together. "It's been *years* since we gave you your Silver Guild Mark. I expected you to apply for an apprentice the very next day."

Telchide twisted his coppola around by the rim and looked down.

"Yes, erm, the thing is that I was rather busy for a while after that. Our lives grew hectic."

He saw Teresina's glare but couldn't look her properly in the eye. She huffed at him.

"What he means to say is that's when mamma *disappeared*."

"Oh, of course," Kesida said softly. "I'm sorry, Telchide. I should think before I let my mouth run away with my words."

Telchide waved a hand dismissively at her apology. Eventually, he managed to look back up at her. She gave him a big smile, but her eyes were full of the pity he'd come to loathe so much.

"Wait here a moment. I'll get the list."

Not knowing how long Kesida would be, or how long Teresina's patience would last, he gave his daughter permission to look at the displayed inventions after securing a promise that she wouldn't touch any of them.

He watched his daughter from a distance. She stopped at the ones she found most interesting and peered closely at the descriptive plaques on the wall next to them. It was the one thing he'd done right by her. Teresina was literate at a young age. She read everything she could get her hands on in their household, which was usually only the newssheets. It had forced her to learn much longer and more difficult words than any six-year-old should know, even if their parents were Guild members and had been taught to read during their apprenticeship.

Telchide turned at the sound behind him. Kesida had returned with a folder full of paper.

"These are our current hopeful apprentices. Some are older than others, but none over fifteen years. In truth, most of the older ones get snatched up as soon as their names are put on the list. I suppose Inventrici don't want children messing around with their work."

Kesida placed the folder on the desk and opened it. Telchide's mind reeled when he saw how many young people were waiting to be called up for an apprenticeship. How could he possibly choose between them?

It was clear Kesida faced this situation on a regular basis.

"What age are you after?"

"A younger one will do, if that's what you have more of."

"Boy or girl?"

"I don't suppose I mind," Telchide answered, slightly baffled. "Perhaps Resi would like it if we had another girl for her to play with."

Kesida crossed her arms over the open folder and leant towards him.

"Telchide, your apprentice will *not* be a playmate for your daughter. They will be your student, first and foremost. Many Inventrici give their apprentice a cot at the back of the workshop rather than a room in their household."

"No, no, that simply won't do," Telchide said immediately. "No apprentice of mine will sleep in the workshop. Absolutely not. We have a spare room upstairs. Serenita will help me clear it out. We only need a month to get things ready."

Kesida blinked then shook her head with a laugh. "Let me guess. It's slightly full of unfinished projects?"

Telchide coughed and tugged at his collar. Kesida turned back to her folder and flipped through the sheets.

"Let's see then, a young female apprentice, ready to wait a month before starting."

Footsteps thudded behind Telchide. He turned to see Teresina running towards him.

"Are you choosing one now, papà?"

"Yes, Resi." He picked her up and helped her look down on the folder. Kesida was scanning her fingers down through the details.

"Not a *girl*, papà!" Resi wailed. "Get a boy."

Telchide paused. He hadn't considered that Teresina would rather a male apprentice – it barely made a difference to him.

"A boy then?" Kesida looked up from her sheet.

Telchide put Teresina down. "Are you sure, Resi? You might not like another boy in the house."

"We don't need another girl in the house, papà."

A nagging thought bothered Telchide. Were Teresina and Serenita concerned another girl would replace Sebetine? Would replace *them*? At least in this, there was an easy solution.

"A boy then," he said to Kesida.

"We have three boys who might suit you. Matteo, Florio and Gaspare. Matteo will be fourteen years next week and won't mind waiting until your room is ready. He comes from a non-Guild family but appears to be quite keen on becoming an Inventore. Florio and Gaspare will be fifteen in two months. They're twin brothers from the orphanage. We've promised to keep them together if we place them."

"Erm, Kesida, I can only take on *one* apprentice," Telchide pointed out. "Silver Guild Mark."

"I know," Kesida sighed. "The problem is that no one ever comes in asking for two apprentices at the same time and the older they get, the more difficult it will be to place them."

Telchide frowned. "Kesida, I don't know what you're expecting of me. You know the rules better than I do. They simply won't allow me to take two apprentices. I've only got my Silver Guild Mark. What if I bungle up training just one?"

"You won't," Kesida told him confidently. "After all the years I've been doing this, I can tell those who will be good maestri and those who will 'bungle' it. You're not the latter."

"I appreciate your confidence in me, Kesida. Truly, I do. But even if I wanted to take these boys, I can't."

Kesida was silent for a few moments. Long enough for Telchide to start absently playing with the rim of his coppola again.

"Leave this with me," Kesida told him, shuffling the papers. "Come back a week before your room is ready so I can get the paperwork ready."

"Erm, I may be going on a trip sometime soon," he told her. "If I do, I may be gone a few weeks, even if the room is ready before then."

Kesida waved her hand. "Yes, not a problem. Just pass by when you return so we can get you an apprentice as soon as possible. I'm sure I'll have everything sorted out by then."

"Thank you, Kesida." Telchide nodded. "You're a gem."

There was a little cough beside him and a heavily stamped foot. Telchide looked down and realised he'd forgotten Teresina was there.

"Of course, my little Resi will always be the brightest gem in my life." He hugged her tightly to his side. This time, she did not push him away to fix her hair.

"Good day, Kesida."

Telchide nodded, put his hat back on and steered Teresina towards the exit.

"A moment, Telchide," Kesida called out. "Do you happen to have any new inventions you're working on?"

Telchide rubbed his chin, surprised by the stubble he found there. He really needed to start grooming himself a little better.

"There's a Lightbox I've been working on," he told her with a hint of pride. "It lasts for four hours, but I want to rig it up so it can potentially go all night or even a whole day. I thought it might be useful in the mines, you know, instead of gas lamps."

Kesida raised her eyebrows appreciatively.

"How much more work is needed do you think?"

"Oh, a day or two if I work on nothing else."

"If you go on this trip of yours, give me what you have so far, even if it isn't finished yet. I have an idea."

"What are you up to, Kesida?" Telchide asked her suspiciously. "You know the Maestri don't like being bothered with unfinished works. They have enough to look at with applications for Guild Marks as it is."

"Don't worry, I won't bother them needlessly. Get it as close to finished as you can, then bring it to me. Agreed?"

"Oh, very well then," Telchide sighed. He did not have the energy or the fortitude to argue with Kesida. "Come, Resi, let's go home. It seems I have more work to do than I thought."

***

On the way back from the Guild Hall, Telchide stopped in on Eduardo. If he were to have any chance of finishing the Lightbox soon, he'd need all the help he could get.

The bell jangled as they walked in. Teresina had already run past the front counter towards the back workshop before the door closed behind them. A bemused apprentice looked up as she bumped him.

"My apologies, Davide," Telchide called out. "You know how much my Teresina loves watching the Alchimisti at work. I wonder if Eduardo might be available for a quick word?"

"Inventore!" Davide bobbed his head quickly. "Yes, of course. I'll fetch my maestro at once!"

Telchide laughed to himself as the apprentice stumbled over his feet in his haste to find Eduardo. It had been years since he'd earned his first Guild mark and the right to his title, but the respect he was automatically granted because of it still took him by surprise.

"Chide, what are you doing here?" Eduardo asked sharply.

Telchide frowned and tried to peer past him into the workshop.

"Is there something the matter?"

"Your constant visits are the matter," Eduardo chided him quietly. "You should use the message box more and visit me less! This is twice in two days. Tongues are bound to start wagging."

The blood drained from Telchide's face. He instantly felt queasy.

"I didn't think..."

"No, you never do. That's the problem." Eduardo said in frustration. "Lucky for you, my apprentices and hired Alchimisti are all loyal to a fault. Otherwise, one or both of us would be hauled away by the authorities for Inter-Guild relations."

Telchide tugged at his collar, which suddenly felt too tight.

"I suppose that means you won't have time to help me work on the Lightbox in the next few days."

"Did Aveline reject you then?" Eduardo asked in surprise.

Telchide looked at him in confusion for a moment.

"Not necessarily. I won't find out until this evening if Lucrezia will agree to allow me to go with them."

"Then why in Caldera's smoke are you working on the Lightbox instead of finishing your promised works?"

"Aveline will be helping me with my orders," Telchide pointed out defensively. "Oh, but I still have the rubber-lined wooden box to do. In any case, Kesida wants me to bring her the Lightbox before I leave – if I leave."

"Why?" Eduardo asked in a rather suspicious tone.

"I confess, I don't know. I went to ask about an apprentice and as I was leaving, she asked if I had anything I was working on. I told her about the Lightbox, and she asked me to bring it to her before I leave, even if I'm not finished it yet."

"I don't like the sound of that. I wouldn't leave my unpatented creations with anyone, even a Guild Amministratrice."

Telchide sighed. "Ardo, I hardly think Kesida will try to pass it off as her own or give it to another Inventore. In any case, the invention is useless without the correct alchemical combination and even *I* don't know it."

"Nor will you be told it," Eduardo huffed. "Not until after we know the entire contraption works properly and you've registered the Lightbox as a Great Work."

Telchide held up his hands in mock defeat and waved his coppola above his head.

"I have to complete a music box tonight, but I'll be working on the Lightbox tomorrow. If you happen to have time to spare, it would be wonderful if you would condescend to join me."

Eduardo huffed. Telchide gave him an impish smile and called out to Teresina. She came out of the workshop with a pout which made Telchide laugh, and Eduardo pat her awkwardly on the head.

"Careful, Ardo, she's already so taken with your workshop. If you start to show her some affection, you may just have Teresina as an apprentice one day."

Eduardo froze with his hand mid-air. He glanced down at Teresina, to his workshop, back at the girl, then over to Telchide.

"Well, erm, she's too young to be thinking about that right now. She'll just have to settle for my company tomorrow afternoon."

"Ooooh! Are you visiting us tomorrow, Eduardo?" Teresina squealed with delight.

"Only if you promise me a nice cup of tea," he said, bending down face to face with her.

"I promise!"

"Very well then. I'll come by the back fence. Mind you leave it open for me."

Eduardo held out his hand and Teresina shook it emphatically. Telchide followed Teresina as she bounced out of the door. She raced ahead of him so that by the time he'd rounded the corner himself, she was already inside their house.

"A boy then?" Serenita confirmed as he stepped into the workshop. "When will he start?"

"Yes, a boy. I don't know which one. Kesida will sort out the paperwork for me to sign when the room's ready."

"And when you get back from your expedition," Teresina added.

"If I go on the expedition," Telchide corrected. "In any case, none of it will matter if we cannot clear the room. And I must finish my projects before then."

Serenita understood what he hadn't said. With a wink, she bundled Teresina towards the stairs.

"Come, Teresina, I'll take you to Greta Sarta's and then we'll see what we can do about that spare room ... and the hallway."

Telchide sighed heavily at the noise that came along with his daughter's excitement as she departed the workshop and left him in relative silence. The pendulum clock ticked noisily, but that sound had never bothered him as he knew it did some people.

He sat down at his workbench and pulled the order for the first elaborate music box towards him. This customer had requested a wooden box with felt lining for her jewellery that played music when she opened it. Telchide thanked his parents for their perseverance in teaching him the basics of carpentry. It meant he could offer his customers the choice between wooden or metallic creations – few other Inventrici had that skill.

He set to work on the box that would play Sebetine's favourite tune. He tried to distract himself from thoughts of her by concentrating harder on what he was doing.

It didn't work. He knew he would eventually need to make certain decisions. No matter what happened, Serenita would always be a part of their lives. He couldn't imagine tearing nonna and nipotina apart. Selfishly, he had to admit that he'd be lost without Serenita's help.

However, none of that changed the fact that he'd need to discuss her disappearance with the authorities at some point. It was a subject he continually avoided. He couldn't believe she was dead without proof, but as the days and weeks, then months and years passed without a whisper of her, the likelihood that she would be found alive and well had dwindled.

As Telchide worked, his eyes passed over the wooden ring on his finger. Sebetine hated the feel of metal on her skin and had insisted on wooden commitment rings for the two of them. Telchide had yet to remove his.

Refusing to let his sombre thoughts ruin the rest of the day, he put the music box to one side and began working on the copper strip which would produce the actual tune with bumps in all the right places.

He had so many projects to finish before he went on the expedition. What would he do if he couldn't complete them all before a break in the Mercantili blockade? Would his customers still pay him for delayed works? Would he need to reduce the prices to accommodate the tardiness of completion?

With a deep breath, he resolved to work on the rubber-lined box that evening and leave his other orders until Aveline had time to help him. She could easily complete the inner workings of the pocket watches for him so that all he would need to do was the etchings on each of them. That would save him a lot of time and he would need all the time he could get.

He hoped she'd have an answer for him tonight. It would not do for him to live in such uncertainty. If he was going to leave, there were things he needed to organise. Serenita's access to funds if he were to be absent was a pressing issue. He could organise that with Kesida when he brought her the Lightbox, whether it was finished or not.

***

Serenita gave Teresina another purple pill that evening. Telchide was surprised that she didn't make a fuss over it. Usually, she kicked and screamed over medicine. She dutifully came to give him a kiss goodnight and was bundled off to bed. Telchide waited patiently for Serenita to return to the kitchen.

"I'm going out for a stroll," he told her.

He did not want to tell her where he was going. She looked at him with sharp eyes.

"A stroll to meet your lady friend?"

"Aveline is *not* my lady friend," Telchide retorted hotly. "She is a fellow Inventrice who has offered me an extraordinary opportunity."

"But you *are* going to meet her," Serenita said quietly. "You could've told me, Chide. I understand, as your daughter does not, that our lives must go on."

Telchide held up his left hand and pointed to the wooden ring.

"I am still committed. I cannot forget that."

Serenita took a deep breath and let it out noisily.

"Yes, you are. You're committed to the woman who disappeared without a trace. No one knows better than I, how much you miss her, how desperately you searched for any information about her. Surely she would've returned by now if she was ever going to."

"What are you saying?" Telchide asked, dropping his hand.

"I'm saying, it's time to stop telling Teresina that her mamma will return one day. It's time to take that ring off. You must accept that she is most likely dead. I accepted that long ago."

Telchide stared at Serenita in disbelief. Sebetine was her daughter. How could she give up hope? Serenita walked over and placed a heavy hand on his shoulder. He looked up into her eyes. They were brimming with tears.

"All I ask is that you don't forget your daughter and you don't dismiss me. We're still your family, no matter what else happens."

Telchide took Serenita's hand from his shoulder and held it gently.

"Serenita, I don't know what you're expecting to happen, but nothing is going to change between the three of us. Even if Aveline and Lucrezia allow me to accompany them, I'll only be away a few weeks at the most. How could I ever forget either of you in that time?"

Serenita squeezed his hand and laughed.

"You really are a fool, Chide. Go for your stroll, then. I'm off to bed."

Bemused, Telchide watched her walk away and stayed listening until her bedroom door was closed behind her. What in Caldera's smoke was the matter with everyone these days?

***

It was drizzling. He like the cool feel of autumn days that ended in a drizzle. Telchide firmly placed his coppola on his head, took his umbrella from the coat stand and locked the door behind him.

The walk to Aveline's workshop was uneventful, though the streets were busy. Telchide rarely went out at this hour. Now he remembered why. Traders had long since closed for the day and only those who were looking for some form of revelry were out and about. He'd never been one of those people. Loud and crowded bars had always made him feel anxious and overly tired.

He passed the people in their finery. Ladies with colourful dresses walking in groups of twos and threes, their gloved arms linked with one another. He noticed the men, bedecked with ruffled shirts or gaudy top hats, walked in pairs or with groups of ladies. Few of them walked alone as he did. Was there some unwritten law he was unaware of that discouraged people from walking the streets alone? He barely had time to ponder the question before he reached Aveline's workshop.

The door opened as he approached. Nevio stood in the entrance a moment and called back inside.

"Yes, Maestra Aveline. I'll be back by nine o'clock. You have my word."

Nevio turned and stared at Telchide as the Inventore stood at the bottom of the steps.

"Telchide Inventore!"

Telchide stepped aside to let Nevio pass. The apprentice did not move.

"Don't let me keep you," Telchide said with a slight bow.

Nevio still did not move, but instead looked back into the workshop through the slightly ajar door.

"For Caldera's sake, Nevio, close the door! You're letting the draught in."

Aveline came to the door herself when the door did not shut.

"Ah, Telchide."

The use of his full name puzzled Telchide. Aveline was usually much less formal with him.

"Nevio, Telchide Inventore is here to discuss the expedition. Go, have fun."

Telchide watched warring emotions flicker across the apprentice's face but couldn't understand any of them.

Aveline sighed loudly. "For Caldera's sake! Take a look at his ring, Nevio. Telchide is not here to court me. Now, please, don't let us detain you."

Telchide felt the heat in his face as he finally understood the apprentice's dilemma. He cursed himself for not formally organising a meeting with Aveline. The distinction that she was a single, available woman did not cross his mind when he thought of the expedition.

Nevio looked back at his maestra hesitantly before pushing roughly past Telchide.

"My apologies, Aveline," Telchide said. "I did not mean to cause trouble. I needn't come in."

"Don't be daft, Chide. Come out of that rain. I'll set the kettle on."

Telchide walked heavily up the stairs to Aveline's workshop. There were so many things other people thought of that never even crossed his mind. The unwritten rules of society often confused him.

He was momentarily distracted by the ingenious contraption Aveline had rigged up around the lit fireplace. Mirrors set at particular angles reflected the firelight over the entire workshop. As long as a steady flame burned, there would be light.

He closed his umbrella and placed it carefully near the door, with his coppola resting atop the handle. Looking around, he realised Aveline was not in the room. He'd never been past the threshold of the workshop before, so he stayed where he was and inspected the various projects she and Nevio had on their respective workbenches.

Nevio's workbench was empty of everything but a handful of tools and the various pieces required for a simple watch. Before he realised what he was doing, Telchide reached out to sort the cogs and gears into the correct order they would be needed.

"Don't touch it!" Aveline called out.

Telchide withdrew his hand and looked around to see Aveline, but she was still not there. He searched the room until he saw what looked like a flexible telescope hanging down over Nevio's workbench – high enough not to be easily noticed but near enough to be effective from whichever room the telescope ended.

Not wanting to tempt himself any further, Telchide sat in one of two chairs against the wall near the entrance of the workshop. Eventually, Aveline returned with a tea tray. She placed it on the small table between the two chairs and seated herself in the empty one.

"Nevio has watched me make dozens of watches and has made a few himself with my help. This exercise is intended for him to put everything he has learnt into practice. If you had put things in order for him, we wouldn't know whether he could do it himself."

Telchide nodded. It was a sound theory. He would need to think of such things himself when he had an apprentice. Would he have had to make extra arrangements if he'd agreed to a female apprentice?

"Excuse me for asking, but what's the difference between Nevio living with you alone and my visiting you alone? We are both men."

Aveline spilt the tea she was pouring and stared at Telchide. He jumped up to find a workshop rag to dry the table before the hot water stained the wood. Aveline had finished pouring both cups by the time he'd dried the table, but she still hadn't answered him. He sat and played with his pocket watch, checking it against the loud bells of the Guild Hall clocks striking a quarter past seven.

"I suppose it's a matter of family," Aveline answered carefully. "Society sees apprentices as part of the household. In their eyes, Nevio is more like my son or my brother than anything else. It wouldn't cross their minds that he could possibly be a suitor."

"But *I'm* not a *suitor*," Telchide spluttered. "I'm a fellow Inventore."

Aveline tilted her head back and laughed softly.

"I'm only too aware of that, Chide. But many others do not know or remember you have a companion. In their eyes, especially in the evening, you're more likely to be calling on me as a suitor than an Inventore."

"Oh."

Telchide put his pocket watch away and picked up the cup of tea instead.

"In fact, I should've thought of that when I invited you on this expedition in the first place. Had you agreed immediately, I would still probably have asked Lucrezia or Dania to accompany us. A lone woman travelling with three men, two of whom are marinai, is not advisable. It could be as dangerous for her as walking the streets of Tor'Esint alone after dark."

Telchide said nothing but blew the steam from the top of his tea. He remembered that Sebetine had never wanted to go out by herself at night either – at least she'd never insinuated that he could ever be considered dangerous.

"I suppose it's a good thing Lucrezia doesn't like me and won't agree to let me join." He looked up at Aveline with a sad smile. "I'll finish the insulated box and bring it to you in a few days. You needn't worry that I'll come after trading hours."

"Don't look so glum, Chide." Aveline reached out a hand to touch his forearm. "I spoke with Lucrezia this morning. After a heated debate, I made it perfectly clear that she didn't have a choice in the matter. She's not the one funding the expedition – I am. You're coming and that's final."

Telchide couldn't decide what flustered him more – the fact that he was really going on this expedition or that Aveline's fingertips were resting lightly on his arm. He took her fingers with his free hand and squeezed them gently, suddenly feeling happy that they would get to spend more time together other than in their workshops.

"Thank you, Aveline. This means the world to me."

Aveline blushed prettily and deftly withdrew her hand. She hid her smile behind her teacup, but Telchide could see nonetheless. It made him smile all the more. In that very moment, he wished he could embrace her – only to thank her, of course. The urge took him by surprise. It simply would not do. Not when they were alone, in this house, in the evening. Suddenly, Nevio's reluctance to leave them did not seem all that foolish.

He finished his cup of tea as quickly as was polite, then took his leave from a surprised Aveline.

"I have much work to finish, you understand. The orders from Mercatodi, the insulated box and the Lightbox Ardo and I have been working on."

"Why in Caldera's smoke do you need to finish the Lightbox before we leave?" Aveline asked.

Telchide shrugged. "Kesida wants me to drop it off to her before we depart. She's finding me an apprentice while we're away."

Aveline frowned at that, but Telchide had no mind to puzzle out why as he tugged on his coppola.

"I'll come tomorrow to help with your orders then," she told him. "After all, you wouldn't need to finish them so quickly if it weren't for me."

Telchide coughed. "Actually, Ardo is coming tomorrow to work on the Lightbox."

Aveline hesitated. "Very well then, the next day. I'll see if I can't leave Nevio to mind the shop for the afternoon so I can help you a little earlier. And I'll bring a list of what you should pack – it won't be much."

Telchide nodded quickly and opened his umbrella to the drizzle. He'd already stayed longer than he should have, though he couldn't deny that he was beginning to wish he could find more reasons to spend time alone with her.

***

On the way back to his workshop, Telchide studied the evening strollers carefully. There were instances of men and women walking out together, sitting at undercover outdoor tables to a cup of something warm. But he saw no sign of a man walking into a house when a woman answered the door.

Most of the women out for the evening favoured a type of dress he found impractical. The skirts were so wide that their companions could barely offer an elbow for them to hold. He'd rarely seen any of the Inventrici or Alchimisti he knew in those sorts of gowns, aside from the annual Guild ball which was hosted by a different Guild each year. This year, the Gioielliere Guild had won the bid to host it.

Was that why it didn't occur to him to think of the Inventrici and Alchimisti as eligible women? Or did he simply focus on their talents rather than their gender? Could it possibly just be that he didn't see himself as a potential suitor because of Sebetine?

The last thought sank in his stomach like a gold weight. More and more often, he felt that Sebetine's disappearance was preventing him from moving on with his life. Either her absence, or his assumption that others remembered he had a companion, caused trouble for him. Perhaps Serenita was right. Perhaps it was time for him to finally let Sebetine go and start living his life freely. He pushed the idea aside before the habitual guilt it caused could grab hold and suck away hours of his life in circling thoughts. There was no time to deal with that now. He would think about that on his return.

Turning his mind to the expedition instead, a growing happiness pushed away all other feelings. His step lightened as he realised he was excited about something for the first time in years. He was really going! There was so little time to prepare. He'd finish the second music box within a few hours, get some rest and work on the rubber-lined box tomorrow until Eduardo came to work on the Lightbox.

The thought of the expedition was suddenly so exciting. Aside from the boat trip itself, he couldn't wait to go to Sentigura Caldera. Perhaps Eduardo could give him something to ease his motion sickness on the journey. In his haste to depart, he'd forgotten to ask Aveline how long the boat ride would take. It mattered little – whether it was ten minutes or ten hours, he would still be sick.

It was too late to call on Eduardo now, and besides, as he'd been reminded recently, Telchide had visited the Alchimista too often in the past few days. Instead, as soon as he got home, he typed a message into the message box.

Cure for motion sickness? T

The message box had been one of the inventions he was most proud of but, just like with the puzzle safe he kept under his floorboards, he'd not shown the Inventrici Guild. There were certain inventions he preferred to keep for his own personal use.

This was still the most convenient way for Telchide and Eduardo to keep in regular contact. Since the Inter-Guild Edict, they'd used it regularly to discuss their combined projects or when one needed something from the other. The Lightbox was just one of those projects. Telchide had come up with the idea after Sebetine's disappearance, when Resi had started waking from dreams more than usual in the middle of the night, but he hadn't been able to work on it much until recently.

Teresina's dreams hadn't started out as nightmares. At first, they were just dreams. Wonderfully detailed dreams that she struggled to explain to him. He'd wished there were a way for her to share them with him the way she wanted to. It was only after her mamma had disappeared that Teresina started having nightmares. Not every night, but often enough that they'd both become sleep deprived. That was when things had gone from bad to worse. It seemed the more tired she was, the more frightening her nightmares became.

Until Eduardo had given them the pills, Teresina hadn't slept an entire uninterrupted night for over a month. Though he still wasn't entirely certain he should be giving her the medicine, the silence in their house these past few nights, and the amount of work Telchide had gotten through in that time, had been a precious gift. One that he was taking advantage of, yet again, that night to complete Signora Angela's music box. A simple child's toy for her son, instead of a key to turn that allowed music to play for minutes at a time, this music box required the child to turn a handle for any sound.

It had been quite difficult to convince a member of the Musicisti Guild to sell him a few sheets of music, and then help him adjust the metal bumps to find the exact right note for the pieces. That had been before the Inter-Guild Edict. Since then, it had become impossible.

The Musicisti Guild was very well aware that he was making a tidy little profit from these music boxes and had stopped selling him their sheet music. If a customer asked for any song that he didn't have, he could only complete the order if they provided him with the sheet music themselves. So now, he always made a personal copy of any new music on a strip of copper so it would be easier the next time he needed to use it.

Telchide placed the finished music box alongside the other two on his workbench. Knowing that some of the customers may come while he was away, he took out his jobs ledger to leave a note for Serenita. He wrote the promised amounts clearly next to each one. Teresina would be there to help Serenita with the ledger, but he was an cautious man and knew Serenita couldn't read. So Telchide drew rough pictures of the music boxes next to their description. Satisfied that he'd completed everything for that evening, he finally went upstairs to bed.

Chapter 12 – Legaramedi 12 Mercantili 230 Years After Implosion

A loud crash above him made Telchide cringe as he finished the inner workings of the pocket watch. Serenita and Teresina had been sorting through the unfinished projects in the spare bedroom. He wished they would be just that little bit gentler with his precious works.

Initially, Teresina had run downstairs every few minutes, asking if he wanted to keep certain items. After the third time, he'd sent her back upstairs with a message for Serenita that he did not have time to sort through his inventions before he left, and she would simply have to find a place for all of them until he returned. That had given him some small reprieve, but the sound of metal and wood dragging along the upstairs floorboards interspersed with crashes and bangs set his teeth on edge.

"What in Caldera's smoke was that?"

Telchide looked up to find Eduardo standing in the back doorway.

"Serenita's clearing space for my new apprentice," Telchide groaned. "Though if I didn't know better, I'd think she was trying to sabotage all of my unfinished projects."

Eduardo laughed long and loud. The sound brought Teresina rushing down the stairs and into his arms.

"Well, little Resi, where's my cup of tea?" he asked, patting her head affectionately.

"Cup of tea?" Teresina asked.

"The one you promised me yesterday," Eduardo said.

Teresina looked at him in confusion. Telchide saw Eduardo's tell-tale eyebrow raise.

"What's wrong, Ardo?"

Eduardo blinked and looked back at Telchide.

"Oh, probably nothing. Tell me, how many of those purple pills has Serenita given you, Resi?"

"One every night since the first one," she answered promptly. "Well ... except for last night. I woke up while papà was out, and she gave me another one to help me sleep."

"I see. Run along now and make me that tea. Mint, if you please."

Telchide waited until his daughter had bounded up the stairs before pressing Eduardo.

"Is there something dangerous about the pills?" he asked in a low voice. "You told me they wouldn't hurt her."

"They won't harm her." Eduardo turned to face him. "However, they weren't designed for such regular use. I'll talk to Serenita about using them a little more sparingly."

"I *knew* something like this would happen," Telchide muttered under his breath. "I should cancel the trip with Aveline."

Eduardo gripped Telchide's wrist firmly.

"You will do no such thing. This is the first thing you've done for yourself since Sebetine disappeared. You cannot continue to allow a little lost sleep with Teresina to stop you from living your life. Serenita will deal with it, and I'll be here if they need me."

Telchide looked into Eduardo's hazel eyes. His friend stared at him relentlessly until he nodded. Eduardo finally let go his vice-like grip.

"Now, why don't you show me what you've got so far with that Lightbox of yours."

Telchide rubbed his wrist absently as he walked over to the Lightbox.

"I've tested it with the yellow fluid from each chamber. It functions as intended, but I want to modify it so that there's no intervention required for the next chamber to open once the previous light has died out."

"How?" Eduardo asked, pulling up a chair to sit by the workbench.

"I thought perhaps a dark-activated switch. When the first light dies out, I need this gear to turn, opening a space to release the next lot of fluid. However, it's easier to have a light-activated switch or a heat-activated one."

As he spoke, Telchide had an idea and turned to Eduardo in sudden excitement.

"Does the light produce any heat?"

"Chide, you must take me for some kind of fool if you think I stuck my hand in there to measure the temperature change over five minutes."

"Come, Ardo, surely you could've stuck a thermometer in there?"

"I had no reason to test the heat," Eduardo replied, crossing his arms over his chest.

Telchide sighed and stood up. "Very well, we'll test it now. Make yourself useful and get the liquids we'll need. I'll find a thermometer."

He eventually found a thermometer in the deepest recesses of his tool drawer. He rarely had a need for it for his inventions.

"We'll need more than one if you plan on testing all the colours," Eduardo said. He pointed to Teresina, who had just stepped down from the staircase, taken the tea tray from the dumbwaiter and was walking slowly towards them. The smell of mint wafted all around her.

"We can send Teresina."

Teresina set the tea down on the workbench and bounced around Eduardo.

"Teresina, can you go to my workshop and find Davide? Tell him you need five thermometers and six beakers. While you're there, ask him for a pinch or two of the powders on the second shelf of the third cabinet from the back door. Can you remember all of that?"

Teresina broke into a smile. "Of course!"

Before Telchide could tell her to be careful, she'd already run out through the back door.

"I'm serious, Ardo, if Teresina spends half her childhood in your workshop, you'll be forced to take her on as an apprentice."

Eduardo waved a dismissive hand. "Bah, she's too enraptured by your inventions to want to work in my stuffy old workshop."

Telchide sniffed and held his tongue. They still had years before Teresina was old enough to become an apprentice. With her strong mind, she would make the decision without consulting either of them and they'd have no choice in the matter.

***

They spent over an hour testing temperature changes, with Eduardo adding small pinches of different powders to the yellow mixture. Some of the powders made no discernible difference, others made the mixture colder, a few made the mixture hotter.

Once they'd found one that would work, Eduardo insisted they test the temperature change with each of the available colours.

"No point in making it work for one, but none of the others. Your machine will be next to useless then."

Telchide nodded. "We just need enough heat for the gears to expand while there is light. Don't overheat my Lightbox."

"Bah," Eduardo huffed at him. "You're too cautious. Why in Caldera's smoke does Aveline think you'll be of any use on her expedition?"

"I beg your pardon, but I'll be of immense use on the expedition. My skills..."

"Must be less than hers," Eduardo interrupted. "After all, *Aveline* is the one with the Electrum Guild Mark, not *you*."

Telchide glared at Eduardo. The infuriating Alchimista only grinned at him, then measured out small quantities of his chosen powder to each beaker, watching the thermometer until it had reached the desired temperature.

"That should do it," he declared, sitting back. "Why don't you try the blue one tonight for Teresina ... without giving her a pill."

Telchide heard the pause. He stared at Eduardo, wondering what he wasn't saying. The Alchimista held his gaze unwaveringly.

"Papà! Eduardo!" Teresina called out from the top of the stairs. "Dinner's ready."

Eduardo was the first to move. "I don't know about you, but I'm famished."

Telchide followed his oldest friend up the stairs, a gold weight falling in the pit of his stomach.

Chapter 13 – Orodi 13 Mercantili 230 Years After Implosion

Telchide woke with a start. He strained to hear the cause. His clockwork alarm showed half past six. He flicked the switch to make sure it wouldn't ring out at seven o'clock and got out of bed.

There was the noise again. Something was being dragged against the floor. He walked down the hallway towards the sound coming from Teresina's room. Not wanting to disturb her, he peeked in through the slightly ajar door.

Teresina, barefoot and wrapped in a heavy blanket, was pulling the Lightbox towards her bed. Once it was close enough to reach from the bed, she hopped up onto the mattress and stared at it. The blue liquid still glowed brightly. Telchide had only filled two segments. He hadn't quite figured a way for it to stop after a certain amount of time without intervention.

He pushed the door open a fraction. The hinges squeaked. Teresina looked up at the intrusion.

"Oh papà! I love this Lightbox! Can I keep it when you go on your trip?"

Telchide sat on Teresina's bed and wrapped an arm around her.

"I promised Kesida I'd bring it to her, remember?"

Teresina looked at him in confusion, then nodded slowly.

"I can ask her to bring it back to you once she's done with it. What do you think?"

"Yes please, papà," Teresina said in a sweet voice, batting her eyelashes up at him.

Telchide couldn't help but laugh and hug her.

"I'll take the Lightbox now. I have other things to discuss with Kesida. Be a good girl for Nonna."

Teresina nodded and hugged herself under the heavy blanket. Telchide patted her cheek affectionately. He bent down to pick up the Lightbox. It was heavier than he would've liked. Perhaps he could refine the invention by using a lighter metal or thinner panes of glass.

"Careful!" Serenita shouted. Telchide stopped in his tracks and saw Serenita standing two paces away from him. He'd been so lost in thought that he hadn't seen her.

"My apologies, Serenita," he said. "I'm just off to the Guild. I have some business to take care of with Kesida before I leave."

"No, not like that you aren't," Serenita said. "You might not be trying to catch any lady's eye, but that doesn't mean you should walk around town as unkempt as *this*."

Telchide blinked at her in surprise. He knew he hadn't taken much notice of his grooming in some time, but it hadn't occurred to him that anyone else had noticed.

"You can bring that box downstairs, but if I hear the front door instead of the sound of you shaving, you can make your own meals today."

Serenita scowled at Telchide as he bent to kiss her cheek.

"What would I do without you, Serenita?" he laughed.

***

An hour later, Telchide found himself outside the Inventrici Guild Hall, leading the Spiderseat that held his Lightbox. At this time of day, there was little traffic, so he chanced a walk across the road to catch a glimpse of the Mercantili Guild Hall.

They had always been the most pretentious Guild. He had very little time for them and, luckily for Telchide, his works had never garnered him enough fame for his wares to be popular in other cities. That had the distinct advantage of not forcing him to deal with the Mercantili Guild very often. Others were not so fortunate.

The Inter-Guild Edict hadn't stopped the Mercantili mingling with other Guilds. There hadn't been a written exemption for them in the Edict, but it was clearly implied – the Mercantili couldn't function without the other Guilds. Telchide wondered how many in the Tor'Esint Authorities owed their positions to the Mercantili Guild. Surely this Edict on inter-Guild relations couldn't last much longer without people realising what had happened.

From his position near the docks, Telchide looked up at the Mercantili Guild Hall. Of all the ostentatious things they could have done! Their Guild Mark seemed made entirely of gold. Telchide was certain it was gold plating – the Mercantili were too miserly to waste money on something hidden from the public eye – but the effect was the same.

Muttering angrily to himself, Telchide walked back across the road, carefully leading his Spiderseat up the steps to his own Guild Hall. The door was closed. Telchide pushed against it, then heard the clock tower strike half past seven.

Was it too early for the Guild Hall to be open? He knew Kesida had lodgings here, as she was too important in their Guild for her to live anywhere else. Surely she would be up by now. He knocked firmly on the wooden door. After a minute or two of silence, he knocked again, this time so hard he grazed his knuckles.

"Hold your horses!" called out a voice from within.

Telchide hurriedly led the Spiderseat back a few steps. He did not intend for his new invention to be destroyed.

Kesida glowered at him as she swung open the heavy door.

"What is the meaning of this?" she shouted.

Telchide drew back from the force of her anger. He gestured towards the Lightbox with his head.

"You told me to bring this to you before I leave," he replied with some uncertainty. "Should I not have come?"

Kesida crossed her arms.

"Do you have any idea what time it is?"

"Yes." Telchide nodded, wondering how she had not heard the clock striking. "It's half past seven."

She stared at him in disbelief. Telchide couldn't understand what he'd said that was so wrong. He shuffled his feet uncomfortably.

"May I come in?" he asked eventually.

Kesida uncrossed her arms and stepped aside to let him in.

"You're lucky I like you, Chide, or I would've closed the door in your face."

Telchide gave her a bemused smile and followed her down the long Hall of Great Works.

"Put it on my desk. I'll get the paperwork."

"Paperwork?" Telchide asked as he followed Kesida towards her desk.

"Just go to my desk," Kesida huffed at him as she hurried past her desk and through the door behind it.

Telchide took the Lightbox and carefully placed it on the wooden desk, covered by a protective cloth. He double checked the vials in his waist pouch. They were unbroken, just as Eduardo had promised they would be. Telchide resolved to study this waist pouch further to see exactly how the Alchimista had designed it to hold such delicate glass vials without them breaking.

Kesida made a great show of returning with her papers. She shuffled through them until she found what she was looking for and placed the entire stack down on her desk beside the invention.

"Alright," she said. "Impress me."

Telchide cleared his throat and removed the cover. The bright blue glow that had delighted Teresina that morning had faded completely, leaving behind a clear liquid on the larger side of the Lightbox.

"The Lightbox will come complete with this clear liquid. Perhaps each of the smaller chambers could be filled with each of the different colours, however, I'm not certain Eduardo will allow it."

Kesida raised her eyebrows. "Telchide, you haven't been breaching the Inter-Guild Edict, have you?"

"Not at all. No," Telchide replied hurriedly, waving his hands in front of his face. "I've simply been a loyal patron of my local Alchimista. For Teresina you understand. She's scared of the dark and Eduardo told me he could create a liquid light for her. He didn't know about this invention until it was already created."

He held his breath as Kesida peered at him closely.

"You might just have been believable if you hadn't held your breath at the end there."

Telchide grimaced. This Inter-Guild Edict was an intolerable nuisance!

"Chide, you really need to be more careful. The only thing that will save you this time is that you won't be here to answer questions when the Maestri study your invention."

Telchide made to protest, but Kesida silenced him.

"Do you have the different colours? Yes? Good. Pass them to me and fill out that form."

Telchide took the vials out of the waist pouch and lined them up in order on the desk, from yellow to blue.

"Why are there two yellow?"

"I want to show you how it works before we fill it up with all the colours."

Before she could argue, he took the first yellow vial, opened the lid to the small chambers and poured it in.

"You can fill all of them later. This yellow one lasts five minutes."

He closed the lid to the small chambers and pointed to a knob at the top between the two sides.

"By lifting this, you allow the yellow liquid to mix with the clear liquid, like so."

He pulled up the knob and the entire Lightbox immediately began to glow a bright yellow. Kesida hurried to douse all the other lights in the room to get the full effect. The liquid emitted a strong glow over ten piedi away, with a lighter glow reaching at least four piedi.

"This is amazing, Chide! A true stroke of genius!"

Telchide found himself blushing despite himself. He *was* rather proud of this particular invention, even if it had needed an Alchimista's touch to work effectively.

Kesida only relit the candles on her desk when the glow had dimmed considerably.

"A little pointless though, if it only lasts a few minutes."

"Ah yes," Telchide replied excitedly. "But only the yellow one has such a short light life. Each colour has a different light life, with blue lasting four hours! I rigged it up yesterday so that you can set a continual glow until all the liquids are used."

He pointed to a lever next to the knob at the top.

"If you flick this to the side, it will lift the knob every time the light dies. That will flush in another lot of coloured liquid, and then so on for as many chambers as you have filled."

He pushed down the middle knob, unscrewed a cover from the bottom of the small chambers and held the empty vial under it to drain the excess fluid.

"The emptying and refilling are the most hands-on part of the working of the Lightbox. Fortunately, it only needs to be done once all the liquids in the small chamber have been used."

Telchide stoppered the vial and placed it in the waist pouch once more. Next, he pulled aside five bits of metal from the side of the small chamber, allowing the first vial to pour directly into the bottom slot.

As he poured each colour in, Telchide pushed another metal barrier back in place before pouring in the next colour. This he did until all six colours were in the small chambers. Finally, he closed the lid to the small chambers and gestured proudly to the Lightbox.

"At this point, the customer can choose either to use a single chamber at a time or to flick this lever to allow for continuous light until there are no colours left to be used. I would like to add a feature that allows for a select number of chambers to be used before that feature stops working, but I don't have enough time now to experiment. My expedition may leave at any time, and I still have much work to do."

Kesida reached out her hand to touch the Lightbox. Telchide rushed to place the cloth cover over it again.

"I don't have any more vials of coloured liquid."

Kesida raised an eyebrow at him. "Yes, fine, fine. I'll show the Maestri how it works when they have a spare moment."

"I need to beg a favour," Telchide said.

"What else?"

"I promised Teresina I'd ask you to return the Lightbox when the Maestri have seen it. The glow helps her sleep at night."

Kesida stared at him in silence for a moment or two.

"Your daughter is lucky to have such a caring papà. I'll do what I can. Now, I need you to fill out that paperwork before you can leave the invention here. Standard protocol I'm afraid. Then you'll need to fill this out for the apprentice application."

Telchide leafed through the papers with a sigh. He should not have left the rubber-lined box so late. He was going to run out of time.

"I need your help with something else," he said, looking back up at Kesida. "I'll leave Serenita with enough money for the first week, but I don't want a large amount of money left lying around the house. Can we set up a system where she can come here on a weekly basis, until I return, to withdraw as much money as she needs from my vault?"

"It would be safer for you to nominate a specific amount of time," Kesida said.

"No." Telchide said firmly. "I don't know how long I'll be away, and I refuse to leave her without money if something should go wrong."

Kesida sighed. "Very well. Start on those forms, I'll get what you need for Serenita."

Telchide thanked her. Before starting on the forms, he placed the empty vials back in his waist pouch to return to Eduardo. It would not do to return broken ones, especially when Telchide hadn't paid for any of the liquids since their joint experiment had begun. He hoped it would be worth their efforts in the end.

This invention, if it were used in the mines or other such working environments, could become profitable. Likely, Eduardo would profit from it more than Telchide, but he was happy to share the success with his oldest friend.

By the time Kesida returned, Telchide had finished filling out all the paperwork. She held out a single sheet of paper. It was thicker than normal. An embossed Inventrici Guild Mark sat in the bottom corner with a swirling gold border running around the edge of the paper. He read the words carefully.

This chit hereby grants_____five silver coins from the vault of_____ Inventrice/Inventore upon presentation to the Inventrici Guild Hall. This chit may be presented no more than once every seven days until further notice.

"You fill in Serenita's name here and your name here," Kesida said as she pointed out the two empty spaces. She paused and took a deep breath. "I still don't think this is a good idea. If something happens to sour your relationship with Serenita and she refuses to relinquish this chit, we'll still be obliged to grant her the money."

Telchide filled out the names and signed his signature at the bottom of the page.

"Kesida, I appreciate your concern, but there's nothing that could happen to sour our relationship. She may as well be my own mamma. If I'm honest, she looks after Teresina more than I do. What kind of person would I be if I didn't provide for them in my absence?

"Now, the only thing I would really like to know is which apprentice will be assigned to me."

Kesida looked away from him and began gathering all the papers on her desk.

"It will all be sorted by the time you return," she told him dismissively.

Telchide felt a sense of unease as Kesida avoided his gaze.

"Have you chosen one?"

"Not yet. I still have a few things to organise before assigning you as a maestro. Now, be off with you. I'd like to have my breakfast before I officially open the Guild Hall."

Telchide looked at her in surprise. His mouth dropped open. Her initial anger now finally made sense.

"My apologies, Kesida. I did not think..."

"You Inventrici are all the same," Kesida interrupted him. "Too wrapped up in your own minds to notice anyone else. Opening is eight o'clock, just like trading! Be off with you now. Have a safe journey and make sure Serenita gets that chit. We wouldn't want it falling into the wrong hands."

Telchide nodded and held the chit tightly as Kesida bundled him back out onto the street with his unburdened Spiderseat. The bright sunlight bouncing off the sea blinded him momentarily.

He turned his gaze away from the bay and quickly tucked the chit into the inner pocket of his waistcoat. Kesida was right – it would not do to lose it. He patted his pocket before heading off to his workshop.

***

By the time he arrived home, it was past eight o'clock. That still left him with the greater part of the day to work on the rubber-lined box. With Aveline coming over that afternoon, he could afford to leave his music boxes until he had finished the box.

"Serenita, Teresina, I'm home," he called out up the stairs.

He should really install a communication device between the upper and lower levels of his house to avoid all this shouting, like Aveline. It simply would not do when he had an apprentice. Nor, for that matter, would it do when he had customers. But, at least in that instance, he'd never yet been embarrassed by Serenita or Teresina calling down to him when his customers were in the workshop.

There were many things that would need to change in their household to accommodate a newcomer, but he did not have the time or the mental capacity to think about that now.

Telchide pulled out the rubber sheets Aveline had given him from the factory. He found himself grinding his teeth over the foul woman they'd encountered there and promised himself he would not treat his apprentice like that.

The unknown apprentice was already a great distraction to him. Instead of keeping his mind firmly fixed on his work, he allowed it to follow a great many pathways all related to this person he did not know. Would the boy fit in with his family? Would he be a respectful, hardworking lad or more trouble than he was worth? Would they get along or would the boy think he was too difficult to work with? This last was the most distressing.

"Right. Wood, measuring stick, pencil."

Telchide often talked aloud to himself. It helped to focus him on what he needed to do. He knew others found it disconcerting at first, but his closest friends and conspirators from the Exploding Beakers group had grown accustomed to it over the years. Now, they rarely looked askance at him when he spoke aloud at random.

He busied himself the rest of the morning measuring and remeasuring the wood and rubber to make sure everything would fit together as he planned. He knew from his own inventions that metal had a peculiar effect with steam and friction power whereas rubber dampened the effect. He resolved to minimise any possible interaction between the energy plant and metal.

There was a pot of hide glue on the corner of his workbench. He rarely needed it for his inventions, but Telchide was as meticulous as he was fastidious. If there was a possibility that he would need it for his inventions, he simply must have it in decent supply. That mindset had saved him a number of times in the past, like the time a single customer had commissioned ten pocket watches at once for his children!

After checking the measurements for a third time, Telchide took his bow saw for the wood and his band saw for the rubber from the shelf beneath his workbench. He cut the wood and the rubber sheets into six sections, then cut the necessary edges into dovetails to interlock the sides and bottom of the box.

Using his router plane, he chiselled out a groove in three of the wooden sections to allow the wooden lid to simply slide into place without the need of metal screws. He made a mental note to add a wooden peg to lock the box before he finished.

With painstaking care, he warmed the hide glue to a malleable state and brushed copious amounts of it onto all six wooden sections, pressing the rubber firmly onto them. Telchide looked around the workshop for something heavy to lay on top of the rubber sheets. Hide glue was fast drying, but he couldn't afford for any mistakes that would make the glue not hold. He settled on his regular toolbox and a few other heavy items.

Telchide put away his woodworking tools and swept the sawdust from the smooth stone floor. It was times like this that he was thankful he hadn't followed in his family's footsteps to become a Falegname. He looked around once more and nodded to himself in satisfaction. It had been a good day's work and he had hours to spare. It was still early afternoon.

He trudged up the stairs. It was time to put his affairs in order.

"Serenita? I need a moment of your time."

Teresina came running and hurled herself into his arms when he was still on the stairs. He pushed her back onto the top step and quickly held onto the rail.

"Teresina, I've told you time and again not to do that! You're getting too heavy for me. What would happen if I lost my balance and we both tumbled down the stairs?"

Teresina frowned at him, her lower lip beginning to tremble.

"Now, now, Resi. Let's not start with the tears. You know I love you. I simply don't want you to get hurt. How could I ever forgive myself if something bad happened to you?"

The lip stopped trembling, but the frown remained.

"Are you finished your work, papà?" she asked softly.

"For now," he said. "I need the glue to dry before I can do anything else with the box. Where's Nonna?"

"She's taking a nap," Teresina whispered. "She takes a lot of naps, papà. You know, she's *very* ancient."

Telchide laughed. "Nonna's not *very* ancient, Resi. She's just older than both of us."

"And older than Eduardo." Teresina pointed out.

Telchide had to think a moment before replying. "You know, I'm not certain that she is. Speaking of Eduardo, can you run along through the backyard and ask him for my motion sickness cure? I may be leaving at any moment and do not intend to be sick the entire way."

At the mention of his trip, Teresina took a big breath and held it. He caressed her cheek and planted a kiss on her forehead.

"You'll have so much fun going in and out of Eduardo's workshop, you'll barely notice I'm gone," Telchide told her.

"Who will read to me before bed?" she asked softly.

Telchide cupped her cheek in his hand. "You can read to Serenita. It will be a nice change."

She looked at him thoughtfully for a moment, then let out her breath with a loud sigh and walked past him down the stairs. He waited until he heard the back door open and close before knocking on Serenita's door. There was no answer. Telchide opened the door a fraction and peeked in. The heavy curtain was drawn across the window, making the room as dark as night.

Stepping carefully, Telchide edged his way towards the window and drew back the curtain just enough to let in a thin stream of light. Serenita was lying on her bed. The gentle movement of her chest rising with her breath was barely enough to see. She stirred when the light hit her face.

"Teresina, I told you not to wake me," she said irritably.

"It's not Teresina," Telchide said.

At the sound of his voice, Serenita rubbed her eyes and sat up.

"Oh Chide, it's you."

Telchide looked at Serenita closely in the sliver of light. She seemed to have aged considerably these past few weeks. How had he not noticed? Why had it taken Teresina's comment for him to see what was right in front of him?

"Serenita, will you be able to manage when I leave?"

"Yes, of course," she replied immediately. "We've been busy lately, if you hadn't noticed, clearing out the spare bedroom for your new apprentice. In between that, with you being so busy and needing peace and quiet to get your work done, Teresina has forced me to play game after game with her. We'll be fine once she can romp around and make as much noise as she likes."

He very much doubted that Teresina romping about would allow Serenita to rest more, but he did not press the issue. Instead, he reached into his waistcoat pocket, pulled out the chit from the Inventrici Guild and placed it on the bedside table.

"While I'm away, take this, once a week, to the Inventrici Guild Hall and they will give you five silver coins. That should provide you with sufficient funds until I return. Can you think of anything else you might need from me before I go?"

"We'll be fine, Chide. Besides, Eduardo has promised to let Teresina spend at least an hour a day in his workshop to give me some peace and quiet."

Serenita winked at him. Telchide chuckled and shook his head. He couldn't deny that much as he was going to miss Teresina terribly, it would be a welcome break not to have to be a papà for a few weeks. It would be the first time he'd ever left Teresina in her short life.

The sound of the back door slamming announced Teresina before her quick steps up the stairs.

"Papà?" she called out softly. Telchide marvelled that she did not realise how much noise she made around the house and still thought she had to whisper for Serenita's sake.

"I'm in here, Resi," he called out to her.

Teresina poked her head through the door hesitantly. When she saw Serenita was awake, she walked in and held out a small brown paper packet to Telchide. He took it from her and read the instruction on the paper.

Take one immediately before departure and another every two hours until the journey is over.

These would be just as precious to him as the chit was for Serenita. He placed the packet carefully in his waistcoat pocket.

***

True to her word, Aveline arrived early that afternoon. Teresina, as usual, immediately hopped up onto the chair next to the coatrack to take Aveline's hat and coat. Today's selection was a dark green coat with silver trimmings. Her hat matched it perfectly, even down to the style of the trimmings.

"Aveline, did a Sarta give you these as a trade for your inventions like Greta Sarta is doing for my sleeves?" she asked, running her hand along the length of the coat as though the touch of it pleased her.

"Actually, I ordered this set when I earned my Electrum Guild Mark," Aveline answered. "It was a sort of present to myself."

Telchide took a second look at the trimmings. From this distance, he couldn't tell if they were silver or electrum. Either way, the ensemble must have been expensive.

Teresina nodded sagely. "It was a good present. Did you do the same for your other Guild Marks?"

"Not in the same way. I gave myself the present of finding and setting up a workshop for my Copper Guild Mark and for my Silver Guild Mark, I took on an apprentice."

"Papà is getting an apprentice!" Teresina exclaimed excitedly. "Nonna and I are clearing out our spare room for him."

Aveline stopped and stared at Telchide with a small smile. He felt her attention on him most keenly and couldn't account for her reaction. In an attempt to break whatever spell she was under, Telchide pointed to his stash of music strips.

"Teresina, could you play those music strips for Aveline. She's to choose one for Greta Sarta in return for your sleeves."

Telchide tried not to notice that Aveline smiled when Teresina took her by the hand to show her the music strips, or how close they held their heads to one another when playing the strips. His heart ached at the sight – Teresina should be showing such affections to her mamma, not a woman who she'd only met a few weeks ago, but it was clear Teresina craved the closeness and Aveline was happy to oblige.

Leaving Teresina and Aveline playing the music strips, Telchide went upstairs to make a pot of tea. He couldn't bear the sight of how well they looked together, as a mother and daughter would look.

Unusually, Serenita was not in the kitchen. Telchide felt a strange relief that he wouldn't have to discuss these feelings with her. Instead, he busied himself making a pot of peppermint tea and laying everything on a tea tray. By the time the kettle boiled, he'd managed to steady his nerves. He could hear that the music had finally stopped, so he allowed himself a deep breath and a moment's pause before sending the tray down in the dumbwaiter and returning to the workshop.

Teresina almost ran into him as he walked to his workstation with the tea tray. She was only held back and stopped from a catastrophic crash by Aveline catching her by the shoulders. The familiar gesture did not earn Aveline even a small scowl from Teresina, as it would have if any other relative stranger had dared touch her. Instead, she stopped and leaned her head back momentarily against Aveline. Aveline stroked her hair affectionately until Telchide cleared his throat.

"Have you chosen one then?" he asked, trying to ignore the painful mixture of affection, grief, and confusion at the sight of them.

"The one on your workbench," Aveline said in an oddly subdued voice. "I think Greta's apprentices will enjoy dancing to that tune. Teresina certainly does."

Telchide nodded mutely. He poured out two cups of tea and sat down to work on the metal strip. Aveline bent her head close to Teresina and said something quietly to her. Teresina disappeared upstairs. The next thing he knew Aveline was standing close by his side, peering down at the copper strip he was smoothing out.

"Will you teach me how to do that?" she asked. "I don't think I'd have the patience to make a music box on my own, but it would be interesting to learn the skill."

Telchide paused. If he taught her, would she steal his clientele? He was immediately ashamed of the thought – it was unworthy, and he knew it.

"Yes, of course," he said after too long.

Aveline hesitated, then sat alongside him and handed him a folded sheet of paper. Telchide unfolded it to see a list of items for the expedition. He placed the list in his work apron with a word of thanks, his heart beating faster in anticipation of the trip.

Trying not to let the expedition distract him, Telchide passed Aveline the prepared strip of copper he'd been smoothing out, the small round-tipped tool he used for every music strip and the tiny hammer.

"Copying a tune is easier than figuring out one from scratch. What you need to do is create dents in exactly the same places as on this template."

He placed the template copper strip just above the smooth one on the workbench. Aveline hesitantly picked up the round-tipped tool and hammer. With no accuracy and too much force, she punched a hole in the copper strip. She gasped loudly, dropped the round-tipped tool, and covered her mouth.

"I'm so sorry, Chide! I've broken it!"

The tension from the afternoon fled. Telchide couldn't help but laugh. Aveline looked cross at first, but then laughed alongside him.

He handed her a metal rolling pin. "Use this to smooth it out again. I'll do Greta's strip myself; you can practise on that one with my awl."

"Your what?" she asked in confusion.

"My awl," he said, picking up the small woodworking tool. "It's round-tipped, so should work just as well for practicing. Just try to be gentle or you'll spend most of your time rolling out your copper than denting it."

He worked side by side with Aveline, sipping tea and preparing the copper strip for Greta's music box. Aveline soon gave up on her metal strip and got to work on the pocket watches Telchide had laid out for her.

"The other day, when you came over and Nevio realised you were committed, he later asked me something I didn't know the answer to."

"Hmm, what's that?" Telchide asked curiously, working on the copper strip.

"Do you think Sebetine is alive? I mean, *really* believe she's alive and didn't just leave you?"

Telchide's hands paused in his work. Aveline laid a gentle hand on his shoulder.

"I'm sorry, Chide. You don't have to answer. It was cruel of me to ask."

Telchide was silent for a while.

"I don't know," he sighed. "I really don't know."

"If you don't mind telling me, what actually happened?"

"She went to visit her mamma in Tor'Dumere. They'd always been quite close, but Serenita hadn't yet met Teresina because she didn't like to travel such a long distance and the funicolare had only just opened. I suppose she didn't trust it. In any case, the sleepless nights Sebetine was suffering from made it difficult for her to look after Teresina. She was beginning to forget simple things. Really, she needed a break.

"The trip was as good an excuse as any for both of them. Sebetine would get a break from Teresina and could try to convince her mamma to come visit us. Teresina stayed with me – she was only three and liked playing in the workshop. If Sebetine had brought Teresina with her, Serenita would've had no reason to come back with her.

"Sebetine was to take the funicolare the entire way, switching over to the Tor'Dumere line at the waystation. She never reached Tor'Dumere. The day after her expected arrival, Serenita got up the courage travel to Tor'Esint to enquire why her daughter hadn't come to see her. That was when we realised something had happened.

"I tried to confirm whether she'd taken the Tor'Dumere funicolare, but no one remembered. The Mercantili Guild investigated it as well, but all we could discover was that she'd caught the Tor'Esint funicolare; and even with a sketch of her likeness, no one remembered which, if any, funicolare she caught at the waystation. I put up posters everywhere I could, sent missing advertisements to the newssheets, but never heard anything."

Telchide paused. He was not crying or choked up. He was numb. He'd never told anyone the full story before because most people who knew had lived through it with him.

"When it became clear that we would not find her, Serenita agreed to stay here. Teresina was still so young that I needed help with her and a nonna is always a good thing to have in your life.

"I think both Serenita and Teresina believe she will never return. I ... don't know what I believe. I sometimes want to believe she is alive somewhere, but if I believe that I have to accept that she left us and never intends to come back. I cannot think so ill of her.

"That makes me want to believe that she's dead. I ... have trouble with that because we never found her body. But if she is dead, then..."

"Then you'll be heartbroken," Aveline finished for him.

"No, it's worse than that." He took a deep breath and held it for a moment before exhaling sharply. "If she's dead, we can all finally breathe again. It's my fault really. I cling to the thought that she might be alive, but that only makes it worse. It keeps everyone hoping that she might return. That we might be able to go back to our lives the way they were.

"If she's dead and we know she's not coming back, we can move on with our lives. Serenita could choose whether to stay with us, and only think of herself in the matter rather than her daughter. Teresina would know that her mamma did not abandon her and feel such intense hatred for her."

He stopped talking. Aveline nudged his arm gently.

"And you?"

And me, Telchide thought to himself.

"I might be able to take this ring off my finger and start anew."

He glanced sideways. Aveline was staring at him, at his ring.

"No one would blame you," she said. He looked at her in confusion. She grimaced. "I mean, no one would blame you if you took off your ring *now*. As you said, it's been three years. If she ran away, for some unknown reason, she isn't coming back. If she was abducted or stolen away, either she died or will never be able to return. If she met with an accident, and no one found her within a few days, she'd be dead."

No one had ever spoken so plainly to him before. Hearing it like that, there was almost no doubt in his mind that Sebetine was dead. *Almost.* And that was the problem.

Before they could discuss it further, the bell to his door tinkled and Signora Angela walked in with her son.

"Signora, what a pleasure to see you again." Telchide rose from his seat to find Angelo's music box and brought it over to the boy. "I have your music box right here. How do you like it?"

The boy snatched it out of his hand and turned the handle. His face turned into a scowl moments before he started yelling. "This music sounds terrible! It sounded much better on Mercatodi. You made it badly!"

Telchide stared mutely at the rude, little boy. Teresina would never dare yell at a Guild member, nor anyone else for that matter. He was so stunned by the boy's reaction, he didn't notice Aveline until she'd taken the music box out of Angelo's hand.

"Angelo, you're forgetting the most important part," she told him. "Remember, it plays best when you put it on a flat surface. Like this table here. Now give it another go."

Telchide watched as the entire atmosphere of the room changed. Signora Angela looked as though she was ready to join in her son's complaint until that point. But when Angelo tried the music box again, this time with Aveline holding it steady on the small waiting table, the music was so rich and full that it sounded like a completely different device.

"Now, I think you owe Telchide Inventore an apology for that little outburst, don't you?" Aveline asked sternly.

Telchide marvelled at her. He would never have the gall to suggest such a thing and, if he did, it would never have been received as well as Aveline's suggestion. A shame-faced Angelo looked up at his mamma who looked down her nose at him and nodded. Angelo stood and brought the music box with him to face Telchide.

"I apologise, Inventore," he said quietly. "It's a lovely music box. Thank you."

Telchide was baffled. "Yes, well, you're welcome. Your mamma picked out a lovely tune for you, so really, you ought to be thanking her."

Dutifully, the boy turned to his mamma and thanked her. Signora Angela melted at the change in behaviour of her son.

"Happy birthday, tesoro. I'm certain your friends will be envious of your new toy." She turned to Telchide. "We agreed on ten silvers, did we not?"

He nodded and extended his hand as Signora Angela held out the coins.

"Signora, be sure to tell your friends that was a Mercatodi special if they decide to purchase one for their children," Aveline said as she quickly crossed the room to join them. "Telchide began teaching me how to make these copper strips today and I now understand that the price of ten silvers does not *begin* to reflect the amount of work that goes into them. I think it would be fair to tell your friends that *fifteen* silvers is the regular price for any music Telchide doesn't already have a template for. He'll have a complete list of currently available songs drawn up before next Mercatodi."

Signora Angela looked from Aveline to Telchide with an odd expression, but then nodded her head in a pleased manner.

"Come, Angelo. Let's go home and show your papà this little marvel. Perhaps his friend's children will also be envious of it when they come to your party."

Telchide waited until they walked out the door before turning to Aveline.

"You shouldn't have done that," he told her.

She frowned at him. "Why ever not? The music box is easily worth fifteen silvers."

He took a deep breath. "Fifteen silvers is lot of money! I don't have my Electrum Guild Mark. I don't have the status to demand such high prices. Potential customers know that, and they won't bother ordering from me now. You've just lost me any business I might have made from that sale."

Aveline paused. "But they're *worth* that much. I'm sure they'll realise that and order them anyway."

Telchide knew she was wrong but didn't want to talk about it any longer. He was suddenly quite tired. Abandoning all hope of continuing work on Greta's music box, he walked over to the pieces of wood that would become the rubber-lined wooden box.

Taking care not to dislodge any of the rubber sheets, Telchide removed the various items he'd used as weights from each section. The rubber appeared to be well-attached to the wood. He heaved a loud sigh of relief. He'd been so worried that it might not work.

With meticulous care, he took the bottom section and laid it in front of him. Next, he slotted in each side of the box, ensuring the dovetailed edges fit together perfectly. Inside the box, he slid thinner pieces of wood to create smaller compartments for the plants. Lastly, he slid in the lid. He went to lock it, only to realise he'd forgotten to put the peg on. Cursing himself for a fool, Telchide painstakingly carved out a semicircle hoop and a peg. He pulled out the pot of animal hide glue and slathered a generous amount on the flat edges of the half hoop. Next, he set the box up at an angle to allow gravity to assist the drying process and pressed the half hoop in place. He set the wooden peg next to the box ready for the next morning.

Standing back to admire his work, he reflected that the box was going to be a little cumbersome to take on the trip. It was more than half the length of his arm and almost as wide as his chest. He looked around to discuss it with Aveline and it was only then that he realised she'd left his workshop. Had she bid him farewell and he had missed it? He refused to feel embarrassed about the way he'd spoken to her – she'd been in the wrong and should have apologised to him. Instead, she'd simply insisted that she was right and refused to acknowledge the difference in their status as Silver and Electrum Inventrici. Perhaps she'd had the luxury, even during her Silver years, to not accept prices she thought were beneath her, but he was not in so fortunate a situation as that.

He should've been flattered, but all he could feel was anger that she'd lost him so many potential sales. He wouldn't have cared half so much if the lost sales were *his* fault. After all, he was used to that. It was the first time that he truly wished Aveline hadn't spent the afternoon with him.

Chapter 14 – Mercatodi 14 Mercantili 230 Years After Implosion

Blockade break on Riposidi. Early morning. Message sent to V and L. E

The message was waiting for Telchide when he awoke the next morning. It was Mercatodi today – that meant they would be leaving tomorrow. He heaved a sigh of relief that he'd finished the rubber-lined box the day before but had a knot in the pit of his stomach at the thought of travelling with Aveline so soon after their *words* the day before.

There was little left for him to do now but to prepare for the trip. He'd fulfilled all but two of his orders – thankfully, the two elaborate music box orders had still not dropped off their sheet music, so he wouldn't be obliged to begin the strips for those until he returned, but they were otherwise ready. He'd tested them with his own template strips and they worked well.

All that he had to do was pack. Aveline's list had been very restrictive

~ *one small bag you'll be happy to carry around the Caldera with you*
~ *one coat or small blanket*
~ *one change of clothes*
~ *food - no more than you can carry*
~ *water canister*
~ *one set of utensils*
~ *one bowl*
~ *tools - necessary ones only*
~ *wooden box for plants*

Telchide rummaged through his belongings until he found a suitable bag. After all, he had many pockets in his clothing in which to bring a few items that might come in handy on a trip like this. He lay the bag on his bed along with his waist pouch. It wasn't as intricate as Eduardo's one, but it would do nicely just the same.

Within a half hour, he'd meticulously laid out the tools and equipment he wanted to bring along with a complete change of clothes.

Once he'd packed the clothing into the larger bag, there was barely any room left for the equipment. He satisfied himself with a measuring stick, a magnifying glass, a ball of leather twining, a spool of copper, a sharp pair of scissors and a sturdy knife.

In his waist pouch, he put his usual assortment of items – a notepad, two pencils, a shaving knife to sharpen them, a handful of coins and a compass.

He walked down the stairs to his workbench and stared at all the things he would be leaving behind. Perhaps there would be room for a few more items.

"Take Teresina down to the market." Telchide turned at the sound of Serenita's voice. "Find yourself a canister and buy as much non-perishable food as you can. Bread will keep a good few days, but it will go stale quickly."

Teresina came running into the workshop.

"Market time!" she squealed. "Can we buy something for me too?"

"Certainly. Put your hat on and let's go."

Telchide took the shopping basket from its perch by the door, donned his coppola, tipped it in farewell to Serenita and took Teresina with him out onto the street. They walked past Eduardo's workshop but, unusually for her, Teresina did not even glance in that direction. Instead, she tugged Telchide's hand until he began to walk faster.

They reached Piazza Mercantile in record time. From there, the roles changed, and it was Telchide tugging Teresina's hand to keep her moving. Every other fortnight, the piazza was full of non-Guild stalls and there was much to see.

"Things for my trip first. *Then* we can look for you."

As they walked through the piazza, Telchide kept his eye out for anything that would be useful on the trip. He bought a loaf of bread, a hunk of cheese, salted crackers and a variety of dried and fresh fruits. In the end, it was Teresina who spotted the water canisters. They were together with a stack of sealed metal cans. Telchide eyed them as he took the water canister from Teresina.

"They're mostly vegetables, Inventore," the shopkeeper told him in an excited voice. "The food keeps fresh for over a month!"

Telchide stared at the man in disbelief. "A month?"

"*Over* a month! We're still testing them. The latest one we've opened is five weeks old and still tastes as fresh as the day we canned them."

"How do you open these canisters?"

The shopkeeper handed him a strange looking tool with a hooked knife at one end.

"They're a little expensive at five silvers, but you'll only ever need to buy one. This little device can open any one of our cans. Let me show you."

The beady eyed man took a hooked knife from the table behind him and held up a can that already had a quarter of the lid cut open. The man turned the can so the closed part of the lid was in front of him and pierced the metal with the hooked knife. Next, he dragged the inner edge of the hook along the metal. To Telchide's surprise, it sliced through the metal as easily as a warm knife through butter.

"What sorts of goods do you have in these cans?"

"Currently we have boiled pumpkin, tomatoes, sardines, and beans. You must understand, the process was only devised a short time ago. We're testing the process with new foods every week."

Telchide looked down at the hooked knife in his hand and his basket half filled with fresh foods. Serenita was right, fresh food wouldn't last long and he didn't know what food they would find on Sentigura Caldera. Aveline had said to bring only what he was happy to carry, but food was important and worth the extra weight.

"I'll take five of each," he told the shopkeeper.

The man's eyes bulged, and he dropped the empty can.

"How much will that be?" Telchide asked belatedly.

"Well, er, yes, just a moment, while I figure it out."

Telchide waited patiently as the man scrawled some figures down on a scrap piece of paper.

"I believe that will be three electrums, Inventore, including the can opener and the water canister."

Telchide raised his eyebrows in surprise. He'd not expected it to be quite so much. He began to pull out some coins when Teresina tugged on his jacket.

"He did his sums wrong, papà," she whispered.

Telchide knew most people would not trust the workings of a child, but he'd schooled Teresina himself and knew her methodology was sound. He smiled at her and peered over at the scrap paper. Teresina was right. He was being overcharged by the sum of an electrum.

"Signore, by any chance would there be a discount involved for buying so many of your canned foods?"

The shopkeeper glanced down at his sums and redid them. He looked up at Telchide, red in the face.

"My apologies, Inventore! Two electrums, not three. Allow me to offer you another can opener. With this many cans, I assume there will be more than one person going on your trip?"

Telchide smiled at the man with good humour and handed him two electrum coins. Together, they repacked his shopping basket to place the heavier cans on the bottom so his other goods would not be squashed.

Once they were a few stalls away from the canned goods, Telchide squeezed Teresina's hand affectionately.

"You saved me an electrum there. I think it's fair to say we can buy you something now. What would you like?"

"Earrings!" Teresina replied without hesitation. "I'd like earrings, papà."

Telchide's loud laugh earned him several reproachful looks from passers-by.

"Earrings? Where in Tor'Esint am I to find you earrings?"

Teresina looked up at him hopefully and shrugged. Telchide looked up and down the street. There were too many stalls for him to search before the end of Mercatodi and there would certainly be no Gioielliere Guild stalls, but he began looking, nonetheless.

At one point, Teresina tugged his hand.

"Over there, papà."

She pointed him to Aveline's workshop. Telchide's stomach flipped.

"We don't want to bother Aveline today," he told her. "She'll be very busy herself."

But Teresina refused to take no for an answer and dragged him up into the workshop. Telchide hung back as Teresina ran up to Aveline and stopped short of hugging her, curtseying in front of her instead. Telchide felt miserable. He was certain Aveline would still be angry with him and didn't want to see her so soon.

Aveline graced Teresina with a large smile. "To what do I owe the pleasure, little Teresina?"

Telchide thought it best that he step in at this point. "My apologies, Aveline, but Teresina and I were doing some last-minute shopping and now we need earrings."

Aveline raised her eyebrows and Teresina giggled.

"Not for papà, Aveline, for me!"

Aveline's face relaxed into a smile. "Ahh, I see. Do you have your ears pierced yet?"

Teresina bit her lip. "No. Does it hurt?"

Aveline knelt in front of his daughter.

"I won't lie to you, Teresina. It will hurt, but not for long. I can do it for you myself if you'd like. Have you found a set of earrings?"

Teresina shook her head.

"In that case, you can pick one of mine."

"We couldn't possibly." Telchide objected. He set down the immensely heavy shopping basket before walking over to them.

"I insist," Aveline said, looking up at him. "It's the least I can do for taking you away from your daughter on this expedition. Nevio, watch the shop while I show Teresina my earrings."

The apprentice nodded dutifully. He shot Telchide an apologetic glance.

"I'm sorry for the other night," he said softly. "I knew you had a child ... but I didn't know about your companion."

Telchide waved him off. "My Sebetine has been missing for so long that you couldn't have known about her. It's times like this I miss her most of all. I didn't have the faintest idea what to do when Teresina told me she wanted earrings, of all things!"

Nevio laughed softly. "Yes, that would've befuddled me too."

"How's your watch going?" Telchide moved closer to Nevio's workbench. "I saw the pieces when I was last here."

Nevio's face fell. "I couldn't put it together. Not without Maestra Aveline putting the pieces in the correct order for me. We've kept it aside for me to try another day."

Nevio motioned to the small box on the far edge of his workbench. Telchide patted his back.

"Perhaps you simply need to believe in yourself. Aveline herself told me that you've seen her put together many watches and put together a few yourself when the pieces are laid out correctly. If you stop and think, which piece do *you* think comes first?"

Nevio pulled the box over and pulled out the large centre of the watch.

"I know this goes in the middle. That's all."

"Come now, I doubt that's all. Which bit goes here?"

Telchide pointed to one side of the centrepiece. Nevio studied it for a moment, then rummaged around in the box until he found the piece he was looking for. He put it in place and looked up at Telchide questioningly.

"Stop second-guessing yourself. You know how to do this. It's only a puzzle. Now, put it together."

"I'm meant to be working on this project for Mistress Aveline." He pointed to another item on his workstation.

"Actually, I'd rather you do the watch if you can." Aveline's voice travelled down to them from the conical device hanging from the ceiling.

There was a moment of silence, then a scream ripped through the air. He knew that scream – it was Teresina!

"Teresina! I'm coming!"

Telchide looked for a way to his daughter. Another scream followed, louder than before. Then the wailing began.

"Blast it all! Nevio, help me get up there."

Before Nevio could move to help him, Telchide heard Teresina's sweet laughter travelling down the conical device.

"Aveline Inventrice, they're simply gorgeous!"

Telchide looked up at the device in surprise. A few moments later, Teresina burst into the room with Aveline close on her heels.

"Papà *look*! Aren't they the most beautiful things you've ever seen?"

Telchide looked at Teresina's ears. The lobes were bright red and starting to become swollen. And there were *things* hanging from raw wounds. What were those things? Surely, they couldn't have been the reason his precious daughter had been willing to let someone punch a *hole* through her ears!

"You don't like them?" Teresina asked in a trembling voice.

Telchide stopped staring at her ears and looked at her crestfallen face.

"No, I mean, I do. Of course, I do. They're beautiful."

Teresina frowned at him uncertainly until he smiled and took a closer look at the earrings. They actually were quite beautiful, once he got past the fact that they'd been the cause of his daughter's pain. Aveline had given her a pair of hanging earrings in the shape of dragonflies.

"Dragonflies are quite magnificent creatures, you know," Telchide told his daughter, drawing her in for an embrace. She forcefully held her head away from him.

"Don't squash my ears, papà," she scolded him. "Aveline told me I'll need to be careful with them until the holes have healed properly. So perhaps by the time you return from your trip, I'll be ready to be squashed."

"Very well then. I promise to squash you upon my return."

Telchide held out his hand and Teresina shook it emphatically.

"Now why don't you watch Nevio at his work while I have a quick word with Aveline?"

He walked over to his shopping basket and motioned Aveline over. She joined him, looking sceptically in the basket.

"Chide, what part of 'pack lightly' did you not understand?" she asked in a hushed voice.

"Why are we whispering?" Telchide asked in confusion.

"I've been trying to convince Nevio to work on that watch for over a week. He keeps looking at it and refusing to touch it, even if I specifically take the parts out of his box of a morning and lay them across his workbench. I don't know how you managed it, but I don't want to distract him now."

Telchide glanced up at Aveline, then over to Nevio in surprise. It hadn't occurred to him that the apprentice lacked confidence after their rather fractious meeting.

Not wishing to distract the boy, he turned his attention back to Aveline.

"Have you seen these before? Canned food! The storekeeper assured me the food will last for over a month. I bought five of each type for our trip. I hope that was not remiss of me. I know you said to pack lightly, but I assumed we would rather bring more food than less."

Aveline pulled out one of the canisters and inspected it carefully, turning it over and over.

"How do you open it?"

Telchide pulled the device the storekeeper had called a can opener and demonstrated it, without actually piercing or cutting the can.

"All the food inside is pre-boiled so we won't need to worry if we can't build a cooking fire."

Aveline laughed softly, relieving all his worry from the previous afternoon. Smoking Caldera – how he adored that sound!

"These will certainly come in useful. Follow me with that basket. We can put all the food stores together. I'll bring them down to the wharf tomorrow morning."

Aveline placed the can back in the shopping basket as Telchide heaved it up once more. He followed her through the workshop and past the threshold into her house. If it had been under any other circumstance, he'd have felt supremely awkward. As it was, he only allowed himself to think of this moment as a duty attached to their expedition and nothing more.

The room they entered was barely more than a storeroom. Stepping around a long coil of lightweight rope, Telchide admired the shelves running along every available wall space. Even the area under the stairs had shelves built into it. One wall was entirely filled with books, another with spare parts, another with larger unfinished works that could easily fit on a workbench and lastly, under the stairs, one for a multitude of hats.

"Smoking Caldera! How many hats do you own?"

Aveline glanced over at the hats and shrugged.

"I live in Zona Sarti. Many of my clients have paid me partly in coins and partly in fashionable goods. Especially since my prices went up alongside my Electrum Guild Mark. Now, put your basket down over here and let's go through everything."

Telchide did as he was told and began pulling out the contents for Aveline to inspect. The olive bread gained him a sound of pure delight, but the canned sardines produced the deepest scowl.

"Well, I think we have all the food we'll need to start with. If only I'd hired a larger boat. This will all be too heavy to take by foot. I'll have to get Nevio to come for a drive tomorrow morning. He'd better not crash my blazermobile on his way home!

"The marinai told me we'll leave at high tide. That will be around half past five in the morning. We'll need to be there at least twenty minutes beforehand to load everything."

She looked at him with an expression he couldn't quite understand.

"You'll need to say goodbye to Teresina tonight, before she goes to bed."

He understood the look now. Aveline did not think he'd be able to go through with this expedition – to leave his daughter.

"That will be fine," he replied coolly. "Serenita and I have prepared her well for this. I've organised for them to be taken care of should anything happen and we don't return."

Aveline stared at him wide eyed.

"I ... I didn't mean to say that we'll never return. I don't think it will really be so dangerous as Claudio and Zaccario suggest. We'll go there, find a few samples of the plant, and come back. That's it."

"Then you think I am so ridiculously attached to my daughter that I cannot leave her. I assure you; I can do this."

Without awaiting her reply, he left the storeroom. In the workshop, he collected Teresina, wished Nevio luck with his watch and practically ran out onto the street. He didn't notice how quickly he was walking until Teresina tugged at his hand to slow him.

"What's wrong, papà?"

"Nothing."

Teresina pulled him to a stop.

"I don't believe you. Did Aveline say something to upset you? I think she's lovely."

Telchide opened his mouth to answer, then paused.

"You ... think she's lovely?"

"Of course! She just pierced my ears and gave me earrings from her very own collection. Oh papà, you should *see* how much jewellery she has. She said most of them were presents from her customers. Why don't you ever get presents like that?"

"Well, for one very obvious reason," he replied, walking again. "I'm not a lady. What use would I have for those sorts of presents?"

Teresina trotted beside him, deep in thought.

"But papà, you don't get *any* presents, do you?"

"No. My customers pay me in coins, just the way I like it. What use have I for presents? I don't think the trade with Greta Sarta counts. I would've ordered your sleeves from a Sarta either way."

Telchide would never tell Teresina, but he was actually quite envious of the fact that Aveline had so many customers who felt the need to bestow her with gifts. Perhaps it was simply her way with people, and his awkwardness with them. More often than not, he said something to offend and had to quickly say something to make up for it. Like the man with the purple hat. If the Silver Guild Mark did not force his customers to pay him more, Telchide was certain a great portion of them would still be paying him the copper fees.

***

When they reached his workshop, there was a woman inside with Serenita. She towered over the older woman and was clearly trying to use her size to cow her.

"Exactly *when* do you expect him to return?" she asked haughtily. "I don't plan to wait for him all day."

"There, signora. Look behind you. He has returned, even though it is *not* a full trading day."

The woman turned to face him. Telchide choked back a groan. He was used to this type of customer. The ones who thought the world of themselves and expected everyone to wait on them hand and foot.

These customers came specifically to the Silver Guild Mark Inventrici who'd earned themselves a reputation for quality craftsmanship, then gave explicitly detailed instructions of what they wanted and haggled the price down to the bare minimum they were forced to pay for a Silver Guild Mark. If they dared behave the same way with an Electrum or Gold Guild Mark Inventore, they would either be shown the door or given an exorbitant price.

"Signora, may I offer you a cup of tea while we talk?"

The woman looked down her nose at him and sniffed inelegantly.

"Tea would be adequate. Your servant can fetch it while you take my order."

Telchide would dearly have loved to tell this self-important woman that Serenita was no servant, but that would likely cost him this job and he was not entirely certain he could afford to do that with an apprentice on the way.

"Teresina, why don't you help Nonna to make a cup of tea for this lovely lady. Please, signora, won't you take a seat."

He gestured to the chairs by the door and the lady sat down brusquely in one of them. Telchide took the other and pulled out his notebook.

"Now signora, what brings you to my humble workshop today?"

The lady looked at him with sharp eyes. He suddenly felt like a bug under an Alchimista's microscope.

"Normally, I would not deign to come to such a lowly Inventore as yourself, but word has spread that you make quite passable music boxes. I wish to see them for myself before we go any further."

Telchide put his notebook away slowly. So, word had spread to the upper echelon of society about his music boxes. Was there any way he could find himself in trouble over that? If he continued to be careful to make the customer source the music for themselves, he could hardly be accused of breaking the Inter-Guild Edict, could he?

"You're in luck, signora. I have two commissioned music boxes awaiting their new owners and another two awaiting the customer's chosen music. Let me show them to you."

Telchide walked over to his workbench and picked up the two smaller music boxes. Ideally, it would've been better for the woman to see the music boxes at his workbench, but he knew this one would create such a fuss if he dared suggest such a thing.

He could hear Teresina's careful tread down the stairs to get the tea from the dumbwaiter. That would mean there would not be room on the small table between the chairs for the music boxes. He brought them both over anyway and placed them on his chair. Telchide waited for Teresina to gently place the cup and saucer down before demonstrating the music boxes.

"This is the simplest one, a child's toy really. You place it on a flat surface like so and turn this handle to play the music."

The lady glared at him.

"Inventore, had I wanted a child's toy, I'd have gone to a toymaker."

Telchide wiped his brow.

"Ah, just so, signora. Let me show you this next one. You turn this key until it can go no further. Once you lift the lid like so, the music plays. This particular one has been requested as a jewellery box, so there are a number of drawers here and a velvet-lined compartment inside for smaller items."

The lady's mouth twitched into something resembling a smile. Telchide took that as a good sign. He left the music playing as he went to retrieve one of the unfinished music boxes.

With this latest artwork, he took particular care. He was so very proud of the ballerina atop the box that twirled with the music. It really was one of the best music boxes he'd ever created. He'd put in one of his own templates until the actual music order was ready. With a smile, he walked back over to the lady. Her eyes bulged as she saw what he was holding. He placed it on his chair and closed the lid of the jewellery music box.

"This one was specially ordered more for the dancers themselves. If you'll cast your eyes this way, you'll see the dancers come to life with the music."

Telchide wound up the music box five turns, just enough for the ballerina to make a decent display before the music stopped. It was a good tactic. The woman leaned forward as much as her stiff corset would allow her.

"You say this one was commissioned?"

"Yes, signora. They all were."

"I'll pay you twice the promised price if you give it to me now."

Telchide stared at her, affronted.

"That's a very generous offer, but it simply wouldn't be fair to my customer."

"You can make them another one," she replied with a dismissive wave of her hand. "They won't know the difference."

He could feel the heat rising to his face. The audacity of this lady! Just because she had money to throw away did not mean she could order people around like that.

"I'm sorry, signora. That simply will not be possible. I'm willing to make you another one, similar to this, but I cannot sell you another person's music box."

The woman sipped her tea noiselessly without taking her eyes off him. Telchide held her gaze steadily. This was not an argument he was willing to lose.

"I need one just like this in three days."

"I fear that's impossible," Telchide replied apologetically.

"Very well then, a week," the lady replied irritably.

"Forgive me, signora, but I will not be able to complete your order for at least ten weeks. I am leaving tomorrow on a lengthy trip. I do not expect to return for four weeks, and it will take me a minimum of six weeks to create a music box with your exact specifications."

It was a blatant lie. He did not expect the expedition to take anywhere near so long, but he would also need time to complete such an elaborate music box when he still had two others to finish.

"Unacceptable!" The lady raised her voice in an unladylike screech as she stood. "I cannot wait *almost three months*. I must insist you sell me *this* music box now."

Telchide drew himself up to his full height, which only brought him up to her nose. He refused to be cowed by her.

"Signora, I will not sell you a commissioned work for another client," he replied in a soft, but strong voice. "If you are not willing to place an order for my return, I must insist that you leave my workshop at once."

He did not wait to hear her reply before returning the ballerina music box to his workbench, well out of her reach. Only when he returned to collect the other two music boxes did he see that she was still there. He ignored her completely as he went to place them on his workbench beside the other one. He took his time in lining them up nicely before turning back to her.

"What will it be, signora? May I take your order, or would you rather find the *second best* Inventore of music boxes?"

With those words, he had her. Telchide hid a smile as he saw the colour rise in her cheeks.

"I will *not* settle for second best," she growled. "If I must wait, then I must wait. But this music box had better be the envy of all my friends at my next dinner party."

"I assure you, it will be," replied Telchide smoothly. He pulled out his notebook once more and carefully wrote down every small detail Signora Loyola – who spelt out her name as though he was illiterate – wanted on her music box, down to the very shade of wood for the dancers and the type of gowns they were to wear.

"As I am certain you must be aware, there is an Inter-Guild Edict that unfortunately prevents me from dealing directly with the Musicisti Guild. I have my own small store of songs available to you, but if you have a particular song in mind, I must ask you to provide the sheet music yourself. Again, I apologise, but the Edict places many restrictions on us, you understand."

At the mention of the Edict, Signora Loyola's features suddenly softened. Telchide wondered if she too had a grudge against the Edict. The city was split into groups of both those for and against it, though few openly spoke out against it.

"There *is* one song I am quite partial to," she replied with the hint of a smile. "I'll acquire the sheet music and have my maid bring it to your workshop in your absence. I expect a note upon your return so that I can organise my dinner party for six weeks later. Is that acceptable to you?"

"Very good, Signora Loyola. If you will mark out your favourite passage of the music, I will do my best to incorporate it all, but you must understand an entire song in a music box is impossible. And now for the price."

Telchide didn't even know where to begin. That specific wood would cost him four silvers at the minimum, then there was the metalwork, the hours of work and lastly, the music strip. He was getting better at them, but he didn't know how he would be able to test such a large strip without an instrument of his own to test it against.

"If this music box is everything you promise it will be, I will give you three electrums."

Telchide struggled to remain emotionless in the face of such a high fee. The woman's face hardened as she glared at him.

"However, if it is anything less than perfect, don't expect more than one electrum. Are we agreed?"

Telchide bowed his head slightly.

"Signora is generous indeed. I promise you will not be disappointed. This music box will be the envy of all your friends."

The lady broke into a full smile at that. She handed him her calling card, nodded, and left his workshop.

"Three electrums!"

Telchide was surprised to find Serenita rather than Teresina sitting on the stairs.

"For that amount, she can behave any way she likes. Do you think she'll keep her word?"

Telchide shrugged. "She'll have no choice. If there are no discernible flaws, I will not allow her to purchase it for less than the promised price. I can put it in my window for anyone else to buy and she won't like that at all."

Serenita's eyes sparkled. "Good! I couldn't stand the thought of her swindling you. Now come up for dinner. You'll need an early night from what Teresina tells me."

Telchide waved Serenita up ahead of him and stayed behind to lock up the workshop. This was the last night he would do this for some time. His stomach tightened uncomfortably as a handful of unpleasant thoughts scurried through his mind. He attempted to banish them all. He could feel them waiting for him but refused to pay them any attention.

Instead, he wound up his friction light and crawled under the workbench. If Serenita was to be limited to five silver coins every week, he intended to give her an additional amount tonight, to ensure she and Teresina would want for nothing in his absence.

He pressed down hard on the spring-loaded floorboard. It swung up, revealing the sliding and rotating puzzle. His fingers automatically moved to solve it – he didn't even have to think about it anymore. He took out his pocket watch and triggered the false knob. With the tiny key that popped out, he opened the lock and peered at the contents of his safe. There was quite a tidy little sum here. It was only a fraction of what he kept in the Guild vault, but nothing to sneeze at.

Telchide knew Serenita felt uncomfortable taking electrum coins to the markets, even though it would mean she carried fewer coins in the first place, so he took out three silvers and a handful of coppers. It was the most he knew she would agree to carry.

From his own coin pouch, Telchide deposited everything but an electrum, three silvers and five coppers into the safe. He doubted there would be a need for coins on this expedition, but he did not intend to be caught unawares.

It took him a minute or two to secure the hidden safe once more. He'd thought of selling this invention but was afraid that he would only make it easier for thieves to rob him and his customers if they had an inkling of where to look.

Telchide debated whether to take his pocket watch with him or leave it somewhere safe in the house. Both options left him uneasy. If he took it with him and lost it, he would potentially need to dismantle the safe entirely to unlock it. If he left it here, there was the possibility that it could be misplaced by Serenita or Teresina, or worse, found by a thief and used to steal his small fortune.

No, it was better for it to remain with him. He'd created the safe himself and knew the way to dismantle it should he lose the key in the pocket watch. The decision made, he put his pocket watch back in his waistcoat pocket.

When he finally trudged up the stairs, Teresina was waiting for him in her nightgown, a blanket draped over her shoulders.

"Papà what took you so long? I was just about to come down to the workshop myself."

Telchide picked her up and held her tightly, being careful not to touch her newly pierced ears. He would miss her dearly!

"I had some last-minute things to take care of. Are you ready for bed?"

Teresina nodded. Telchide slid her back down to the ground and took her tiny hand in his. Together, they walked down the hall to her room. His mind flashed back to the early days, after Sebetine had disappeared. They'd often walked hand in hand to Teresina's room then. She couldn't understand why her mamma hadn't returned and Telchide had little comfort to offer. All he could tell Teresina was that her mamma loved her dearly and would be here if she could.

"You're not going to disappear like mamma, are you?" Teresina whispered as she pulled her heavy blanket over her shoulders.

"No, Resi," Telchide choked out the words. "I would never disappear on you. Never."

He bent down to kiss her cheek.

"I love you so very much, my little Resi. Remind yourself of that every day that I'm gone. I will *always* come back for you."

Teresina flung her arms around him, forgetting momentarily to be careful of her new earrings. Telchide hugged her tightly, fighting back the tears stinging his eyes. He kissed her forehead over and over again. He would miss her too much.

On the way out of her room, Telchide lit a candle lantern for Teresina. It would help her fall asleep. He only hoped Kesida would return the Lightbox soon. Candles were growing increasingly expensive and Telchide did not want Serenita wasting all their money on them.

"Are you finally ready?" Serenita asked when he sat at the kitchen table.

"Almost. This is for you."

He placed the coin pouch in front of her. She opened it curiously.

"That should be enough for the first few days. After that, use the chit I gave you yesterday. Should you have need of more money, I'm certain Eduardo will have some at hand to spare and I can pay him back upon my return."

Serenita closed the coin pouch and left it on the table.

"You worry too much, Chide. We'll be fine. And so will *you*."

Telchide looked up at her in surprise. Serenita laughed lightly.

"Chide, you may have fooled everyone else, but you cannot fool me. I know you're worried about Teresina, and even myself, but I also know you were using your daughter as an excuse not to go on the expedition in the first place. You're scared. And you have every right to be. But don't you dare let that stop you tomorrow morning when you must leave before we wake up."

Serenita got up, took the coin pouch, and patted his cheek before heading down the hallway to her room. Telchide looked after her in amazement. Sometimes he wondered if Serenita knew him better than he knew himself.

Almost too tired to move, Telchide slowly spooned up the plate of pasta that had been left for him. He cleaned his dishes and went to his bedroom to set the alarm for half past four in the morning. That should give him enough time to gather his things and walk down to the docks. Before hopping into bed, he set out clothes for the next day next to his bag of necessities.

Chapter 15 – Riposidi 15 Mercantili 230 Years After Implosion

The clockwork alarm rang loudly in his ear. Telchide slammed his hand down on top of it, afraid that Teresina might hear. It would not do at all for her to wake up now. As quickly and quietly as he could, Telchide changed out of his night clothes and into the fresh set of clothes he'd laid out for himself the night before. He struggled to fit the night clothes into the bag of necessities. Who knew under what circumstances they would be forced to live for the next few weeks? Would he even need his night clothes?

Hugging the over-stuffed bag, Telchide wound his friction light, moved carefully down the stairs and ensured the shutters were locked into place. He would not leave Teresina and Serenita unprotected in his absence. He would never be able to forgive himself if something happened to them while he was away.

He kept his eyes firmly averted from his workbench, knowing that something else would catch his eye and his already over-stuffed bag would burst open. Instead, he walked straight to the wooden box and tested the wooden peg again. It held firmly.

Telchide put on his long coat and coppola, then shouldered his bag and bent to lift the box. It scraped noisily against the floor. Telchide held his breath, straining his ears for any sign that Teresina had heard him. After a few seconds of silence, he let out a long breath. As quietly as he could, he left the workshop and locked the door shut behind him.

Once out on the street, he placed the friction light in his coat pocket. The gas lamps were just bright enough to light his way. He headed down towards the docks feeling uneasy. It took him a moment to realise that it was because the streets were empty. He didn't usually walk out at this time of the morning. The only shop lights he passed were the pasticcerie, who were already busy getting the day's breads and pastries ready for their customers. He did not envy them their trade.

As he was nearing the docks, a blazermobile sped past him. Telchide startled and lost his grip on the wooden box. It hit his shin and scraped down his leg to his outstretched foot.

"Smoking Caldera! I hate those infernal contraptions," he muttered, rubbing his shin. He picked up the wooden box and examined it. There was a slight dent on one edge, but nothing that would compromise its integrity.

"Telchide!"

He peered down the street to find the owner of the voice and walked closer until he realised it was Aveline. She was leaning out of the window of her blazermobile.

"You?" he asked incredulously. "You almost ran me down!"

Aveline tossed her head back. "I did no such thing. It's not my fault you're afraid of blazermobiles."

Telchide heard a muffled laugh coming from inside the blazermobile. Aveline *had* mentioned Nevio would need to drive the blazermobile back to the workshop for her.

"Hurry up and get in or we'll be late," Aveline said.

Telchide's stomach flipped. There was no point in arguing. He'd have to endure an entire boat trip of motion sickness. It wouldn't make a difference if the journey started now.

Nevio hopped out of the blazermobile and opened a compartment in the back for Telchide to put the wooden box. Together, they found space for it in amongst the other things Aveline was taking with her.

As they walked back around to the side door, Telchide fumbled in his pocket for the motion sickness cure. He opened the small brown packet and picked out a single pill. It was a pale yellow, like the sun on a winter morning. As he began to chew it, he felt a sharp tang on his tongue and the taste of ginger flooded his mouth. So startled by this was he, that he barely resisted when Nevio ushered him into the blazermobile.

He only realised once he was already seated that he was wedged between Aveline and her apprentice. He couldn't help the fact that his leg was pressed up against Aveline's. Before he had time to rectify the situation, the blazermobile roared to life and they lurched forward. Telchide chewed harder on the yellow pill, trying not to think of how his stomach would fare on the short, violent journey to the docks.

Aveline took the corner onto Corso delle Gilde so tightly that Telchide was thrown practically on top of her, with Nevio clinging to the side rail just to keep his seat. Telchide tried desperately to find his seat once more, but every time he tried to push himself into place, he accidentally touched a part of Aveline's body. His cheeks burned so hotly that he thought his face might explode. Thankfully, neither Aveline nor Nevio seemed to notice.

As soon as they arrived at the docks, Telchide practically threw Nevio onto the street in his haste to exit the blazermobile. Nevio glared at him as he smoothed down his coat.

"Maestra Aveline, are you certain Telchide Inventore should join you?"

"Nevio, there are more important things to being an Inventore than keeping your head and quieting your stomach in a moving vehicle."

Aveline exited the blazermobile lightly and quite easily in her work pants, face flushed with excitement. Telchide would never understand her love of the ridiculous vehicle.

"Are you certain *he* has any of them?"

Telchide was shocked by the boy's impertinence. If he weren't still recovering from the ride, he'd have had a word or two to say to that young upstart apprentice. Instead, it was Aveline who quietened him.

"Tell me, Nevio, how many days did I try to get you to make that watch?"

Nevio didn't answer.

"Then let me ask you this. How long after Telchide spoke with you about it did you actually manage it?"

Telchide looked over at him to see the young man's lowered eyes.

"I knew you could do it!" Telchide grinned despite his anger. "It was all in your head. You had too many other things clamouring for your attention."

Nevio smiled almost shyly.

"Thank you, Inventore. I'm not finished it yet, but the fiddliest parts are done."

Telchide caught the smug look on Aveline's face as Nevio's attitude changed. It would have been a perfect moment had it remained just the three of them.

"About time the two of you arrived," Lucrezia shouted at them from one of the docks. "Captain Corrado says it's almost high tide. We need to load the boat and go."

Telchide rolled his eyes. If only *anyone* other than Lucrezia was joining them, this entire expedition would be a thousand times more enjoyable. As it was, he had to content himself with being allowed to come after rejecting Aveline's initial offer.

Nevio opened the back compartment of the car and all three of them loaded up with as many things as they could carry. Telchide wondered exactly how they were going to be able to carry all of this when they got to the Caldera, though he had little time to dwell on the matter.

The briny sea air slapped his face as he followed Aveline down a wooden dock. Every few steps, he was forced to stop for balance. The smoking dock was moving! Trying not to let it affect him, Telchide swallowed the final lingering taste of ginger. There was nothing he could do about it now. If he were going to be sick, at least he could lean over the water and try not to make a mess everywhere.

"This is it," Aveline said, nodding towards a wooden sailboat with large round paddles on the sides. It was larger than Telchide had expected, but at least a quarter of the boat was taken up with what he assumed was the motor room for the circular paddles.

The two marinai were waiting for them. One on the dock, the other on the boat. Telchide noticed their shared look with rolled eyes.

"You ain't taking all that, signora," the one on the boat called out. "Specially the heavy stuff."

Aveline turned to look at the procession behind her. Telchide well understood the problem. They'd need to sort out their priorities.

"This box needs to come," Telchide pointed out immediately. "If we do find the plants, we won't be able to take them back any other way."

Aveline nodded.

"Yes, go ahead and put that on. We'll need the food as well, and my rope."

Telchide stepped awkwardly onto the boat. The marinaio grabbed hold of his elbow as Telchide lost his balance.

"Give it 'ere," he growled.

Before Telchide could protest, the marinaio took the wooden box out of his hand and dumped it unceremoniously in a compartment at the front of the boat. He returned to take Nevio's large basket of food. The marinaio heaved it over the edge of the boat, took one look inside and dragged it to an open door at the back of the boat.

Telchide watched the efficiency with which he worked in some wonder. His rough tongue did not inspire confidence, but his movements did. At a third pass, the marinaio roughly pushed past Telchide.

"Out the way! Sit there."

Irritated, Telchide quickly went to sit on one of the wooden seats lining the side of the boat. He watched the rest of the loading with a strange sort of detachment. He still couldn't believe that he was on a boat which would take him all the way to Sentigura Caldera.

At one point, Aveline and Lucrezia raised their voices at each other. Telchide strained to hear what they were saying from his seat. The water amplified the sound of their voices, but they were facing away from him.

"I *need* this," Lucrezia insisted as Telchide walked towards them. "We don't know what we'll find there. If you or that lavalump you asked along get injured, how will I treat you otherwise?"

"Lavalump indeed!" Telchide yelled at her. "I'll have you know *I'm* the one who thought of a way to safely transport the plant back with us."

Lucrezia turned to him with a scowl. "A ridiculously large box and heavy food stores. It's *your* fault we don't have enough space on this boat."

"Stop yer fightin' or the Mercantili Guild'll be on our tails before we leave," the captain told them. "Get it sorted and let's go."

Aveline replied in a low voice. "I would rather have enough food and a way to transport the plant back than anything else. The trip will be pointless if we find the plant and have to leave it behind because we have no way to bring it back and have run out of food."

Lucrezia opened her mouth, presumably to protest.

"Take *two* boxes of your potions and pills. We don't need *five*." Aveline cut her off. "Telchide, help me up."

Immediately, Telchide held out his hand to Aveline. She grasped it tightly and pulled to haul herself over the side and into the boat. Telchide held her hand a moment longer than was necessary – he didn't mean to, it just happened. Aveline looked up at him, then quickly lowered her eyes as she stepped away.

In an attempt to treat both ladies the same, Telchide held his hand out for Lucrezia. The Alchimista looked at his hand in disgust and, instead, stepped onto the boat without holding onto anything. She fell to one knee as the boat drifted away from the dock and was pulled back sharply by the thick ropes holding it in place.

Telchide walked away without offering to help her up. If she disliked him enough not to accept his help in the first place, she would certainly not accept it after her embarrassing fall.

"Nevio, mind the shop well. Take any orders you think you can reasonably do and tell any special orders they'll have to wait until my return to discuss them."

Aveline waved farewell to her apprentice. Nevio tipped his hat to her and stood back while the marinaio on the docks unravelled the heavy ropes and threw them onto the boat. He jumped on deck before the boat had a chance to move too far away.

Telchide quickly found a seat and gripped the side of the boat tightly. He couldn't swim and did not intend to fall out of the boat if it moved anywhere near as quickly as Aveline's blazermobile.

"Secure the ropes, Roque!" shouted the captain.

"Aye, Captain!" shouted back Roque as he wound the ropes around a wide wooden pole towards the back of the boat. "Ropes secure."

Telchide clenched the side rail tighter and watched in silence as Corrado and Roque worked around each other seamlessly. Roque got the motorised paddles going as Corrado headed to the raised helm to guide the boat away from the dock.

Telchide couldn't see how the paddles were made to move, but move they did. As they cleared the docks, the paddles switched direction and now they drifted slowly out into the bay. It was not a lurching, sporadic movement like the blazermobiles. In fact, Telchide found he could bear this boat tolerably well in comparison.

He gazed out at the horizon. Sentigura Caldera was a smudge in the morning mist. He couldn't estimate how far away it was. Whatever the distance, the boat would not cover it quickly. He doubted they were travelling much faster than a person could walk.

After a few minutes, Telchide spied more ships on the horizon. Apparently, so did the marinai. In a flurry of activity, the sails were raised, and their boat lurched away from the oncoming ships.

"Smoking Caldera! I ain't seen this many ships coming in all year!" Corrado fumed.

"It's the Inventrici Convention," Aveline called out to him. "It's tonight. All Inventrici in travelling distance will be there."

The Inventrici Convention! Telchide was meant to escort Aveline there tonight. He'd promised! Or was that promise only a ruse on Aveline's behalf to hide this trip from Teresina?

"I'm sorry you're missing it," Telchide told her.

Aveline shrugged, but her eyes were sad. "There'll be another one next year."
"Not in Tor'Esint there won't," Telchide said quietly.

She didn't answer.

After a few minutes of watching the Caldera, Telchide pulled out his notebook. There was no point in wasting precious time just because they were forced to endure a boat trip before their adventure really began. He opened the notebook but had barely looked at more than a few of his diagrams before the contents of his stomach squelched uncomfortably.

Telchide hurriedly closed the notebook and placed it back in his jacket pocket. No matter. He could do with a rest. The past few days had been a torrent of activity. Telchide gazed back out over the bay. The water was smooth. He leaned back against the seat to enjoy the ride to the best of his ability.

***

A few hours later and Sentigura Caldera was a solid mass ahead of them. Telchide had watched it tirelessly the entire journey. Eduardo's chewy ginger pills appeared to work to a limited extent. He'd taken careful note of the time when he took the first pill and had followed the Alchimista's instructions to take another every two hours. He was just finishing his third one now.

The pills deadened the churning within his stomach, but if he looked in his notebook or took his eyes off the horizon ahead of him, he instantly felt worse. It hadn't been much of a chore to stay seated where he was and facing ahead. He did not wish to speak with Lucrezia after her insult and Aveline ... well he didn't trust himself to even look at her without blushing at the memory of her hand grasping his. Not to mention his accidental touches in the blazermobile.

His face flushed at the very thought. He would need to do something about that. He wouldn't last this journey without Aveline noticing and Lucrezia teasing him. Perhaps he could simply keep himself to himself and only talk to Aveline during the evening when the sun couldn't betray the colour of his cheeks.

Of course, he couldn't stop Aveline from talking to him. He glanced over at her approach and tried not to look at her delicate hands. She sat next to him, blocking his view of the Caldera. Telchide shifted slightly to keep it in view.

"I need to see the Caldera," he said without meeting her eye. "It appears to make the motion sickness bearable."

"I'm rather impressed you found a way to keep the contents of your stomach, well, in your stomach," Aveline jested with him.

Her comment made the contents of his stomach roll around, making him nauseous. Telchide placed his hand over his middle to dull the feeling.

"Do we have a plan for when we arrive?" he asked, trying to keep all emotion from his voice. He should not have to remind himself that he was *not* a suitor.

"My reports tell me there's a series of handholds leading up the cliffs. We'll use those to get up," Aveline said confidently. "Then, if we can't find a good place to shelter, we may need to make the boat our base of operations."

"That's a ridiculous idea," Lucrezia snapped from across the boat. "If we're planning to be here more than a few days, it's bound to rain in that time. I'm not going to lounge outside in the rain, get soaked to the bone and come down with a lung disease simply because *you* couldn't be bothered thinking up a proper plan."

Aveline sighed loudly. "Then what's *your* plan?"

"We leave everything on the boat and find a place to shelter before nightfall. If we can't find anywhere, *he* can build something for us. If he can build you a box, he can build you a simple shack at the very least."

Telchide ground his teeth in an effort not to yell at Lucrezia. She rubbed him up the wrong way every time she opened her mouth. He wondered if she did it on purpose or if that was just the way she was. Either way, it was irritating beyond measure.

"She's right. We can't stay on this 'ere boat overnight," Corrado piped up from the wheel. "Me and Roque'll sail 'round 'til we find a good enough place to tie 'er up. Then you'll need to find a place to sleep."

Lucrezia crossed her arms and lifted her head arrogantly. Telchide could've slapped the captain for agreeing with her, even if he himself thought it the best plan. Any time he was forced to agree with Lucrezia was not a good time.

"Fine," Aveline conceded with good grace. "Once we find a place to dock, we'll set out and meet back at the boat after two hours and report our findings. We'll split into two groups to cover more ground before nightfall. We'll go with Telchide and the marinai can go together. If neither group finds anything suitable for even a single night, we'll *all* work together to build a shack."

Telchide saw Lucrezia was about to protest but, at an angry look from Aveline, she kept her peace. He did not relish spending so much time in close proximity with her either, but there was nothing they could do about it on this trip.

It was close to eleven o'clock when Corrado angled the paddle sailboat into a small cove. The shore could barely even be called that, Telchide thought. Sharp, jagged rocks shot out at all angles over a smoother black surface. The light caught the rocks at certain angles, and they glittered like millions of little jewels. Just inland, at the very edge of the cliff, stood a row of tall, thin trees.

Roque took a look and shouted up at Corrado on the raised helm. "Too tricky."

Telchide eyed the cove. It certainly didn't look like a good landing place. He exchanged glances with Aveline.

"Captain Corrado, there are meant to be handholds from the Sant'Elba expeditions. Can we sail around the island to find them?"

Corrado and Roque exchanged rough words, but eventually a course of action was agreed upon.

They sailed for over an hour, passing by sheer cliffs that rose from the water, without even a narrow shoreline. The tops of the cliffs were lined with trees and shrubs. There was definitely vegetation – all they had to do now was get up there somehow and find the plant they were looking for.

"I ain't seen no handholds yet. We're going back to the western side," Corrado told them. "That rocky cove was the safest place to anchor."

"*That* was not a safe place," Roque argued. "There ain't no safe places here. I *told* you we shouldn't't've taken this job. There ain't nowhere to dock and there ain't no time to get back to Tor'Esint before dark. The night monsters'll get us out here!"

"Night monsters?" Lucrezia asked incredulously. "You believe in children's stories?"

Roque turned sharply to face her. His eyes were wild.

"You ain't a marinaia. You don't know what lives in these waters. There *are* night monsters and if we don't find a safe place to dock, they'll take us while we sleep!"

Lucrezia laughed loudly. Telchide didn't. He looked from Roque to Corrado and saw fear in both their eyes. Even if night monsters were just children's stories, they may have been based on something real. It didn't seem as though they wanted to find out, and Telchide was beginning to agree with them.

"Let's go back then to the western side. Tell us what you need us to do, and we'll do it," Telchide said.

He pulled another yellow pill out of his pocket and popped it into his mouth. He didn't know how much longer these pills would work, or even how many he had left, but he couldn't afford to be sick now when it was most important.

When neither of the marinai answered him, he turned to Aveline. There was a hint of uncertainty in her own eyes. He walked up to her and held her gaze.

"Aveline, should we go to the western side?"

He could read her fear of failure so clearly in that moment. And he knew she could read him – his absolute faith in her ability to lead this expedition. The uncertainty in her eyes lessened. She saw what she needed to do.

"Captain Corrado, take us back to the western side," she told him. "I know those handholds are somewhere, so everyone must keep a keen eye out for them."

The captain stared at her for a moment, then shrugged. Without saying a word, he turned the boat around and headed back the way they'd come.

The water was rougher on the western side of the Caldera, closer to the opening of the cove. Corrado dropped anchor, but strong currents swirled around the opening, and he struggled to get the paddle sailboat in a good position for Roque to disembark and further stabilise the mooring with the rope and avoid crashing into the rocky margins. It was looking too perilous.

Roque, standing at the ready, leaped from the boat holding the thick rope. He missed his footing and slipped, slicing his left hand and leg on the glittering rocks. He screamed in pain and dropped the rope.

"Get the rope!" Corrado yelled.

Telchide could see Roque was in too much distress to obey. Careful not to make the same mistake as the rough-mannered marinaio, Telchide held onto the side of the boat and lowered himself over the side, searching for purchase on the rocky surface as waves washed over his feet and filled his ankle boots with water.

Glad not to have sliced his feet or legs on the sharp surface, Telchide kept a tight hold on the side of the boat and made his way towards the Caldera to retrieve the fallen rope. He grabbed it before the current could drag it out past the cove. The anchor was not enough to hold the boat in place in the current, it needed the security of an additional mooring line before the others could risk disembarking with their supplies. Taking firm hold of the rope, Telchide finally let go of the boat and, watching his step carefully, made his way slowly through the sharp volcanic rocks until he reached a narrow strip of black sand.

"Now what?" he called out to Corrado.

"Tie it to something firm!"

Telchide looked around him. Something firm. What in Caldera's smoke was firm and reasonable amongst these sharp, jagged rocks? There was an uncomfortable burning sensation along his feet and calf muscles. He looked down and realised there was steam rising from the sand underneath his boots. Likely looking a fool, he hopped from one foot to the other.

"What in Caldera's smoke are you doing?" Lucrezia shouted at him.

"The ground is burning!"

At that exact moment, Roque stood unsteadily from where he had fallen. Telchide thought he looked like a madman, as he stumbled, flailing his arms for balance as he took the few steps he needed to reach the boat. Telchide watched as the marinaio pulled himself up and over the side of the boat and hit the deck with a thud and a groan that Telchide could hear even from his position.

Telchide spotted a tall, thin tree not too far from the shore where the ground looked softer. He tripped and hopped his way over to it, pulling the heavy rope behind him. Finally, he reached the tree, pulled the rope to get as much slack as possible and tied it firmly around the trunk.

The burning sensation had disappeared from his legs. He looked down and saw the ground had changed. He was no longer standing on the dark, hot sand. Or if he was, it was covered with a dense black ash. The ash must have been insulating the heat, keeping his legs from burning.

From where he was, Telchide shouted out to the others.

"It doesn't burn over here. Hold the rope to keep your balance on the way."

They shouted something back at him, but Telchide couldn't hear over the sound of waves crashing on the rocks. When they waved him over, he used the rope as a guide to keep himself upright.

As soon as he reached the boat, he heaved himself over the side. He fell awkwardly onto his stomach and lost the horizon from view. Scrambling to get up, he only succeeded in tripping over his feet. Clinging to the side of the boat, Telchide leaned heavily towards the water and vomited. It didn't make him feel any better. He stayed in that position, staring at the rocky bay, trying to get his stomach to settle.

"We can't stay anchored here," he heard the captain say, as though from a distance. Roque eagerly agreed with him. Telchide tried to concentrate on the argument they were having with Aveline, but lost part of it when he vomited again.

"My boat'll be smashed to bits!" Corrado shouted. "You didn't pay me *that* much!"

Not caring if it was too soon for another yellow tablet, Telchide popped one into his mouth and bit down hard, concentrating on the sharp ginger on his tongue.

"Captain, do you have any rubber or thick rope?" Telchide asked.

"Yeah, more rope." Corrado looked at him quizzically.

"Good. Fetch it."

Telchide saw the man's eyes bulge for a moment before he sent Roque to find the required item. Telchide could not understand Corrado's sudden anger but was grateful he hadn't lashed out.

The marinaio soon returned, dragging a large coil of rope behind him. He dropped it at Telchide's feet and looked at him angrily. Telchide quickly explained his idea and the two of them set about hanging the rope over the side of the boat at regular intervals, looping it through hoops on the rail. Most of the work fell to Telchide, as Roque was still hobbling around on his injured leg.

When they were done, Telchide stepped back and looked at their work appreciatively. They had effectively created a buffer between the boat and the rocks. Even if the turbulent waves pushed the boat against the rocks, the risk of harm would be reduced.

From the corner of his eye, Telchide saw Aveline's smile. He followed her gaze to the cliffs beside the rocky shore.

"The handholds were there all along, just hiding. Captain, can you manoeuvre the boat under them?"

"Aye, but how's that going to help? I ain't climbing all the way up there."

"Leave that to me," Aveline said with a grin. "Where did you store my lightweight rope?"

While the captain manoeuvred closer to the cliffs and sent Roque to get the rope for her, Aveline rummaged through her bag. Telchide was only mildly surprised to find that she'd brought a hand cranked pulley wheel with her. She attached it to her belt and slipped a hammer and large pin into two small loops on the belt.

When Roque returned with the rope, Aveline tied it around her waist, looping the rest of it over her shoulder. With Lucrezia holding her steady, Aveline stepped up onto the railing and leaned out to the cliffs. Telchide held his breath as Aveline caught the first handhold and heaved herself onto the cliff. He now understood her decision to wear work pants instead of skirts. She stayed where she was for a moment before reaching out her left hand to find another, higher, hold.

Aveline inched herself up the cliff face as Telchide and the others waited in the boat. Lucrezia roughly patched up Roque as he complained at her. When the marinaio made a lewd comment about the angle of Aveline's rear as she climbed up the cliff, he felt Lucrezia's anger as she slapped his face.

Though he was glad Lucrezia had reprimanded the marinaio, Telchide tried to tune out their argument as he watched Aveline's painstakingly slow progress. At times she moved sideways rather than up, following the direction of handholds attached to the cliff. By the time she reached the top, she'd travelled so far sideways that she was no longer near the rocky beach.

"What's she want the rope for?" Roque eventually asked. "I ain't climbing a rope up a cliff if that's what she's thinkin'."

Telchide looked at him in surprise. "She's going to create a pulley system, to lift us up the cliff, of course."

Roque looked at him doubtfully. "Oh yeah, and how's that going to work?"

Telchide explained the principle to him. Roque's eyes widened and he let out a low whistle.

"Still sounds mighty dangerous," Corrado ventured. "We'll be cut up pretty bad by the time we reach the top."

Telchide studied the cliff face once more. Corrado had a point. Sharp rocks jutted out at odd angles all over it. He walked purposefully to the storeroom. Corrado followed him.

"Captain, can you manoeuvre the boat under Aveline?"

The captain nodded.

"Good, then ask Roque to help me empty this basket while you do that," Telchide said.

To his credit, Corrado did not object, but gave orders to Roque as he took to the helm.

Telchide and Roque began taking food out of the basket and placing it on the shelves of the storeroom instead. When the basket was empty, Telchide carried it out onto the main deck. Lucrezia looked at it suspiciously.

"I'm not getting in that, if that's your idea."

Telchide shrugged. "Suit yourself. But you'll be the only one of us who gets cut on the way up."

Lucrezia looked about ready to protest when a rope fell right in front of her. Telchide hid a smile and set to work tying the end through the handles of the basket to split the strain. When he was done, he offered Lucrezia the first trip, but she impolitely declined.

To Telchide's surprise, it was Roque who jumped into the basket. Telchide told him to hold the rope and stand in the middle, and signalled Aveline. She signalled back to him, and the basket lifted off the boat. Roque shouted in surprise and held to the rope so tightly that his knuckles turned white.

"Roque, yer flying!" Corrado shouted out to him gleefully as the basket lifted slowly into the air.

The captain laughed loudly as his first mate was hauled away from him. It took over five minutes for the basket to reach the top. Poor Aveline had to hand crank it the entire way. Telchide watched for her signal then quickly cleared Corrado and Lucrezia to the other side of the boat. He joined them and then signalled back to Aveline. The basket fell towards the boat with incredible speed. When it was almost upon them, Telchide signalled back to Aveline. The basket instantly jerked to a halt then continued in a much slower manner onto the deck.

"Who's next? Lucrezia? Corrado?"

Corrado patted his boat affectionately.

"Captain's always the last to leave the boat. Let the Alchimista go first."

Lucrezia shook her head mutely. Her face had turned a chalky white. Telchide felt a pang of pity for her, but it passed quickly when he thought of how she usually treated him.

"Lucrezia, you can't stay on the boat the entire trip. And I don't think you climb as well as Aveline. The basket really is your best choice."

"I can't," she whimpered.

"You don't have a choice," Telchide tried to reason with her. "Come with me, I'll help you in."

Telchide held out his hand to her, she looked at him, then down at his hand. After a long pause, she finally reached out a trembling hand. Telchide squeezed it gently and led her over to the basket and helped her into it. Her eyes were wide with fear as Telchide signalled to Aveline.

The basket moved up a few piedi into the air and jerked to a halt. Lucrezia screamed. Telchide tried to calm her, but his words had no effect. The Alchimista rocked the basket wildly, trying to get out. Somehow, she managed to tip it and fell headlong into the water, narrowly missing the rocks jutting out around the cliff.

Corrado was instantly hanging off the side of the boat with a large white circular object. He threw it to Lucrezia. To Telchide's amazement, it floated right in front of her. Lucrezia splashed out to reach it. It took her several attempts in her panicked state. Once she had a firm hold on it, Telchide helped Corrado pull the floating circle back to the boat and haul Lucrezia over the side.

She lay in a coughing heap, shivering and whimpering. Corrado threw a cloth over her and emptied her sturdy boots of water, but the shivering continued.

"If she don't change out of them wet clothes, she'll catch her death," Corrado told Telchide uncomfortably.

Telchide looked at the marinaio incredulously. Exactly which one of them was supposed to tell her that? Corrado kept his eyes firmly averted from Telchide's stare. Lucrezia couldn't stop shivering. Telchide knew the captain was right, but he also knew he could absolutely not do this.

"Lucrezia, you need to change your clothes."

She looked at him but didn't answer. Her teeth chattered against each other. Telchide set Corrado to look through Lucrezia's bag. Surely she'd packed a spare change of clothes like Aveline had told them to. In the meantime, Telchide struggled to peel off Lucrezia's coat. He could feel her eyes on him, but knew she was in no position to stop him. She couldn't control her movements – she was in shock.

"I found these." Corrado held up a pair of trousers and button up shirt.

"No undergarments?"

Corrado flushed deeply and held up his other hand. Lucrezia's undergarments were a deep crimson. It was a glimpse into Lucrezia's personal life that Telchide wished he'd never had to know. How were they to manage this?

"Corrado, I know you're the captain, and the captain does not leave his ship while others are on board, but under the circumstances ... perhaps you could go up and ask Aveline to come down?"

To his relief, Corrado readily agreed. The captain waved his hands madly up at Aveline, who dropped the basket down to him. Corrado climbed in and waved at her once more. The basket lifted off the boat. Telchide paid no more attention until Aveline arrived in the basket. Lucrezia was still shivering, though Telchide was rubbing her cloth-covered back and trying to keep the worst of the wind off her.

"What's the matter?" Aveline asked as she hopped out of the basket. "Corrado wouldn't say anything other than I was needed down here."

Telchide made a point to only look at her face, holding up Lucrezia's spare clothes in his hands. Aveline looked at them, then at the shivering Alchimista. She sighed and took the clothes from Telchide.

"You can turn your back, but don't go up in the basket yet. I may still need your help."

Telchide thanked her and went to sit on a bench with his back to the two ladies. Never in his life would he have imagined himself in this position! Behind him, he heard Aveline's grunts of effort and Lucrezia's muffled whimpers.

"You can come over," Aveline called out after what felt like an age. "She's decent."

Telchide turned, expecting to see Lucrezia on her feet and ready to go. Instead, the Alchimista was sitting on a side bench, hugging herself and rocking back and forth.

"We can't take her like that," he whispered to Aveline.

"We can't leave her by herself either and up there is better than down here."

Telchide looked up the steep cliff, eyebrows raised. He'd not been up there yet so couldn't contradict Aveline, but he highly doubted the Caldera would be any place for a person in Lucrezia's state.

"Chide, listen to me. She needs more warmth than the boat can provide. There's plenty of vegetation up there. We can build her a fire to warm her up."

Telchide nodded his assent to the plan. Aveline gave him a half smile, then grimaced.

"There's one other thing. She can't walk well – she's hurt her ankle – and I cannot lift her."

"You can't be serious! Aveline, she'll *never* forgive me for that."

Aveline sighed. "Let's not be childish. Lucrezia already loathes you. This can't possibly make things any worse than the time you exploded one of Nestore's beakers in front of her."

Telchide knew he had no choice. He walked resolutely over to the Alchimista and, without looking her in the eye, placed one hand under her knees and the other around her back and under her arms. He lifted with all his might.

He groaned audibly. Lucrezia was most certainly a good deal heavier than Teresina. Not trusting the strength of his body, he carried her as quickly as his legs could carry him towards the basket. He awkwardly placed the Alchimista within it and signalled up to Corrado before she had a chance to object. The basket began to ascend, more smoothly, but a good deal slower, than the last time she was in it.

Telchide kept his eyes on the basket for a few moments, then knelt to gather the rest of the things they would need up on the Caldera. Roque and Corrado had taken their bags with them. Aveline's was still here somewhere, as was Lucrezia's and his own. He found them all and put them in a pile at Aveline's feet along with the food. The movement got her attention, and she looked down at him. In that moment, the heat rushed to his face. Before he could think better of it, he took her hand and pressed it lightly with his own.

He would dearly have loved to kiss her hand instead, but that would be beyond indecent. He was not available to court her and she was most certainly not interested in him. Except she didn't pull her hand away as he expected her to. She held his hand tightly and pulled him up to his feet. For a moment, she drew his hand nearer, as though she meant to kiss his fingers. Telchide's heart beat so wildly he thought she must have heard it for she let his hand go suddenly and without explanation.

Aveline frowned and turned her attention to the packs, reorganising her clothes and stuffing in her water canister and as much food as would fit. Confused by his emotions, Telchide followed her lead and squeezed the food into the bags.

Lucrezia's basket had still not reached the top of the cliff when they ran out of things to distract them. He caught her glance at him and turning away as soon as their eyes met. He was hurt by the fact that she appeared to be purposely avoiding talking to him.

"My apologies, Aveline, for being so familiar with you. I was simply trying to express my thanks to you for helping with Lucrezia. Nothing more. I assure you."

It wasn't true. Not in the least bit. But he didn't want Aveline shying away from him because of this one impulsive act. It would simply not do, especially when they were to spend a great deal of time together on this Caldera.

Aveline coughed. "Of course. Your gratitude for Lucrezia. I see."

It was difficult to tell, but Telchide thought he saw a sudden spark of anger in her eyes.

This uncertainty was going to be his undoing. If he knew for certain that Sebetine was never coming back, would he pursue Aveline? Would she even accept his advances? Telchide shook his head. He doubted she would. She'd made it quite clear that he should not have touched her hand, that he should not have visited her alone that evening back at her workshop, that she was now angry with him for the hint of intimacy between them.

The basket thudded suddenly onto the boat.

"I'll go up first, with the heavier bags. You can come up last and bring the rest of the things we'll need."

Aveline did not even wait for him to reply before piling in the bags, hopping into the basket and signalling to Corrado. The basket whirled away. Telchide couldn't keep his eyes off it. This was going to be a difficult expedition if both Lucrezia *and* Aveline were angry with him.

Very well, he could deal with it. He would talk to them as little as possible. He would allow Aveline to take the lead on all matters, after all, it was her expedition. There was nothing else he could do.

He gathered the last of their required possessions and shouldered the bags in anticipation of the basket. It soon came travelling back down to him. With a last look around the boat, he hopped inside the basket.

His stomach lurched as the basket was heaved into the air. Desperately, he clung to the sides. He suddenly understood now how Lucrezia had panicked on her first journey, especially if it had jerked to a stop suddenly. Telchide found that he was not breathing – could not breathe.

The basket rose ever higher into the air. Soon, the boat below him was but a fraction of its original size. The sea beyond it was tinged a deep orange as the sun began its slow descent. He hadn't realised how many hours had passed since they'd first reached the Caldera.

Out in the distance, he could see another landmass. Without anything to judge it by, he couldn't tell its size. He thought it appalling that he didn't know enough about the outer lying islands to know which one it was, as there were only two options: Ontigura or Sant'Elba. Everyone on Beltigura knew that their island was the largest of the three since the implosion of Sentigura had created a rift in the land with the Caldera in the centre. Many Mercantili travelled the Circle Run around Beltigura, Ontigura and Sant'Elba, but few of them travelled further than that.

He focused on these thoughts and tried to ignore the fact that he was hovering in a basket high in the air. Below him were only sharp rocks and water to break his fall. From this height, he doubted he'd be as fortunate as Lucrezia to miss the rocks.

When he reached the top of the cliff, Telchide was hoisted up out of the basket by the captain, much to his mingled terror and joy. He stood transfixed by what he saw. Sentigura Caldera was nothing like he'd imagined. Before seeing the trees on the shore, he'd always expected to see a black island of volcanic ash and stone, not a sunken jungle. From his vantage point, he could only see tall trees and dense brush to either side. In front of him, the land cascaded down into the centre of the Caldera. The very middle rose up again, as though the Caldera had grown again after the last cataclysm. However, it too was covered with heavy jungle.

With a last look, he turned to the rest of his companions. Aveline and Roque had already set about building a fire. Telchide saw them throwing sparks on the leaves, but they were not catching alight.

"Are they perhaps too wet?"

His question earned him nothing but an annoyed look from Aveline as she continued to draw her knife against a stone. Telchide went for a closer inspection. They'd selected a variety of leaves, but no sticks. He looked around at the plants surrounding them and noticed a distinct lack of dry kindling. No wonder Aveline had given him that look.

Not knowing if their first day on the Caldera was the best time to use it, Telchide looked through his waist pouch for Eduardo's special lighter fluid. He'd agreed to take it the night Eduardo had come over for dinner. It was the first time in his life he would be willing to use it.

"A few drops of this should help," he said, stepping towards Aveline. She looked up as he drew out the lighter fluid.

"What is it?"

"Eduardo's lighter fluid. It should do for the fire what blazer solution does for your blazermobile."

Corrado held out his hand before Telchide could unstopper the vial.

"Not here. You don't have a lot of that stuff. Don't waste it all now. Let's find somewhere to camp, bring the Alchimista there and *then* light a fire."

Telchide had to admit it was a better plan, but he was not about to agree to anything if Aveline was against it. He was already in her bad graces and did not want it to get any worse.

"It's up to you, Aveline. I'm happy to explore with Corrado if you don't need us here."

She looked at the two of them, irritated.

"Go then. We'll try to light the fire without you. But if you don't find anything, I want you back here within an hour. I'll try to keep Lucrezia as warm as possible in the meantime."

Telchide motioned to Corrado, and they left before Aveline could change her mind. There was a narrow lip all around the Caldera. Telchide doubted they would find a cave or any such shelter along there. He undid the rope from the basket and tied it to his waist instead. He did not intend to get lost.

With Corrado by his side, Telchide tried to walk through the dense jungle. After only a few piedi, he realised they would not get far. He pulled out his knife and tried to cut his way through the vines and leaves, but it was so small that it barely made a difference.

"Let me through."

Corrado pushed past him, brandishing a machete. In long, sweeping movements, the marinaio began to cut a path in front of them moving downhill. Telchide hurried to follow him, though he stayed back from the swinging knife.

The further they got from the sea, the quieter everything became, that was, until his ears adjusted. Birds called out to each other, leaves rustled in the air, and foliage crashed down in front of Corrado. Telchide was certain he could hear running water.

"Stop!"

Corrado halted mid-stroke. Telchide put his finger to his lips, and they stood in silence.

"There's water over that way."

He pointed to their left. Corrado looked hesitantly in that direction.

"Water don't mean caves. Could just be water. Maybe not even fresh."

"It can't hurt to look," Telchide insisted.

Corrado shrugged and changed direction, heading towards the sound. It was indeed running water, though Telchide could only wonder how there could be running water in a place like this. As they drew closer to the sound, the air changed. It was warmer here. He was beginning to sweat. Not only that, but there was a peculiar odour in the air – like one of the Exploding Beakers' experiments gone wrong, though not quite as potent as the concoctions Nestore produced.

Telchide was so distracted by this that he walked into Corrado. The captain had stopped suddenly in front of him. Telchide peered around his side and drew in a sharp breath.

Before them was a large pool of water, but it was not just that which drew their attention. The lake was not a clear blue or green in colour but looked as though a prism was suspended over it with coloured specks floating everywhere, and the water was steaming – truly *steaming*. Telchide took a step closer, but Corrado held him back.

"I ain't ever seen anything like this before. Is it safe?"

Telchide studied the lake further. There was a stream feeding into it and a waterfall off the far end. Brightly coloured birds swooped down over it, but only skimmed the water. There were no dragonflies or mosquitos hovering over the water. No frogs croaking on lily pads. In fact, there was no vegetation in the water at all.

"We won't know until we try."

Without touching the water, Telchide held his hand out over the top. The heat was enough to instantly take the chill out of his bones, like a roaring fire. He did not dare touch it with his bare hands.

"We won't need a fire," he said. "All we need to do is bring Lucrezia here to warm her up."

"Oh yeah, and when we get back there, how do we find our way here again? It's already getting dark!"

"We follow the rope."

Telchide untied the rope from his waist and tied it instead to a tall tree near the steaming lake. He placed a hand on the rope and followed it back the way they had come. Corrado walked behind him, his knife sheathed, but as they continued it became clear that the rope had shifted as they walked. As the ground grew steeper, Telchide and Corrado used the rope to help them clamber their way up the side of a scree slope.

"And how're we going to get yer Alchimista down there?" Corrado asked out of breath once at the top.

Telchide looked down at the steep, rocky slope dubiously, wishing the rope hadn't shifted.

"Let's just get back to them and worry about that later."

Corrado raised an eyebrow but said nothing. He took the lead once more and cut the vines and leaves out of their way. They had definitely *not* come this way before. Telchide looked at his pocket watch. It was already over an hour since they'd left the others. Aveline would not be pleased.

When they finally returned, it was over an hour after their agreed time. The sun had almost entirely dipped down behind the outlying islands. Aveline was sitting with her arms around Lucrezia's shoulders, rocking her back and forth, muttering something under her breath. Roque sat on the other side of their failed fire looking at them both with a strange expression. Telchide couldn't quite place it, but he didn't like it. The marinaio's eyes darted to the jungle every few seconds, then back to the women.

Telchide took in the scene and drew a deep breath before coming into view. Roque instantly stood and moved towards them. Aveline looked up and Telchide was caught off guard by the wariness in her eyes. He'd expected to see a smouldering anger.

"Where have you been? Do you know how long we've been waiting? Did you find shelter?"

She didn't stand up but seemed to squeeze Lucrezia tighter. The Alchimista groaned under the sudden restriction.

"I'm soaked, with a sore ankle – don't give me a broken rib as well!" Lucrezia scolded.

"My apologies, Aveline. We didn't find shelter, but we found something else that may help Lucrezia."

Aveline raised an eyebrow at him.

"It's a lake, steaming water. It's bound to warm her up."

"I don't trust it," Corrado muttered beside him. "It's coloured water, and ain't no animals anywhere near it. I *don't* trust it."

Aveline looked from Telchide to Corrado and back again, weighing her options.

"Lucrezia still needs more warmth than we have here. Let's go to the lake. We can worry about shelter later."

Telchide decided now was not the time to tell her he doubted they would find shelter *anywhere* on this island. From what he'd seen, it was covered with this same jungle everywhere. The only breaks had been at the cliffs and the water. There would be time enough later to discuss that problem. For now, he helped Aveline lift Lucrezia to her feet.

The Alchimista was cold to the touch, even through her clothing. Her ankle was so bad that she couldn't put much weight on it. Without assistance, she would never make it to the water that could warm her.

Telchide motioned for Roque to bring the empty basket over. The marinaio helped him lift Lucrezia into it and then the two of them lifted the basket up by the handles. It was awkward and heavy, but it was better than trying to get Lucrezia to walk by herself. Thankfully, the Alchimista had the sense not to argue the decision.

They carried the basket, taking turns to swap in and out with Corrado. Aveline led the way slowly, following the rope with her hands and watching her footing until the moonlight was of no use.

"What now?" she asked.

Telchide passed his side of the basket over to Roque and followed the rope with his hand down to Aveline. When he reached her, he rummaged around in his bag until he found the friction light. With nimble fingers, he wound and wound until the crank would go no more. The glass bulb atop it emitted a bright yellow glow.

"That should last for up to five minutes at a time," he told her. "Just wind it up again when it goes out and watch out, there's a rocky slope somewhere nearby."

He passed it to her, being careful not to touch her hand. There had already been enough awkwardness caused by his undue familiarity with her. Aveline leaned her head close to his until they could see each other's eyes properly. There was something wary in her large, hazel eyes as she flicked them at the marinai behind him, but also something else. Something he couldn't understand – a softening at the corners of her eyes that made him not want to look away. She remained close for so long that Telchide felt the sweat bead at the back of his neck, but this time it had nothing to do with the steaming water. He tugged the material around his neck nervously. Aveline blinked and moved away.

"Thank you, Telchide. This will do nicely," she said, oddly formal.

She stepped back again and gasped his name. Telchide instinctively reached out and grabbed her wrist with both of his hands, her weight dragging him to his knees. The scree! She must have slid on the loose rocks in the dark. His heart pounded in his ears as he struggled to keep hold of her.

"Aveline, grab hold of the ledge!"

She twisted and reached with her other arm for the ledge.

"Help us!"

Roque and Corrado came to his side, reaching out for Aveline. Between them, they dragged her back over the ledge, one gripping her free hand and the other the back of her shirt to bring her up and onto solid ground. The four of them sat in a heap for a moment, breathing heavily, before Aveline lurched toward Telchide and tucked her head into his shoulder.

"Are you alright?" Telchide asked urgently, unable to bring himself to release her.

"There's a drop there, Chide" she replied shakily, her words muffled against his shoulder.

"I *told* you this was a bad idea," growled Corrado.

"We didn't have a choice," Telchide retorted sharply. "It would've been easy enough to get down if we could see."

"But we can't see now, can we? She dropped the *smoking light*."

Aveline leaned back, craning her neck. When he realised she was leaning towards the ledge once more, he tightened his grip and braced himself to support her.

"The light is still down there; I can see it from here. I don't know how it didn't break, but we can use it to climb down."

He pulled her back from the edge, not yet ready to let her go.

"Yer Alchimista's still a problem," Corrado pointed out. "How're we going to get her down?"

Telchide looked at Lucrezia. Her eyes were on him, but slightly unfocused. They couldn't take the basket down and she couldn't climb.

"Does anyone have a spare belt?" he asked no one in particular. "Or any long lengths of cloth?"

"What are you thinking?" Aveline asked him before Corrado could argue again.

"If Lucrezia's already angry with me, there's no point in the social niceties now. I can take her down the rope with me. It should be strong enough to hold the two of us. I need both hands free, though."

Aveline gave an amused huff.

"You want to tie her to your back?"

Telchide coughed. "Well, erm, yes. You can use my nightgown. I don't think I'll be needing it anyway."

"I can help you there."

Aveline proceeded to tear his nightgown into long strips. Corrado and Roque brought Lucrezia over and explained the plan.

"Absolutely not!"

Telchide rolled his eyes, thankful it was too dark for her to see.

"Crez!" Aveline snapped. "If you hadn't struggled with the basket in the first place, we wouldn't be in this mess. Telchide is willing to help you, and you're going to let him. No argument."

In a rare display of equanimity, the Alchimista agreed and wrapped her arms around his front. Aveline set to work lashing Lucrezia to his back with strips of cloth. The inelegant work often brought her into much closer proximity with Telchide than she would ever otherwise have cause to be. Telchide found himself breathing hard, though he could hardly feel Lucrezia's weight on him while her feet were still on the ground.

"Corrado, Roque, you two go down first. If anything goes wrong, try to catch Telchide and Lucrezia. I'll come down last."

Telchide waited patiently for the marinai to descend. Aveline stood close by his side. So close that he could feel the heat radiating through her shirt. So much for his intention of keeping well away from her.

Perhaps she was still shaken by her fall. He could understand that. Teresina always wanted to be cuddled after a nightmare. He reached out an arm to hold Aveline close but realised what he was doing just in time. He dropped his arm quickly, accidentally letting his hand slap his leg. Aveline turned at the sound. Her face was so close to his now.

Telchide's heartbeat thudded loudly in his ears. He did not look at her. He focused all his attention on the dark slope before him and listened out for

Roque. The marinaio was to call out when the pair reached the bottom. The climb was taking a lot longer than Telchide expected.

"Chide?"

Aveline's breath was warm on his neck. Telchide did not move.

"Yes."

She touched his fingers ever so slightly. His own fingers reacted to her touch. He knew it must seem like a flinch, and it was, but that was only because he'd felt a spark when she touched him. Aveline drew her fingers back. He desperately wanted to reach out to touch her lovely hand, to turn his face towards her, to take one step closer to her.

"Thank you for catching me," she said, taking a step away. "I just wanted to say thank you."

Telchide was confused by her tone. She sounded hurt rather than grateful. And certainly not full of the longing that he himself felt with her so close to him. But she was now two steps away. Out of reach unless he stretched out towards her. Had he imagined her so close before? Had that really been her breath on his neck or just the warm air wafting up from the steaming lake?

"It was instinct," Telchide replied.

Lucrezia huffed at that, making him cringe. Aveline nodded and crossed her arms. Telchide wanted to kick himself. Yes, of course it had been instinct – but that instinct was only there because he cared for her. He doubted his reaction would have been quite so quick had it been Lucrezia or one of the marinai. Why did his words always come out wrong?

"Your turn!" Roque called up just as Telchide was about to try to explain what he'd meant. "Don't fall!"

Telchide couldn't see Aveline properly now that she was standing so far away from him. The moon and stars were shining, but he could only see glimpses of them through the patchy jungle canopy. They did not provide enough light to see properly more than an arm's length in front of him.

"I'll see you at the bottom of the cliff," he said. He couldn't see if she reacted at all.

Taking hold of the rope, Telchide put one leg on either side and eased himself over the edge. As he shifted position, Telchide felt Lucrezia's weight drag him down. It took all his effort and concentration to keep himself upright on the scree. If he slipped, his shoulders would roar in pain and his palms would be shredded by the rope. The threat of that pain was enough to keep him walking slowly and carefully down the rocky surface, his hands burning with the strain of holding up two people. He tried to keep his mind off the pain and just focus on his feet. And *not* on his conversation with Aveline or the fact that he couldn't stop thinking about her face nestled in his shoulder.

His foot slipped on loose rock.

"Watch it!" Lucrezia shouted in his ear.

Telchide shook his head sharply at the volume. The last thing he needed was to fall and crush Lucrezia – she'd hate him even more than she already did.

With Lucrezia on his back, he couldn't even look back over his shoulder to see how close he was to the bottom. For all he knew, he was almost there, but every step proved him wrong. His hands were sweating. It became ever more difficult to keep his grip on the rope. His foot skidded on a loose stone, and he slipped forward. Before he could do anything, his head slammed forward onto rock. Something warm and wet trickled down his face and he lost his grip on the rope and twisted sideways. He slid down the slope until he landed on something hard and rolled. There was a heavy weight atop him. He could scarcely draw breath!

Rough hands dragged him sideways and started pulling at his clothes. Something was taken off him, but he was still clothed. He patted himself down. Yes, he was certainly still clothed. But a weight had been lifted off him. As Telchide drew in a deep breath, his thoughts cleared enough to remember Lucrezia had been lashed to him. He drew several more breaths. A salty, copper taste seeped into his mouth. He wiped it away only to find his hand covered in blood.

"He's over here," someone said. Telchide knew he should recognise that voice, but his mind was so clouded.

"Chide, can you hear me?"

He looked for the owner of the voice. She was right in front of him. Her face glowed yellow. Why did she have yellow skin? Wasn't it normally a lovely bronze? She dabbed something cold onto his head.

"Smoking Caldera!"

The sharp pain brought Telchide out of his stupor. Aveline was hovering above him, wiping his head with something that whiffed of menthol and pepper.

"What are you doing?" he asked between sneezes.

"I'm stopping your wound from bleeding," she answered harshly. "Unless you'd like to bleed to death."

Telchide pushed her hand away roughly.

"I'm fine."

Aveline rolled her eyes. Instead of leaving, she took one of the abandoned strips of cloth and wrapped it around his head. He went to push her away again, but she was finished before he could. Perhaps he'd hit his head harder than he thought.

Aveline looked at him closely then stood up.

"Right, you two carry Lucrezia in the basket. She's too heavy for me. I'll try to help Telchide – at least he can walk, I think. Just help him to his feet."

Telchide felt himself being dragged to his feet. He'd have fallen over but Aveline was by his side, draping his arm over her shoulders and tugging down on his hand to keep it in place. With her other hand, she held the light in front of her, found the rope and began walking. She tried to keep them moving but Telchide kept stumbling and forced her to slow down.

It seemed to take such a long time to reach the steaming lake. Telchide could feel it before he could see it. Warm sweat dripped from Aveline's face onto his hand. It tickled, then itched, but he was in no state of mind to do anything about it.

Without warning, Aveline released his hand and he fell to the ground. His arm fell into hot water. The longer he lay there, the warmer his arm became until it was unbearable. Telchide felt so weak. He could barely move.

"His arm!"

He heard a muffled shout, and his arm was yanked out of the water. Too tired to wonder what had happened, Telchide closed his eyes.

Chapter 16 – Gildadi 16 Mercantili 230 Years After Implosion

"He needs stitches."

"Then give him stitches."

"I can't! I don't have my supplies. You must have left them with his box."

There was a pause. Telchide strained to hear what was being said.

"I'll go back and get them. I'll bring everything back. This is a better campsite anyway."

"Begging yer pardon, Alchimista, but you won't be able to carry everything on yer own, not with that ankle."

"I'm an Alchimista. I think I can manage to strap my ankle so it isn't a problem," she replied scathingly.

"I'll come with you just in case," Corrado insisted. "It's daylight now and I can see the first path that we took to get here. There was no slope then. We'll take the basket with us and fill it with everything we left behind."

"It's settled then." That was Aveline's voice. "I'll stay here with Telchide and Roque. You go with Corrado and bring everything back."

Telchide tried to open his eyes, but they were swollen. He heard leaves rustling loudly, as Lucrezia argued with Corrado about who would take the lead. Then nothing except for the rushing water.

He lifted his hand to his eyes and winced at the pain. He tried once more to open his eyes and succeeded, but the bright sunlight hurt. As he rolled to the side, shielding his eyes, the world tilted at a strange angle, and he vomited.

"Help." He could barely hear his own whispered voice. He tried again. "Help me."

Soft hands took his.

"Chide? Chide, are you awake?"

"Yes," he croaked out. "My eyes."

Fingers gently probed his face. He bit his lip not to cry out in pain.

"They're fairly swollen. I'll see what I can do. Give me a moment."

Aveline left him. He heard sounds nearby. Perhaps she was looking for a water canister.

"Roque, would you watch Telchide? I'm just going to see if I can fill this with water without burning myself."

Telchide strained to hear what was happening. He tried to sit up but was pushed back down roughly. His head hit the ground hard. There was a blow to his stomach. Telchide gasped, trying to catch his breath.

"Roque, what are you doing?" Aveline asked warily, an odd note in her voice. "I asked you to watch Telchide."

"Yer Inventore's sleeping. It's just us now. No one'll hear a thing."

Telchide couldn't cry out. Roque had winded him, the smoking ash-sucker! He couldn't open his eyes, couldn't help her.

"You will maintain your distance, marinaio."

Telchide could hear the sharp edge to Aveline's voice, but a quiver at the end indicated all was not well. He tried to sit up, but his head swam with the movement. He rolled to his hands and knees instead.

"What's the harm? We'll be done before they get back. Now be a good lass and come here."

Telchide heard a sickening crunch and a yelp of pain.

"My nose! You broke my nose! You'll pay for that!"

As Telchide struggled to crawl towards them, he could hear the impact of blows against flesh, but he couldn't tell who was on the receiving end. Aveline's sharper cries were punctuated by Roque's guttural grunts of anger.

There was a splash, and the sounds of fighting stopped. Telchide strained to hear what was happening. There were cries for help and frantic splashes, but the sounds grew fainter and fewer, until Telchide heard something else. Something he'd never wanted to hear.

Aveline was crying. Muffled sobs, but he could hear them. Each sound tore at his heart. He still couldn't open his eyes without feeling sick. He did not attempt to stand again. Instead, Telchide listened to the pitiful sound and crawled towards it.

When he judged he was close, he stopped. What had Roque done to her?

"Aveline? Did ... did he hurt you?"

The crying ceased for a moment. Deep breaths replaced sobs. Deep, trembling breaths, like she was trying to calm herself.

"Not the way he wanted to," she finally replied.

Telchide wanted to hold her close, to tell her she was safe. But he couldn't. She was hurt because of him.

"I'm sorry I couldn't help. I'm sorry I put you in this position – where he thought he could treat you that way because I was in no fit state to stop him."

Aveline sniffed loudly.

"Chide, this is *not* your fault," Aveline said, voice trembling angrily. "It's not mine either. The fault is all his. I've met men like him before and it's never ended well, for either of us."

Telchide didn't know what to say. He couldn't decide which was the worst part of what she'd just told him.

"Not all men are like him."

"Yes, I know," she spat out. "But men like him are one of the reasons I have a male apprentice. It makes them think twice about treating me like a common whore."

Telchide put the pieces together.

"So, Nevio thought I was one of *those* men that night?"

Aveline did not answer. Not immediately. And when she did, she avoided the question entirely. It did not put Telchide's mind at ease. Not at all.

"Let me try clean you up."

Even with the warning, he was unprepared for the hot cloth pressed against his eyelids. It stung more than he expected. The water was so hot! After a few swipes, he could tell that Aveline was being too gentle to be effective. The next time the cloth was pressed against his face, he took it from her, trying so hard not to touch her hand – after what she'd said, he didn't know how she'd react. She quickly relinquished the cloth.

Telchide rubbed at his face far more roughly than Aveline had. The remnants of blood and vomit began to come away. When he felt it was no longer making a difference, he held the cloth out to her. She took it, sloshed it in water and returned the wet cloth back to him. They repeated the procedure twice before Telchide had the courage to try and open his eyes again.

He avoided looking at Aveline. Instead, he peered over at the water.

"You won't find him," Aveline told him flatly. "Strange for a marinaio, but he apparently couldn't swim well. He was dragged out towards the waterfall. I lost sight of him before he got there. I don't know if he drowned or went over the side. Good riddance to him either way."

Of course, she had every right to feel as she did, yet Telchide couldn't help thinking that she'd caused his death and didn't care. Then again, had he been in her position, he doubted he would care either. In fact, he wondered if he'd have been able to fight off the marinaio as well as she had.

"Is there ... is there anything I can do? For you, I mean. While we wait, that is." He stumbled over his words.

He finally looked at her. She did not seem to notice that her bodice was ripped, allowing him an unfettered view of the top of her breasts. The blood rushed to Telchide's face. He looked away too quickly and Aveline noticed. From the corner of his eye, he saw her look down at herself before he completely averted his gaze.

"For Caldera's sake, pass me a shirt or your waistcoat – something!"

Telchide looked around for their bags before remembering they'd left all of them back at the landing site. There were no spare clothes! He immediately unbuttoned his waistcoat and passed it to Aveline, with his eyes averted. She snatched it out of his hand and hurriedly put it on.

"You can look now. I'm as decent as I'm going to be before those bags arrive."

Telchide glanced up. Aveline was sitting before him in her workpants, a ruined bodice and his green waistcoat. It was an odd sight – he choked back a laugh.

"Is there anything else I can do?" he asked.

Hand-shaped bruises were beginning to show on her arms and her left eye was already swollen. She stared unflinchingly at him, roughly brushing away at the few tears on her cheeks.

Telchide thought of Teresina again. If this had happened to her, he wouldn't hesitate to take her into his arms and hold her close. He would promise her that he would never let anything like that happen to her again, but it would be an empty promise and he knew it. He hadn't wanted to believe until now just how vulnerable women were to men like Roque, but he couldn't hide from the reality anymore.

"Who taught you to fight?" he asked.

Aveline seemed caught off guard by the question. She hesitated before answering.

"My papà, actually. He didn't like the idea of me joining the Inventrici Guild. It meant that I couldn't stay in our home and he wouldn't be able to protect me. He used our final weeks together to teach me to fight. It was the best parting present he could've given me. One I've used more often than I like to admit."

Telchide regarded her with some awe. His own parents had always made him shy away from fisticuffs. A Falegname's hands were critical for their artistry, for their livelihoods. Fighting was simply not allowed in their household and was strongly discouraged by their Guild. Any scuffles with other children on the street were only ever had by use of the feet. It made for a very silly fight and most of the children gave up after their first few scuffles.

"When we get back, will you teach Teresina how to fight?"

"Shouldn't you?" Aveline asked.

"I couldn't see what happened with you and Roque, but I don't think I could teach her whatever it was you did. I ... haven't been in many fights."

Aveline raised her eyebrows. "Very well then. I'll teach your daughter to fight, but not until she's a little older. We don't need to make her afraid of men. Especially not if you've requested a male apprentice."

Telchide hadn't even thought of that. Would his daughter be safe with a male apprentice? Should he have taken a female one, despite Teresina's protests? He lapsed into silence, torn by thoughts that couldn't be tended to until their return to Tor'Esint.

***

"What in Caldera's smoke happened here?"

Telchide was startled awake. Lucrezia's tone was enough to tell him that something was terribly amiss. He looked over to Aveline and breathed a sigh of relief. She was still there. But the bruises that had only begun to show earlier were dark now.

"Roque attacked me," Aveline stated flatly.

"He never would!"

"I heard him!" Telchide instantly felt the need to come to Aveline's defence.

"*Heard* him?" Corrado asked, his voice raised angrily. "You didn't *see* him?"

Telchide shifted uncomfortably. "No. But I know what I heard. Roque tried to rape Aveline. Just look at the bruises on her."

"Lies! How do I know it weren't you?"

"What?!" Telchide spluttered, trying to get to his feet. A wave of dizziness overtook him, and he fell down. Aveline came to his side but did not touch him.

"Aveline, where's Roque now?" Lucrezia asked in a gentler voice than Corrado.

Her eyes flittered to the steaming lake. "He fell into the water. I haven't seen him since."

"Fell in my arse! You threw him in!"

Telchide looked angrily at Corrado. He was being completely unreasonable.

"Aveline is not a large woman. Exactly *how* do you think she threw him in?"

Corrado ignored him and ran to the water's edge calling Roque's name over and over again.

"You people!" He rubbed his hands over his face. "I'm leaving! The pay isn't worth it."

"You can't," Aveline protested, her arm reached out as if to hold him back. "I hired you to take us to the Caldera and back again. We're not ready to leave yet. We only just got here."

"I don't care! I. Don't. Trust. You." He emphasised each word slowly. "You threw Roque into the water. You *killed* him. How do I know you won't do the same with me?"

Corrado, shoulders slumped, turned towards the forest. Lucrezia stood in his way.

"I don't think you want to do that," she said in a low voice. "Aveline Inventrice paid you good money for this journey. You are honour bound to see out your contract."

"Honour be damned! Get out of my way Alchimista."

Lucrezia did not move. Telchide could feel the tension building in the air. He was in no fit state to do anything to alleviate it. Aveline moved to stand beside Lucrezia, her feet in a fighting stance.

Corrado looked between the two of them.

"How're you going to stop me? Throw me in the water like Roque?"

Aveline's face flushed. "I told you, he *fell* in. Besides, you haven't tried to attack me. We need you now. You're the only one who can sail the boat back to Tor'Esint."

"Who says I even *want* to take you back now? I should just leave you here, by yerselves, without a boat."

Aveline crossed her arms and stared at him.

"You won't though, because you know I'm not lying. You can see the proof all over me."

Corrado refused to meet her eyes; his shoulders sagged.

"Aye, I can see it," he said quietly.

"You'll stay then?"

He looked around at all of them, weighing his options.

"I'll stay." He nodded.

Aveline rubbed her arms. "Thank you, Captain."

"What now?" Lucrezia asked. "Are you happy to make this the base of our operations?"

Aveline nodded.

"Good. Then let's eat and make a plan."

Lucrezia brought the basket over to where Telchide and Aveline had settled, on the rocks further from the jungle. Aveline, Lucrezia and the marinaio sorted out some food, Aveline passing Telchide a generous slice of bread with cheese. He ate it gratefully, his stomach rumbling at him for not having eaten yet that day.

By the time every had finished, Aveline and Lucrezia had come up with their exploration plan for the day. As Telchide stood to join them, another wave of dizziness struck along with a wave of nausea. This time, he couldn't keep it in. He turned away from their possessions, fell to his knees and hurled up the contents of his stomach.

"Crez, we can't take Chide with us. Besides, you still need to stitch his head."

Telchide wiped the vomit from his mouth and looked at the mess he'd made. At least it wasn't over any of their clothes, or his rubber-lined box.

Lucrezia stomped towards him. Telchide was ready for the tongue-lashing he felt he was bound to hear, but there was only silence. He looked to the side to see the Alchimista going through their bags, looking for something.

Eventually, she pulled out a few of her supplies and led him towards the water. She sat him down and set to work on his head. He felt the pressure relieve as she unwrapped the makeshift bandage. Silently, he watched as she rinsed out the blood from the strips of cloth.

He stifled a flinch as she wiped away the dry blood encrusted on his head. The water didn't seem to be quite so hot now. He wondered if that was his imagination or if he was simply getting used to the heat.

"Close your eyes. I don't need you flinching as I work."

Telchide looked down at her needle and thread. He swallowed the bile in his mouth and closed his eyes.

To her credit, Lucrezia worked quickly and smoothly. She slathered on a small amount of numbing cream, but Telchide still bit his lip to stop from making a sound – it was more uncomfortable than painful.

"There," Lucrezia said in a satisfied voice. "That should do the trick. At least it will stop you from bleeding. I don't know how hard you hit your head, but hopefully if you rest today, you'll be ready to explore with us tomorrow."

Telchide opened his eyes to see both Lucrezia and Aveline sitting near him. Aveline had changed into a new shirt – not the ruined one – and was looking towards the jungle, where the rope led. She'd laid his waistcoat by his side.

"How are we going to make sure we don't get lost? This might not be the only lake and the rope isn't long enough to take on a full day's journey."

Telchide followed her gaze into the jungle. The multiple trips back and forth had well and truly created a path now, but it wouldn't be visible from a distance. He turned to look at the lake. There was vegetation all around it.

"Why not walk around the lake today?" he suggested. "If you keep the waterfall within earshot, you should be able to find your way back easily enough."

Lucrezia huffed. "He isn't as stupid as he looks."

Telchide rolled his eyes. It seemed like their temporary truce was over.

"And you aren't as useless an Alchimista as you first appear," he retorted.

"Enough!" Aveline clapped her hands once. "This morning has been difficult enough without the two of you bickering. Telchide makes a good point. We may as well follow the lake around. Who knows? We might even make it to the stream and find out where the main source of water is coming from. The water in our canisters won't last forever."

She stood and looked down at Telchide.

"Chide, will you be alright by yourself?"

Telchide waved her concerns away. "I have enough water to last me until you come back, and I might even try my hand at preparing a meal for us all after I clean up ... *that*."

He motioned to the mess he'd made earlier. Lucrezia snorted but held her tongue. Instead, she picked up her bag and took out the non-essentials to lighten her load for their day's exploring.

"I don't think you should be left alone." Aveline bit her lip.

Telchide huffed, ready to protest when another wave of nausea hit him. He closed his eyes to keep his stomach.

"Suppose we can't leave him to cook all by hisself if he can barely stand. I'll stay with him," Corrado announced. "You two go exploring. Yer the ones who know what yer looking for anyway."

Aveline nodded. "We'll be back by sunset."

"Safe exploring," Telchide muttered as they set off.

Telchide sat and watched as the Inventrice and the Alchimista walked away from him, towards the stream. This was not at all how he'd expected their expedition to begin.

He looked at the mess he'd made and scratched the back of his head. Nothing for it but to clean the mess. He found a small pot Aveline had brought along, but before he could do anything with it, Corrado took it from him and made him sit down out of the way.

Too tired to argue with him, Telchide lay down and closed his eyes.

***

Yawning, Telchide opened his eyes. The midday sun was blazing through the jungle leaves. He'd not intended to doze off, but his head wound had taken that decision away from him. In a belated effort to keep everything cool, Telchide began to move their possessions further into the shade. Corrado quickly joined him.

Telchide sorted through the bags he'd just moved. His was the easiest to spot – Teresina had stitched on a dragonfly when she got bored one day. He pulled out his water canister and shook it near his ear. There was a little liquid left. He took a sip, saving the rest for later.

"How's yer head?" the marinaio asked.

Telchide touched it experimentally. "She did a good job stitching me up. But I still feel sick if I move too quickly."

The captain nodded. "You rest. I'll get you something to eat."

Telchide smiled gratefully and watched as Corrado searched through the bags, eventually pulling out two apples. He handed one to Telchide and bit into the other himself.

"I should've known something would happen with that marinaio," Corrado said contemplatively. "He had a bad reputation, but his mamma's an old friend of my family. She begged me to give him a job. Don't know what she'll do without his pay now."

Telchide grunted. He couldn't condone hiring someone disreputable just to help his family. He also didn't want to insult the captain, giving him any reason to leave.

It was tiresome resting all afternoon. Telchide wanted to be out there, exploring with Aveline and Lucrezia, but knew he needed to recover or he'd be useless the next day too. He settled for cutting the leaves off the fat section of a palm stalk and began whittling away.

In the early evening, he looked through their food stores. He set aside all the canned food, knowing they would need it later. He gathered the fresh fruit and vegetables they'd brought along and sorted them into those he knew would last well and those that needed to be used within the next day or two.

It was a wonder he knew anything of the sort, but Sebetine had insisted that cooking together at the end of the day would be good for them. She'd been right – it had forced Telchide to stop thinking about his work, even just for an hour each day. When Serenita had realised he knew how to cook, she'd taken advantage of it once a week to visit the small group of friends she'd made in Tor'Esint since her arrival. He thanked his lucky stars for both of them and set to work.

Someone had brought along rice and dried pasta – both were easy enough to cook. He settled on the rice then realised he would need water. A good deal more water than he had left in his water canister.

Telchide got up and wandered over to the lake with a pot. He eyed the colourful water then shrugged. They were going to be here for longer than they could possibly survive without using water. They'd have to try the lake water at some point. He scooped up a potful and sniffed it. It certainly smelled different to the water back in Tor'Esint, but that was not to say it wouldn't be drinkable. Taking a deep breath to steady himself, Telchide brought the pot up to his mouth.

"What are you doing?" Lucrezia shouted. Telchide looked up to see his companions had returned.

"You're back!" He smiled at them and lowered the pot away.

"And you're about to kill yourself," Lucrezia retorted sharply.

"Whatever do you mean?" Telchide spluttered. "I was not!"

"So, you *weren't* about to just drink that water without letting me test it first for dangerous substances?" she asked, crossing her arms.

Telchide looked guiltily at the pot full of water in his hands.

"Test it then." He held it out to her. "I was going to cook us some dinner, but I'll wait until you've cleared the water first."

Lucrezia took the pot with a huff. From the corner of his eye, Telchide saw Aveline stifle a laugh. It made him smile. The fact that she could find anything amusing after what she'd gone through that morning was astounding to him. He left Lucrezia to her own devices and walked over to Aveline.

"Did you find anything of interest?"

She shrugged. "There were many interesting things, just none of them were the plant we're looking for."

"It's a large island," Telchide pointed out. "Much larger than I realised from a distance. It could take us a few weeks to find the plant. No point doing it all on empty stomachs. If you help me light a fire, I'll cook something for dinner as soon as Lucrezia has approved the water."

Aveline smirked at the irritated sound that escaped Lucrezia. Together with Corrado, they set about trying to find things to burn. By the time Lucrezia was done testing the water for toxic substances, they'd gathered a decent amount of vegetation. Again, none of it looked particularly long-burning or flammable, but it was the best they could come up with.

Telchide arranged it all on the warm rocks, away from the jungle itself. If it did somehow catch alight, he did not intend to set the entire jungle on fire. Then they'd never find the plant they were looking for.

He fished out the flint and steel kit from his bag and set to work trying to get it to light. It was no use – the plants were simply too green. With a sigh, he pulled out Eduardo's lighter fluid.

"Lucrezia, do you know how much of this I need to use?"

He waved the vial around above his head. Lucrezia looked over and gasped.

"Don't wave it around, you lavalump! Did Eduardo tell you *nothing* about lighter fluid?"

Telchide stopped waving it and looked at the fluid with renewed distrust.

"Erm, no, not really. Just that a few drops help to light fires."

"Inventrici and their lack of respect for alchemical liquids!" she exclaimed loudly.

"Alchimisti and their bizarre fondness for unstable liquids!" Telchide retorted, his temper rising.

"Are they always like this?" Corrado asked Aveline. His amusement only irritated Telchide further.

Aveline rolled her eyes at Corrado and stepped in to stop the argument. "Now, now, you two. Let's just get the fire going. Crez, was the water drinkable?"

"Yes. It will make everything taste slightly strange, but there's not much we can do about that," replied Lucrezia, carefully taking the lighter fluid from Telchide and holding it steady. "I'm taking this away until you learn to treat these things with the respect they deserve. We'll use *my* lighter fluid today."

Telchide bristled at her tone. Another time, he may have retorted – however, he held his tongue on this occasion because he did not, in fact, know how to use the lighter fluid and did not intend to waste the opportunity to see how she did it.

Lucrezia unstoppered her vial. It had a glass dropper attached to the lid. Using the dropper, she dripped out three precise drops on various parts of the vegetation. Then immediately replaced the lid and secreted the vial away in her waist pouch.

"Use your flint now. Just be careful – this fluid is potent."

Telchide did not need the extra warning. He still remembered Eduardo's singed eyebrows after his demonstration. It had taken weeks for them to grow back!

He held the flint and steel out towards the vegetation, ready to jump back at a moment's notice. He dragged the steel over the flint over and over. Small sparks flew down to the vegetation below. A few sparks fell onto the lighter fluid and the flame spread quickly to the other drops.

Not willing to give Lucrezia the satisfaction of knowing that he thought her lighter fluid might be that little bit superior to, or at least more reliable than, Eduardo's, Telchide stepped away. It really was a very stable flame. Perhaps their chemicals weren't quite so bad.

Whoosh!

Telchide fell back from the sudden heat of the fire, knocking over Aveline. Scrambling to get out of that awkward situation, Telchide shuffled himself off her and, in his haste to be disentangled, he almost missed Lucrezia's smirk.

"Your alchemical liquids are just as unstable as Ardo's! I should *never* have trusted you."

Aveline sat up and moved away from the roaring fire. She sighed noisily.

"We've barely been together two days and you two are already fighting like rival apprentices. If you don't strike a truce, I'll end up thumping one or both of you into silence."

Aveline was right. He knew she was, but that would not make it any easier to get along with the infuriating Alchimista. At least Eduardo had a decent sense of humour and knew when he was taking things too far. They'd come to a mutual understanding long ago. That's why they worked so well together. Telchide and Lucrezia had *never* gotten along.

"A truce then."

Telchide held out his hand. Lucrezia groaned but limped over to shake his hand anyway.

"Just don't think this makes us friends."

"I wouldn't dream of it," Telchide said through his teeth.

They gripped each other's hand tightly for a few moments longer, then released the handshake simultaneously. Aveline clapped, probably in mock delight.

"Now, Chide, you were about to cook something?"

Telchide grunted and set about his task without further interruption. He poured two handfuls of rice into the pot of water and placed it as close to the flames as he dared get. With no other option, he chopped some vegetables on the hot black rocks then tossed them in the pot. He rummaged through the bags for a moment pulling out the utensils and bowls Aveline had instructed them to bring.

With nothing else to do while the food cooked, he walked a little way into the jungle, searching for anything that might be useful to them. Corrado joined him.

On the jungle floor, he found a large roundish object. It was yellowish-green and oval in shape. If he could split it in half, perhaps it would make two decent bowls. He hefted it from one hand to the other. Liquid sloshed around inside it. Already presuming it wouldn't work, he tried to cut the yellowish ball with his knife. It went through the green outer skin but hit a hard interior layer and the knife stuck.

Corrado came up behind him.

"You can't open a coconut like that," he said with a laugh. "Give it here."

Telchide handed it over. "I thought coconuts were brown, hard balls."

"Aye, when *you* see them, they are because they ain't as fresh then," Corrado agreed. "But this is what they're like before that."

He hacked off one end to create a flat edge to rest it on, then proceeded to shave off the green exterior until he'd exposed the top of the coconut. With practised ease, he hit the top at an angle and the entire top came off. Inside was a thin layer of bright white flesh and a clear liquid filled the entire centre. Telchide huffed in surprise.

Corrado looked at him curiously. "Haven't you ever had one before?"

"No. Sebetine had a bad reaction to one when she first came to Tor'Esint, so we never had them in our household."

Corrado shrugged. "Well, I'll get one ready for each of us and you can try one today."

They brought the four coconuts back to their campsite. Corrado handed one to Aveline.

"What's that?" Aveline asked.

She sniffed it and went to take a sip of the liquid. Lucrezia immediately held out a hand to stop her.

"You Inventrici are useless! Is your first instinct to taste every possible poisonous substance on this Caldera?"

Aveline laughed. "Crez, not *everything* on this Caldera will be poisonous."

"And coconuts are definitely *not* poisonous," Corrado told her, rolling his eyes. "You can drink the water and eat the inside, though there ain't much flesh on these ones."

"I've seen coconuts at the markets and they don't look like this." Lucrezia gestured to the fruit. "They're brown and fibrous on the outside."

"*Under* the yellow bit they're brown and only when they're riper," Corrado sneered at her. "Ain't you ever seen the inside? I'll be your poison tester. Let me eat it first. I don't mind, it'll mean less for you."

Lucrezia, clearly unfazed by his last comment, motioned for him to try it. Corrado made loud slurping noises followed by the most irritating lip sucking sound.

"Now *that's* a good coconut."

Lucrezia snatched one away from him. She sniffed it, still distrustfully, and took a sip.

"You know? It's actually not bad."

Aveline and Telchide sampled their own. The water was quite sweet and left a slight tang in his mouth afterwards. He drank it all and tried to scoop the flesh from the inside with his fingers.

Corrado laughed loudly. Telchide looked up to see Aveline trying the same thing.

"You can't eat it like that. You need to cut it off the shell with a knife."

Corrado took Telchide's coconut and hacked it in half with his machete before handing it back.

Telchide was not above taking advice from the marinaio. He flicked out his knife and began to peel bits of the white flesh from the shell. He popped a small piece in his mouth and chewed. And chewed. And chewed.

"Are you sure this is edible?" he asked, still trying to grind down the fibrous white flesh.

"Takes a bit of getting used to," Corrado admitted, "but it ain't poisonous."

Aveline handed her coconut to Corrado and elbowed Lucrezia to do the same. The Alchimista sighed heavily and placed her coconut next to Aveline's

Telchide left them to eat their coconut flesh and went back into the jungle to find more. It was surprisingly easy now that he knew what he was looking for. They were scattered in clumps around certain trees.

He picked up an armful and brought them back to the campsite. Even if the steaming lake's water was not poisonous, he did not fancy drinking it too often. These would do quite nicely as an alternative.

By the time the rice and vegetables were cooked, they'd managed to eat the white flesh from all four coconuts. Aveline directed Telchide to bring her their bowls and proceeded to pour the contents equally into them. The meal was certainly not as tasty as Serenita's – the water was almost unbearably salty – but it was edible, and he was hungry.

"Too salty," Corrado said when he'd eaten the last grain of rice and licked the bowl clean.

Telchide raised an eyebrow at him. He felt proud of the edibility despite the taste.

"How about *you* cook the next meal then?"

"I could do a damn sight better than you, but at least it was edible."

He thought about the marinaio's situation. He'd changed his tune considerably since that morning. Even had he still wanted to return to his boat alone, without Aveline's pulley, and someone to work the crank, Corrado was effectively trapped unless he trusted himself to descend with the hand holds.

His thoughts rested on Aveline. He already admired her for so many things, but this trip had already given him further insight into a very complex personality. Her past was a mystery to him, which he was keen to learn more about, and she was clearly an extremely skilled person. It all made her more alluring. If only he were free to court her and if only she had *any* interest in him. He shook his head to clear his thoughts.

The sun had dipped down behind the lip of the Caldera. There was very little light left aside from the fire, which they had to keep refuelling with vegetation every half hour to keep it aflame. Without large logs to create simmering coal, it would die out very quickly.

"Are we set for the night?" Telchide asked, laying out his blanket.

"I still don't trust him to stay," replied Lucrezia not quite under her breath.

Corrado heard her, but just rolled his eyes rather than reply.

"There isn't a way for him to get down to his boat without our help," Telchide pointed out. "I really don't think he could leave us here."

There was a moment of silence as the ladies looked at him.

"Well, he can't, can he?"

"I ... suppose not," Aveline replied slowly.

"Signora Inventrice, I promise I won't leave you and ... I'm sorry."

She looked up at his words, an eyebrow arched questioningly. Corrado sighed.

"I'm sorry I ever doubted your side of the story. I knew his reputation. I just don't know what I'm going to tell his mamma. But I promise I won't tell the Authorities what happened. All they need to know is he went overboard in rough waters and drowned. All of us at the docks knew he couldn't swim."

Aveline gave him a half smile. "Thank you, Captain. I appreciate it."

Lucrezia looked between them and nodded. "Right, we'll sleep on this side of the fire, you two on that side."

Telchide quickly agreed and lay on his blanket atop the rocks, wondering how the sun's heat hadn't yet disappeared from them.

Chapter 17 – Ramedi 17 Mercantili 230 Years After Implosion

The sun had yet to reach the lake when Telchide awoke, but he could see it on the inner lip of one half of the Caldera. And the black rocks between the jungle and steaming lake were still warm to the touch. He placed his hand on rocks, trying to understand how they retained their heat. As he got closer to the lake, the rocks grew even warmer to the touch.

"You know the volcano inside this Caldera's still alive, don't you?"

Telchide turned at the sound of Corrado's voice.

"I beg your pardon?"

"Yer wondering why everything's so warm here, ain't you?" the marinaio asked. "It's because the volcano's alive. There's probably lava under the whole island. Why do you think the lake's so hot?"

Telchide thought about it a moment.

"But *you* were the one who was scared of the lake water. Why are you scared of it if you know so much about it?"

Corrado drew himself up straight.

"That water ain't blue, or even green. It ain't natural."

Telchide laughed. "Your dinner was cooked with that water, you know that!"

Corrado paused. "It weren't coloured in the bowl."

"No, you're right there," Telchide admitted. "But I have a feeling it's the alchemical components in the water that make it such interesting colours. Whatever it is that gives it that interesting odour and taste may make it change colour, in vast quantities."

"Telchide, leave the surmising about alchemical properties to the Alchimista," Lucrezia called out in a sleepy voice. "Aveline, are you up yet?"

There was no answer. Telchide looked around their campsite but couldn't see Aveline anywhere. Then he heard splashing.

He stood and ran across the smooth black rocks to the lake's edge, scanning the water to find the source of the disturbance. Aveline was *in* the water, not ten piedi away. Telchide moved closer and held his hand out to her. She looked calmly at the hand but did not take it.

Telchide noticed a pile of her clothes abandoned on the rocks and couldn't see anything other than a bronze sort of shadow under the water.

"Telchide, if you don't mind, I'd like just a *little* privacy."

"Yes, of course," he spluttered and turned away. He could feel the heat rising on his cheeks. His heart beating wildly. He took a moment to catch his breath then walked back to the campsite.

"She's ... fine. She'll be along in a minute or two."

Lucrezia peered around Telchide and snorted with laughter, which made Corrado turn to see what was happening. He chuckled and turned away. That was better than Lucrezia who kept looking at his face, which he was certain was still flaming red. How could it not be?

"Good morning," Aveline said lightly as she joined them, fully clothed. Her bruises did not seem quite so dark this morning and the swelling in her eye had gone down considerably. Perhaps Lucrezia had used some of her alchemical salves on Aveline last night.

"Good morning," Telchide replied stiffly. Aveline looked at him oddly.

"I've been thinking, and I have a new plan. The Caldera is roughly round, we can plainly see that. If we keep walking in the same direction every day, we're bound to return to this point. So why don't we try that?"

"Walk in a circle?" Lucrezia asked incredulously.

"Yes. Until we find what we're looking for. We can't just stay within half a day's walk from here. Rumour has it the sparking plant is towards the centre, but we probably have a better chance of spotting them from higher ground. One of us can map it out so it's easier to find if we come back again."

"I can do that," Telchide volunteered. "I don't know if there will be many striking landmarks, but I can try."

He pulled out his notebook and drew a rough outline of what he remembered the island to look like from their journey around part of it and the view from the lip that first day. He sketched their landing point and any other details he could remember, including the walk down to the lake.

"The slope you slid down was probably closer to here."

Aveline pointed to the map. Lucrezia and Corrado came over to have a look.

"The other path went around there," Lucrezia pointed out. "And yesterday, we walked over here. There was nothing of note there. Not even large animals, aside from the birds."

"So today, we head north, keeping the sea on our left side," Aveline declared. She smiled down at Telchide as he took out his compass. "Thank you for volunteering to draw the map, Chide."

Lucrezia didn't comment, and Telchide noted a distinct lack of derisive sounds. Instead, she walked over to inspect Aveline's bruises.

Telchide began to pack their things into the bags. The most awkward item to carry was his insulated box. If only he'd thought to put a handle, or a strap, something to make it easier to hold. Aveline came over to him as he tried out different ways of carrying it.

"Hold it out."

He did as he was instructed and watched as Aveline took a few lengths of cloth and tied them around the box until she'd effectively turned it into a bag. She stood back and smiled at her efforts. Telchide returned the smile automatically.

"Ever the Inventrice," he remarked, shouldering the makeshift bag.

He went to clap her on the back, as though she were a man but realised what he was doing just in time and lowered his hand. Aveline noticed his hesitation and laughed lightly.

Telchide smiled uncomfortably at her laughter, not understanding what caused it. He quickly turned to Corrado and handed him both marinai bags. Corrado took the extra burden without complaining.

They fell into an easy order with Aveline and Lucrezia leading the way and Telchide and Corrado bringing up the rear. Telchide knew his head wound was healing quite quickly under the circumstances, and he was beginning to wonder if the water from the lake had some alchemical properties that Lucrezia could study.

It wasn't until later that afternoon when his thoughts were confirmed. Aveline's bruises and swollen eye mostly healed. Those sorts of injuries should have taken days, possibly weeks, to heal naturally.

"Lucrezia, what did you find in that sample of water from the lake last night?" Telchide asked during a short rest.

"More things than I could identify without a full testing kit. The main alchemical properties were sulphate, that's what gives it the rotten egg smell, calcium, sodium and chloride. Why?"

"Do any of those things have accelerated healing properties?"

He pointed first to his head and then at Aveline. Lucrezia followed his motions and smirked.

"Noticed that, have you? Chloride is used to clean wounds. Perhaps together with the others, it might accelerate healing, but I've never heard of such a thing. However, there were small amounts of many other alchemical properties, some of which I've never come across before. In such small quantities, they can't be poisonous, but I know little else without proper tests."

Telchide knew they were now both wondering if these other alchemical properties were the key to their accelerated healing and whether Lucrezia could bring enough of the water back to Tor'Esint to manufacture it somehow. After all, Lucrezia wouldn't be here only for the sparking plant, it didn't sound like something Alchimisti could utilise. To him, it seemed more like an Inventore's plaything.

***

The day passed quietly. They poked around all over the jungle in a northerly direction, not finding any plants that matched the description of the one they were looking for. Telchide had quickly fallen into the trap of wondering whether they would find it, or if they had come here on a fool's gambit with nothing more than rumours.

Later that evening, Aveline came to sit by him when Lucrezia and Corrado were already fast asleep. They sat together in comfortable silence. Telchide was missing Teresina terribly and beginning to think he'd made a huge mistake by coming along. Aveline, perceptive as always, gave him the silence he required for a good long while.

"Don't give up hope, Chide," she said, mistaking the reason for his silence. "There's so much of this Caldera to explore. It could take us weeks to cover every pollice of it. Besides, we don't even know if you can see the energy plant by day. Perhaps it's a nocturnal plant that doesn't work until there's complete moonless darkness. We could be surrounded by them and not even know it until the new moon."

Her words did little to comfort him. He did not like the idea of being played for a fool by nature. It wasn't pleasant. They lapsed into silence once more. Telchide found himself taking sidelong glances at Aveline. One of those times, she caught his gaze and held it. He abruptly looked away.

"Did he ... hurt you more than those bruises?"

Aveline looked down at herself, turning her arms.

"To be honest, I probably hurt him more than this before he fell into the lake. A punch to the nose is usually a good way to stop them in their tracks, that or a swift knee to the groin."

Telchide stared at her open-mouthed. She shrugged.

"I wouldn't expect you to understand. You're ... not like that." She smiled fondly. Telchide didn't know what to make of that. "I've seen you avert your gaze or blush bright red when you thought you saw something you shouldn't have. Men like you don't do things that men like Roque do."

Telchide was glad for the darkness – it hid the blush that he could feel rising to his cheeks. It was times like this that he knew she did not care for him, but only respected him as a person and fellow Inventore. He coughed to cover his embarrassment and briefly wondered what it would be like not to have the burden of another four years looming over him.

He sighed, shoulders slumping down. He'd looked into it and there was a restriction of seven years before you could claim a missing person as dead, legally – that left four more years. Absently, he twisted the wooden ring on his finger and only noticed when he realised Aveline was watching his hands.

"It wouldn't be fair for me to take it off yet," he told her. "Imagine I take it off and court a woman and then tell her we cannot have a commitment ceremony for another four years."

Aveline looked at him oddly. "Four years? That's a very *precise* timeframe."

"I *am* technically still committed and will be so until the day Sebetine is found, in whatever state, or declared dead. A missing person cannot be declared dead until seven years after their disappearance. Unless there was an accident or evidence of foul play – neither of which are present in her case.

"I suppose that's the real reason I keep the ring on. To remind myself that I am not truly free to do as I please. However much I might want that."

Aveline did not reply. Telchide didn't really expect her to. It was a morbid topic and had nothing to do with her at all.

He closed his eyes and leaned back against a tree. He was so very tired, so why couldn't he sleep?

Something brushed his cheek. Something warm and soft that sent sparks down his spine. He opened his eyes and sat bolt upright, knocking Aveline off balance.

"Aveline?" he turned to look at her as she pushed herself back up off the ground. "What in Caldera's smoke are you doing?"

"I ... I'm sorry, Chide. Forgive me."

Before he could reply, she got up and walked away to lay down beside Lucrezia – the one place he would not follow her.

Why in Caldera's smoke had she just kissed him?

Telchide had tossed and turned all night. He'd tried to blame it on the uncomfortable rocks, but in truth it was quite pleasant to lie on their smooth warmth. The black rocks lay in meandering lines running away from the centre of the Caldera. Corrado told them it was a petrified lava stream. In fact, Corrado seemed quite knowledgeable about the Caldera.

"How do you know so much about this place?" Telchide asked him as they walked. "Have you been here before?"

"No," Corrado replied. "Sant'Elba marinai come here sometimes. They like collecting coconuts and those sharp, glittery rocks. I've spent a lot of time on Sant'Elba. I listen to their stories.

"When that younger Alchimista started asking about the trip, I knew she wouldn't find anyone else in Tor'Esint to take her here – I'm the only marinaio that travels as far as Sant'Elba to know about their secret handholds." He winked at Telchide. "Thought it'd be a good chance fer me to come and see it fer meself."

"Did any of these stories tell of a plant that shocks people?"

Corrado shrugged. "Not that I heard. But I didn't talk to all the marinai, just some of them."

Telchide was only half listening. He was trying to overhear the hushed conversation between Lucrezia and Aveline, but any time he got close enough to catch a word, Lucrezia silenced Aveline and turned to glare at him. Aveline had often taken the opportunity throughout the day to take side routes into the jungle only to reappear ten minutes later, flushed from exertion but looking calmer.

Was she upset? Over the kiss? The kiss. Telchide tried to recall what had happened. Had she really kissed him or was it something else? After all, his eyes had been closed. Perhaps it was a leaf brushing past, or he'd imagined it? Though that would not explain why she fell when he had sat up suddenly, nor her immediate retreat and continued silence.

Aveline's behaviour confused him no end. She'd given no sign that she felt anything other than friendship for him. He'd just told her that he wouldn't truly be free to court anyone for another four years. What then? Had she felt sorry for him? Had it been a pity kiss, to give him the hope of something from someone years in the future? None of it made any sense to him. Why were women so difficult to understand?

"Inventore? Did you hear me?"

Corrado tugged his shirt sleeve. Telchide turned to the marinaio in confusion.

"Do you want to add this to the map?" Corrado pointed to the small steaming lake off to the side of them. "That's the third one today. I think they're linking up to each other."

Telchide took out his notebook and drew in the lake. That made four. The first one was still the biggest they had found yet. Two of the others today had been only a few piedi across each, but all of them had at least a trickle of water running away from them.

"I wonder if they run the entire way around the Caldera," Telchide mused aloud.

"If they do, it will make tracking our progress easier," Lucrezia pointed out. Aveline had wandered off again and the Alchimista seemed to be taking the opportunity to join him and Corrado while she waited.

"Tell me, Telchide, whatever did you do to her last night?"

"Me?!" Telchide spluttered. "*I'm* not the one who did anything."

The leaves of the jungle rustled and Aveline appeared.

"You would do well to hold your tongue, Telchide," she advised him coldly.

Telchide closed his mouth angrily and held it firmly shut. How could he be in trouble over this? He hadn't done anything!

Lucrezia looked from Aveline to Telchide and threw her hands up in the air.

"Oh, for Caldera's sake, you two had a lover's spat, didn't you?"

"Lover's spat indeed!" Telchide shouted, angry and confused. He and Aveline were not lovers.

"We did not have a 'lover's spat' as you call it," Aveline said in a steady voice. "We are not courting, nor did we in fact argue."

Telchide clenched his fists at his sides. That part, at least, was true. Aveline had apologised and walked away before they could even discuss it. Telchide still had no idea what was going on and couldn't possibly piece it together without her help.

"Indeed, we did not. Perhaps it was a *misunderstanding* which could be cleared up if we had but a moment to talk."

Aveline waved her hand dismissively.

"We don't have time to talk. I want to see how much farther we can get before nightfall."

There was no point in protesting. If Aveline didn't want to talk, there was nothing he could do about it.

They walked on for another few hours. This time, there was no lake and no black rocks, but they came to a clearing of sorts. They decided not to attempt lighting a fire to cook. Instead, everyone agreed to try the canned food that Telchide had brought along. He called out the choices of boiled pumpkin, tomatoes, sardines, and beans. Everyone but Corrado opted for the pumpkin. The marinaio chose the sardines.

Telchide opened only one of the pumpkin cans. He didn't know what it would taste like, or whether there would be enough to feed more than one person. There was no point opening more than what they needed to.

He lifted the lid off carefully, as the vendor had warned him about the sharp edges of the cut metal. Inside, as promised, were boiled pieces of pumpkin. They floated in an orange-tinged liquid. Telchide sniffed. It really did just smell like pumpkin.

Lucrezia laid out their bowls. Telchide thanked her warily, Lucrezia did not usually help him without prompting. Telchide poured the pumpkin equally into three of the bowls. If it was edible, one can would not be enough for the three of them.

He quickly opened a sardine can and poured some into the last bowl. They looked slimy and unappetising to him, but Corrado's eyes lit up at the sight. He took the bowl without waiting for the others to take theirs and popped one sardine after another into his mouth, sucking his fingers after each bite. It was a revolting display.

Telchide grimaced. The sight was almost enough to put him off eating at all. However, hunger won him over. He took the last bowl and very hesitantly tasted a chunk. To his surprise, it just tasted like pumpkin boiled in salted water. A few herbs or spices wouldn't have gone amiss, but it was perfectly edible on its own. Apparently Aveline and Lucrezia thought so as well. They finished their bowls quickly and fetched out another can.

Corrado wasted no time polishing off his sardines and began to empty the rest of the can into his bowl. As an afterthought, he held up the can and asked, "Does anyone want to try the sardines?"

Telchide shook his head, as did the ladies. Corrado shrugged and poured every last sardine into his bowl.

By the end of the meal, three empty cans lay in the middle of their campsite. Telchide stared at them unhappily. He hadn't thought of what he would do with the cans once they'd served their purpose. Had he been at home, he'd have washed them thoroughly then melted them down into something he could use for his inventions. But there was no chance of that happening out here. Not only would he not have a fire hot enough to melt them, he didn't have the necessary moulds to shape and cool the molten metal.

"We can't very well leave them here. I'll put them with the other cans," he decided aloud. "I'll find some leaves to wrap them so no one cuts themselves on the edges."

No one objected. The canned food had been a brilliant find and would undoubtedly save them days of hunger when they couldn't light a fire or find coconuts.

It had been a strange day. Aveline's silence seemed to have taken its toll on all of them. Once he'd safely packed the empty cans, Telchide busied himself with his notebook, determined to stay awake until it was only himself and Aveline. They needed to talk about last night.

Aveline did not see things the same way. As soon as she returned from relieving herself away from the campsite, she laid out her blanket and went to sleep. Or feigned sleep. Either way, Telchide understood there was no chance of them talking that night. He lay down miserably on his blanket and tried to get to sleep.

Chapter 19 – Mercatodi 21 Mercantili 230 Years After Implosion

The next two days passed in much the same fashion – the only highlight being Telchide's inventive curses as Lucrezia removed his stitches. Aveline spoke to Lucrezia and Corrado, when necessary, but was otherwise silent. Telchide mapped out any significant features and they all kept their eyes peeled for the elusive plant that had drawn them all the way to this smoking Caldera.

On the third afternoon, Telchide realised that they were now on the eastern side of the Caldera. At this time of day, the sunlight still reached most of the Caldera except the inner side of the western lip. It really was a beautiful sight. From this vantage, the Caldera looked like a sea of emerald-green, broken with bright streaks of red, yellow and blue as noisy birds flew from tree to tree.

For the first time, he noticed there were more lakes around the base of the inner peak. He took a closer look. In fact, they didn't look like the other steaming lakes they'd seen, shimmering in the sunlight. Telchide thought they looked more like miniature lightning flashes.

"Do those lakes look like the other ones we've seen to you?" he asked Corrado, pointing to the valley.

Telchide and the captain had become quite companionable over the past few days, as he had no other options. Lucrezia and Aveline were always together.

Corrado looked over.

"Those don't look like lakes."

"Lucrezia, Aveline, come here!" Telchide called out loudly.

They had walked a decent way ahead when Telchide and Corrado stopped to inspect the view. As they got closer, Telchide could see angry lines on Aveline's face. He nervously plucked at the buttons on his shirt to distract himself.

"What is it?" Lucrezia asked in a tired voice.

The constant walking, and the disappointment of not yet finding the plant, was taking its toll on all of them. Telchide pointed out the flashes he'd initially mistaken for sunlight reflecting off a lake.

"Telchide, don't waste our time," Aveline said shortly. "I saw those two days ago. They're just more lakes near the main peak."

"They're not though," Lucrezia told her, shading her eyes with one hand. "*Those* definitely aren't lakes. They're lights of some sort."

He was *right* and Aveline was *wrong*. Telchide smiled in satisfaction, but then lost his smile with a pang. His crowing over being *right* would not solve the problems between them. It might only serve to make things worse.

"It's too late to get there now. Why don't we camp here and then walk down tomorrow?" Telchide suggested in what he thought was a very reasonable tone.

"No," Aveline replied shortly. "If they're the plants we've been looking for, I don't want to waste any time."

"It's a rather steep climb." Lucrezia peered down into the valley. "I don't fancy getting stuck half-way at night, or worse, falling down there in our haste. I agree with Telchide."

"Me too," said Corrado. "Well, if my vote counts for anything."

"Tomorrow then," Aveline huffed angrily.

Tensions were high as they made camp. Keeping the odd lights in their sight, they retraced their path to one of the smaller lakes they'd passed earlier that afternoon. Aveline's constant dour mood must have been grating on Lucrezia – she speedily volunteered to look for firewood with Corrado.

While Corrado and Lucrezia set about getting fuel for a fire, Telchide prepared the meal itself. This was the last of their fresh vegetables. The fruit had all been eaten during walking meals when they did not want to stop to rest.

It was the first time in days that he'd been alone with Aveline – she'd made certain of that. But things couldn't continue like this. If they didn't sort this out before returning to Tor'Esint, Telchide doubted they ever would. The problem was, he had no idea how to even begin and so he hadn't been able to even speak a word to her by the time the others returned.

While their meal was cooking, and throughout the evening, Telchide stared out at the lights. While the sun still shone on them, they produced light. Even after the sun dipped down behind the Caldera, the lights still twinkled. It must have been a good hour at least before their light died out.

"That's the last of them gone out," he said quietly.

He didn't realise that their fire had burned out and he was talking to himself. How long had he been staring at those lights? Telchide was used to less sleep than most people. Teresina's nightmares had forced him to make do with only a few hours a night for so long. On this trip, it had meant that everyone fell asleep before him every night. Tonight, it was no different.

Out of habit, he counted the sleeping bodies on the ground. One was missing. He peered through the dark and realised it was Aveline. For a panic-stricken moment, he couldn't find her. Then he heard the telling splash of her bathing. He breathed a sigh of relief. Aveline had made a habit of bathing in the hot waters of the Caldera. Both Lucrezia and Corrado had tried it once, but neither had managed to stay immersed for even a minute before jumping out again. Telchide himself hadn't tried. He was too ashamed to admit that he couldn't even tread water to stay afloat.

Absently, he walked over to the steaming pool, barely more than a pond. Telchide stood there for a moment wondering how deep it was. His question was soon answered when he saw Aveline's outline in the moonlight. She was leaning against the rocky edge, facing him, and appeared to be sitting with her knees – her *bare* knees – visible above the water.

"Aveline, for Caldera's sake, will you please stop bathing naked!" He wrung his hands together in desperation. How was anyone meant to avoid catching a glimpse of her body if she insisted on this nonsense!

She tilted her head up in a defiant way, but to him, it only served to make her more alluring.

"What difference does it make to you what I do? *You* are not courting me, nor do you have any wish to!"

Telchide drew himself up to his full height. If she wanted to have this discussion while she was naked, he refused to let it distract him.

"You misunderstood me that night," he told her firmly. "I was surprised. That was all."

Aveline raised herself a little in the water and Telchide shut his eyes.

"You can open your eyes now," she told him mockingly before launching into an angry tirade. "Surprised doesn't cut it. You asked what in Caldera's smoke I was doing! Any other man in that position, and I mean literally *any other man*, would have kissed me. Without hesitation!"

She scowled at him furiously. Telchide blinked and swallowed hard.

"You ... *wanted* me to kiss you? But you never ... I didn't know ... I'm *committed*."

Aveline sank down into the water, as far as she could, until only her face and fingertips were visible. Telchide knew he'd said the wrong thing. Again. Why did he always say the wrong thing to her? Not willing to leave things the way they were, he knelt by her side, close to the edge of the pond.

"Veli, *please*. I need you to understand, I didn't think you cared for me – not like that. I was so careful to hide my own feelings, and I'd just told you that I can't court anyone for four years. *Four years*! How was I supposed to know you would kiss me after that?"

Her laugh had a bitter edge. She looked up at him with mournful eyes.

"You're not very good at hiding your feelings, Chide. Not from me, anyway."

Telchide paused.

"You knew? Why did you never say anything?"

"How could I say anything when all you ever do is talk about your daughter and, on occasion, your missing companion? You have a family, even if it's a broken one. How could I ever presume to be a part of it?"

She had a point there. No matter their feelings on the matter, Telchide really was not free to court Aveline for another four years.

"But ... you still kissed me."

"I did," she whispered, lowering her eyes.

Telchide couldn't think with the sound of his heartbeat thrumming in his ears. The rules of their society were so unfair! Why should he be punished a thousandfold because his companion had disappeared? He knew she was likely dead, just as everyone else presumed she was. Why was he forbidden from forming any other attachment?

Damn the rules! There were only the four of them on this island anyway.

Telchide reached out and took hold of her fingertips. Carefully, he drew her hand out of the water. She did not stop him. He pressed a light kiss onto the back of her hand. When he tried to let go, he realised she'd curled her fingers around his. He chanced a look at her and saw a hesitant smile spread across her face. She pulled his hand towards her mouth and returned the kiss. *This* time, he did not flinch away.

Telchide cleared his throat.

"It's getting late. We should probably get some sleep."

"Chide?"

"Hmm."

"What happens now?"

His shoulders slumped. What happens now indeed?

"I don't know. All I know is I don't want to wait four years to court you."

Aveline nodded. "The law says you would have to wait at least four years before you could *have a commitment ceremony*. You could still court me, couldn't you?"

"I ... suppose I could. But would you really be happy with that?"

He was almost too scared to hear her answer. No one could really be happy with that, could they?

"I would be happy with that, for now."

Chapter 20 – Riposidi 22 Mercantili 230 Years After Implosion

The next morning proved that things were not going to be easy between them. Although he was sure Aveline had meant what she'd said the night before, it did not change facts. He *was* still committed. Numerous times that morning, while they were packing up their gear, he saw her glance at his hands. It was only when he looked down that he realised what constantly drew her attention – the wooden ring.

He'd thought of taking it off so many times, but it just didn't seem right. It was his reminder, his increasingly uncomfortable reminder, that Sebetine might still be alive. If he were ever going to take it off before the requisite years had passed, he'd need to talk with Serenita and Teresina.

And then it dawned on him. Serenita knew. That's what all the fuss had been about before he left. How could he not have seen it himself?

Telchide tried to smile when Aveline caught his eye, but it was a false smile and quickly dropped from his face. This was not going to be easy for either of them. His thoughts were interrupted by Lucrezia.

"I don't know what's going on between the two of you, and I really don't care, but have either of you realised that the lights aren't there anymore?"

Telchide looked over at the inner peak. There was a distinct lack of anything out of the ordinary. He shrugged.

"The lights went out about a half hour after sunset. Perhaps they're fuelled by the sun's rays."

"A light that only works when it's light. What use is that?" she scoffed.

Telchide felt the usual anger the Alchimista provoked rising.

"It's not the light we're after," he said through clenched teeth. "It's the power it could provide."

"Only during the day."

Telchide threw his hands up in the air.

"There are plenty of things that need power during the day. Even blazermobiles could run on this if we learn to harness it properly. That would negate the need for your infernal blazer solution!"

Lucrezia froze. Aveline moved quickly across to stand between them. Her hand was warm on his wrist. The sudden contact startled him into silence. He looked from Aveline to Lucrezia. The Alchimista had turned quite pale. Telchide wondered exactly what it was he'd said to cause her reaction.

"You mean to negate any advantage the Alchimisti Guild has gained," Lucrezia said with ice-cold fury.

"Why in Caldera's smoke would we want to do that?" Telchide frowned. "The Alchimisti are our closest allies."

Lucrezia dismissed him. "Aveline?"

"Crez, we don't even know what this plant does other than produce light at some point. It's only rumoured to have a shocking effect and even that might not be of any use to us."

"Did Dania know what you meant to do when she agreed to come?"

Aveline looked at Lucrezia calmly. When she did reply, her voice was low and steady.

"Dania was the one who told me the rumours. She was just as excited about it as I was but did not have the means to hire the marinai, which is why *I* secured the boat. We planned it together. For Caldera's sake, it's a *plant*, Crez. It may benefit the Alchimisti as much as the Inventrici."

It all finally clicked into place for Telchide. Why Aveline continued to plan the expedition with Dania even when the boat hire turned out to be so expensive. She didn't wish to take advantage of the young Alchimista.

"Don't know if anyone cares, but the lights are back again," Corrado called out to them.

The marinaio had wisely kept out of their argument. Telchide spotted some lights around the inner peak. It was much more difficult to see in the early dawn light, but they were certainly there. Aveline and Lucrezia weren't looking – they were still staring at each other.

"It's a long way down," he told them. "If we don't start soon, we may still find ourselves on the descent at sunset."

Aveline joined him at the lip of the Caldera, her fingers lightly brushed against his. The familiar touch made him smile. He fought the urge to take her hand in his. They hadn't exactly discussed how open they were willing to be.

Drawing his attention away from her, Telchide peered down the slope. It was steeper here than further north on the island. He pulled out his notebook and opened it to his map.

"It will be an easier descent from there." He pointed to a spot where the land dropped away at a gentler angle. "It's perhaps half a day's walk from here."

Aveline looked to Lucrezia. The two of them had made most of the decisions together.

"Don't ask me." Lucrezia crossed her arms. "I'm more likely to destroy the plants than help you take them back with us."

Aveline glared at her. Telchide wondered why she'd ever agreed to let the Alchimista along in the first place.

Aveline turned back to Telchide and lightly brushed the scar on his forehead.

"I suppose half a day to be safe is worthwhile. Let's go back."

Telchide barely heard her with the sound of blood rushing through his ears. Her open touch effectively paralysed him. At the same time, it shone a bright ray of hope through his chest, bringing with it a confidence he hadn't felt in years.

Belatedly, he shouldered his pack. Everyone else was already ready. Aveline left enough time for Lucrezia to join her at the front, but the Alchimista was now well and truly in a mood. Telchide shrugged and took her usual place next to Aveline. They'd not spent quite as much time together on this expedition as he'd hoped they would, and he was keen to make up for it.

But they walked in silence most of the morning. There was little he could say that he was happy for the others to overhear. So, for now, it was enough just to walk by her side.

By a quarter past eleven, they reached the gentlest slope on this side of the Caldera. Telchide motioned for everyone to stop. This part of the Caldera's lip looked as if it had split in two, with one side overlapping the other. He meant for them to go down the inner split.

Aveline looked at it dubiously when he pointed it out to her.

"It's no worse than when you climbed up the outside of the Caldera," Telchide pointed out.

"Yes, but that was before I almost fell to my death on the *inside* of the Caldera," Aveline answered, not taking her eyes from the descent.

"That was at night," Telchide reminded her, "and I caught you."

She blushed prettily at the memory. "Yes, you certainly did."

Telchide couldn't help but smile at the double meaning in Aveline's comment.

"Will you two lovebirds quit reminiscing," Lucrezia said as she shoved past them. "I don't intend to stay up here all day."

Telchide tried not to take offence at her comment. Calling them lovebirds! The cheek of her! He refused to take that as a sign that she knew of their agreement.

Not wanting to be left behind, Telchide followed Lucrezia down the inner lip of the split. It was more difficult than he'd anticipated. The trees and brush were thicker here than on the flatter surface of the wide lip. Though it meant there was more to hold onto, there were also fewer places to step without the risk of falling. He slipped often and scratched the palms of his hands trying to hold onto the rough fibre of the hanging vines.

The others were not having a better time. He saw Lucrezia's stumbles and could hear the yelps of surprise from behind him as either Aveline or Corrado lost their footing.

Keeping on their feet was not their only problem. The further down they went, the more humid it became. Telchide was sweating profusely, and not just from physical exertions. He wished they'd just get to the bottom so he could pause to drink. He was not ashamed to admit that he was too afraid to get his water canister out in this gully.

The inner section of the Caldera was so humid that Telchide felt like he could almost sip water out of the air itself, but that wasn't the worst of it.

Stinging bugs flew all around him, landing on any bit of unclothed skin and biting him. He soon had bites all over the backs of his hands, around his neck and on his face.

"This is ridiculous!" he shouted, swatting the infernal insects away from him as ever more took their place. "Is there any way to stop them?"

"How should I know?" Lucrezia shouted back at him, slapping her bare arm and killing two of the stinging insects.

"Peppermint oil, or something citrus, like lemons or orange," Corrado called out to them as he reached the valley floor.

Like Telchide, he was wearing long pants and a long-sleeved shirt. The two of them had less skin to protect, as both Aveline and Lucrezia were wearing short-sleeved shirts.

"That would've been good to know *before* we finished our oranges a few days ago," Aveline said in frustration, slapping at the insects on her arm. "Crez, do you have any of those sorts of oils in your stores?"

"I am not a walking alchemical store! You made me leave three of my bags behind," she retorted furiously. But at least she began looking through her vials, calling out the names of things as she went.

"That one!" Corrado called out excitedly. "I've heard lavender oil works too, just not as well as the others."

"It's worth a try," Telchide said when Lucrezia looked up sceptically.

With a huff, she pulled out the vial and tipped a few drops into her hand. She then spread it over one arm and held it out. Telchide watched hopefully as he continued to swat away the pesky bugs.

"Looks like it's working, but I don't have very much of it."

Lucrezia covered the rest of her exposed skin with the oil, then passed it to Aveline. Telchide waited impatiently for his turn. The vial was more than half empty by the time she gave it to him. He looked at it worriedly. Using it as sparingly as possible, he rubbed the oil on the backs of his hands, around his neck and over his face.

The scent of lavender was overpowering. It reminded him of the purple tablets Eduardo had given him to help Teresina sleep. His thoughts ran away to his daughter. It must be near to a week since he'd left. Was she missing him? Were Serenita and Eduardo managing to keep her occupied? Or was she running them ragged? Was she still sleeping through the night?

"It's working!" Aveline breathed a loud sigh of relief.

Telchide looked at his hands. There were no insects on them, but they were covered in small bite marks. The lavender oil was already working to soothe the angry welts.

"Don't get too used to it," Lucrezia told her, holding up the empty vial. "That was the last of the oil and I don't know how long it will keep those infernal insects away."

"Then let's get to the plants as quickly as we can. I don't want to spend any more time down here than we need to."

"Which way then?" Corrado asked.

Telchide looked at the jungle surrounding them. Down on the valley floor, they couldn't see where they were going. He pulled out his notebook and worked out the rough direction. With his compass, Telchide turned around until he was facing north-west.

"That way."

He pointed and began walking towards the light plants. The others followed close behind him. The valley floor was marginally easier to walk along. There were more runs of black rock, though Telchide quickly learned not to walk on these ones. They were hotter than the ones on the lip of the Caldera. When he stayed on them for more than a few moments, the heat went straight through his shoes and his calves started hurting, just like on the rocky shore they'd landed on.

In the early afternoon, they reached a decent sized lake, but even Aveline did not attempt to touch the water. Steam billowed off it in constant waves. The one benefit was that the stinging bugs were nowhere to be seen.

"We'll have to go around it," Aveline pointed out.

"That will take us too far off course," Lucrezia argued.

Telchide put the compass away and took out his notebook instead. He did not intend to be part of their argument. It was better to spend his time mapping the area they'd walked through so far. The main problem was that he couldn't judge the distance between the lip of the Caldera and the inner peak. He drew in the main landmarks to the best of his ability, with Corrado reminding him of some of the runs of black rock he'd missed.

"We're going around and that's final," Aveline said firmly. "If you want to stay here, that's *your* decision, but the rest of us are going."

Telchide raised his eyebrows at her tone. Usually, *he* was the one to lose his temper so thoroughly with Lucrezia. Things had definitely gone badly wrong if even Aveline couldn't stomach her anymore.

He quickly replaced the map and retrieved his compass. He waited until it was pointing north-west again. The lake was shorter on the southern end, so they turned that way and began walking. This time, Corrado walked in front of them. The lake was surrounded by jagged black rocks so they couldn't follow the banks of it completely. Corrado took out his machete and began hacking a way through the foliage.

As he followed Corrado, Telchide risked a look behind him. Lucrezia was walking in small circles, intermittently stamping her foot. He tugged on Aveline's sleeve and flicked his head back towards her.

"It's her decision, Chide. If she wants to stay by herself at the lake, she's perfectly free to do so."

This was a new side to her that he did not recognise.

"Aveline, we cannot leave her alone. It's not a good idea to get separated right now. Especially when we can't see each other through the trees."

"I'm not going back for her, and Corrado is already well ahead of us."

"*I'm* going back," Telchide told her.

Aveline sighed but did not stop him. He saw that she didn't follow Corrado either. At least she was going to wait for him to get Lucrezia. Telchide hurried over to the Alchimista. She'd finally stopped stamping but was still walking around in a fury.

"Lucrezia, let's go. Corrado is already a good way ahead of us and I don't want to lose him."

"No," she replied firmly. "I don't think we should be going around the lake. Surely we can find a way to get over it. We're going to lose our way."

"Go on and touch the water," Telchide prompted her. "See how close you can get to this lake, or how long you can stay on the black rocks."

To his surprise, Lucrezia actually took his suggestion. She walked out over the rocks, towards the lake. She'd not reached halfway before turning and stumbling back to his side.

"These rocks are a lot hotter than the ones up there," she said in a matter-of-fact tone.

"Indeed," Telchide responded dryly. "Now, will you hurry up before we lose the others?"

"Fine, fine," Lucrezia mumbled.

Telchide turned back where he could see Aveline waiting for them. He reached her and they began to follow the path that Corrado had carved out.

As they walked, Telchide kept an eye on his compass, but it became apparent that something was amiss. Either Corrado had misjudged where they needed to go, or the three of them had missed where he had changed direction. Telchide held out a hand to stop the ladies.

"Can either of you hear Corrado?"

He strained his ears, but all he could hear was the gentle rustling of leaves and the calls of wild birds. Aveline and Lucrezia both shook their heads.

"Corrado!" he called out. "Corrado, where are you?"

Telchide listened for a reply but didn't hear one. Soon, the ladies followed his lead and started calling out for the marinaio. They waited for a minute or two, but there was no reply. No sound to give away which direction he'd gone.

"I *told* you this was a bad idea. Now what?" Lucrezia crossed her arms defensively.

"This would never have happened if Chide hadn't had to go back and get you!" Aveline snapped. "This is *your* fault."

Telchide clapped his hands loudly, drawing their attention.

"We're not going to find Corrado like this. I don't think he came this way – I can't see any slashed branches or leaves. I say we follow the compass and try to get back to the plants."

No one objected, so Telchide took the lead and began to follow the compass. He led them in a north-westerly direction again, hoping to meet Corrado along the way.

By sunset, they'd neither reached the light plants, nor found any trace of Corrado. Telchide felt the mood dampen as the time dragged by. When they reached another smaller lake, Telchide stopped.

"Let's camp here and build a fire. Perhaps the light will draw Corrado to us."

Again, there was no objection. The three of them set about gathering fuel for the fire in silence. There was nothing to say. If they didn't find Corrado, how would they get off the island? Would they be able to sail his boat themselves? And could they stomach leaving him behind as the marinaio had previously threatened to do to them?

"What if he's going back to his boat, to strand us here?" Lucrezia asked suddenly.

Clearly her thoughts had gone a slightly different direction to Telchide's.

"He can't get down to the boat without us," Telchide reminded her. "Besides, I think we're past that stage now. He doesn't seem to be so angry about Roque."

At the mention of the other marinaio, Telchide saw Aveline shudder.

"Let's just light the fire and see if he finds us by morning," Aveline said firmly. "We can figure out what to do then if he still hasn't appeared."

It was as good a suggestion as any. Lucrezia dripped her lighter fluid on the piled plants. At least down here they'd managed to find some larger branches, though with the humidity, they were all as wet as if it had just rained. Telchide used his flint kit to spark the flames. Having learnt his lesson from last time, as soon as the flames took, he stepped back as far as he could from the fire. He was just in time. A few seconds after he reached the edge of the clearing, the fire flared up.

Telchide busied himself trying to get something together for dinner. They'd agreed not to use the canned food unless they couldn't find anything else to eat. It was to be kept as an emergency food supply.

That didn't leave him many options. He scrounged around for coconuts, knowing the others must be as sick of them as he was. The best thing about them was the water inside – it saved them from having to drink from the steaming lakes. True, he'd grown used to the odd alchemical tang of the water, but he did not relish drinking vast quantities of it.

He gathered some fruit and berries and brought them back to their campsite. Lucrezia sifted through them and tested each and every unfamiliar one for toxins. It seemed like that was the only alchemical solution she'd brought along in great quantities. He wished she'd thought to bring more of the lavender oil. The stinging bugs were still being kept at bay, but Telchide did not hold out much hope that they would remain so for much longer. The only relief was that the bugs did not venture near the lakes, so they stayed as near the steaming water as they dared. This lake had fewer black rocks around it, so they could huddle in closer.

He tried to focus on these thoughts. He did not want to think about Corrado. If the captain were anywhere near them, he couldn't fail to see the glow of the fire or smell the burning vegetation. They'd stopped calling his name hours ago as it seemed to serve little purpose.

When he had nothing else to occupy him, Telchide sat at the edge of the black rocks and pulled out his notebook. He filled in the final details of his map, hoping that his directions were accurate. Aveline came to sit by his side.

"What do you think? Will we reach them tomorrow?" she asked him hopefully.

He sighed. "Honestly, I don't know. I don't even know if we're heading in the right direction anymore. I can't tell how far around the other lake we detoured when we thought we were following Corrado. For all I know, we're just as far away from them now as we were this morning."

Her shoulders slumped. Telchide knew he probably shouldn't, but he needed to comfort her. He reached his arm out around her shoulders and pulled her in for a sideways embrace. Aveline nestled her head in the crook of his neck. Her hair, frizzy from the humidity, tickled his nose. He tried to smooth it down with his other hand to no avail. All it did was allow him to hug her tighter.

"Don't I get a hug too?"

Lucrezia stood in front of them, hands on hips. Telchide looked up at her but did not remove his arms from around Aveline. Amazingly, Aveline did not try to struggle out of his embrace.

So that was it – they weren't trying to hide their courtship.

"I don't really care what happens between you here, but we all know Telchide's committed. When we get back to Tor'Esint, you'll need to stop ... whatever this is."

She gestured towards them with carelessly.

"His companion is dead, Crez." Aveline lifted her head but stayed close.

Lucrezia raised her eyebrows. "You *hope* she's dead. That's not the same thing. And honestly, hoping that someone is dead so you can be with her companion is one of the lowest things I've ever heard. You should be ashamed of yourself.

"And you, Telchide, not only are you committed, but you have a child. What will she say when she finds out about this? And doesn't your companion's mamma live with you? Do you really think she'll be happy to stay in a house with her son-in-law's mistress?"

Lucrezia handed them the berries she'd deemed edible and went to sit by herself, closer to the fire. During her tirade, Telchide had felt Aveline stiffen at the insults slung at them. It was one thing to say she was happy to be courted for four years but clearly, it was quite another for others to find out about it and bear their hostility.

"I ... *You* don't think that do you?" Aveline asked, her voice trembling. "If I thought Sebetine was alive, I would never dream of..." She trailed off.

Telchide couldn't blame her. He was thinking the same thing. It was the very reason that he found himself wishing that he knew one way or the other if Sebetine was dead or alive. He didn't want to think that he was cheating on her. It seemed unreasonably unfair of Lucrezia to say she didn't care what they did and then to badger them about it.

"I know," he said helplessly.

It was all he could think to say. But he knew it wasn't enough. He tried to hold Aveline close, but she sat up straighter and pushed away from him. Lucrezia's cruel words were enough to fracture their new and fragile relationship. And she was right. They could do whatever they wanted on this island where only Lucrezia and Corrado were their witnesses. The rules of society were suspended here. But that would only make things more difficult for them when they returned to Tor'Esint. If they *could* find their way back.

Where was Corrado?

Chapter 21 – Gildadi 23 Mercantili 230 Years After Implosion

Corrado did not turn up during the night. Telchide tried to hide his disappointment. He'd really thought that the marinaio would be drawn towards the fire, but if he were realistic, he knew there was not much chance Corrado had even seen the flames. He wondered if the captain kept a compass on him. If not, Telchide didn't think they would meet up again soon.

Aveline looked up at him as she stirred awake.

"Are you alright?" Telchide asked.

Lucrezia was still asleep and would not be bothering them. He reached out to stroke Aveline's cheek, but she moved her head fractionally away.

"I'm fine," she replied shortly.

Telchide drew back his hand, hurt by how much Lucrezia's words had affected her. *He* was not the one who had made the first advance. *He* was not the one who'd grown angry when that advance was initially rejected. It was not *his* suggestion that they court for four years while he was still committed. So why was Aveline the one backing off now?

"Do we go on towards the plants?" he asked Aveline, abruptly changing the subject.

Her shoulders sagged. Was that in sadness or relief for him not pressing her? He could no longer tell. If only Sebetine had been found, alive or dead! His mind tried to take him down the treasonous path of whether he would have fallen for Aveline if Sebetine was still in his life, but he shut the thought down ruthlessly.

"Yes, we go towards the plants," Aveline said decisively. "If Corrado can see them from where he is, he'll likely head there too."

"Unless he heads for his boat."

Lucrezia had woken. Why did she always have to air such negative opinions?

"Lucrezia, we've been over this. He knows he cannot reach the boat without us. I agree with Aveline. Let's head towards the plants."

Lucrezia scoffed, standing up. "*Of course,* you agree with Aveline. You're not going to side against the only person who is stupid enough to allow you to court her while you're still committed."

Telchide wanted so badly to slap her, but he stayed his hand. Aveline was not so controlled. She walked over to Lucrezia and slapped her face. Or tried to. The Alchimista caught her wrist before it connected.

"I only point out the truth," Lucrezia said bluntly. "I don't say it to be cruel. Let's get going to your cursed plants. Then we might be able to leave this smoking Caldera."

Telchide watched the whole thing happen with a lurching stomach. Aveline and Lucrezia hadn't really been friends before this, but they'd gotten along much better than he and the Alchimista did. How awful Aveline must feel to allow Lucrezia to affect her so much.

No one was in the mood to eat, so they got their things ready and left. Telchide led the way with an eye on his compass, walking in single file. They had to detour around more steaming lakes, but Telchide tried to keep them heading in the right direction.

***

It was late afternoon when he saw them. There was a clump of the plants emitting a pale blue jagged light that arced across from one leaf to another, or one plant to another.

"There they are."

He pointed them out to Aveline and Lucrezia, when they came up behind him.

"Across another steaming lake," Lucrezia sighed. "And this one looks like it goes for miglia in both directions."

Aveline walked over to the black rocks surrounding the lake and let her hand hover over the water. She kept it there for half a minute before stepping onto the rocks. Telchide refused to follow. He knew the rocks had been getting hotter the closer they came to the inner peak. How Aveline was walking on them was beyond him.

When she reached the water, she dipped her fingers in and jerked back almost at once.

"Let's just walk around," Lucrezia called out to her.

Aveline shook her head firmly.

"*You* talk to her," Lucrezia said more quietly to Telchide. He looked at her in shock.

"She won't listen to me," he said angrily. "Not after what *you* said. She's barely talking to me anymore."

Lucrezia raised an eyebrow but did not push the matter. Telchide wondered if she really didn't know the effect her words had. He turned his attention back to Aveline. She was trying the water again. This time, she held her hand over the water for a minute before touching the surface. To Telchide's surprise, she did not pull her hand back.

"Turn your back, Chide," she called out.

"Oh, not again!" Telchide sighed, turned around and sat at the edge of the rocks. He took the opportunity to update his map once more. Whether he was sketching any of it accurately was anyone's guess, but he did it all the same.

Over a half hour later, Lucrezia nudged his shoulder with her knee. He looked up at her and she nodded towards the lake. Telchide risked a glance. Aveline was almost completely submerged, her clothes a rumpled mess at the side of the lake.

"Aveline, this is madness!" he called out to her. "You don't have the box or your leather gloves. And what if the plant shocks you into the water? We won't be able to reach you before you drown!"

Aveline turned back towards them, stooping just enough to cover her breasts in the water. Telchide couldn't help but stare. She held out her hands towards him. He swallowed.

"Put the gloves in the box and pass it to me. I'll take it across."

Momentarily disappointed that she hadn't been holding her hands out to him, Telchide did as she asked. He also took the liberty of putting her clothes in the box but was scolded for that.

"I don't want my clothes to get burnt on the way back. Leave them out."

Telchide looked up at Lucrezia for support.

"I agree with Aveline," she said unapologetically. "If you put her clothes in there, she'll either have burnt or wet clothes by the time she gets back."

Defeated, Telchide took the clothes back out. He secured the box using the peg, with a set of leather gloves inside, and walked over to Aveline. As she reached up to get the box, she rose up out of the water until it was only waist high. Telchide gasped and very nearly dropped the box on her head. He fumbled and steadied his hold on it. Lucrezia cackled while Aveline sighed.

She took the box from him and held it well above the water as she waded further from the bank. It appeared as though this lake was shallow enough for her to walk across. Towards the midpoint, she slowed and stopped.

"Is this watertight?" she called out.

"I doubt it!" Telchide yelled back.

He couldn't quite hear her muffled reply, but it sounded like a curse. Telchide held his breath, waiting to see what she would do. Aveline held the box as high up as she could and took the next step. She sank down to her neck. Her movements were jerky and awkward.

"She's in too deep," Lucrezia muttered by his side. "What will happen if she gets the box wet?"

"I don't know," Telchide admitted. "We don't know how the plant reacts to water, but I wouldn't trust it. See how the light jumps from leaf to leaf and plant to plant? I can't imagine water would stop it jumping."

"Will the rubber inside it?"

"Well, it should," Telchide replied hesitantly. "This isn't exactly the way I'd have tested it, given the choice."

"We should've gone around," Lucrezia said.

Telchide found himself nodding. It felt odd to be agreeing with Lucrezia about anything. But he would not have been so hasty as Aveline. Perhaps she was done with this island and just wanted to get off, but that was not a good enough reason to compromise her safety.

The box dipped into the lake several times before Aveline reached shallower water. Telchide couldn't tell how wet the box was from this distance, but he hoped Aveline had the good sense to check the inside before trying to put a plant in it.

Eventually, she reached the other bank. Telchide forgot to turn away as she lifted herself out of the water and onto the rocks. He could see her naked form quite clearly, if in less detail than if she were standing in front of him.

"Are you just going to stare at her then?" Lucrezia teased.

Telchide flushed but did not immediately turn away.

"I want to see if she gets the plant."

"Mm hmm, I can tell you what happens. Turn around now."

Telchide's heart was beating so loudly that he could barely hear her. It was only when she laid hands on his shoulders and physically turned him away that his heart began to slow.

"She's taking the box further up the rocks. Now she's taking the gloves out and turning the box upside down. I can't see any water dripping out, but it's hard to see that far. The lid is back on now. She's taking it closer to the plants. Well, that's an awkward way to hold it," Lucrezia snickered. "I wouldn't want that squished up against my bare breasts."

Telchide fought the urge to turn around and look. He wished Lucrezia would keep her comments to the task at hand rather than Aveline's body.

"She's close to the plants now. The box is on the rocks. The lid's off."

"Has she got the gloves on yet?"

"Yes, of course. She put them on when she took them out of the box."

"You didn't say that!" Telchide answered peevishly.

"Assumed action." Lucrezia waved dismissively. "Now, she's walking towards the plants. No, she's changed her mind. Looks like she's going to one by itself."

Telchide nodded. "Smart move. She won't want any of them arcing out to her."

"Ouch! Too late."

Telchide could not be damned with decorum any longer. He turned to see Aveline heaving herself up from the rocks.

"Where did it hit her?"

"What difference does it make?" Lucrezia asked in annoyance.

"Did it hit her gloves or her body? Did she try to dry herself? Is the water making things worse?"

Lucrezia answered slowly, keeping her eyes on Aveline. "Actually, it arced towards the nearest foot when she was close to it."

Telchide watched in horror as Aveline was struck again, this time on her arm above the glove. It must not have been so bad as her only reaction was to step back and rub at the spot.

"Aveline!" he yelled as loudly as he could. She hesitated a moment but walked back towards the plant.

"Aveline!" he yelled again, prodding Lucrezia.

She joined him in yelling her name. This time Aveline stopped and turned, shaking her head.

"Dry yourself!" he screamed at the top of his lungs.

Lucrezia added her voice to his own and Aveline looked at her wet skin. Then at the environment around her. Telchide did the same thing. There was nothing available to dry herself with.

"The rocks," Lucrezia breathed out. Telchide watched curiously as Lucrezia dipped her hand in the water, then dragged it against the hot rocks.

"Dry," she said, holding her hand up. She stood again and yelled out to Aveline.

"The rocks! Use the rocks!"

Aveline cupped her hand to her ear. Lucrezia pointed down at the rocks. Aveline looked down in confusion and back at Lucrezia, who made odd movements with her hands and body. Aveline paused, then lay herself down on the rocks.

Telchide had trouble breathing as he watched her roll around on the hot rocks.

"You know, you *could* look away now."

Telchide tried to huff indignantly, but all that came out was a squeaky cough.

"I told her to bring her clothes. That would've sorted the whole problem without ... this."

He gestured to the naked woman across the lake, draping herself across the rocks to dry off. Eventually, Aveline stood up and inspected herself. Obviously happy with the result, she walked back towards the lone sparking plant.

Telchide held his breath as she reached out her hand towards it. The plant sparked towards her. The only difference this time was that she was closer. Aveline was thrown back and fell to the ground. She did not move.

"She's dead!" Telchide cried in despair.

Lucrezia peered across the lake, her hand shading her eyes.

"No. I think she's breathing. This is ridiculous. How's she meant to get to the plant if it shocks her no matter what?"

Telchide frantically turned the thought over in his mind. Trying not to think how hurt Aveline could be.

"That's it!" he shouted, startling Lucrezia. "The plant loses its spark overnight. All she has to do is wait until after sunset."

"That's hours away yet," Lucrezia pointed out.

"Precisely! That will give us time to find a way around this lake without swimming across it. We'll bring her clothes with us."

For once, Lucrezia did not argue with him. He knew neither of them was willing to jump into the steaming lake. No one else had managed to bear the heat as well as Aveline.

"Aveline, stay there!" Lucrezia shouted. "We're coming to you."

There was no movement. Telchide hoped that she had suffered no permanent harm. He gathered up her clothes, stuffed them into her bag and shouldered it. He looked in both directions along the lake. It looked almost the same, but there appeared to be a slight narrowing on the eastern side.

"That way."

He began walking without giving Lucrezia a chance to voice her own opinion.

***

They walked all afternoon and well into the evening before reaching the tip of the lake. It tapered down to a stream where they could probably jump over to the other side. Telchide went first, almost losing his footing on the slippery surface and pitched himself forward to fall on the rocky bank instead of in the stream. He got to his feet and held out his scratched hands to Lucrezia. She looked at the stream with scepticism.

"Lucrezia, we don't have time for this," he said impatiently. "Either Aveline is still lying there in need of your assistance, or she's woken to find we aren't across from her anymore. Imagine how hurt she might be right now and you're too afraid to jump across this trickle of a creek."

He could see the blood rushing to her head. It was exactly what he was counting on. Lucrezia pursed her lips together, took a few running steps and leapt over the stream. She teetered on the edge of the rocks, and Telchide caught hold of her arms to pull her to safety.

"Thank you," she said with uncharacteristic gratitude.

Telchide tipped his head in surprised acknowledgment.

They picked and stumbled their way over the black rocks. The starlight was not bright enough to see clearly by and the moon was refusing to make an appearance. Telchide was determined to not stop walking, but when he heard Lucrezia begin to struggle behind him, he turned back, silently drew her arm through his own and supported her as they continued on.

***

Hours later, Telchide thought he saw a lump just ahead that was definitely not rock-like. He dropped Lucrezia's arm and dashed towards it, catching his feet on the sharp rocks sticking out at odd angles. The sharp pain barely slowed him. He knelt by Aveline's side. She looked to be sleeping peacefully. He powered up the friction light and pulled her clothes out of her bag. As he covered her with the clothes, his fingers brushed her skin. It felt wrong for him to find such pleasure in the sensation when she was in this horrid situation – he did not know if she would ever wake again.

"Chide?" Aveline said softly, without opening her eyes. "Where's Lucrezia?"

Telchide almost cried in relief, his hand clutching at her shoulder.

"She's coming, just a few steps behind me."

"Could you turn around until I'm dressed?"

"Oh." He snatched his hand away. "Of course."

He hurriedly stood and moved away, turning his back from her covered form. Lucrezia laughed mockingly as she passed him. Telchide waited impatiently as Lucrezia helped Aveline dress. He found it inordinately odd that their situations were now reversed. Aveline had been dressing a half drowned Lucrezia only a week or so ago.

It was taking a long time. Longer than he'd expected. Females had more complicated clothing than men most of the time, like Aveline's long green coat with silver trimmings that showed her figure to great advantage – but here, she only had work pants and shirts.

Telchide yawned. He hadn't realised how tired he was until now. The strain of the day was catching up with him. He sat down and closed his eyes to rest them a moment while Lucrezia helped Aveline dress.

***

Telchide flinched at the hand on his shoulder. He was no longer sitting but lying on the warm black rocks. Lucrezia was hovering over him. He looked up at her in surprise.

"You fell asleep," she told him.

"That's because you were taking such a long time." He yawned widely. "Why *were* you taking so long?"

Lucrezia did not answer immediately. Telchide sat up quickly to find Aveline still lying on the rocks. At least her clothes were on now.

"Lucrezia, is she ... well?"

"I can't tell exactly what that plant did, but the least of it are burns along her arms and leg where it sparked out at her. I did what I could for the burns. I even tried wiping the burns with water from the lake – it seemed to make a difference with both of your injuries when we first arrived." She shrugged. "I'm hoping that, and a good night's rest will help her."

Telchide couldn't take his eyes off Aveline. He should have insisted they go the long way around, found a way to be more careful. He should've ... done more to protect her.

"This isn't your fault, Chide," Lucrezia said gently, resting a hand on his back. "You couldn't have stopped her any more than I. You should go to her now. I think you can provide more comfort to her than I can."

"Not after what you said to her," Telchide replied woodenly. "You had no right to treat her like you did. And now I've lost any hope I had."

He felt Lucrezia remove her hand from his back. She took a step away.

"I apologised to her. I didn't want to have those words be our last, just in case."

A spear of ice tore through Telchide's heart.

"You think she's going to die tonight?" he asked in a panic.

Lucrezia sighed. "I don't know. Probably not. But I think she would rather have you by her side than not. Do as you please."

Telchide watched as Lucrezia went to lay down as far away from the light plants as she could. He almost laughed at the sight of them. They looked like normal plants in the starlight. He should harvest a few now – that was why they were here – but he did not want to waste time. If this were to be his only night with Aveline, he would spend every minute with her.

He walked carefully across the warm rocks until he reached Aveline. Her chest rose and fell in regular, but shallow movements and her burns were wrapped. Telchide stared down at Aveline a moment longer before using his bag as a pillow and lying down beside her.

She was warm to the touch, but that was not surprising, given she was lying on a bed of heated rocks. Usually, Telchide would avoid such a warm spot, preferring to lie at the edge of the rock bed. But that was impossible here – the sparking plants were on the edge, and he refused to go near them.

He expected some kind of reaction from Aveline when he lay next to her, but there was nothing. Not a sound, not a movement. Telchide carefully lifted her head and placed it in the crook of his shoulder so that he could hold her close without hindering her breathing. She murmured something but did not try to pull away. Perhaps he imagined it, but Telchide thought she nestled her head in closer to him.

He stayed awake as long as he could, cradling her gently in his arms, not wanting their time together to end.

There were pins and needles in Telchide's arm as he tried to wipe the sleep from his eyes. The sun was blazing down on him, forcing him to shield his face with the one hand that was working. What in Caldera's smoke was wrong with the other one?

He opened his eyes properly and turned his head to the side. Aveline's face was so close to his that he could easily kiss her. So, he did. He kissed her forehead, her nose, her cheek.

She startled awake.

Telchide almost cried out in surprise. He was so overjoyed to see that she was alive that he kissed her cheek again and again. It was only after the third kiss that he realised she wasn't pulling back. She was staring at him with a strange look. He closed his eyes and risked everything by kissing her lips. She did not stop him, but the kiss tasted saltier than he had imagined it would.

Aveline was crying. Not sobbing, not whimpering, she just had tears running down her face. Telchide stopped kissing her.

"What's wrong? Should I not have kissed you?"

Aveline shook her head, a tear flying off onto the rocks below.

"Lucrezia probably didn't think I heard, but I knew she thought I might die last night. And here I am, alive and kissing you. I couldn't be happier. I really couldn't."

Telchide frowned. His confusion was swept aside as Aveline leaned forward to kiss him. Her lips were so soft and smooth. He put his free arm around her waist and pulled her closer to him. All that was between them now were thin layers of clothing. He could feel every curve, every muscle. It was almost more than he could bear. In surprise, he realised that he too was crying. It had been so long since he'd felt anything that could even come close to how he felt to have her in his arms, warm and alive and kissing him back.

Aveline ran her fingers through his hair, and he couldn't help but frown at the sight of her bandaged arms. He ran his fingers up gently past her bandages, to her smooth, bronze neck, pulling her in for a kiss. Her moans of pleasure only made him pull her ever closer to him. He forgot about her injuries until she winced in pain.

"I'm sorry," he whispered, pulling back.

"No, don't stop!" Aveline sighed.

Hearing the urgency in her voice, he wished he could rip off her clothes but, no, *that* would definitely be going too far. Kissing any skin that was already bare though, how could there be any harm in that?

Gently, he slid her off his arm and bent down to kiss her jawline, the crook of her neck, her shoulders. How far down did her shirt go? Not far enough!

He pulled at it with his teeth. It easily moved aside. He took the opportunity to kiss her clavicle, the bare skin just below the neckline. Her chest was heaving up and down heavily. He kissed every bare part of her that he could, running his tongue along her neck, nibbling on her ears.

She pulled him down on top of her and held him close. So close that he could only kiss her neck and her incredibly bare shoulder.

"No more," she whispered. He felt her feet curl as she pulled him closer. "It's too much. I ... want you too much."

Telchide nodded automatically.

"Yes, you're right. It's too much. Just. One. More. Kiss."

She turned her head towards his and he kissed her, gently biting on her lower lip. Her groan made him want her even more. But she pushed her hand against his chest.

"No more," she panted. "No more."

Telchide drew away from her. It was the only way. If he touched her, he knew he would start kissing her all over again. And that would certainly lead to more than just kisses. They were on a dangerous island and ... they were not alone.

Telchide looked around their campsite for Lucrezia but couldn't see her. He frantically wondered if she'd been a witness to anything that had just happened. Aveline saw his panicked reaction and mistook it.

"I didn't mean no more ... ever. Just not right now."

Telchide smiled at that. "Believe me, I understood you. I was just looking for Lucrezia. She was here last night, after all."

Aveline froze.

"Do you think she saw? Or heard?" Aveline covered her mouth with her hand, eyes darting everywhere.

When he couldn't spot Lucrezia, Telchide started to relax. After all, it was the Alchimista who'd told him to comfort Aveline, to spend time with her. Did it really matter whether she'd seen or heard anything?

There was a loud splash from the lake. Telchide looked up and down the bank but couldn't see anything. Another loud splash drew his attention in a different direction. Corrado was across the lake, throwing rocks to get their attention.

"Corrado!" he shouted. "How did you find us?"

When the marinaio shook his head, Telchide motioned for him to walk up the east bank and then back down to them. The marinaio nodded and began walking.

"Are you two lovebirds decent?"

Telchide and Aveline sat up to see Lucrezia in amongst the energy plants. They were not alight yet but Telchide's heart nearly skipped a beat, nonetheless. He did not want Lucrezia getting shocked by the plants any more than he had wanted Aveline to.

"Of course, we're decent," Aveline replied, pulling her shirt back up over her shoulder. "Get out of there before you hurt yourself!"

Lucrezia held up a small plant in her gloved hand. "I can feel them warming up. But they aren't quite there yet. I've dug up this little one to put in your box, Chide. Bring it over here."

Chide? Had things changed so much between them last night that Lucrezia had lost her animosity towards him? Not wanting to give her any reason to revert to her usual caustic form, Telchide quickly located the insulated box.

As he walked over to her, he held it down low in front of him. He did not need her to see how aroused he'd become with Aveline. That would simply not do. Unfortunately, by the smirk she gave him, Telchide thought it entirely possible that she'd not only seen but heard everything.

Telchide cleared his throat and placed the box on the ground to open it. Lucrezia gently settled the young plant into one of the compartments of the box.

"It will need soil," Telchide told her. "The soil here is vastly different to Tor'Esint."

"Well, now, look who's been brushing up on his horticulture."

Telchide rolled his eyes at her. Lucrezia smiled and went back to scoop up some of the dark soil. Telchide could feel the plants warming up from where he was. Lucrezia was too close to them. He reached out a hand and pulled her away just as the first plant arced a spark out towards her.

It missed her and caught another plant instead, starting a chain reaction between them all the plants in the clump.

Lucrezia got to her feet unsteadily and handed the lid to Telchide. He covered the box up quickly. This little one might not be as close to the hot rocks as the others, but that did not mean it would not warm up with the sun's rays alone. He did not mean to give it the chance to shock any of them.

Carefully, he pegged the box shut and took it over to where he'd left Aveline. She still had a gorgeous flush to her cheeks, but her attire was in order now. Telchide noted with some amusement that she appeared to be wearing even *more* clothing now, a plain brown coat over her work pants and shirt. She smiled shyly at him, and his stomach flipped. How did she have so much power over him?

"I take it you two sorted things out between you this morning," Lucrezia said in an offhand manner.

Telchide did not know how to answer. He hoped things were, but that might only be while they were here on Sentigura Caldera, not back in their normal lives in Tor'Esint.

"I think we're well on the way to sorting things out," Aveline replied evasively. "That doesn't seem to bother you anymore."

Lucrezia shrugged. "It never bothered me in the first place. I just wanted you to know how people back home will react. You actually suit each other well enough, I suppose, though I would never want to spend my life with anyone like either of you."

"Yes." Aveline nodded. "That's why you never did find a companion. I don't think you'd be happy spending your life with, well, *anyone*."

Lucrezia laughed. "My standards are higher than yours, that's all."

Telchide followed the bouncing conversation. Had he ever said these things to Lucrezia, it would have earned him a sound scolding. Now, it appeared he was part of an inner circle of friends which he found both pleasant and strange.

"Shall we take a look at the plant, then?" he asked.

Aveline and Lucrezia both looked at the box sceptically.

"I don't think we have what we need to protect ourselves from it," Aveline admitted. "I managed to get closer to the plants when I was dry, but they still sparked out at me."

"And they'd have gotten me just now if you hadn't pulled me away," Lucrezia added.

Telchide thought on it for a while. Bits and pieces of information were floating around his mind, he just needed to stitch them together the right way – he just knew it. It all had to do with the leather gloves. They'd protected Aveline up to a point. Could it be so simple?

"Did anyone bring needle and thread?" he asked.

They didn't answer. Lucrezia looked at him then glanced at Aveline.

"See how long it took him to ask a bizarre question? He's got a plan, he just hasn't explained it," Aveline said.

Telchide frowned. "Isn't it obvious? We need to stitch the three pairs of gloves into one pair of much longer gloves."

Aveline laughed lightly and patted his cheek. Lucrezia stared at him in surprise.

"You didn't hear any of our conversation, did you?"

Telchide shook his head.

"We were discussing the fact that we ought to wait until night to study the plant."

"Oh," he replied disheartened. How had he missed that conversation? He must have been thinking too hard. "I really do think the long gloves will work. I have scissors to cut them to shape, if anyone has a way to put them back together again."

Lucrezia rubbed the back of her neck. "I *do* have needle and thread, but it's meant to be used for stitching flesh, like the ones I used on your head. I doubt the needle will go through toughened leather gloves and, even if it did, it would go dull too quickly to be of any use if someone is injured again."

She was right, of course she was, but Telchide was so certain his idea would work. He did not want to study the plant at night. He wanted to be able to see how it worked during the day. Test if the spark could provide energy in any way that they could harness.

"I have another idea!"

He ran over to his bag and fetched his friction light. The lightbulb only worked with the energy created from the friction when the handle was wound up. If the plant could make the lightbulb glow, then they could be certain that it was indeed a power source, and not simply a health hazard.

He pulled on the gloves and took the friction light closer to the sparking plants. When he was a few piedi away, he got down on his stomach, with his arm stretched out in front. He pushed the friction light along pollice by pollice.

When he was about two piedi away, the nearest plant sent a spark arcing out towards him. It hit the friction light. He felt the force of it through the leather glove, but the spark did not travel up his arm. Telchide sighed in relief. He left the friction light where it was and crawled back a safe distance before sitting up to watch.

Aveline and Lucrezia soon came to join him. The three of them sat and observed the friction light for a half hour. The bulb lit up every time a spark of light reached it. Sometimes it glowed for seconds at a time, other times, it lit up for minutes. The plants really did seem to provide it with the energy it needed.

Telchide ducked and covered his face as the lightbulb exploded with a tinkling crackle.

"What just happened?" Lucrezia asked, checking herself for bits of glass.

"The light exploded," Telchide replied. Really, he didn't understand why people asked such ridiculous questions.

"For Caldera's sake!"

Aveline placed a hand on Lucrezia's arm and turned to Telchide.

"She means, *why* did the lightbulb explode?"

"Oh well, that's obvious. There was too much power."

Aveline nodded, but Lucrezia only looked at them both in confusion.

"Lightbulbs, especially ones as little as this, don't need much power. If they get a bit too much, the wires inside melt. If they get quite a lot more than they need or the glass heats up too quickly, they explode."

"I see," Lucrezia replied slowly. "So, the plants are powerful."

"Well, yes," Aveline answered. "We knew that from last night. What we need to see is if we can control it at all. Does a single plant like this spark out like the groups do? Does it produce as much energy on its own? Does it need the hot rocks and that specific soil to survive? There are just so many questions!"

"And we need to be on the Caldera to answer them?"

"Of course!" Telchide nodded. "What if we take this little one home with us and it dies on the way, or soon after we return, because we don't know what it needs to survive? Then the entire trip would've been a waste of time."

He saw Aveline's eyebrows shoot up. He fidgeted with the buttons on his shirt.

"Well, of course, I don't mean the *entire* trip would be a waste of time. Many good things have happened here too."

Lucrezia laughed. "It's rather too easy to make him react like that, isn't it?"

Aveline smiled mischievously and nodded. Telchide couldn't help but feel that he was being made fun of. He stopped playing with the buttons and took the box away from the ladies in a huff. He wanted to see how this little plant would react on its own.

"Chide, I don't think that's a good idea," Aveline called out to him.

He ignored her and plunged into his experiment. With a gloved hand, he unlocked the box and slid the lid out. The little plant was not sparking inside. Telchide held up the lid as a sort of shield, with the rubber section facing towards the plant.

Nothing happened.

For a long time.

Just as Telchide was growing bored waiting, a tiny spark arched from one leaf to another. He leaned in closer to get a better look. Pale blue jagged lines of energy shot from one leaf to another, often sparking off chain reactions. The sparks were much smaller than when grouped together with larger plants. He tentatively reached out a gloved hand and held it above the plant.

There was no reaction.

He touched one of the leaves with the leather glove. Still no reaction to the glove. But he noticed that as one leaf bent onto another, a sharp zap rang through the air. He could taste the scent of ozone in his mouth – like the air in a lightning storm. His nose wrinkled up in distaste.

"Any luck?" Aveline asked from behind him.

"It does work by itself, and it might be easier to tame away from the other plants. I just wish I had another lightbulb to experiment with."

Aveline did not answer. Telchide turned to see her walking away. Decidedly odd behaviour.

He caught a small, green leaf floating by in the lake and dropped it onto the plant. Within seconds, it burned down to ash. So, still quite powerful then. If only there were other things to test with it. Telchide wished for his entire workshop, then thought better of it. He did not want such an unpredictable plant in his workshop. It made him cringe just to imagine the damage it could do.

"Try this one."

Aveline held out a larger bulb than the one he'd destroyed.

"I only have one more of these, so don't break them all today."

Telchide took it with his gloved hand and held it carefully high above the plant. It sparked out towards the bulb but did not connect. He lowered it bit by bit until the light arced out and touched it. The lightbulb glowed brightly the entire time the spark was touching it.

Experimentally, Telchide lifted the lightbulb away. It glowed for another few seconds before going out. Once more, he lowered it to the plant. This time, he left it there for as long as his arm could stay in one place. When he pulled it away and let it rest in his gloved hands, it continued to glow for a few minutes.

"That's remarkable!" Telchide exclaimed.

Lucrezia wandered over to see what the fuss was about.

"Not *so* remarkable," Aveline replied glumly. "It means we would need to sell these plants along with our inventions because the charge doesn't last."

"The charge doesn't last," Telchide said slowly. "But what if we could make the fuel cell I mentioned?"

He placed the lid back on the box and handed the lightbulb to Aveline. The three of them sat together, lost in thought.

"What about a liquid store?" Lucrezia suggested. "It seems to have an exaggerated reaction to water. Do you think it might keep its charge in some sort of solution?"

"Like the blazer solution?" Telchide asked.

"No. That's more of an alchemical reaction. The blazer solution reacts to..." Lucrezia hesitated, "...something in the engine and creates energy. If the water keeps its charge, you wouldn't need it to mix with or touch anything in particular for the energy to be produced."

"It's worth a try," Telchide admitted. "Do you have an empty vial?"

Lucrezia nodded and went to look through her bag. She held up an empty vial and went to fill it with water from the steaming lake. Telchide looked at it dubiously.

"This water's different to the water in Tor'Esint."

"True, but we don't have any of our home water left," she told him. "Just try it."

Shrugging, Telchide put his gloves back on and took the lid off the box. Aveline held up the lid as a shield to give him two free hands to work with. He took the vial of water from Lucrezia and placed it in an empty compartment next to the plant. Eventually, the blue light sparked out to the water, making it bubble. Telchide knew it would not take much heat for that to happen as the water was already quite warm to begin with.

"How long do you think we need to leave it there for?" he asked.

The ladies both shrugged. Telchide reached out to get the vial. He may as well try it now. Aveline passed him the lightbulb and he placed the coiled section carefully into the water. Was that a brief spark of light? Lucrezia sat up straighter.

"Try it again, for longer this time," Aveline said. She looked confused. Perhaps she'd not seen the light.

Telchide returned her lightbulb and placed the vial back in its compartment. He looked at his pocket watch and timed five minutes. With his gloved hand, he couldn't tell how much heat was in the water, or if that would make the difference.

Aveline handed him the lightbulb, which he placed in the water. It glowed, continually, for precisely five minutes. Perhaps he'd looked incorrectly at the minute hand. He gave the watch to Lucrezia, the bulb to Aveline and put the vial back in the box.

"Time it for ten minutes," he instructed Lucrezia. "This is too much of a coincidence."

Ten minutes later, Lucrezia called out the time. Telchide nervously took out the vial and put the bulb back in it. The effect was immediate. The light was no brighter than the last time, but it did last for ten minutes.

He stared at the pocket watch that Lucrezia dangled in front of him. It really was ten minutes. But how could that be?

"Let's do one more test today," Aveline suggested. "Charge the water for another ten minutes, then leave it for an hour before putting the lightbulb in. See if it still holds its charge then."

Telchide put the vial back in the box while Aveline put the bulb away and Lucrezia scrounged around for a stopper. She eventually found one. Telchide was not confident that a cork would be the right material, but they had no other option.

***

"What took you so long?" Telchide asked when Corrado finally appeared. It was already late afternoon and Telchide had begun to lose hope that the captain would find his way to them.

"Do you know how far I had to walk to find somewhere to cross?"

"Not more than a few miglia," Telchide replied confidently.

Corrado laughed at him. "Try eight miglia!"

Telchide stared in confusion. "No, Lucrezia and I found a narrow stream not more than two or three miglia from here."

"The place I would've broken my neck if I'd jumped?"

"That's the one," Lucrezia called out from the side of the lake, drying her hair. With Aveline's guidance, she'd finally managed to submerge herself without getting burnt. Aveline's burns were significantly better than they ought to have been and Lucrezia had begun theorising about the healing qualities of the water. Telchide refused to bathe in the water but had been persuaded to at least rinse his clothes in it and scrub himself down from the bank, suffering their amusement at his embarrassment as he did so.

"If Chide hadn't caught me, I would've broken *my* neck last night."

Aveline looked at him in surprise. "Becoming quite the dashing hero, aren't you?"

He brushed off the comment. What could he say? That he'd only saved Lucrezia because she was the best chance he had of saving Aveline? No, that would not do. And, if he was honest with himself, that wasn't entirely truthful. He simply couldn't let someone be hurt or die.

Days ago, when Aveline had slipped off the ledge, he thought he'd only reacted so quickly because of his affection for her. That was true in a sense, but it turned out that he couldn't knowingly let anyone come to harm.

"Well, whatever the delay, you're here now. How did you find us?"

Corrado pointed to the sparking plants. "I was going to go to higher ground, but figured I'd only get lost again. Took me a while, but I managed to climb these coconut trees. Do you know how far you can see from the top of one of them?"

Telchide shook his head.

"Well, a *long* way," Corrado continued. "I climbed one every now and then. They led me straight here. Well, almost. I went up and down a lot trying to find you. And here I am."

The marinaio gave him an impish grin. Telchide found he liked the fellow more and more with every passing day. It wasn't Corrado's fault that his first mate had been a wretched character. The captain had quickly come to his senses and been quite reasonable since then.

"So did you get one of them plants?"

Telchide in all his excitement, showed Corrado the little plant Lucrezia had managed to harvest then put the lid back on.

"I was just about to see if the water held its charge."

He put the gloves on and looked expectantly at Aveline and Lucrezia. The ladies shared an exasperated look but soon returned with the required elements. Telchide unstoppered the vial and dipped the bulb into it. To his disappointment, it did not glow.

"Where did we go wrong?" he asked no one in particular.

"Perhaps we misunderstood the elements," Aveline suggested. "Rubber appears to work well as an insulator, and water is certainly a conductor. But perhaps it isn't useful as a permanent fuel cell."

Telchide pondered that. But where was he to find a fuel cell? He didn't have a blazermobile, nor did he know what the actual fuel cell in that looked like, or what the components were.

"What happens if you dunk it in water?" Corrado asked.

Lucrezia laughed. "Don't you know anything about plants? You would only succeed in killing it."

"How do you know?" he asked, crossing his arms. "These plants are different to what you're used to. If I'm right, then all you need is a plant in water."

It was an interesting idea. But Telchide was not willing to kill their only specimen just yet.

"What about a leaf?" he suggested. "What if we submerge a charged leaf into the water?"

"That might work while the sun is up, if you leave the vial in direct light," Aveline said. "But I doubt it will be of any use in the dark, even if the leaf produces any power when cut off the plant."

"It can't hurt to try," Lucrezia said. "Where are those other gloves? I think we might need more than one person for this."

Telchide waited impatiently for Lucrezia to return. Aveline placed a hand on his knee. He hadn't realised he was tapping his heel until she stilled him with her touch. Lucrezia passed the last set of gloves to Aveline as she put her own pair on.

As Telchide unlocked the box, Corrado stopped him.

"Won't you need a knife or something to cut the leaf?"

"Metal will likely increase the effect," Telchide explained. "I don't want to risk it burning a hole in my gloves. I'll just try breaking one off."

He took hold of a leaf from the plant and pulled. It was a lot tougher than he'd thought. He bent it back and forth, weakening the joint. Eventually, it came off in his hand.

Lucrezia unstoppered the vial of water and held it out to him. He dropped the leaf in. There was an immediate reaction. Light sparked all through the water, with bits of it shooting out of the top of the vial. Lucrezia quickly stoppered it. Telchide stared at it in shock. He'd not expected that to happen.

Corrado, foolish man that he was, reached out a finger and touched the glass. With a yelp, he pulled his finger away and sucked on it.

"That's *hot*!"

Aveline took off her gloves and reached out a hand but stopped short of actually touching the vial.

"I can feel the heat radiating off it," she said excitedly.

Telchide wanted to feel the effect but held himself back. There was more experimenting to be done. He pulled out his pocketknife and held it close to the vial. The sparks of light intensified dramatically. The strange thing was, they were now concentrated on the side of the vial nearest the knife. He moved the knife around and watched in fascination as the lights moved along with it.

"Is it any hotter?" he asked Aveline. She placed her hand near the vial again and shook her head.

"Interesting. Well, I suppose that's enough experimenting for today. The sun will go down soon, and we can't light a fire here."

"We could try burning one of them plants." Corrado pointed to the sparking plants. "You know, after they finish glowing."

Telchide stared at him. "I'm not certain that would be the wisest thing to do."

Corrado shrugged. "Let's have some of them sardines before night then. I've been missing them."

Well, that was it then. There was nothing else they could do until morning. Telchide fetched his bag of canned food. Once again, Corrado had the sardines all to himself while the rest of them shared two cans of vegetables. It really was an ingenious way to store food for an extended period.

A sudden thought struck him. What if they were to put a leaf inside one of the empty cans, without water. Would it have a similar effect as the glass vial? Of all the things he'd brought with him, a pair of long handled tongs was not in the list. He hardly dared try it with only a pair of gloves to protect him. It was something he could work on tomorrow.

It was getting dark now. Time to sleep. He set out his blanket closer to the water than the plants and lay down upon it.

Chapter 23 – Argentodi 25 Mercantili 230 Years After Implosion

Telchide's arm was wrapped around Aveline's waist, holding her close. Bemused by how she got there without waking him, he breathed in the scent of her. It was a rather interesting mixture of sweat and singed hair. That did not bother him. He was just happy to have her so close to him and already mostly healed – Lucrezia was probably right about the water. He kissed the tangled mess of hair and hugged her tighter.

Aveline turned her head to face him and kissed him, so close to his mouth that he could almost taste it. She was the most wonderful person to wake up to. It felt so right to have her there, with him. No one there to judge them. No reason they couldn't stay with one another. At least on this island. That thought niggled at him, but he ignored it. He would savour every moment he had with Aveline before they got back to Tor'Esint.

"Hey, lovebirds, the plants will be starting to warm up again soon. If you want another one, we should get it now."

Aveline turned away from Telchide to stick her tongue out at Lucrezia.

"Go and get one, then. Chide doesn't need to save you every time."

Lucrezia laughed and walked off. Telchide marvelled at how much their relationship had changed. Aveline rolled over to face him and he kissed her softly on the mouth. She parted her lips ever so slightly and traced her tongue across his lips. He shivered in pleasure and pressed his tongue against hers.

They stayed in each other's embrace, kissing intensely until a nearby cough interrupted them. Corrado! Telchide had forgotten the marinaio was with them again.

"Begging yer pardon," he said with a smirk, "but the Alchimista's on her way back with two more of those plants. I reckon you'd better get the box ready for her. Seems like they're already starting to spark."

Telchide groaned as Aveline disentangled herself from his embrace and nodded to the box. Wishing he could have spent more time with her, he went to perform his Inventore duties. Before opening the box, he pulled on the leather gloves.

Lucrezia hurried forward, holding the two plants out at arm's length on either side of her. They were larger than the one she'd brought him yesterday. He hoped they would still fit in the box. They were already sparking out by the time she reached him, though the sparks were not reaching her skin.

She put the plants in two of the empty compartments and quickly stepped back. Telchide did not blame her. As soon as they got near each other, the three plants started arcing across to each other. Telchide frowned. It certainly seemed that the more plants there were, the more exaggerated the effect of the sparking. He carefully slid the lid back on, trying not to crush the plants inside.

"Right, well, let's see if the water kept its charge with the leaf in it," Lucrezia said, clapping her gloved hands together.

Aveline found the lightbulb and brought it over to them. Lucrezia held up the vial. There was no sparking light in it now. Aveline touched it with her bare hand.

"It still feels warm, but that could just as easily be from the heat of the rocks."

Telchide passed her a pair of gloves. She quickly put them on before nodding to Lucrezia. The Alchimista unstoppered the vial and held it out. Aveline placed the lightbulb in the liquid. It glowed, but only dimly and not for very long.

"What a waste!" Aveline cried out in defeat. "If the sparking plant only works during the day, when we don't need as much power, what use is it?"

Lucrezia crossed her arms. "Oh, but when *I* said that you didn't agree."

Aveline glared at her.

Telchide refused to get pulled into their spat. He had more ideas to try out and refused to be distracted. He fetched one of the cans from the night before – one with the lid still partially attached – and went to rinse it in the lake. When it was as clean as possible, he brought it back to their experiment site and dried it with a spare shirt, being ever so careful not to cut himself, or the shirt, on the sharp edges.

He waited patiently for the plants to be at full sparking capacity before making his move. He reached out and broke off a leaf from one of the larger plants and placed it in the metal can. It had an explosive effect that did not ease until he closed the lid. Even then, sparks flew through the smallest gaps where the can opener had bent the metal to a point where it would not connect.

"Do you have any spare rubber or leather?" he asked Aveline.

When she did not answer, he turned to find all three of his companions staring at him open-mouthed.

"Your gloves then, if you have nothing else."

He waited, but she did not move.

"Aveline!"

Aveline blinked. "Yes. Of course. My gloves."

She took off the gloves and threw them at his feet. Telchide knelt and placed the can, lid down, on one of the gloves. He wrapped the other glove around it and looked for a way to tie them both in place.

"I need twine, cloth, something," he told them.

Corrado fished a length of twine from his pocket and threw it towards Telchide. It did not reach him. The marinaio growled and bent to pick up the twine. With exaggerated caution, he stepped closer to Telchide and held it out to him.

Telchide took it gratefully and tied the gloves in place. He inspected his handiwork with some small amount of pride.

"Now, I just need that lightbulb."

"Chide, I only have one more if you break this one," Aveline reminded him.

"Yes, yes. I know, but this could be the key to everything. Don't you want to find out?"

Aveline hesitated. Telchide waited. He knew she would agree with him. The curious Inventrice within her would not let her miss out on this opportunity to learn something new about this plant.

His patience was rewarded. She handed him the lightbulb and hovered as near as she dared to watch. Telchide stood on the opposite side of his experiment, so they could all have a decent view of what happened.

He carefully touched the lightbulb to the can. Nothing happened. Telchide rubbed his stubbled cheek in confusion. There was plenty of energy in the can. Why wasn't it working?

"Perhaps it needs more points of contact," Aveline suggested. "It was different with the liquid because the entire bottom of the globe was submerged."

Telchide nodded. "Do you have a length of copper or any metal? If not, I have a few coils of copper in my bag. Clip off a length of perhaps half a piede."

Aveline rushed to do as he requested. Telchide did not waste a moment in continuing to experiment. He placed the end of the globe in different positions on the bottom of the can. When he laid it down and had the most contact, there was a soft glow.

He smiled in satisfaction – Aveline was right. There was more than enough energy inside this can for the light. They just needed to harness it properly.

Aveline returned with a length of copper. Telchide took it with a word of thanks then proceeded to wrap the copper in a winding coil around the bottom of the globe. He left a decent portion hanging off the end and twirled that into a large circle.

Once again, he placed the lightbulb, with the extra copper, on the can. It immediately glowed brightly.

"Time it!" he called out frantically. Lucrezia pulled out her pocket watch and noted the time.

After a few minutes of holding the light globe in place, Telchide realised this really might be the key. The light did not dim at all. He called Aveline over.

"Can you hold the lightbulb in place for me? I'm going to see if I can't wind the copper around the can so that we don't have to keep holding it. I have a feeling it's going to stay lit for a longer time than any of us want to sit here with it."

Aveline took the globe from him, being careful not to let it lose contact with the can. Telchide examined the remaining wire and decided it would not be long enough to wrap around the actual can sufficiently. He went to his pack and pulled out the copper wire. Instead of clipping off a length of it, he brought the entire coil over. He lowered the glove around the can a little and wound the copper wire around it three times. Next, he attached that wire to the bottom of the globe.

When he was done, he took the bulb back from Aveline and placed it atop the can so that it still had contact but was safely nestled within the wires and would not fall and break.

He stepped back to survey his handiwork. It was quite impressive if he was being truthful. Aveline would eventually have figured it out herself – she was the most intelligent Inventrice he knew – but her mind worked in a different way to his. She was much more cautious and less prone to trying things that she wasn't already certain would work.

Perhaps that was why Nevio had such trouble with his pocket watch. If he'd taken note of how Aveline worked, he was certain to adopt some of her traits, whether consciously or not.

"How long's it been?" Corrado asked.

Lucrezia looked at her pocket watch. "Seventeen minutes."

"What now?" Corrado asked. "Are we just going to stand here and watch it all day?"

Telchide startled at the question. He would indeed be perfectly happy to do that.

"We can take it in shifts to keep watch on it. The others can spend the rest of the day as they please," Aveline stated.

"I want to hike up the inner peak," Corrado replied instantly. "No point coming all the way here and not looking in the Caldera itself."

"The peak?" Aveline asked incredulously. "It's still smoking. I don't think it's safe."

Lucrezia laughed loudly. "Safe? Veli, if the Caldera blows, *nowhere* on this island will be safe. It won't matter if we're on the peak or not."

"But how are you going to get there?" Telchide asked. "It's surrounded by these plants."

Corrado shrugged. "Mebbe not the whole way around. Mebbe I can find an easy way up. I'm going fer a walk. Anyone want to come with me?"

Lucrezia got to her feet.

"I'll come," she said. She handed the pocket watch to Telchide. "Aveline, are you coming?"

"Absolutely not!"

"Fine, then. Stay with your lover."

Telchide grinned as Aveline's face flushed crimson. He noticed that she did not dispute the label.

He made himself comfortable on the warm rocks and settled in for a long day of watching the light.

***

Telchide started in surprise as Aveline knelt behind him and wrapped her arms around his waist. He'd been so focused on watching the light that he hadn't noticed Lucrezia and Corrado leave. He was alone. With Aveline. He carefully placed the pocket watch on the coat in front of him and held her hands. They were so soft on top, but the strong fingers were evidence of the hard worker that she was.

There were some industries that were mainly dominated by one sex or the other. There was no strict rule about it, of course, but that did not stop it from happening. More women worked in the Sarti Guild. More men worked in the Inventrici and Mercantili Guilds. There were a few Guilds, like the Alchimisti, where the split was fairly even.

It was quite an achievement for Aveline to have earned her Electrum Guild Mark. She would likely have been marked harder than her male counterparts, which was entirely unfair. But Telchide knew the same occurred with the other Guilds that were dominated by one sex or the other. He knew of no way to change it, especially not now with the Inter-Guild Edict in place.

"Chide, does your mind ever stop working?" Aveline murmured in his ear.

"What a question to ask," he replied, his train of thought interrupted. "How do you even know I was thinking anything?"

"You have a tell. Every time you're consumed by your thoughts, the entire world around you disappears. If you're not writing something in your notebook, your hands clench and you freeze up."

He instantly released her. He hadn't hurt her, of that he was certain, but he'd not realised how tightly he was holding her hands until she mentioned it.

"You know ... we're quite alone now," she whispered, her breath tickling his ear.

Her hands drifted up to his chest slowly, then her nails ran down his front. Telchide groaned in pleasure, closing his eyes for the briefest moment.

"We ... need to ... keep watch," he stammered out.

"It hasn't dimmed at all in over an hour. I think we can risk at least a few minutes of pleasure without the light going out."

Aveline stood up and walked around in front of him. Telchide swallowed hard as he looked up at her beautiful figure. He tentatively reached out and touched her leg.

A lady would normally have stockings on, but Aveline had taken to wearing workpants that she'd torn off at the knees to keep cool.

She stood where she was for a few moments more, tracing the toes of her other foot around his fingers then sliding her leg along his hand. He did not know what to do, what was allowed or what she expected of him. Then she made it perfectly clear by sitting on his lap. He instinctively moved to make the two of them as close to each other as possible, only belatedly realising that she might not like that.

He tried to move her away, but Aveline wriggled herself down onto him, making the blood rush to more than just his head. Telchide pulled her in for a passionate kiss, not wanting to move from where he was.

Aveline left him in no doubt of what she wanted. She moved in such a way he had no control of what his body did, and she knew it. He'd missed this type of intimacy much more than he'd realised. Absurdly, he couldn't help wondering if he was somehow taking advantage of Aveline, even though *she* was the one who had begun this.

"Chide," Aveline murmured, running her fingers through his hair, "stop thinking so hard and just kiss me."

Telchide hadn't realised that he'd stopped kissing her when those thoughts began. All thoughts halted as he reached behind her head and pulled her in for a long, intense kiss. She responded by pushing him down onto the rocks and lying on top of him, her legs straddling either side.

He winced in pain and arched his back as the uncomfortably warm rocks irritated him. Aveline laughed and pulled out a blanket from her nearby bag. She rolled them both over so that she was the one lying on the rapidly warming blanket. She deftly removed her clothes and spread them around her blanket so that Telchide wouldn't burn himself again.

Telchide marvelled at the sight of her. Aveline gave him an oddly shy smile as she unbuttoned his shirt and pulled him down on top of her.

***

Telchide lay beside Aveline, on a heap of discarded clothing, panting heavily. He brushed the hair out of her face and kissed her once more. He hadn't felt so satisfied and at peace in such a very long time.

"Well, the light is still bright," Aveline murmured.

Telchide stared at her in confusion.

"I told you we'd have time before the light went out," she said mischievously.

Telchide couldn't help but laugh. Never in all his days had he been so wonderfully distracted by something, or someone, that he'd forgotten about an experiment or invention. It was a delightfully liberating experience. One that he was more than willing to relive again.

"You were correct indeed, my love," he replied.

Aveline tensed beside him.

"Is ... something the matter?" he asked, worried.

"My love?" she asked in a soft voice.

Telchide frowned. "Are you not?"

"I ... suppose I am," she replied softly. "I've just never been the object of anyone's affection before – not to that degree."

She sat up and began to retrieve her clothes. Telchide followed her lead and tried to make himself presentable once more.

"I thought you knew my feelings," he said quietly. "At least, I *assumed* that you knew."

Aveline looked at him with an odd expression.

"Yes, you did make it clear. I suppose I just didn't really believe you."

"Why in Caldera's smoke not?"

Aveline shrugged. "There have been many men in my past who said things to try to get what they wanted. I never gave them more than I was comfortable with, but all their words turned out to be false in the end. All of them lied to get more than they deserved from me."

Telchide looked at her for a long time, trying to decide if he wanted to know what these men wanted and what she'd agreed to give them. It was none of his business really. He'd given everything to Sebetine, and Aveline knew that. After all, he had a child, didn't he?

"Whatever those men said, whatever was done, *I* am not like that. You are my love. I have no reason, no need, to lie to you. My life is complicated enough without adding lies to it. I would never do that to you."

Aveline frowned briefly, but then smiled. Telchide couldn't read her expression.

She got up, holding her clothes close to her, and walked a distance away from him to the steaming lake and dropped her garments on the rocky shore. He did not look away this time, nor did he feel embarrassed by her nakedness anymore. Once she was submerged in the water, he turned his attention back to the light. He checked the time – it was now two and a half hours that the light had been on.

***

Hours later, the light was still glowing brightly and there was no sign of Lucrezia and Corrado. Telchide was not worried. They couldn't have gotten lost going up to the peak.

"I'm going to find some food," Aveline announced. "I'll take my clothes this time and swim across. Lucrezia showed me the safe berries and fruits. I'm sick of the canned food. I need something fresh."

Telchide almost protested, but he couldn't deny that he was longing for some fresh food. But he doubted that was the reason she was leaving. She'd barely said a word to him since bathing in the river. Telchide was not a fool. He knew it was likely because of something he'd said but couldn't understand why it had elicited such a reaction from her.

Did she not love him? He did not get the chance to ask her. She was gone for hours.

Lucrezia and Corrado finally returned as the sun began to set. It almost seemed as though Aveline was waiting for them to appear before she returned. When she did, it was with a bundle of fruits wrapped in a spare shirt. Many of the berries had leaked onto the light material. They were certain to leave a stain.

"Who's hungry?" she called out brightly.

Her clothes were dripping wet and clung to her slender form, but that did not seem to bother her. She laid out her spare shirt on the rocks and everyone immediately dove into the pile. Within minutes, the precious treasure trove of fresh fruits and berries were gone. It was not nearly enough to fill everyone, but it was a good start.

The plants lining the foot of the Caldera's peak began to dim. Their sparks grew less frequent, eventually dying out altogether. The lightbulb was still glowing. Admittedly it was dimmer than before, but it was still alight. Telchide wondered if it would've worked all night had they taken a leaf just before the sun set. No point wasting thought on it now. That was an experiment for tomorrow. Now all he could do was continue to watch this light until it stopped glowing.

"Did you find a way up to the Caldera's peak?" Aveline asked.

Lucrezia shook her head. "We walked the entire way around the peak, but there are plants everywhere. If neither of you object, we're going to start out early tomorrow morning, before the plants start sparking. That way we can cross through them and climb up to the peak without danger."

"So, you'll be gone all day?" Aveline asked, a hint of worry in her voice.

Lucrezia looked from Aveline to Telchide.

"Did I miss something?" she asked. "Is there a reason we shouldn't be gone all day?"

"No," Aveline said a little too quickly.

Telchide risked a glance in her direction. She was rubbing her arms in the same distracted manner she always did when she was worried about something.

"Telchide, what happened?"

Telchide rubbed his stubbled cheek. He was not about to reveal their activities.

"Aveline?" Lucrezia asked more insistently. "If you don't tell me then I shall take it upon myself to be your chaperone the entire rest of the trip. Is *that* what you want?"

"Crez, *please*. It's not like that," Aveline said quietly. "You know Chide would never take advantage of his situation."

Lucrezia threw her hands up in the air. "Then what?"

Telchide saw the harried look Aveline shot at him. Somehow, that look made up her mind. She took Lucrezia by the hand and led her well away from them.

"What did you do?" Corrado asked curiously.

Telchide tore his eyes away from the outline of the ladies in the low light.

"I called her 'my love'," Telchide said. "Apparently, that was the wrong thing to say."

Corrado started laughing. He laughed so loudly and for so long that Telchide grew quite frustrated.

"You lavalump!"

"I beg your pardon!" Telchide replied indignantly

"Well, you two just started fooling around, didn't you? You can't tell a woman you love her so soon! It makes them all jittery-like. They get scared. I dunno what else happened today, but she sure as Caldera's smoke don't want to be left alone with *you* and she *don't* want to have a conversation about it."

Telchide stared at Corrado in horror.

"It's settled," Lucrezia announced upon their return. "Aveline will join me tomorrow. Corrado, you're still more than welcome to come along."

Corrado looked at Telchide with a pitying expression.

"I'll stay here. Just don't go finding anything too exciting without me."

"Oh, don't worry. I only intend to be the first of us to look inside the Caldera." Lucrezia winked at him. The marinaio shook his head and laughed.

Telchide felt a gnawing sense of irritation that Lucrezia and Corrado seemed to have fallen into a very easy and friendly relationship. They never seemed to have any lasting disagreements or misunderstanding. Why couldn't things be that easy for him and Aveline?

He ate his food silently. Before anyone could involve him in any further discussions, Telchide bundled up his coat into a pillow and lay himself down on his blanket to sleep. He did not expect that Aveline would join him at any point tonight. Not after she'd reacted so badly to his declaration of love. He hugged himself tightly, a sudden wave of homesickness sweeping over him. He found himself wishing for the tiny, but affectionate, embrace of his daughter. How he missed her!

Chapter 24 – Legaramedi 26 Mercantili 230 Years After Implosion

Telchide kept to himself. He was not in a mood to talk to anyone, not even the affable marinaio. Aveline and Lucrezia crossed to the base of the Caldera's peak early in the morning, well before the sparking plants warmed up. Telchide watched in furious silence as they made their laborious way up the steep peak.

He should have been running more experiments, he knew it, but he was seething with something akin to anger. With Aveline or himself? If he knew that, then perhaps he could stop. Perhaps he wasn't angry with Aveline at all. She had every right to react as she did, especially given the fact that he was still committed.

Was he angry with himself, then, for expecting things to go so smoothly when there was nothing at all ordinary about this situation for either one of them? He should not have expected Aveline to fall into the place of Sebetine, to act like they had been in a relationship for years rather than days. And back in Tor'Esint, was Aveline to come and live with him and Teresina ... and Serenita? How would they manage their workshops? Would she keep her workshop and her apprentice in their current location, or would they merge everything?

He shook his head in frustration. It was all too much to think about.

The only way he knew to take his mind off other matters was to dive headlong into work. Telchide took out his notebook and flipped through the pages. He looked over the findings from the past few days of experimenting. The most successful by far was the leaf in a metal can, surrounded by the leather gloves. It had lit the lightbulb for an entire day. Now to see how to harness that energy in a delayed fashion. Customers would not want to tinker with their power source, so he'd need to make it as simple for them as possible.

He sought out his makeshift fuel cell. The lightbulb was still attached, but there was no longer a glow. Nor did there seem to be any heat coming off the can itself. Telchide pulled on his gloves and got to work.

Carefully, he uncoiled the copper wire from around the can and placed the lightbulb on his coat. He didn't want to crush it. Aveline had warned him often enough that this was the second last bulb they had. Things would not go well for him if he broke it now.

Keeping the metal as far from his skin as possible, Telchide untied the twine from around the leather gloves and carefully opened the can. To his surprise, the leaf wasn't dead. True, it was no longer sparking, but he hadn't expected it to survive the night.

Telchide reached in to pull it out. His arm scraped the lid of the can, and he felt a jolt.

"Ouch!"

"What happened?" Corrado cried out, startling Telchide further. He turned to find the marinaio running towards him.

"Oh, it's nothing." Telchide rubbed his arm, where a small red line was growing darker by the second. "The metal must have retained some of the energy, that's all. I didn't expect it to shock me."

Corrado stared at him flatly. "Then why'd you wear the gloves?"

"Precaution," Telchide replied evenly. "I don't intend to kill myself because something doesn't meet with my expectations."

"You're a funny man, Inventore."

Telchide raised an eyebrow but said nothing. He turned back to his work. There was so much more he wanted to do. So many things he wanted to try the plant with. But all he had was this lightbulb.

"Corrado, how is your boat powered?"

"Coal."

"You haven't converted it to blazer power?" Telchide asked in surprise.

Corrado coughed uncomfortably. "The conversion's too expensive. Them Alchimisti know a good thing when they see one and they charge a right pretty price for it. Do you actually know anyone other than Alchimisti who have blazermobiles?"

"Aveline has a blazermobile," Telchide pointed out.

Corrado shrugged. "Then she's either got Alchimisti friends who did it cheap or she saved a mountain of money for it."

Telchide frowned. Aveline didn't *flaunt* her money, but she didn't exactly hide it either. She'd funded this entire expedition herself without a second thought. And her parents had been wealthy when she was young. He wondered if her wealth was so very great that she could afford the conversion if it was so expensive or if Corrado was correct in his assumption that her friends had given her a good price.

Refusing to let his thoughts go back to Aveline, Telchide made a proposal instead.

"How would you like your boat to be the first fuelled by a sparking plant?"

Corrado did not answer for a long moment.

"I'll pass."

"Come now, where's your sense of adventure?" Telchide prodded.

"Don't take this the wrong way, Inventore, but I don't want you burning my boat or shocking me to death."

"I assure you; I have no intention of doing either. Now, explain to me how it works."

Telchide forced Corrado to tell him as much as possible of the paddle mechanism. He drew a sketch of it as the marinaio explained how it worked, adjusting it slightly whenever Corrado pointed out an error.

"Yes, I think I can work with this." He nodded to himself. "All I need to do is direct the power from this can to that cog to make it turn. Once that's done, the rest is simple."

"Long as you can make it run and stop when you need to," Corrado pointed out unhelpfully.

"Yes," Telchide replied slowly. "We could always see if I can provide you enough power to get around the Caldera."

Corrado shook his head. "Sorry, Inventore. I'd like to help you, but I can't let you convert my boat. What'd happen if you mess it up and we can't fix it? You'll strand us on this island. Don't know about you, but I can't swim to Sant'Elba from here – and she's the closest island."

"Ah, yes, I see your point."

Telchide hated to admit defeat, but there was nothing for it. All he could experiment with was a lightbulb. He didn't even have enough material to create a music box or a watch. He fervently wished he had something else he could use.

"No matter. No matter. I'll make do with this light then. I can do that."

He turned back to the makeshift fuel cell to continue his experiments. Corrado came to sit by his side to watch. Telchide felt sorry for the marinaio – it must have been a sore blow to be stuck with him all day. He knew he was not a great conversationalist when he was working. Telchide grimaced. Nor at the best of times.

"What do you think'll happen if you put a whole plant in the can?"

"I presume it would die from lack of sunlight," Telchide mused.

"So, it's the sunlight it needs? Not just warmth that gives it a spark?"

Telchide paused.

"How're those plants in yer box? They ain't seen the sun or had any water in days."

"There's been no rain," Telchide pointed out. "The other plants haven't had water either."

He carefully wrapped the metal can back in the gloves – he did not intend for anyone else to get shocked or burned by it. Once he was satisfied that it would remain safe, he got to his feet and stretched out. How long had he been sitting there? He looked at his pocket watch. Four hours! How had he not realised the time?

The wooden box was closer to the water. Telchide walked over to it with Corrado trailing a few steps behind. The marinaio was certainly a cautious man, though it made sense not to get too close if he had no gloves as protection.

Telchide knelt and unpegged the lid, carefully placing the wooden peg in his pocket for safe keeping. He slid the lid open and was astonished to see that the plants were still alive, and sparking.

"How is this possible?" he cried out.

Corrado came up for a better look and whistled appreciatively.

"You've found some magic plants there. You sure they're powered by the sun?"

Telchide shrugged. "I don't know what to think anymore."

He carefully pulled out the smallest plant – the first one Lucrezia had harvested – and closed the lid. With Corrado staying well away, Telchide held out the plant at arm's length and carried it back to the metal can. There was one last experiment he wanted to run today.

With great care, he placed the entire plant inside the can and sealed it up with the extra leather gloves. He then reattached the lightbulb and left it. The bulb instantly began glowing brightly.

Telchide smiled and made a note in his notebook. He would leave the lightbulb attached all day, all night and then observe it again in the morning. He presumed it would dim overnight, but if it relit itself the next morning, then his theory would be confirmed.

He closed the notebook and put it away with a sense of satisfaction.

"Now what?" Corrado asked.

Telchide shrugged. "Did you happen to bring a book?"

Corrado laughed. "No, Inventore. I know my letters well enough to read maps. That's all."

Telchide laughed along until he realised the marinaio was serious.

"Oh. Well. I could teach you if you like."

"Begging yer pardon, but I don't think so. Besides, there ain't no point fer a marinaio to know how to read. I don't get much free time."

Telchide could not understand this him. Corrado was being offered a gift – a true gift – and he was rejecting it. He knew not everyone learned to read, especially if their parents did not know how and it was not necessary in their trade, but to refuse to be taught at all. He couldn't abide it!

"Unless you can think of any other way to pass our time, then I'm afraid I must insist. Who will teach your children to read if you cannot yourself?"

"I ain't got children," Corrado pointed out desperately. "Nor a companion."

"No, well, of course not yet. How could you possibly maintain a relationship when you're at sea so much and do not have the means to write letters?"

Corrado took a step back, hands held up. "Inventore, really. I don't want to learn more'n I already know."

Telchide threw his hands up in the air.

"Then how do *you* propose we spend the rest of the day? The ladies won't be back until after sunset. It's only just past two o'clock. Sunset won't be for at least another three hours and then another half hour or more before the plants stop sparking enough for them to get back past safely."

Corrado did not reply. But his eyes were wide with something like fear.

Telchide turned to the back of his notebook and held it out to Corrado with a pencil.

***

An hour later, Corrado began protesting in earnest. Telchide had managed to go through the alphabet with him – the marinaio knew most of his letters already – and the sounds associated with them. It was the same way he'd taught Teresina years ago.

The marinaio had then opted for copying the letters over and over rather than attempt to read anything. Telchide knew he was stalling – reading aloud could be a most daunting venture, but he refused to let the captain weasel his way out of it.

"Corrado, I promise I will leave you to your own devices when you prove to me that you can read two simple sentences on your own."

"Two sentences?" Corrado asked, holding up two fingers in confirmation.

Telchide nodded, likewise holding up two fingers. "Two sentences."

Corrado handed him back the notebook and pencil, which they'd already had to sharpen twice with how hard the marinaio was pressing on the paper. Telchide wrote the words: *My name is Corrado. I am a marinaio.*

He handed the notebook back to Corrado. The marinaio stared blankly at the words.

"These ain't two *simple* sentences. That word's got *seven* letters!"

Telchide frowned.

"Corrado, can you spell your name?"

The captain turned a deep shade of red, his lips narrowing to a thin line. He did not answer.

"I see," Telchide said slowly. "Why don't we start with that, then? It will make these sentences easier for you."

They spent the next five minutes labouring over the sounds and letters in Corrado's name. Eventually, the marinaio held up the notebook with a look of pride.

"Corrado. C – O – double R – A – D – O. There it is. That's my name!"

Telchide couldn't help but smile at the marinaio's joy. He called an end to their lessons for the day, though there were still hours left until the ladies would return.

"What now?" Corrado asked.

Telchide was wondering the same thing.

"If Aveline can swim across this lake, perhaps one of us can too."

"No," Corrado said firmly.

"No," Telchide agreed glumly. He took out his compass and studied it for a moment, then pointed west across the lake. "Your boat's that way. If we can build a bridge, it would make things easier. Perhaps we can set up a system where we travel back and forth to the island when we need new plants to experiment with, or once we're ready to start using them in actual inventions.

"We could create a rope ladder and attach it to the cliff where we first landed. That was a safer port for your boat as I recall. Then we'd have an easy way to get up to the lip of the Caldera and a quick way to get across this lake."

He looked at Corrado with excitement. The marinaio was staring at him with wide eyes and a slack jaw.

"Inventore, does yer mind ever stop working?"

"Erm, no, I don't think so. Do you think it would work? You'd then have a fairly regular source of employment and could potentially focus on starting a family."

Corrado sat heavily on the rocks. Telchide could hear the thump from where he stood a few piedi away.

"Don't you need to talk to Aveline Inventrice about that? I don't come cheap is all."

Telchide scratched his stubbly chin. It was a good point. He knew Aveline was paying Corrado thirty electrum coins for this trip alone. Any ongoing contract was bound to be expensive. It was something they would need to discuss later.

Before the plants around the Caldera's peak began sparking that morning, Telchide dug up another four and added them to his collection. With the one still in the repurposed can, that made seven.

The lightbulb on the can was still glowing. It appeared an entire plant, whether it saw the sun or not, began sparking again during the day, renewing the energy that was spent throughout the night. Telchide was pleased with that outcome. It meant the plant was a more viable source of power than he'd thought from initial experiments.

"We'll need to set up a safe location to experiment with these plants," he told Aveline when she awoke. He'd tried to talk to her when they'd returned the previous night, to brush her cheek with his thumb, but she'd turned her face away. Defeated, he'd related the results of his experiments to her – she had no trouble with *that* kind of conversation. "I wouldn't like an accident with them in my workshop. If they don't burn my house down, they'll still likely ruin every one of my inventions and I cannot afford that."

"Perhaps the Guild will be able to allocate a safe testing area for us," Aveline suggested. "Surely we cannot be the only ones in all of Tor'Esint who need a larger testing area than their workshop can provide."

"We could work there together on specified days," he suggested hopefully.

Aveline nodded slowly, chewing on her lip. "Or we could take turns so that we can still run our own workshops efficiently."

Telchide's shoulders sagged. The others were still asleep – he'd heard Lucrezia and Corrado talking late into the night.

"We must talk," he said in a firm, but quiet, voice. He did not want to rouse the others.

"No, we mustn't."

"Veli, *please*. I did not mean to scare you off. I … it just felt such a natural thing to say. I'm sorry."

Aveline was silent for so long Telchide began to fidget with his buttons. He did not want things to remain unresolved by the time they returned to Tor'Esint. Then he'd *never* get to clear up the mess they were in. Nevio would ensure that Aveline was never left alone and Aveline herself would never come to his workshop. The only time they would meet would be their dinners at the Exploding Beakers, which would not afford them any privacy. If she did not agree to work with him in the larger workshop, then he'd never see her again. Not in any meaningful way.

"You have nothing to apologise for," she eventually told him. "I know I started this, but I really shouldn't have. I was caught up in the moment – we both were. Wonderful as it was, I can't do this. I can't return to Tor'Esint knowing that you love me and that I can't be with you for another four years."

Telchide sputtered. "But ... you ... I never ... This is the *very reason* I never pursued a relationship! I knew it would come to this." He paused. "But then you kissed me, and I felt, well, hopeful."

"I know," Aveline said, her eyes shining with tears. "But we have to be realistic about this. When we return, *this* cannot continue. You won't live in my workshop with Teresina, and I certainly won't live in your workshop with Serenita. I would feel an intruder in the house. And just imagine what would happen if Sebetine returned from wherever she went!

"Chide, I can't do this. And I can't promise to wait four years. Not if I find another man who loves me as much as you do."

Telchide stared at her in confusion. "But you said..." He shook his head and took a step back. "Of course. We'll pretend none of this ever happened. Lucrezia won't tell anyone, and neither will we. It's done."

He walked over to his blanket and rolled it up, ready to pack into his rucksack. Aveline's hand on his shoulder stopped him.

"I'm sorry, Chide. Truly I am."

He did not reply. He had no choice in the matter, so what was he to say?

"We have enough plants now and it looks like they'll survive in my box. It's time we leave. Tell Corrado I've borrowed his machete. I'm going to the other side of the lake to build a bridge."

Aveline stood where she was and watched him. He couldn't bring himself to look at her. It hurt too much. Instead, Telchide rifled through Corrado's possessions until he found the oversized knife. Without another word, he walked along the stream towards the point where it narrowed.

***

By the time he'd reached the narrowing he and Lucrezia had used, Corrado had caught up with him.

"No, not here. I ain't jumping across *that*." The marinaio pointed to the stream. "There's a narrower point up there. Let's keep going."

Telchide shrugged and followed Corrado. He wasn't in a rush. There was no one injured on the other side of the stream this time. They walked up the stream until they reached a narrower point and jumped over.

As he walked back up the other side of the stream, he kept his eyes on the distance to the other shore and the height of the trees. Just when they reached the first narrowing, Telchide stopped. There was a tree here that looked like it could work. He turned to find Corrado, but the marinaio was not behind him.

"Corrado!" he called out loudly. "Where are you?"

There was a whooshing sound before some branches came crashing down further in the jungle. Corrado appeared, his machete swinging beside him.

"So, you think your machete can cut through two of these tall trees?" he asked the marinaio.

Corrado turned his attention back to the jungle and scratched the stubble on the side of his neck.

"Dunno. What're you thinking?"

"If they stretch across one of the narrowings, we could use them as the sides of a rudimentary bridge."

Telchide followed Corrado's gaze up the coconut trees. The taller they were, the thicker they were, but none of them were thicker than Telchide's own body.

"Inventore, I'm tired. Can't we just rest now?"

"Fine, fine. Rest now. We'll cut down this tree later." Telchide laid a hand on the selected tree and smiled. He saw Corrado's eyes travel up the length of the trunk. The marinaio said nothing but sat down with his back against the tree. Telchide took his cue from Corrado and did likewise.

They sat in silence for a long while. Telchide didn't mind except for the fact that it gave him too much time to think. He was just growing restless when Corrado turned to him.

"What happened with Aveline Inventrice?"

Telchide choked and started coughing. Corrado slapped him on the back so roughly that Telchide could barely catch his breath. He pushed the marinaio's hand away from him and breathed deeply, which only served to make his ribs ache. That man certainly was strong!

"I'm a committed man with a missing companion," Telchide sighed. "What can possibly happen?"

Corrado thought for a moment. "Can't you say you don't want to be committed to her anymore? Begging yer pardon, but how'd you know she didn't scarper off with another man?"

Telchide stared at him in shock before the blood rose to his cheeks. "She most certainly did *not* 'scarper off' with another man!"

Corrado shrugged. "She's missing. You don't know what happened to her. I could be right and then what?"

"I ... don't know," Telchide admitted sheepishly. "I honestly don't know."

He got to his feet suddenly and dusted himself.

"If you've got the energy to make up stories about my companion, you've got the energy to chop down a tree. Let's get on with it."

Corrado stared up at him with a look in his eyes that Telchide couldn't place. He shrugged and hefted his machete. It was not an axe, nor a saw, but when he started hacking into the base of the tree, it still did a decent amount of damage. After the first chips of wood flew at him, Telchide stood back a safe distance. Only when Corrado showed signs of fatigue did Telchide offer to help.

"No offence, Inventore, but I don't trust you not to cut yer leg off."

Telchide crossed his arms angrily, though he knew Corrado was probably right, and positioned himself away from the flying chips *before* they had a chance to flick at him, and on the side of the tree he would need to push from. It was tall and he did not like their chances of moving it if it fell in the wrong direction.

Corrado stopped chopping before Telchide heard any groaning or creaking from the tree. He looked around at the marinaio questioningly.

"Let's see if we can't push it now. I don't want to get caught underneath it if it..."

Corrado collapsed. Telchide saw the coconut which had hit the marinaio's head rolling away from his fallen body. The tree creaked loudly. In a trance, Telchide grabbed Corrado under his arms and hauled him away from the tree. He put him down, ran back to the tree and pushed with all his might. This tree *needed* to fall across the stream now. He needed Lucrezia and did not have time to run the long way around to the narrowing further upstream.

As he pushed, he felt the silence of Corrado. Not a groan, or even cursing. The silence scared him. It gave him the strength to push even harder on the tree.

It started to lean, slowly at first then suddenly it began to fall. Telchide held his breath as he watched the tree fall over the stream and drop onto the other bank. It was long enough!

"I'm going to get help!" Telchide shouted as he ran towards the edge of the steaming water.

He stepped up onto the trunk. It was narrow, but at least as wide as his feet. Carefully, he began the walk across. The rising steam stung his nose and made his eyes water. He was soaked with sweat before he was even a quarter of the way across.

The trunk became slippery from the steam. Telchide struggled to keep his footing. It was no use. The soles of his shoes couldn't grip the trunk.

Hoping he would not fall in, Telchide sat on the trunk with his feet in front of him. As quickly as he dared, he took his shoes and socks off. His bare feet would have better grip than his shoes.

By the time he reached the other side, his feet had been rubbed raw by the trunk. He stepped onto the black rocks, relieved to be on solid ground. Instantly, he regretted the decision and jumped back onto the trunk. His feet felt like he'd dipped them in a lava bath.

Biting his lip to stop from screaming, Telchide pulled his socks over his ruined feet. It took all his self-control to shove his feet into his shoes. But he knew he needed to do it. Corrado was unconscious on the other side of the lake, and he needed Lucrezia.

***

Telchide arrived limping and hobbling at their campsite. He reflected bitterly that perhaps he'd have taken the same amount of time had he gone the long way around.

"What happened?" asked Lucrezia, dispensing with her usual banter.

"A coconut fell on Corrado's head!"

Lucrezia stopped and stared at him. "Oh, *really*, Telchide! A coconut? For Caldera's sake, you had me worried for a second."

"You *should* be worried," Telchide replied angrily. "He's unconscious and he's the only one who knows how to sail his boat."

The blood drained from Lucrezia's face. "Where is he?" she asked urgently.

Telchide described where he'd left Corrado and didn't bother suggesting she take their makeshift bridge. She could navigate her way to the marinaio however she liked. Telchide was too sore to care.

He found his coat in his rucksack and eased himself down onto the black rocks, arranging his coat under him. With great care, he removed his shoes and peeled his socks off, wincing as the material rubbed against his raw feet.

"Would you like me to have a look at them?"

Telchide looked up to see Aveline standing over him. He'd been in such a rush to find Lucrezia that he hadn't even noticed her.

"Don't bother. I can wait for Lucrezia," he replied coldly.

"Don't be daft, Chide. Let me help you," Aveline fumed. "Just because I can't find a way out of our sticky situation, doesn't mean we can't talk to each other."

Telchide said nothing but moved slightly so that she could assess his feet. He remained silent the entire time that she examined him, and still said nothing when she first washed his feet with water from the steaming lake, then rifled through Lucrezia's things to find a balm to slather over his soles.

"There, that should help," she said, examining her handiwork. "It might take a few days to heal properly, though. How did you do it?"

Telchide swallowed. "We were trying to make a bridge across the lake, so we wouldn't have to go so far around if we returned to the Caldera. I didn't realise how difficult it would be to cross with shoes. I had to go barefoot most of the way for fear I'd fall in the water. Then I burnt my soles on the rocks."

As he said that, he looked down at Aveline's feet. They were bare. Again.

"Why don't the rocks burn you?" he asked enviously. "Or the water?"

Aveline shrugged. "I don't know. It just doesn't. Maybe I built up a tolerance to it. You never bothered to try."

Telchide huffed and turned away from her. He looked across the lake, trying to see the spot where he'd left Corrado, but it was too difficult with all that jungle in the way.

Lucrezia didn't return. Not for hours. When she did, it was only to tell them that she couldn't move Corrado. He'd woken briefly but his words were incoherent and slurred. They'd have to wait to see if he recovered.

"We may as well move camp," Aveline suggested. "If we have everything we need, there's no point staying on this side of the lake anymore."

Telchide said nothing but carefully put his socks and shoes back on so that he could pack. Most of his things were already in his rucksack. He took it upon himself to pack Corrado's things as well. Lastly, he found the strips of cloth Aveline had used to strap Lucrezia to his back all those days ago. They would work just as well to strap the insulated box to his back.

"Let me help you with that," Aveline said, walking up to him.

Telchide couldn't move away in time – not with his feet in their current condition. She took the cloth strips out of his hand and motioned for him to hold the box in place. The procedure brought her close. Too close.

He could feel her breath on his skin. Telchide closed his eyes and tried not to lean in towards her. No matter how they'd left the situation, it hadn't dissolved his feelings for her. And she was so close. So very close.

"There. All done," Aveline said.

She patted him awkwardly on the shoulder. Telchide opened his eyes to find her backing away from him. His hand involuntarily reached out to her before he realised what it was doing. He made an overt movement to show he was actually going to pull his pocket watch out to look at the time. Though he doubted she was fooled.

Telchide cleared his throat noisily. "Erm, well, it's getting late. We should go now if we want to reach him by dark."

***

It took longer than he expected to reach Corrado. He'd sent Aveline and Lucrezia ahead of him. His feet were simply not in a good enough condition to keep up with them. The salve Aveline had slathered over his soles at least made the pain bearable enough to walk, but he couldn't move quickly.

It was well and truly night by the time he arrived at their new camp. Corrado was still unconscious. Lucrezia and Aveline had lit a small fire and organised themselves a meal of canned beans and tomatoes. They were just finishing up as he arrived. He noted, sourly, that there was none left for him. Aveline looked up at him guiltily.

"There's a pumpkin and two sardines left. Would you like me to open one for you?"

"I'll have the pumpkin, thank you," Telchide said as he began unwrapping the cloth strips keeping the insulated box in place.

"No wait!"

Aveline put her hand out to stop him too late. The box slid from Telchide's back and landed heavily on the ground. Telchide jumped away from it quickly, but his leg was struck by a thin bolt of energy that sparked out at him.

He hobbled quickly away from the box and only stopped when he reached a tree to hide behind. Telchide peeked out from behind the tree to see little sparks of light jolting around the box. Thankfully, he'd made it well enough that the box hadn't come apart when he dropped it, but the wooden peg had slipped out and allowed the lid to slide fractionally open.

Aveline and Lucrezia had taken it upon themselves to drag Corrado out of the way. They were a safe distance back now – Telchide was glad for that. He did not want to have to worry about them as he attempted to close the box.

He searched for a stick on the ground but couldn't find one. This jungle had an abundance of palm trees – quite a variety of them. But none with branches that would break off into sturdy sticks. He had to make do with a palm frond. He broke it off at the top to remove the weakest section.

Standing as far back as possible, Telchide pointed the frond's spine towards the box. It reached, but the frond was too long, and he didn't have enough control over it. Grumbling, he broke off another section of the frond to make it more manageable.

This time, the movements were controlled enough to reach the box and touch the lid, but he couldn't put enough force behind it to close the lid.

"Smoking Caldera!" Telchide yelled angrily. "This is pointless."

He threw the frond aside and rummaged through his rucksack to find his leather gloves. They likely wouldn't be enough protection, but there was nothing else he could do.

"Chide, it's not worth it," Lucrezia said. "Just wait until the plants stop sparking. It can't be much longer now. The sun set a while ago."

Telchide turned to her wondering how she could be so stupid.

"Do you want those plants to start a fire?"

"What in Caldera's smoke is he talking about?" Lucrezia asked Aveline.

Telchide barely listened as Aveline explained to Lucrezia that the sparking plants could start a fire if they sparked onto a dry piece of vegetation. He was consumed by his current task.

A few piedi away, Telchide lay down on the ground and inched his way forward. The sparking plants were gaining momentum now that they were out in the open. He needed to hurry.

He reached his hands out towards the box hesitantly. He'd yet to be shocked badly by the plant itself, but the shock he'd had from the can the previous morning had been painful enough that he didn't want to feel the full force.

The plants sparked out at him and hit above his gloves. Heat seared up Telchide's arm in almost unbearable pain. He pulled back instinctively.

His rapid breath did nothing to calm him. There was no other way.

As quickly as he could, Telchide reached out to the box. The plants sparked out at him again, snaking along his arms. Telchide did not pull back. He firmly closed the lid ... and only then did he hear the screams. It surprised him to realise *he* was the one screaming.

A shower of pain burst across his cheek. He looked up to see Lucrezia standing over him, hand raised.

"Sorry, Chide," she said softly. "You were in shock."

Aveline pushed Lucrezia aside and knelt beside him. She hugged him unreservedly and covered his face with kisses. Telchide couldn't react. He was too sore to move and too confused to understand what was happening. His arms remained flaccid by his side.

Eventually, Aveline pulled away from him. She did not look at him, though he thought he saw tears running down her face. His eyes followed her movements as she located the wooden peg and replaced it.

"Let me have a good look at you," Lucrezia said, drawing his attention away from Aveline. "Follow my finger."

Lucrezia moved her finger from one side of his face to the other. Telchide found it difficult to concentrate but managed to follow the movements. She dictated a series of other tests which Telchide performed tiredly.

Finally, Lucrezia pulled off his gloves. Telchide looked at the arms she held up in front of him. His hands were pristine, but his arms were covered in burns. He noted with some interest that the pattern of burns looked like a sheet of red lace.

"Aveline, pass me my salves."

Telchide lay there impassively until the salves were applied. The coolness of them against the burns brought a much-needed relief from the pain. He closed his eyes as Lucrezia worked. He barely noticed when she took off his socks and shoes to attend to his ruined feet.

Chapter 26 – Mercatodi 28 Mercantili 230 Years After Implosion

"We need to get back to Tor'Esint. These two need better care than we can give them here, and my clients won't wait for me much longer. If I don't return soon, they'll begin using another Alchimista."

"Look around you, Crez. Our marinaio is unconscious and Chide's feet haven't healed properly. He cannot walk all the way to the boat."

Telchide listened to the two of them arguing back and forth. He could barely remember how long they'd been away. It must be close to two weeks now.

He opened his eyes and looked around. The sun was peeking over the lip of the Caldera, which placed the time at around eight o'clock. Aveline and Lucrezia were sitting to one side of the camp. Telchide turned his head to find Corrado by his side. The marinaio was breathing steadily.

"I can walk," Telchide said softly, as he pushed himself to sit up.

The ladies stopped talking and stared at him. They weren't looking at his face, but lower on his body. Telchide followed their gaze to his arms. The bright red lattice of burns that had adorned his arm last night had darkened considerably, somehow making the burns look worse.

"It doesn't hurt so much," he reassured them. "No worse than Aveline's burns, and she's healed up fine."

Their stares did not stop. He'd misjudged what they were looking at. Telchide bent his legs to look under his feet. The skin that had been burned and rubbed raw was practically healed. He probed the soles of his feet inquisitively but felt no pain. Testing his limits further, Telchide stood and walked around. It really didn't hurt.

"You have magical salves Lucrezia," he said, smiling at the Alchimista.

Lucrezia shook her head. "My salves don't work *that* fast. Neither does the water, from what I've seen, though it certainly has been working wonders."

"Perhaps it's the combination," Aveline said. "I washed Chide's feet with water before I put the salve on."

"You forget, the water burns everyone but you," Telchide told her.

"No, it doesn't," Aveline replied. "Not if you're careful about it. Crez, let's try it on Corrado's head. You never know, it might just work."

"I did that yesterday," Lucrezia sighed "but it won't hurt to do it again."

She walked to the water's edge with a few strips of cloth. Telchide watched her dunk them carefully into the lake then wrap them around Corrado's head. The marinaio moaned as she moved him around, but he did not stir otherwise.

"Chide, pass me your water canister. I want to take as much of this water back with us as possible and study it further."

Telchide found his water canister and handed it to Lucrezia. While she was filling it in the steaming lake, he rummaged around in Corrado's bag and found the marinaio's canister as well.

Once all the canisters were full, Telchide inspected his feet. They really weren't hurting at all. His arms were another matter. Lucrezia suggested he rinse them down with the water to speed the healing process before she bandaged them. The burning sensation had faded, but not enough. He knew it wouldn't disappear completely until he was properly healed. He needed to keep busy, to keep his mind off the burning.

"Let's go to the boat," Telchide said. "If Corrado wakes up on the way, all well and good. If he doesn't, we'll see if we can't work out how to sail that boat of his."

Lucrezia cocked an eyebrow at him. "Uh, Chide, you know he can't walk. Exactly *how* are we meant to get Corrado to the boat?"

Telchide coughed uncomfortably.

"I thought I could carry him the same way I carried you when we first arrived. You know, on my back."

Lucrezia nodded appreciatively. "Yes, good idea. Aveline, come and help me with Corrado."

Telchide wanted to protest. He did not want Aveline so close to him again. Instead, he said nothing and stood there helplessly as Lucrezia held Corrado against his back and Aveline strapped him on.

Once again, they were face to face. Aveline was too close to him. He couldn't stand it. He closed his eyes, thinking that to remove her from his sight would help. It did not. All it made him do was focus on her movements, her scent, the touch of her hair as it tickled his nose.

Finally, she moved away from him.

"It's okay, Chide, you can open your eyes now," she sighed.

Telchide opened his eyes. From the corner of his vision, he could see Lucrezia busying herself as far away as she could.

"Aveline, I cannot keep doing this," he said softly. "You've told me this can't work, and however much I may wish it were otherwise, you're probably right. But if we both know that, then I can't have you kissing and hugging me then pulling away. Telling me that we can't be more than friends and still have you so close to me that I can feel your breath on my skin. I can't do it."

There were tears in her eyes. She wasn't so far away from him that he could miss it. Her lips were trembling.

"Just because I know what the sensible thing to do is, and I made that choice, doesn't mean I don't still have feelings for you, Chide."

He could feel the heartache in her voice. It was the same way he'd spoken in the early days after Sebetine had disappeared. The same Sebetine who was now the cause of his further unhappiness. If only he could find a way out of this mess – for all of them.

A tear trickled down Aveline's face. Telchide reached out a hand to wipe it away. Aveline clasped his hand to her cheek and kissed it. It was more than he could bear to see her so unhappy. He pulled her in and hugged her awkwardly with Corrado on his back.

With a light kiss on top of her head, he released Aveline and went to make sure Lucrezia hadn't forgotten to pack any of their belongings before they left this place.

***

It took them most of the day to travel back to the western side of the Caldera. This close to the lip, the sun disappeared earlier in the afternoon. By five o'clock, they began looking for a steaming lake or stream to camp at before complete darkness fell.

Aveline was the one to find it. By some awful coincidence, it was the same lake they'd found that first night on the Caldera, with the waterfall tumbling off one edge. The same one where Roque had decided it was his right to rape Aveline.

"We don't have to stay here," Lucrezia said. The same memory had clearly crossed her mind. "We can do without water for one night."

"No." Aveline said firmly. "I'm not going to let the memory of one ash-sucking marinaio drive me away from the warmth of the lake. We're stopping here for the night. At least from here we know our way back to the ship and, if Corrado is conscious, we can set sail tomorrow."

Telchide shared an uneasy look with Lucrezia, but neither of them argued with Aveline. She was the one who'd had the experience, not them. If she was comfortable to stay, who were they to disagree?

Chapter 27 – Riposidi 1 Alchimisti 230 Years After Implosion

Telchide woke early. He'd had an uneasy night. Though the burns on his arms were healing, any time he moved, the bandages had rubbed against his blanket, irritating him.

Taking matters into his own hands, he knelt by the water's edge, took off his shirt and held his hands out over the water. Ever so slowly, he lowered his arms until they were just above the steaming water. Slowly, he submerged his arms. He'd realised the day before that water did not burn him if he went slowly. The heat ran through his body, warming even the tips of his toes. It was a curious sensation.

A splash further out grabbed his attention. Telchide looked through the steam to see Aveline swimming in the water. He remembered, with a smile, how annoyed he'd been with her at the beginning of their trip when she stripped down to her bare skin to swim or just lay in the water. That was before they'd made love. Her naked body did not embarrass him anymore, but it did cause some very unwelcome feelings.

Hoping that she hadn't noticed him, Telchide kept his head down and concentrated on his arms. The heat was dwindling now, as though his arms were adjusting to the heat. He wondered if, just this once, he could try to submerge his entire body in the pool.

He was contemplating taking the rest of his clothes off when he heard a cough behind him. He turned to find Lucrezia standing not far away.

"You've done well not to succumb these past few days, Chide. If you go in there now, I don't like your chances of staying away from her."

Telchide felt the blood rush to his cheeks but knew Lucrezia would not be able to see his blush. His entire body must be bright red from the heat of the water. He pulled his arms out and hurriedly pulled on his shirt as he got to his feet, suddenly embarrassed to be half naked in front of a woman.

"Erm, yes, I thought I'd see if this water can heal my burns any faster. That's all." He shuffled his feet for a moment, then made a show of peering behind Lucrezia. "How is our marinaio doing? Has he woken up yet?"

"For a few minutes, yes, but he's out again."

Telchide twisted the hem of his shirt. He fought the urge to look back towards Aveline.

"Well then, let's see if we can't reach the boat today," he said with a forced smile. "If you rebind his head with wet cloths and help to put him on my back again, that should give Aveline enough time to finish her swim."

Lucrezia looked as though she was about to say something, instead she nodded and walked back to the marinaio. She unbound his head, dipped the cloth in the steaming water and rebound it. Telchide kept his eyes firmly on her movements and not on the naked lady in the lake.

Telchide found he had more strength than the previous day. He managed to hold Corrado in place as Lucrezia fastened the marinaio to his back. Somehow the Alchimista didn't make him feel uncomfortable, despite their closeness. Telchide wondered if Aveline had purposely been moving closer to him when she was the one tying the marinaio to him the day before.

***

By the time they were ready, Aveline had returned from her final swim. There would be no more steaming water now that they were about to ascend the lip of the Caldera. Telchide hadn't wasted the time. He'd scanned the trees and cliffs for the rope he knew was still there. With the *situation* created by Roque, no one had thought to undo the rope that fateful day. It must still be tied up somewhere along here, leading them straight back to Aveline's pulley system.

"There it is!" he cried, pointing to a tree near the edge of the hot rocks.

"There is what?" asked Lucrezia, turning to scan the jungle.

"The rope," replied Telchide happily. "The rope that will lead us back to the boat and home. I can't wait to see my little Teresina again!"

Saying his daughter's name out loud brought a genuine smile to his face. It had been too long since he'd seen her. He knew Serenita and Eduardo were more than capable of looking after her, but it didn't stop him from missing her. He so badly wanted to hug her, to have her little arms wrapped tightly around his neck. For a moment, his heart hurt so much he almost cried. But the moment passed. Eventually.

"Let's go."

Without waiting to see if the others were following, Telchide walked over to the tree and untied the rope. He wanted to pull it to the side, away from where he knew the little cliff was, but there were too many trees in the way. With a sigh, he began to coil the rope in front of him as he followed it into the jungle.

"Chide, wait!" Lucrezia called out as he disappeared into the jungle. He stopped and waited for her to catch up.

"You can't climb the scree slope with Corrado on your back."

"Why not? I came down it with you, didn't I?"

Lucrezia rolled her eyes at him. "Do you forget that you smashed your head against the rocks, and we fell in an ungainly heap at the end?"

"Erm, actually, yes. I *had* forgotten that." Telchide scratched his neck. "But that was in the dark and I was already tired from carrying you all the way from the start."

Telchide made to start walking again but Lucrezia stopped him.

"No. Think what you will of your strength, but Aveline and I will not be able to carry both you and Corrado should anything else go wrong.

"Let's just follow the path Corrado cut until we reach the rim. Then we can pull in the rope after us."

Telchide began to protest, but Lucrezia put up a hand to forestall him. He had no choice but to listen to the Alchimista. Without her help, he knew he'd never make it up the cliff with the marinaio. Annoyed with the perceived delay, Telchide dropped the rope and followed Lucrezia into the forest with Aveline close behind him.

Lucrezia swung Corrado's long knife in front of her, widening the path for Telchide and Aveline to follow. It was a steep path and the muscles in Telchide's legs began to burn from exertion. No matter what he'd told Lucrezia, his strength was not unlimited. Every step up to the lip of the Caldera became more and more difficult.

"Crez, I need to stop," he panted. It felt like he'd been walking up the steep path for hours. "Just a short rest."

"Twenty more steps, Chide," she called out from ahead of him. "Then you can stop."

Twenty steps. She may as well have asked him for a hundred steps. Telchide shook his head, ready to sit where he was. It was only Aveline pushing him from behind that made him keep going. He kept his head down, focusing only on the undergrowth. If he looked at the height of the slope, it made the journey seem unbearable.

Ten steps. He was half-way, and the burning in his calves was excruciating. He felt Aveline push past him and take him by the hand. She pulled him along until his final ten steps were taken.

"There, rest now," she told him.

Telchide finally stopped and looked up. He began to laugh, quietly at first, then uncontrollably. Twenty steps had brought him to the top. The sea stretched out in front of him for miglia, broken only by the islands that surrounded the Caldera. But these were the unfamiliar islands. He'd never been to Sant'Elba and Ontigura.

He waited impatiently as Aveline and Lucrezia untied Corrado from his back, then sank to his knees and stared out at the sight of the sun beginning its descent through the western sky. Until that moment, Telchide hadn't realised how much he'd missed the sight of the sea. Not just water – there had been plenty of steaming lakes and streams on the Caldera – but the vast expanse of the sea that stretched away from the docks near his home. The breeze smelt different up here, sharp and briny. It was a relief not to breathe in the scent of whatever alchemical properties were in the steaming water of the Caldera, no matter how healing they may be.

An open coconut was placed in front of him. He noticed with gratitude that the flesh had already been carved from the side so that all he had to do was pick up the pieces and pop them in his mouth. It had taken him a while to get used to the fibrous texture of the coconuts. Though Telchide enjoyed the flavour, he would not be sorry to get back home and devour one of Serenita's plates of pasta and leave these coconuts here.

"I should bring one back for Teresina," he said.

"Bring one what back?" Lucrezia asked.

Telchide turned to look at her in surprise, not realising he'd said that aloud.

"A fresh coconut," he replied. "When I tell her about our trip, I'm certain she'll want to taste one and will be disappointed if I don't bring one back for her."

"We could fill the basket with them," Aveline ventured. "It's practically empty now that we've eaten almost all the food."

Telchide shrugged in a non-committal way without looking at her. He found her closeness too difficult. With any luck, this would be their last night on the Caldera. By tomorrow evening, they would be home and things would return to a semblance of normality.

For Telchide, that meant living in his house with Teresina and Serenita, pretending that he was still waiting for his companion to come home, though he now accepted the fact that she never would. He would try to avoid openly interacting with the Alchimisti but continue to meet them at the Exploding Beakers once every three weeks with his fellow Inventrici.

What he would *not* do was see Aveline every day. Or Lucrezia. That thought was oddly sad. He and Lucrezia had never gotten along well. And at the beginning of this expedition, he was more than happy to see her come to some misfortune. But somewhere along the way, they'd begun to somewhat see eye to eye. He hesitated to call it respect, though this was the closest they had ever come to it.

But his treacherous thoughts kept going back to Aveline. He'd heard of arrangements where committed couples could no longer get along and parted ways – they called it a disunion. Was that a possibility for him if his companion were not there to consent to it? It was not worth mentioning to Aveline right now. Not until he knew whether it was possible. Even if it was, Aveline had put her finger on a more important point – he would not leave Serenita to move in with Aveline and she would not move into a house where his current companion's mamma lived with them. They were at an impasse, and he could think of no way around it.

Chapter 28 – Gildadi 2 Alchimisti 230 Years After Implosion

Telchide lay still for a moment, eyes barely open. It was still dark. The crash of the waves against the rocky cliffs beneath them drowned out almost every other sound. Almost.

He sat up quietly and looked around the camp. Lucrezia and Corrado were lying close together, their chests moving rhythmically up and down. Still asleep. Beside them was the neatly coiled rope that Lucrezia had pulled along behind them out of the jungle the day before.

Telchide searched for Aveline and saw her seated with her back against a tall palm tree. She was shivering. Telchide picked up his coat from where he'd been using it as a pillow and brought it over.

As he draped it over her, he realised that what he'd mistaken for shivering was trembling. In the dwindling starlight, Telchide could see the tear stains on her face. She looked up at him with watery eyes as he knelt before her.

"Aveline, have you hurt yourself?" he asked in concern.

She bit her lip and shook her head.

"Then whatever's the matter?"

Aveline did not answer but turned her head away. Telchide could have kicked himself. How had he not understood that Aveline was hurting inside as much as he was?

"I'm sorry, Veli," he mumbled. "I should've seen. I didn't know you felt as badly about it as I do."

She trembled out a laugh.

"You're so blind, Chide. So very blind. You think I give my heart away so easily to every man I meet? That I'll soon forget about you and be on my way?"

Telchide's shoulders slumped. He reached out a hand to wipe the tears from her eyes. She did not stop him, but the tears only flowed faster. He leaned forward and tenderly kissed her cheek, the saltiness of her tears sharp on his tongue. She did not move away but sucked in quick breaths as she attempted not to cry.

If it was their last morning together, Telchide refused to waste it. He would not presume to do anything Aveline would later regret. Fighting down all other urges, Telchide sat by her side, wrapped his arm around her shoulders and pulled her in tightly. He kissed the top of her head, then rested his cheek there. If he could do nothing else, he would hold her until it was time to go.

***

By the time Lucrezia awoke, Aveline had stopped crying and had finally fallen asleep, leaning against Telchide's shoulder. Telchide hadn't slept. He was still holding her close, as though if he didn't let her go now, perhaps he would never have to.

He watched the Alchimista rise and stretch her arms up to the sky. She froze as her eyes came to rest on Telchide. He did not shy away from her pitying gaze.

"It will be time to go soon," she said softly. "I'll be trying to wake Corrado soon."

Telchide nodded. "If that's all the time I have left, I'll hold her for those few minutes."

Aveline stirred at the sound of his voice, but she did not wake. Telchide kissed the top of her head, ignoring Lucrezia's expression. It was an expression he was familiar with – the same one people had given him when Sebetine had first disappeared, when he was still searching for any sign of her. It was a hopeless kind of sadness. They knew he was broken inside and there was nothing any of them could do to fix him.

In truth, he'd mended months ago, but had been wandering around in limbo. Aveline had brought him out of that and now, after years of feeling numb, he was painfully alive. If her response had been different that night – the night when he'd told her that he could not commit to her for another four years – would they still have fallen headlong into the mess they were now in?

"Probably," he whispered aloud.

Aveline stirred again. Telchide held her closer, and she snuggled into his shoulder, like it was the most natural thing for her to do. It felt wonderful. He would miss that. He would miss everything they had yet to do. The stolen kisses when no one was watching, their first meal at a ristorante as a couple. The rushing of his heart at the sound of her voice when she called his name.

Telchide looked down to see Aveline looking up at him with a smile in her eyes.

"Good morning," she said softly.

"Good morning," he replied, then bent his head down to kiss her forehead. He hadn't meant to do it, but it felt so natural. Telchide could have kicked himself. This was exactly how she didn't want him to act. He closed his eyes and leaned his head back against the tree.

Her mouth touched his so softly he thought it was his imagination. He leaned forward to feel her lips more firmly. She pulled him closer and kissed him with an urgency that surprised him.

Telchide wanted to keep kissing her, to pull down the neck of her shirt and feel the smoothness of her skin under his lips. Instead, he drew her gently away from him. He was already aroused and knew he was approaching the point of no return. If he did not stop now, he would not be able to.

"Good morning," he said once more, gasping for breath. "We'll be leaving soon to find your pulley system. Lucrezia is rousing Corrado."

Aveline did not pull away, nor did she lean in again. Telchide couldn't read her.

"It's not fair," she murmured into his shoulder. "I wanted more time with you. How are we supposed to go back to Tor'Esint and go on as though nothing happened? I don't want to have to pretend that I don't care for you. I don't want to do it."

"Nor do I." Telchide brushed his thumb against her cheek. "I could visit you of an evening, after Teresina goes to bed."

Aveline looked at him with a spark of hope in her face. But it quickly faded.

"Nevio does not go to bed as early as I assume Teresina does."

"He's not your companion, nor your papà. I don't care if he sees me coming."

Aveline bit her lip. "But I do."

Telchide pursed his lips in anger.

"You mistake me, Chide. I don't care if he sees us together, Tor'Esint is fairly liberal. But you *are* still committed. *That* is what he will find unacceptable. I trust him, but his tongue might wag and where would that leave us? My Electrum Guild Mark will mean nothing if I have no customers, nor will your Silver one."

"We'll find a way, Aveline. We must, or neither of us will be happy. What's the use of finding someone you love if you can't spend any time with them?"

There was a loud cough. Telchide looked towards the sound and saw Lucrezia leaning over Corrado.

"Time to wake up, marinaio."

She shook him not so gently. The marinaio stirred and reached out a hand to strike whatever had woken him.

Telchide let out a huff of laughter as Lucrezia slapped Corrado's hand away from her. Aveline turned towards them and gave a small smile. Telchide used the change in her mood to get to his feet, help her up and gather his things. They couldn't stay here forever, and he dearly wanted to get back to his daughter.

"Crez, it's no wonder you don't have a companion!" Corrado grumbled. "No one'd want someone who wakes them so rudely."

Corrado got to his feet. Lucrezia turned her back on him and did not see the captain stumble. Telchide ran forward to hold him steady. They had only just got their marinaio back. It would not do for him to be incapacitated when it was time to go home.

"I'm fine, I'm fine," Corrado assured him, once he was steady on his feet. Telchide moved away but kept his eyes on the captain in case he should stumble once more. It would be a perilous drop should he fall over the edge of lip.

It was light enough now to assess the situation. Telchide laid himself down and looked over the side of the cliff. The pulley system, unsurprisingly, was still intact. Aveline had secured it very well to the rocks at the top of the cliff.

"The boat's still there," he said.

"In one piece?" Corrado asked worriedly.

Telchide shrugged. "I can't tell from here. It's still floating, though."

"That's something," Corrado muttered. "I'll go down first. Empty out yer basket."

Telchide shuffled back from the cliff edge and got to his knees.

"There's nothing in the basket but the box and a few coconuts for Teresina. We've eaten all our food and everyone else's supplies are in their rucksacks."

"Then let me into it."

Lucrezia laughed mirthlessly. "Are you so keen to be the first to fall to your death?"

Corrado stared at her, his face going red. "No, I want to get back to the love of my life."

"That!" Lucrezia pointed down at the boat. "*That* is the love of your life?"

Telchide stifled a laugh as Corrado patted Lucrezia's cheek and turned to help Aveline. Eager not to be the only one available to bear the brunt of Lucrezia's ire, Telchide offered his assistance to Aveline as well.

Between the three of them, they took out the insulated box and managed to tie the basket to the rope attached to the pulley system. Carefully, Telchide and Corrado pushed the basket over the side of the cliff. It dangled precariously above the crashing sea.

"Are we sure there's no other way down to the boat?" Lucrezia asked, looking nervously at their escape route.

Telchide thought for a moment. "Veli, what if we move the pulley?" She looked at him in confusion. "What I mean to say is, the only reason the pulley is here is because it was the easiest route for you to climb to the top with the handholds. But now that we're leaving, what's the harm in moving it over to the rocky beach?"

"You're a lavalump, Chide," Lucrezia said flatly. "Instead of letting us drown, you'd have us fall onto hard, black sand, then walk over sharp, burning rocks to get back to the boat."

Telchide huffed and crossed his arms. It was a *good* idea. Lucrezia was just unreasonably scared.

"If we leave everything in place, it would make future trips easier," he said firmly.

"He has a point, Crez," Aveline said. "The cliff over the rocky beach was not so high as this one. And there was a patch of ash near the cliffs to keep the heat from becoming unbearable."

"Begging yer pardon, but none of this is safe fer my boat," Corrado pointed out.

"We could safeguard your boat," Telchide told him. "All we need to do for future trips is reinforce the hull and create proper bumpers for the sides, with rubber. That will keep it from being damaged by the rocks or the heat. Then you could even drag the boat up on shore so there isn't a chance of it drifting away."

Corrado tilted his head from side to side, considering the option. "Yeah, well, sounds like a better option, though she's a mite bit heavier than you think. Let's go to the beach."

"Done!" Aveline ordered Telchide and Corrado to haul the basket back over the top of the cliff then set to work unbolting her pulley system from the rocks.

In a matter of minutes, she'd disassembled the contraption and they were ready to go. Lucrezia grumbled the entire time. Telchide could understand her reticence, but there was nothing for it. No one had ever said the Caldera was a safe place to visit. If it were, the sparking plant and the magnified healing properties of the steaming waters would already have been discovered and harnessed.

Aveline fumbled with the awkward load she was carrying. Telchide let his fingers brush against hers as he took charge of the pulley. He carefully placed the contraption, rope and all, into the basket and hefted it onto his shoulder.

They set a gentle pace for the day, Lucrezia leading them with Corrado close behind, regularly arguing that *he* should be the one using the machete as it belonged to *him*, thank you very much!

Telchide was happy to walk alongside Aveline, chuckling softly whenever he heard the marinaio cursing the Alchimista. Aveline squeezed his fingers affectionately. Telchide looked down and wondered when they had started holding hands. He did not recall it happening but made no move to let go.

"I think our captain is suffering from a little case of infatuation," Aveline whispered conspiratorially.

Telchide nodded with a smile. "I've heard it said that people who spend an inordinate amount of time with each other sometimes succumb to feelings that would otherwise never arise. The feelings are said to increase dramatically should one or the other be in a perceived position of rescuer."

"Is that so?" asked Aveline pointedly. Telchide thought he detected a hint of anger in her voice.

"Oh, Veli! You *know* I wasn't referring to you and I." He brought her hand up to his lips and kissed it tenderly. "Why is new love always so insecure?"

Aveline laughed. "New love?"

"Well, yes," Telchide said slowly. "You know, I mean, the initial stages of a relationship."

"Yes, I understood you, Chide. But I think you misunderstand what has happened here."

Telchide looked into her hazel eyes but couldn't fathom what she was talking about.

"This isn't the initial stages – not for me, anyway."

"Whatever are you talking about?" he asked in confusion. "I think I would remember if something had happened before we came here."

"Oh, but you don't," Aveline said. "It's very clear that you never really saw what was happening. I couldn't tell you how long I've felt this way. I'd be lying if I said it definitely only started after Sebetine disappeared – I simply can't remember. But I don't exactly treat you the same as every other man I know. I never collaborate with other Inventrici, even within our closed circle of friends, not really. I share my ideas, I comment on others' ideas, but haven't worked with anyone but you. Have you never realised?

"I would never have asked any of the other male Inventrici to come on an expedition I was organising. I've never allowed any man, committed or otherwise, to be in my house without Nevio there. That's not to say I haven't enjoyed myself with them on occasion, but never in my own home."

Telchide was silenced by this information. He really hadn't seen it. All this time he'd thought they were just friends. He'd thought she would never welcome his advances, even if he were free to make them. It had never occurred to him that perhaps he'd been encouraged in more serious contemplation of their situation by Aveline herself.

"You..." He coughed. "I remember you placed your hand on my arm a few times. I thought you were just being friendly."

"In *our* society?" Aveline laughed. "Chide, honestly, do any of your customers or acquaintances lay their hand on your arm?"

"Well, no. No, they don't."

He was lost in a swirl of thoughts. Aveline had only done those things of late.

"Did something change recently? I don't recall it happening before you asked me to collaborate with you after trading hours."

Aveline was silent for a while. Telchide did not press her. Sometimes, she just needed time.

"*You* changed," she said eventually. "When Sebetine disappeared, you became a shell of a man. You still functioned, but it seemed as though you were only performing the tasks that needed performing because it was ingrained in you. If you weren't such a creature of habit, I doubt you'd have survived.

"Then, slowly, things changed. Every now and then, a smile would creep on your face when someone made a joke, or when Nestore created a new concoction to keep prying eyes and ears away from our meetings. Then there was the night you offered to escort Dania and myself home with Eduardo."

"I remember that night." Telchide frowned. "Wasn't that when your carriage was in for conversion to a blazermobile?"

Aveline nodded. "But if that had happened any earlier, it wouldn't have occurred to you to offer to walk us home. That's what I meant when I said *you* changed. You became human again and I re-discovered what an incredible person you were."

"But that was weeks ago," Telchide pointed out. "We walked you and Dania home over a month ago. And you didn't act like this then."

"True," she admitted slowly. "But months ago, you wouldn't have left Teresina to come on an expedition with me. You were starting to heal, but you had a long way to go."

Telchide only half listened. His head was a swirl of thoughts ticking away. It was only after he'd agreed to go on the expedition, in fact begged to be allowed to come, that Aveline began to treat him in an obviously different way.

"You, *you* tried to make me feel this way!"

He said it a little louder and a little sharper than he'd intended. Aveline withdrew her hand from his. Telchide cringed at the hurt expression on her face. He took her hand again.

"I ... I didn't mean it as an accusation, Veli," he said softly, bringing her fingertips to his lips. "I simply didn't realise what had happened. All that time, I thought I was the one accidentally showing how I felt to a woman who was not seeking my advances."

Aveline was silent for a moment.

"You *do* know I couldn't have made you feel anything that wasn't already there, don't you?" she asked hesitantly. "I was just hoping to let you know how I felt so that if you felt anything at all, you'd understand that I would accept your advances."

"Of course, you couldn't," Telchide laughed softly. "Can you imagine the same thing happening with Lucrezia even if she'd laid a gentle hand on me?"

She smiled. It was a precious sight. One he would miss seeing every day. Was there any chance he could make this work? Teresina seemed to like Aveline well enough. Surely, they could come to an arrangement of some sort?

But then there was Serenita. She'd done so much for them since Sebetine's disappearance. He couldn't ask her to go back to Tor'Dumere. Nor would it be fair for him to ask her to live under the same roof as the woman who was taking her daughter's place.

No matter how he looked at it, Aveline *was* taking Sebetine's place. If he allowed her into his life, she would become his companion – eventually – and mamma to Teresina. Everything that Sebetine had been, except for Serenita's daughter.

He tried to keep his deep thoughts from view, but Aveline noticed the change in his mood. She smiled bravely, her eyes tearing up.

"You see, every time you think of it, I can tell. We can't make this work back home. It isn't possible."

Telchide did not answer. He just kissed her fingertips once more and kept following Lucrezia and Corrado.

***

Within a half hour, the land began to slope down.

"We're close," Corrado shouted over his shoulder. "Keep yer eyes open."

The captain managed to take command of his machete as Lucrezia took a moment to look around. It left her at somewhat of a loss. Telchide saw her hesitate, then hurry to catch up with the marinaio.

"It looks like Corrado might not be the only one who's infatuated there," Telchide whispered to Aveline as he nudged her playfully.

"And as odd as their relationship would be if they chose to pursue it, they'd have less trouble than the two of us." There was a bitter edge to her voice. Telchide glanced sideways at her.

"Aveline, *please*, I can't worry about it anymore. We will figure something out, I promise."

Telchide knew his comment had hurt her, but he couldn't go over the same argument again. He didn't have the stamina. They'd be back in Tor'Esint soon. There would be time enough then to figure something out.

Aveline pushed aside some branches and looked down the cliff.

"We're already there," she said. "We can walk to the bottom of the slope if you like, but anywhere here will do."

Telchide relayed the information to Lucrezia and Corrado. They agreed on the bottom of the slope. As Lucrezia put it, the shortest drop would be the safest. Telchide decided not to tell her that any drop onto the hard, black sand would likely end her life. There was no point terrifying her into inaction.

When they reached the bottom, Telchide put the basket down. Aveline quickly set to work putting the pulley system in place. As Telchide watched her work, he reasserted to himself that she really was worthy of her Electrum Guild Mark. There was no hesitation, no hint of doubt in her movements. She knew what she needed to do, and she got on with the job.

Of course, he'd seen some of her inventions, but they'd never had reason to watch each other working until the weeks leading up to this trip. Somehow, the way she worked endeared her to him all that much more.

Sebetine had never been part of a Guild. Her name had ever remained Sebetine di Serenita. There was nothing wrong with that. Plenty of people never took on an apprenticeship. Not every job required one. When he'd met her, she'd been working in a haberdashery, cutting material and ribbons, wrapping buttons and spools of thread for customers. It had earned her a tidy little sum but hadn't required the years of apprenticeship followed by the time it took until she could produce a Great Work to submit to her Guild for a Copper Guild Mark.

When they'd had their commitment ceremony and she'd moved into Telchide's house, she'd helped around the workshop instead. He had fared better when she was around. Had he not garnered a reputation as the best music box maker in Tor'Esint, he doubted he'd have many repeat customers without her.

Dealing with him once was usually enough for most people. He knew this but had found it difficult to modify his behaviour accordingly. There should've been a disconnect between what he was thinking and what he said. Unfortunately, he tended to speak before he could stop himself and often ended up insulting his customers without meaning to.

"Ready," Aveline said.

Telchide looked down to see Aveline kneeling in front of the pulley system, with the basket hanging over the side of the cliff.

Corrado wasted no time in climbing into it, with Lucrezia warning and chiding him by turns.

"Lower me down," he said once he was settled in with all their rucksacks, the insulated box and the coconuts.

Telchide took Aveline's place near the pulley and began cranking it.

"Veli, how is the last person going to get down?"

There was a pause.

"I think I can climb down the rope if we leave the basket down there. It can't be very different from climbing up the rocks themselves."

She did not sound entirely certain.

"I'll go down last," Telchide said suddenly. "I couldn't bear it if something happened to you."

Lucrezia cuffed the back of his head.

"Telchide, *please*, you're one of the clumsiest people I know," she told him. "You'd kill yourself for certain. Let Aveline do it. She's the better climber."

Telchide gritted his teeth and concentrated on the pulley. He didn't have a choice in the matter. With Aveline and Lucrezia on the same side, he'd never win this argument.

It only took him a few minutes to lower Corrado to the rocky beach. He waited until the marinaio had emptied out the basket before reversing the direction on the pulley and turning it again. As the basket lifted towards him, Telchide watched Corrado use the taut rope between the tree and the boat to keep his footing across the treacherously sharp rocks. The fact that it was still taut gave him hope that the thick ropes he and Roque had tied to the side of the boat had saved it from destruction.

The empty basket was easier to crank up. By the time it reached them, Corrado had still not reached the boat. Telchide had no more time to pay attention to the marinaio. It was Lucrezia's turn.

"You go next, Chide," Lucrezia told him.

"Lucrezia, it will be easier for you to get in the basket with Aveline and I helping you. Please, let's not make this more difficult than it has to be."

The Alchimista stared at him with wild eyes. Her face was deathly pale.

"Just don't make any sudden moves, and you'll be fine," Aveline said. It wasn't what Telchide would've said. He assumed any reminder of what had happened last time would be the worst thing for Lucrezia.

"I can't do this," Lucrezia whispered.

"Of course, you can do it," Aveline said soothingly. "Now take Chide's hand. That's the way. And step over here. I'll hold the basket steady."

Telchide lay on the ground to steady himself and held out his hands to Lucrezia. Aveline pulled the basket as close to the cliff edge as possible so Lucrezia could get in more easily. Lucrezia lowered herself to the ground and slid herself into the basket, tightly holding Telchide's hands.

"That's the way," Aveline said. "Now let go of Chide's hands and we'll lower you."

Telchide felt Lucrezia squeeze his hands at the mention of her letting go. He tried to loosen her grip, but she yanked him forward instead. Telchide slid towards the edge of the cliff.

"Let go!" he shouted, trying to prise his fingers away from hers.

Aveline's grasp on the basket failed, lurching Lucrezia away from the cliff face. Telchide felt Lucrezia's grip loosen as he was pulled over the edge. In a desperate attempt not to fall, he swung his arms towards the basket.

He caught the lip of the basket with his left hand, but his right hand missed. Telchide dangled precariously. He'd never been the most athletic person and had trouble swinging his other arm up to support himself.

"Drag him up! Hurry!" Aveline screamed from the cliff.

Lucrezia snapped out of her stupor and leaned out over the basket. Telchide felt her hands grab his shirt and start pulling. All that happened was his shirt untucked from his pants.

"Catch my hand!" he yelled, swinging his arm wildly up.

Lucrezia dropped his shirt. He felt her hands grasping for his – he couldn't see them. All he could see were the sharp rocks glinting maliciously beneath him. His fingers were slipping. If Lucrezia didn't help him soon, he'd find out just how sharp those rocks were.

Telchide swung his arm up again and felt cold fingers wrap around his wrist. He immediately twisted his fingers to grip Lucrezia's arm.

"Pull me up!" he called out to her.

Lucrezia pulled, he could feel that, but nothing happened.

"I can't," she whimpered. "You're too heavy for me."

"Smoking Caldera!" Telchide cried out. "Aveline, lower us, quickly, before the rope snaps."

The basket immediately began to lower. Telchide held onto the basket and

Lucrezia for dear life. His fingers were sweaty and so were hers. He could only hope that Aveline lowered them before they both lost their grip.

As they went further down the cliff face, the basket swung unevenly. Telchide twisted into the rocks. They weren't as sharp as the ones on the shore, but they still hurt as they sliced through his shirt and scraped against his back.

The ground was much closer now. Aveline lowered them quickly. But it still wasn't quick enough. Telchide's hand slipped from the basket. He reached up and tried to grab it again, but his fingers, slick with sweat, only slid off again. He wiped his hand on his pants and tried again. As he reached up, his fingers lost their grip on Lucrezia's arm – she couldn't hold his weight!

He screamed as he fell. He hit the ground hard. It knocked the breath out of him and his vision went black. Everything hurt. He tried to suck in air. It was too painful.

There were noises near him, but he couldn't hear them properly. It sounded like someone was trying to talk to him, but the words were too soft.

Telchide tried to breathe again. This time he managed a short breath. It hurt, but he could hear the voice now.

"Chide, can you hear me?"

It sounded like Lucrezia. Telchide tried to reply but only managed a groan. He couldn't see anything. Everything was black. He didn't try to move – it was all he could do to keep breathing.

His vision began to clear in blurry patches. At first, he couldn't distinguish anything, only the brightness of daylight. Slowly, colours resolved into shapes. The angles looked odd. It was only then that he realised he was lying on his stomach. That explained why he couldn't breathe properly.

"Smoking Caldera, Chide! You scared me for a minute there," Lucrezia said as she leaned away from him. "No, don't move. You took quite a tumble. I need to check where you hurt yourself."

Lucrezia began to prod and probe him – his neck, his arms, his ribs. Telchide gasped and closed his eyes as pain exploded down his leg.

"I was afraid of that," Lucrezia muttered. "Chide, I'm going to turn you over. It's going to hurt, but I need to see if you've done any damage other than to your leg and back."

Telchide want to stop her, but he couldn't.

Instead, he lay still as Lucrezia turned him by the shoulders. He was dreading the amount of pain he would be in when she moved his legs. Not wanting to be forewarned of what she was doing, he closed his eyes. Perhaps it wouldn't hurt him quite as much then.

He was wrong. A roar escaped his lips as too many hands moved his legs. Telchide opened his eyes to see Aveline there as well. He couldn't understand how she was there. He couldn't understand anything through the pain.

"Give him something for the pain!" Aveline shouted.

"Shouting at me won't do any good," Lucrezia said in a much calmer voice. "Find my rucksack and bring it to me."

Telchide whimpered in pain while Lucrezia continued to press her hands against different bits of him. She lifted his arms, checking all the joints.

"Move your fingers. Good. Now the other hand."

Telchide followed her orders. It gave him something to focus on other than the pain.

When she was happy with the movement of his fingers, she went back to her prodding – this time on his torso. Telchide drew in a sharp breath as she pressed on his ribs. Instead of leaving him be, Lucrezia focused on his ribs, pressing each one in turn on his left side, then his right. Telchide couldn't tell where he was sore. The pain blended everything together.

"I know this will be difficult, Chide, but I'm going to remove your boots. I need to see if you can wiggle your toes."

"Please, no," he whimpered. "*Please!*"

Lucrezia paused and lay a gentle hand on his shoulder. "I'm sorry, Chide. We need to do this."

Aveline returned with the rucksack. "Can't you give him something for the pain first?"

"Not if we want to understand the full effect of the damage he's done." Lucrezia's voice was gentler than Telchide had ever heard it. "Help me with his boots, Veli. Carefully. Bite down on this, Chide."

A leather-covered rod was put between his teeth. Telchide didn't understand why until the pain began again. He bit down on it hard, trying not to cry out. He couldn't tell whether it made a difference to the pain. He wavered on the brink of unconsciousness.

"Can you wiggle your toes for me?" Lucrezia asked him. Telchide did as she said. It hurt more than he expected. Lucrezia started to prod and poke again. Telchide bit down harder on the leather rod. He could feel tears streaming down from the sides of his eyes.

"Well, as far as I can tell, you have two broken ribs and a broken leg – your left one. You're lucky not to have broken both. Your arms will be sporting rather impressive bruises soon and you've cut up your back fairly badly."

Telchide spat out the leather rod. "Something for the pain. Give me something!"

"Yes. Of course."

Lucrezia searched through her alchemical kit and sat on her haunches staring at the contents for a long minute.

"The liquid will work best, but it will likely knock you out. Chew this tablet for now."

She popped a hard tablet into his mouth. Telchide chewed hard through the bitter taste covering his tongue. The pain dulled slightly, but it was still there.

Every time he breathed, it felt worse but at least it was now almost bearable. He did not want to try moving his leg.

Lucrezia got to her feet and motioned Aveline to join her. They moved a short distance from Telchide, but he could still hear them.

"I'm going to fetch Corrado. We'll need his help to set Chide's leg. You won't be strong enough to hold him down by yourself. Stay with him. Try not to let him move too much. I don't think he's damaged his spine, but we can't be too careful."

Telchide listened in mounting terror. The only reason Corrado would need to hold him down was if setting his leg would hurt more than anything Lucrezia had already done. He tried not to think about it, but he couldn't help himself. His breath came in short, rapid gasps. It hurt his ribs, but Telchide couldn't stop. His vision began to cloud again. There was a voice near his face.

"Slowly, Chide. Breathe slowly. In ... and out. In ... and out. That's the way."

Telchide's vision cleared. Aveline's face was right there. Worry lines creased her forehead. The sight made Telchide sad. He knew he was the cause of her worry.

"I'm sorry," he whispered.

"Sorry? For what?"

"For making you worry."

Aveline bent down and kissed his brow. Tears fell from her eyes onto his face.

"We're just going to have to find a safer way for you to be a hero," she said with a trembling laugh. "Seems every time you try to save someone, we end up having to fix you as well."

"I'm sorry," Telchide repeated himself.

"Stop saying that," Aveline chided him. "I couldn't have helped Lucrezia into the basket myself. You did what you had to do. If anyone should be sorry, it's Crez for pulling you over the side of the cliff. I'm just glad you didn't die."

"No, I just broke lots of bones," Telchide replied bitterly.

Aveline drew a sharp breath. "Yes, but at least you didn't badly damage your arms or your hands. You'll still be able to work when we return. Be thankful for that."

Telchide did not reply. He did not feel thankful. He felt increasingly angry. This trip was taking more of a toll on his life than he'd expected. First it had broken his heart, now his leg and ribs. What more could it take from him?

He couldn't move when Aveline began to stroke his hair. It felt nice, but he didn't want anything to feel nice now. He felt the pain and he wanted to feel the misery. He should be allowed to feel sorry for himself. There never seemed to be time for him anymore. He always had to give time and spend energy on everyone else. It wasn't fair.

It felt like an age while they waited for Lucrezia to return with Corrado. In truth, Telchide wanted them to hurry to get the pain over and done with. The tablet was doing its job well. He could only feel the sharp edges now. All the duller throbs had disappeared.

"How's he faring?" Lucrezia asked.

Aveline mumbled something but Telchide couldn't make it out.

Lucrezia sighed. "Yes, that's one of the side effects of this tablet. But I still think it was the better option if we don't want to carry him ourselves to the boat."

Telchide couldn't hear Aveline's reply, if there was one. He was surprised by the appearance of Corrado above his head. The marinaio put firm hands on his shoulders and pushed down.

"You're hurting me," Telchide told him sharply.

"Yeah, well, you'll be hurting a lot more soon. Give it time." The marinaio's reply did nothing to assuage his fears.

He felt someone hold down his right leg and could only assume it was Aveline. Lucrezia lifted his left leg and shoved something under it. He screamed in pain and thrashed about. Or tried to. Corrado held him down firmly. Aveline was not so fortunate. He kicked and hit something soft. He didn't care. The pain was unbearable. Something was shoved into his mouth. He bit down on it to stifle the pain.

Lucrezia counted out loud to three and a shower of pain burst through Telchide. His world went black again.

***

When he awoke, only Lucrezia was with him.

"What happened?" he asked her.

"I should've given you the liquid is what happened. You've been out for so long that I sent Aveline and Corrado to load everything onto the boat. They'll be back for us soon."

Telchide was almost too scared to move, but he shifted his head to get a better vantage point. His left leg had a wooden board under it that was tied in place with eight strips of cloth. The cloth looked vaguely familiar.

"Is that *my shirt*?" he asked in horror. His eyes landed on his bandaged chest. "Lucrezia, you used my shirt!"

"Would you rather I used your pants?" She gave him a wry smile. "I had to use something, Chide. Besides, I needed to get to your ribs. Now, this is going to be hard, but you're going to have to walk to the boat. Try to sit up."

He tried. Everything still hurt, but at least his leg stayed firmly in place. Lucrezia shifted over to help him. They sat back together against the cliff. Telchide eyed the black shore.

"Erm, I'm not sure I'll be able to manage that."

Lucrezia shrugged. "We'll figure something out. It's high time we were off this smoking Caldera. I'm not going to let a broken leg stop us."

Telchide took a deep breath – and instantly regretted it. The pain made him cough, which only made things worse.

"Try not to laugh," Lucrezia said with an impish smile. "I've heard that hurts more than coughing."

Telchide looked at her in shock. This Alchimista had a wicked sense of humour. Thankfully, he was spared more of it by the arrival of Aveline and Corrado. One behind the other, they followed the rope leading towards the ash-covered section of the shore.

"Can I help you up?" Corrado asked when he reached them. Telchide nodded mutely. He was not looking forward to this.

"How's the boat?" he asked, trying to stall the inevitable.

"Ah, well, she's a bit worse for wear, but she'll get us back to Tor'Esint." He rubbed the back of his neck. "I'm sure I'll find someone I trust to fix her there."

"I'm sorry, Corrado," Aveline said in a quiet voice. "I didn't realise it would be so difficult for your boat here."

"Well, that's why I charged you so much," he replied smartly. "I should still have a little profit after I use yer fees to mend my boat. Now if we ever come back again, I know what to prepare for."

Telchide looked up at the marinaio in surprise. "You're still willing to come back? After everything that's happened?"

Corrado looked up the cliff, then down to Telchide's leg.

"If one of you figures a better way to get up and down this cliff, I'll come back."

Lucrezia laughed mirthlessly. "You won't get me coming back, even if you *can* find a safer way into the jungle. If you come back again, I'll pay you well for the privilege of staying home myself while you bring me some more of the water." She got to her feet. "Come on, Chide. Time to get going."

Telchide could not remember much about the short journey to the boat. He was overwhelmed with pain. Corrado walked beside him with Lucrezia behind to catch him if he fell. They had agreed amongst themselves that Aveline would be the one to undo the rope and bring it to the boat when the others had safely embarked.

When they were finally on the boat, Telchide lay down and caught Lucrezia's arm.

"The liquid now, if you please."

Lucrezia left him for only a minute or so before returning. Telchide did not listen to any of her warnings before swallowing the entire contents of the vial she handed him. Aveline hadn't yet arrived before he slipped into the blissful embrace of unconsciousness.

Chapter 29 – Ramedi 3 Alchimisti 230 Years After Implosion

Telchide woke to the sound of someone running across floorboards. He opened his eyes. He was in a room – a familiar room. There was a feather mattress beneath him and gloriously soft blankets atop him. For a moment, Telchide smiled. It must all have been a dream.

Then he turned on his side.

The pain returned in sickening waves. He leaned over the side of the bed and vomited. The footsteps stopped.

"Nonna! Come quick!"

Even through the pain and the nausea, Telchide was glad to hear his daughter's voice. The door to his room opened and Serenita bustled in and drew the blinds. Telchide squinted in the sudden sunlight.

"I was sick," he said in a raspy voice. "Sorry."

"At least you're alive," she replied with a smile. She took a red tablet from a glass jar on his bedside. "One every three hours. Lucrezia's orders."

"Lucrezia," Telchide repeated. His memory came back in patches.

"She and Ardo had quite the argument over your leg. Seems they couldn't agree on who should put it in a cast. She'll be back this evening to do the job."

"They've left me without a cast," he said slowly. "Isn't that a bad idea?"

Serenita shrugged. "Apparently, if you've waited this long, a little longer won't hurt. In the meantime, bed rest has been ordered and one tablet every three hours."

Telchide's mind felt fuzzy, but he could still tell Serenita was keeping something from him.

"How was everything in my absence? Teresina wasn't too much trouble, was she?"

Serenita did not answer immediately, which made Telchide nervous.

"She had a little trouble sleeping the first few nights. Then I don't know what happened, but she *changed*."

"What do you mean she *changed*?" asked Telchide, suddenly scared.

"Papà!" shouted Teresina as she ran through the open door. "I've missed you."

She kissed his face all over. Even though it hurt him terribly, Telchide hugged her close. He couldn't help but smile at how much his daughter loved him.

"I've missed you too, my little Resi." Telchide buried his head into her shoulder and held her tightly. "I don't want to ever spend so long away from you again!"

Teresina drew back from him, her face a mask of confusion. "What do you mean so long? It's not even been *one* week, papà!"

"Your papà had a fall, Teresina, and bumped his head. He doesn't know what he's talking about. You go and have breakfast in the kitchen. I'll be there in a minute or two."

Telchide's mind was a jumble.

"Serenita, what's going on?"

Serenita rose and closed the door gently before returning to his bedside.

"In those first few nights, she had such bad dreams of terrible things happening to you on the Caldera. I tried everything to calm her down, but even Eduardo's purple tablets did little to help. We increased the dose and eventually, she could sleep," she said guiltily. "It wasn't until a full week later that we realised something was wrong. Her temperament changed completely. Instead of the sulky little girl we'd been dealing with for the first few days, she became completely carefree and oblivious to the fact that you'd be gone for long.

"She started forgetting things. Just little things at first, so that I passed it off as nothing. It was only when you returned late last night that I realised it was much worse than that. Teresina doesn't remember how long you've been away. She seems to have lost the past few weeks, but not entirely. She can remember bits and pieces, just not everything. I don't know what's happened to her."

Telchide stared at her in silence. The one time he agreed to leave his daughter and *this* is what happened! He would never be able to forgive himself for it. Never! How could he have thought an expedition to the Caldera was more important than being a papà to his daughter?

"She doesn't know then?" he asked in a detached kind of curiosity. "She doesn't know that she's losing her memory?"

Serenita shook her head. "I've been trying to prompt her to remember certain details since last night. If she's prompted enough times, it seems to jog something inside her and sometimes she remembers. But that doesn't happen with everything."

Telchide lay his head back on his pillow, irritated by how comfortable it was. He shouldn't have the luxury of comfort now that he knew there was something wrong with his daughter.

Serenita got to her feet. "I'll fetch something to clean this mess. You rest."

As though he had a choice! He could do nothing but rest until he had a cast on his leg. Was that why Lucrezia and Eduardo had argued? Did Eduardo want to keep him immobile so that he couldn't do anything about Teresina? Did he know what had happened to her? How could this be happening?

After her breakfast, Teresina returned to Telchide's side and snuggled in next to him on the bed.

"Did you have a fun trip, papà?" she asked him excitedly. "Apart from your accident."

Telchide thought about the trip. What could he possibly tell her about it?

"Did you know there's a jungle inside the Caldera?"

"Really?" she squealed. "A real jungle?"

Telchide nodded. "Indeed. With plants I've never seen before. I brought something back for you. Fresh coconuts. They're all over the Caldera."

"Coconuts. I've always wanted to try one!" Teresina said excitedly.

"We'll open one up later and you can see how we stretched out our food to last so many days."

Telchide resolved to be around when she tried it in case she had a similar reaction to the coconuts as her mamma.

"Oh papà, you're too funny," Teresina laughed. "You brought so many cans of food with you. How could you possibly run out in just a few days?"

Telchide paused. How was he going to explain any of his trip to her without making her understand that her memory had holes in it?

"I'm a little tired, Resi. I'll tell you all about it later. I promise."

Teresina nodded happily and lay quietly by his side. Telchide wished he could fix her just by lying beside her. He closed his eyes, hoping for an answer. He was certain it had to do with the purple pills. Eduardo had told him they weren't designed for regular use. If Serenita had increased the amount she was giving Teresina, then it could only be that which was causing the problem. What wasn't Serenita telling him?

"Teresina, tell me, did Nonna give you a purple pill every night while I was away?"

"Yes, papà," she answered into his chest. "Every night. Sometimes two if I woke up with a nightmare. I kept dreaming something awful would happen to you. I was so scared for you."

Telchide squeezed his eyes shut, trying to prevent tears.

"Well, I'm here now. No need for bad dreams. Did you use my Lightbox at night?"

"No. Don't you remember we left it with Kesida?"

Telchide paused. If Teresina's memory was failing, would she remember if Kesida returned the Lightbox?

"Could you do me a favour? Run along and find Nonna. I need to ask her something."

Telchide braced himself for the pain as Teresina got out of his bed. She was as gentle as she could be under the circumstances, but even the movement of his mattress hurt.

He heard Teresina run along the hall and down the stairs. Of course, it was daylight. Serenita would have the shop open by now to attract customers in his absence. There was muffled discussion and Serenita came up the stairs.

"What's wrong, Chide?" she asked tiredly.

"*Please* tell me Kesida brought the Lightbox back. Teresina said she didn't, but I don't know how much I can trust what she says."

Serenita sighed. "Yes, she brought it back a few days ago. You're to see her as soon as you return, but I think she'd be happy to wait for your leg to be plastered first."

"Did she say anything about my apprentice?"

"That's what she wants to talk to you about," Serenita explained. "I showed her the room we got ready for the apprentice and she's happy with the arrangement."

Telchide breathed deeply and groaned from the pain. When would he stop making that mistake? He gritted his teeth and made a decision.

"If I'm to stay in bed until those smoking Alchimisti return to plaster my leg, I don't want to be lying down all day. Help me sit up."

Serenita hesitated. "But the pain..."

"The pain will subside eventually."

Unfortunately, his body did not see things the way he did. When Serenita put his arm over her shoulder, pain bloomed over his ribs. It was only masked by the pain in his leg when he eased himself towards the head of the bed.

Telchide looked around his sunlit room, chest aching too much to breathe properly.

"Can you bring me something to work on?" He wished Aveline was here working on the sparking plants with him. "Were there any orders for pocket watches in my absence?"

Serenita sighed. "Chide, I know I've been living under the same roof as you for three years, but I don't know one cog from another. I cannot get you any projects to work on."

"Then send Teresina to Eduardo. He can come and plaster my leg now."

"He was the one who wanted to wait until tonight," Serenita told him. "I think he knows you better than you know yourself. You'd never agree to bed rest if you're capable of moving around."

"Serenita, you'll be the death of me!" Telchide cried out. "Is there nothing you can give me to do?"

"I can bring you your notebook. That's as much as you can expect to do in your condition."

Telchide smiled automatically and waited impatiently for Serenita to bring him his notebook. He spent the rest of the day consumed with thoughts about the sparking plants. There were so many things he wanted to try with them.

***

It was past six in the evening when Telchide heard voices in his workshop. His heart beat faster as he recognised one of the voices as Aveline's. He thought it was in excitement to see her until thoughts of Teresina and Serenita intruded.

Would they be able to tell that something had happened between the two of them? Teresina would hopefully still think kindly of Aveline, since his fellow Inventrice had pierced her ears and done her hair. But what of Serenita? Had she guessed something had happened between them when he was returned home, unconscious, last night?

"Ardo, I don't care if he climbs to the top of the Inventrici clocktower tomorrow. We're putting that cast on him tonight. It's too dangerous not to."

Telchide smiled. Lucrezia was a force to be reckoned with. Before this trip, he would never have expected her to advocate for him in any way. Now, it seemed she was more on his side than his best friend.

The door to his room burst open. Teresina jumped up onto his bed and Telchide screamed.

"Sorry papà!" she whispered as she slid off. "I forgot."

Telchide clenched his teeth and smiled, tearfully. He couldn't speak.

"Teresina! Let me see those piercings." Aveline took Teresina by the hand and drew her away from the bed. Telchide tried to catch her eye, breathing through the pain, but she appeared to be studiously avoiding his gaze.

"There now, your ears are healing quite nicely. And those dragonflies suit you perfectly."

Telchide smiled as Teresina proudly tilted her head from side to side, preening happily.

The two of them were bundled off to the kitchen by Lucrezia as Eduardo set up the equipment they would need. It all looked very alchemical.

"Erm, exactly what are you planning on doing with that?" he asked, pointing to the green liquid.

"It will harden the cast once we're done," Lucrezia explained. "But first, we need to lubricate your leg so the plaster doesn't stick to your skin. Eduardo, I'll leave that to you while I beg Serenita for some hot water."

Lucrezia left the room in a flurry of bright red skirts. Telchide wondered if she chose the colour to disguise any bloodstains from her clients. He'd never taken the time to wonder about it before, but he knew many Alchimisti wore red when they went to visit patients.

When the colourful skirts had vanished from sight, Telchide's gaze turned back to Eduardo. His old friend hadn't said a single word to him.

"Serenita told me there may be a problem with Teresina."

Eduardo mumbled in agreement as he began to spread a gooey solution over Telchide's leg.

"Tell me truthfully – is her memory loss caused by your pills, Ardo?"

Eduardo's hands paused for only a moment, but Telchide noticed it.

"It's a possibility," Eduardo answered, his face carefully blank. "I told Serenita to use them sparingly. I didn't design them for such regular use. It makes me wonder..."

"What?" Telchide asked sharply. "*What* does it make you wonder?"

Eduardo shook his head and kept working. Telchide couldn't get another word out of him, try as he might.

Lucrezia returned with a bowl of steaming water and set it down on the floor next to Telchide's bed. Eduardo excused himself to wash his hands.

"What was all that about?" Lucrezia asked. "I could cut the air with a knife."

Telchide crossed his arms angrily. "He's hiding something from me – about the purple pills he gave me for Teresina."

"Purple pills?" Lucrezia asked as she began to soak the bits of plaster.

Telchide sighed and told her everything that had happened since the night Eduardo had given him the pills until that morning when he'd discovered Teresina's memory problems.

Eduardo hadn't returned. Telchide thought perhaps the old Alchimista was purposely avoiding him.

"What do you make of it?" Telchide asked Lucrezia.

She put the last bandage on, rinsed her hands in the cloudy water and dried them on a white cloth. Only then did she answer him.

"Do you know if Teresina's had any dreams at all since taking those pills?"

Telchide nodded. "She's had a few nightmares. That's when they increased the dose."

"And after that?"

Telchide shrugged.

"I see." Lucrezia poked her head out of the door, looking sideways down the hall. For a moment, Telchide thought she was going to leave his cast half done. "If you prefer not to have him in the room right now, I can do the green paste by myself. But it will be easier with another Alchimista to help me."

"Get him in here," Telchide said. "Maybe *you* can get some answers out of him."

"Excuse me a moment then," Lucrezia said. She walked out and left Telchide wondering what in Caldera's smoke was going on.

He heard the hushed sounds of a heated argument before Lucrezia pushed Eduardo, none too gently, into the room.

"Tell him what you just told me."

Telchide looked up at Eduardo expectantly. The Alchimista rubbed his arm nervously.

"Teresina stopped dreaming entirely when Serenita started giving her two pills a night. I *did* try to warn her that it might not be the best idea, but she was getting so tired with Teresina waking so often with her nightmares. She's getting on a bit, you know."

Telchide stared coldly at him, not giving him any room for prevarication.

"Yes, well." Eduardo rubbed the back of his neck. "It appears her memory problems became much worse after that. I told Serenita to stop the pills, but she wouldn't listen."

"*You're* the Alchimista, Eduardo. If you thought they were unsafe, you should've taken them away," Telchide said angrily, trying to dismiss the fact that Serenita omitted that fact.

"And so, I did," Eduardo added quickly.

Telchide was about to make another angry retort when Eduardo's answer registered.

"But if you took them away, why hasn't her memory come back?" Telchide asked, curious despite himself.

Eduardo didn't answer. Lucrezia elbowed him firmly. He gave her an injured look, but she only glared at him.

"What's going on?" Telchide felt a chill run down his spine. "Eduardo, what aren't you telling me?"

Eduardo coughed. "Serenita told me last night that she found another stash of the purple pills."

"Where?"

"Chide, please try to understand, I didn't know of this side effect until a week or so ago," Eduardo told him.

"What is it?" Telchide roared, his ribs aching with the effort.

Eduardo stumbled back, but Lucrezia did not let him leave the room.

"Tell him," she said firmly.

Eduardo looked at her fearfully. Then over to Telchide who had a sinking feeling in his stomach.

"Months before she disappeared, Sebetine asked me for something to help her sleep. She couldn't handle the restless nights when Teresina was so young. You must understand, she was exhausted."

Eduardo hesitated. Telchide let everything sink in.

"Are you ... can you possibly be telling me that my companion disappeared because you ruined her memory?"

"It's possible," Eduardo said quietly. "But I didn't know. You didn't say anything about her memory to me."

"Don't you dare blame *me* for this! We had a sleepless toddler. Both of us were sleep deprived and I was working hard to earn my Silver Guild Mark so I could charge more money to provide for my family. I barely even saw Sebetine!"

"I know, I know." Eduardo held up his hands in a placating manner. It did nothing to soften Telchide's mood.

"I'm too angry to even talk to you about that right now. But I will. I *promise* you. I will." Telchide took a steadying breath, wincing at the pain in his ribs. "Are you telling me Serenita and Teresina found what was left of Sebetine's pills and used those without you knowing about it?"

Eduardo nodded. "I thought it was strange when they stopped asking me for help. Everything went silent. I came over every few days to check on them, but Serenita quickly sent me away. I should've pushed for more information, but she wouldn't let me in."

Telchide didn't know who to be angrier with – Serenita for going against Eduardo's recommendation to stop giving Teresina the pills, or Eduardo for ever suggesting them in the first place.

"Is there anything else?" he asked in a cold voice. "Is there any other way you've ruined my life while I've been away?"

Eduardo looked down but did not answer. Telchide couldn't keep his temper any longer.

"What else!" he roared through the blinding pain of his ribs.

"We're not in trouble," Eduardo answered quickly. "Not yet anyway. But it seems as though the authorities don't quite believe that we didn't collaborate with your Lightbox. I tried to convince them that you simply asked me for alchemical solutions and I sold them to you. Nothing more, nothing less.

"They can't prove that we've been working together so they can't punish us. But they'll be watching us closely now. We won't be able to work together anymore."

"Why in Caldera's smoke would I *ever* want to work with *you* again?" Telchide knew he was being cruel, but he didn't care. Eduardo had lost him his companion and ruined his daughter's memory.

There was a moment of silence. Telchide realised the entire house was silent. There was no sound, even from the kitchen. Lucrezia was effectively barring the doorway so Eduardo could not escape.

"Tell me one thing," Telchide said in a quieter voice. "If you suspect Sebetine was taking too many of your pills, what do you think happened to her?"

Eduardo seemed to shrink in on himself. "You understand, this is merely conjecture?"

Telchide didn't answer. Eduardo's shoulders sagged.

"I would assume she set out to visit Serenita and forgot what she was doing on the way there. If she fell asleep before she reached the waypoint, that could easily have happened. She would've wandered off somewhere and gotten lost.

"Depending on how bad the situation was, even if she didn't continue taking the pills, her memory could've been permanently damaged. She wouldn't remember anything much. If she resurfaced in any of the cities on Beltigura, they would've found her."

"You think she's dead then?"

Eduardo nodded unhappily. "With this new information, I can't see any possibility where she's still alive. She wouldn't have brought many coins with her for that journey, and she wasn't a Guild member. I doubt she would've been able to keep down a job, even if she found one in the first place."

"Dead," Telchide mumbled to himself.

"I'm sorry, Chide," Eduardo said pathetically.

"Get out," Telchide said in a dangerously low voice. "Get out, *now*. I don't want to speak to you. I don't want to see you. Get out of my house and do not come back."

Lucrezia made way for the old Alchimista. There was a hint of pity in her face, but more anger.

Telchide didn't watch as Eduardo left. He heard the heavy footfalls on the stairs. Eduardo went down alone. Even Teresina's light footsteps didn't follow. Had she heard? Did she know what had happened to her? What had happened to her mamma?

"I'm sorry, Chide," Lucrezia said softly. "If it's any consolation, I'm sure Eduardo didn't do any of that on purpose."

"I don't care if he did it on purpose," Telchide answered angrily and loudly. "He ruined my entire family!"

There was a sound by the door. Telchide looked up in time to see Teresina's heartbroken face.

"I'm not *ruined*, papà."

He didn't have time to say anything before she ran to her bedroom and slammed the door shut.

"Well, you made a right mess of that," Lucrezia stated plainly.

Her manners did not improve upon befriending her. Telchide waited impatiently as she covered his cast in that hideously green paste. Curious despite his anger, he watched as it hardened instantly upon contact with the plaster strips on his leg. He'd never seen such an alchemical reaction between two substances before. It took Lucrezia a half hour to do the entire cast, carefully lifting his leg to do the underside as well.

"I'm done here. I've left a pair of crutches in your workshop. Serenita can bring them up to you when you're ready to walk. It will take time for you to learn to use them, and it will be a strain with your broken ribs. Don't be a lavalump and fall down the stairs. Much as I enjoy spending time with you, I don't want to come back to put your other leg in a plaster."

Telchide didn't have the heart to smile at her bad joke. The most he could manage was a short nod.

Lucrezia hesitated before gathering her things.

"Aveline came to keep me company. Do you ... would you like to see her before we leave?"

Telchide shook his head. As much as he wanted Aveline in his life, now was not the time. Not when he'd realised that his companion really was most likely dead – that his best friend had unknowingly caused her death. He wouldn't know what to say to Aveline. He didn't think there was anything *she* could possibly say to him. Not right now.

"Very well," Lucrezia said quietly. "I'll be back in a week or so to check on your progress. If you have any trouble in the meantime, I'd say Eduardo can help, but I doubt you want him to. Just send me a message and I'll come."

Telchide nodded and closed his eyes as she walked out. It was so difficult to keep the angry tears at bay. He listened as muffled voices spoke for a long while in the kitchen. Telchide wondered what Serenita thought of the whole mess, where she'd found Sebetine's pills. There were too many people to blame, including himself.

It had been selfish of him to go on the expedition and expect her to look after his child. He could have insisted that Teresina come on the expedition, but she would've been in just as much danger there – all of them had experienced some danger on the Caldera. The only thing he could have done differently was to simply not go.

"Chide?"

Aveline stood in the doorway. Telchide fought down the happiness at seeing her – he did not deserve to feel anything but anger and guilt. He'd specifically told Lucrezia that he didn't want to see Aveline, yet here she was.

"You don't have to say anything, but I do. I heard what happened with Teresina, and Sebetine. And I know how your mind works. Right now, you're berating yourself for going on the expedition, thinking that if you hadn't gone, none of this would've happened."

Telchide huffed. He wouldn't admit to her that she was right.

"Once you've thought about it reasonably, you'll realise it's probably a good thing that you went. If you hadn't, the problem with Teresina's memory may not have surfaced so soon. After all, you barely noticed it with Sebetine. You've managed to catch it a lot sooner with Teresina precisely because you went away. Just think on that. And please don't dismiss what I've said just because it makes you feel better to take on responsibility for everything."

She turned to go. Telchide couldn't remain angry with her, especially as she was right.

"Thank you, Veli."

Aveline paused and turned back to him, in a hesitating manner.

"I heard Kesida wants to see you as soon as possible. If you'll permit me, I'll accompany you to the Guild hall tomorrow. You can see what she wants, and we can tell her about the trip and ask for an isolated workshop."

Telchide nodded. "That would be good. Thank you."

Aveline looked at him for a long moment. She opened her mouth and Telchide leaned forward waiting for her to say something, anything else. But she shook her head and quickly turned away, leaving him alone with his thoughts.

Chapter 30 – Argentodi 4 Alchimisti 230 Years After Implosion

Telchide looked at the crutches leaning against the wall next to his bed. He could reach them easily enough, though it strained his ribs to stretch out to them.

He didn't hear voices. In fact, he hadn't heard Teresina at all since she'd slammed the door to her room the night before. And Serenita had made herself scarce after bringing him a plate of pasta and later helping him to the water closet. He'd been forced to sleep in his day clothes.

With the crutches on either side of him, Telchide heaved himself up out of bed. He limped unsteadily towards the kitchen. It was only as he got closer that he heard the whispering.

"Don't be ridiculous, Resi. Your papà loves you. He really doesn't think you're ruined. Stop this nonsense and eat your porridge."

Telchide awkwardly pushed open the door and stumbled into the room. Teresina didn't look up at him. Serenita glanced his way, slopped some porridge into another bowl.

"Good morning," he said stiffly.

There was no reply. He bent over Teresina and kissed the top of her head. She wriggled out away from him and moved her bowl closer to Serenita.

"How did you sleep last night? I didn't hear you wake up."

"I didn't take another purple pill," Teresina said in a petulant tone. "Lucrezia gave me a sleeping tablet instead. She said if I was forced to sleep, maybe I wouldn't wake up during the night even if I had nightmares."

"I see," Telchide said, not knowing what else to say. But then something dawned on him. "That means you remember something from yesterday. Your memory is working again."

Teresina paused, spoon halfway to her mouth, and looked over at Serenita. She nodded her head almost imperceptibly.

"But I can't remember everything," Teresina told him. "Just bits and pieces. I can't remember them bringing you home, even though Nonna says I was awake, but I do remember seeing you in your bed yesterday morning."

"Yes, but that's what I mean," Telchide insisted. "You can remember from yesterday because you stopped taking the purple pills."

Teresina looked at him angrily. "No, papà. You don't understand. I only remember bits and pieces, even from yesterday. I don't even know if it's more than any other day."

Telchide sagged back into his chair. He'd hoped that she'd be cured as soon as she stopped taking those accursed pills, but it just couldn't be as simple as that.

The conversation died. Teresina, quite pointedly, told *Serenita* that she was going to play outside. Telchide couldn't help feeling hurt. He knew he'd made a mess of things, but he missed his daughter. He loved her. But he'd let her down, made her feel broken, ruined. That was solely *his* fault.

"Do you think she'll forgive me any time soon?" Telchide asked Serenita with a defeated smile.

She gave him an odd look. "Of course, Chide. Teresina will forgive you as quickly as you forgive me."

Telchide wanted to protest that he didn't blame her, but he did.

"Just tell me one thing," he said, trying to keep the anger from his voice. "Where did you find Sebetine's pills?"

Serenita drew a sharp breath. "Ardo told me to stop giving the child those pills. He even took them away from us. *I* was the one who asked Teresina to help me search everywhere in the house to see if somehow we could find something else that would help us. We both needed sleep. In truth, we weren't even looking for the pills. Neither of us had any idea that Sebetine had been taking them too. We were looking for something that smelled of you – an unwashed shirt, an old blanket – anything.

"I gave her your blanket and then decided to clear Sebetine's things from your room while we were cleaning up for your apprentice. I found the pills at the back of the drawer in her bedside table. Once we realised what they were, we kept it a secret from Eduardo. I knew he'd take them away if we told him. If you want someone to blame, blame *me*. *I* did this to your daughter. Me. No one else."

Telchide stared at Serenita trying to find a way to let go of his anger with all of them. But he couldn't do it. He'd put them in this situation. He was the one who'd been so desperate to go on his adventure that he'd left a vecchietta in charge of a six-year-old child with sleeping problems. Eduardo had prescribed dangerous pills and Serenita had purposely abused them.

"I *am* angry," he admitted. "But you gave up your entire life in Tor'Dumere to help me find your daughter and then further to help me look after Teresina. You did the best you could. I shouldn't have asked so much of you. It won't happen again."

He wanted to say more, as though his words might fix everything. But he knew they wouldn't. His attention was drawn to a loud knocking at the front door.

"I'll go," Telchide said, struggling to his feet.

"And whoever it is will be long gone by the time you get downstairs. Go clean yourself up. I'll open the shop."

He nodded and reached over the table to drag his porridge towards him. He quickly ate his breakfast and made his way to the sink to wash his face. He was drying himself off when Aveline walked into the room. Absurdly,

Telchide felt a blush spread over his cheeks. Aveline had seen him in much more compromising positions than drying his face.

"I'm sorry," she mumbled. "Serenita told me to come up while she minds the shop."

"No, of course, that's fine, of course, yes," Telchide stumbled over his words as her eyes stayed fixed on him. "Did you have a pleasant evening?"

Aveline smiled prettily. "Indeed. Nevio's so glad to have me home again that he offered to make me more tea and coffee than I could possibly drink in one sitting."

Telchide grinned. "That's an ... interesting reception."

"Well, he knows how much I enjoy warm drinks." Aveline laughed.

"I don't suppose I can offer you one now then?" Telchide asked, eager to spend more time with her.

Aveline bit her lip and looked down for a moment. "I actually have a lot of orders waiting for me at home. Nevio was busy promoting me to anyone who walked in the door. I only have time to go down to the Guild Hall to work out an arrangement with Kesida."

"Of course," Telchide said too quickly, trying to hide his disappointment.

Serenita had only managed to take two commissions for pocket watches in his absence. If he didn't already have the elaborate music boxes to work on, he'd have no work by the end of the week.

He accepted Aveline's help down the stairs with a comment that her chair lift would certainly come in handy if he had one now. The slow trip brought them in much closer proximity than he would've liked with Serenita watching them like a hawk from the fireplace.

"Slowly, Chide," Aveline told him as he tried to rush. "If you break your other leg, Crez will never let me forget it."

"Yes, *Chide*, we wouldn't want you to fall again," Serenita said.

Telchide frowned at her tone. She was definitely trying to hide a smile. Did she know what had happened? Could she possibly suspect? He tried not to panic. None of it made sense. If she knew, she wouldn't be so happy. Would she?

It didn't matter. Aveline had seemed quite adamant about the fact that she couldn't live with his companion's mamma, even if that companion proved to be dead, seemed highly likely now.

"I should have him back to you within an hour," Aveline told Serenita with poise and serenity. Telchide admired that in her, but also envied her people skills. "We have some Guild business to attend to and will return immediately from there."

"Yes, yes. Take your time." Serenita shooed them out the door. "I'll tell any customers that you're back in town, Chide. Now go and sort out what's happening with your apprentice."

Telchide barely had time to nod before Aveline whisked him away. He belatedly realised that he'd not bothered to farewell Teresina. He balanced on his crutches, his leg swinging with indecision, but didn't go back. His daughter was still clearly hurt and angry with him. He'd have time enough that afternoon to make amends.

He couldn't help but think of Eduardo out here on the street. On any other day, he'd have suggested going in on their way back. Not today. Perhaps not ever again. That thought hurt him more than he thought possible.

His silence lasted much longer than it should have. Aveline's expression was uneasy when he glanced at her.

"Is anything the matter?" he asked with concern.

"No more than it was when we were planning to leave Sentigura Caldera, and your leg wasn't broken. Everything's still the same – only worse."

"How is it worse?"

Telchide stumbled with his crutches over a crack in the street pavement. Aveline caught his arm steadied him.

"Well, I suppose it isn't. It just won't change any time soon. You can't make any more commitments in your life. Your daughter will need all the attention you can give her, especially now, and I don't suppose your broken leg and a new apprentice will help matters."

Telchide sighed. "Veli, Teresina will *always* need my attention. The only difference right now is that I need to find some way to help her memory return."

He paused. "I think Serenita may suspect something."

Aveline laughed. "Oh Chide, of *course* she suspects something. She knows you better than most of us."

Telchide coughed. "Well, erm, she doesn't appear displeased. I think she likes you."

"No." Aveline waved her arms in front of herself like a shield. "No. No. *No*. I don't care how much you think she likes me. I could never do what you're thinking. Aside from the fact that I don't trust her after what happened with Teresina, it would be a unreasonably unfair situation for Serenita ... and me."

"Fine, fine," Telchide mumbled, trying to quash his own anger with Serenita. "Forget I said anything."

He kept his silence the rest of the way to the Guild Hall. It wasn't usually a long walk – just a few blocks – but his arms were aching from managing the crutches by the time they arrived. With Aveline's help, he managed to make his way to the top of the stairs.

The doors to the Guild Hall were open, unlike the last time he was here.

Telchide hobbled in behind Aveline. They walked through the Hall of Great Works. As always, Telchide couldn't help but look at the inventions along the shelves on the walls.

"Look, there's your zipper!"

Telchide pointed at the left wall. He turned to Aveline. She was blushing quite brightly.

"It was nothing," she said modestly.

"Ah, Aveline, you'll have trouble convincing *anyone* that it was nothing. It revolutionised clothing!" he said as they approached the desk where Kesida sat busily filling out paperwork.

The Guild Amministratrice looked up at that comment.

"Another reason you Inventrici keep making the Authorities knock on my door and breathe down my neck."

Telchide stopped in his tracks, suddenly remembering Eduardo's comments about the Lightbox.

"Chide, I'll deal with you in a moment. Aveline, what do you want?"

Aveline cleared her throat. "Well, actually we've come together to ask if you have any isolated warehouses or empty workshops that are available to rent. We found something on our expedition that could revolutionise power sources, if we can find a way to make use of it."

Kesida eyed them carefully. "You both have workshops of your own. Why do you need another space?"

"The, ah, item we found can be quite ... erm ... dangerous," Telchide told her. "We don't want to ruin our other work."

He immediately tried to fidget with his buttons, but that only succeeded in making him drop one of his crutches. Aveline stooped to pick it up for him.

"What's this item, if I may ask?" Kesida looked at Telchide. Telchide looked at Aveline.

"Oh, for Caldera's sake," Aveline muttered under her breath and pulled up her sleeve to reveal her mostly healed burns. "It's a sparking plant. We know it produces energy because of the tests we conducted on the Caldera. But it's dangerous. The energy of the plant can cause severe burns, potentially fatalities, and generates so much power that it can make lightbulbs explode. We need a safe and clear area to carry out our experiments so that we can harness the power of these sparking plants without damaging everything in sight."

Kesida's mouth hung open. She closed it slowly.

"The Guild does own a few properties throughout the city," she told them after a moment of consideration, "but it'll take some time for me to locate one that's suitable for your purposes. I suggest you keep these plants safely locked up until further notice. Come back Orodi afternoon, just before five o'clock. I should've found something for you by then."

Telchide nodded.

"Aveline, if you bring your blazermobile, I'll direct you there and explain everything you'll need to know about your building. Are we agreed?"

"Agreed," Telchide said in unison with Aveline. He was already dreading the ride in her blazermobile.

"Right then. Aveline, you can go." Kesida dismissed her with the wave of her hand. "Chide, we have some other business."

Aveline looked at Telchide in concern.

"I'll be fine. I'm sure Kesida can help me down the stairs and I can walk back to my house perfectly well by myself."

"Very well. I'll see you Orodi evening then."

Telchide nodded affably. He turned his attention to Kesida, but the Guild Amministratrice did not move until Aveline had left the room. She then rang a bell and waited. Her odd behaviour set Telchide on edge.

"Is something the matter, Kesida?"

She waved him to silence. A young man who looked to be less than twenty years old came into the room.

"Zeno, I need you at the desk. I have business to address with Telchide. You know the routine. If anyone wants to lodge a Great Work, get them to fill out the paperwork before leaving it. If they have requests, write them down and tell them they can wait until I return or I'll send a message for them later."

"Yes, Kesida," Zeno replied obediently.

Telchide felt the young man's eyes on him and shifted uncomfortably.

"Telchide, come with me."

Kesida didn't wait for him to reply before walking towards a side door. Telchide had never been through it. With Kesida using his full name, he was beginning to fear that all was not well. He didn't want to go through that door but had no choice.

He followed Kesida through two more rooms before an elaborate staircase spiralled up ahead of them. Kesida silently began to climb it. Telchide coughed.

"I'm not very good with these crutches yet."

Kesida turned around and sighed. "Sorry, Telchide, but we need to go upstairs. I'll help you."

"What's going on, Kesida?" Telchide asked nervously as she helped him navigate his way up the stairs.

"Not here, Chide," she whispered. "The walls have ears."

Her manner disturbed him, so he remained silent until they finally reached the room which Kesida was adamant that they use. She closed the door behind them and locked it, pointing to the walls.

"They've been soundproofed, you see. It's the only room where I can say what I like without the Maestri, or anyone else, overhearing."

Telchide looked around. It was a well-furnished room, with several chairs. He immediately headed for the nearest one. His good leg wouldn't last much longer. When he was settled, with the crutches beside him, Telchide finally faced Kesida again.

"*Now* will you tell me what in Caldera's smoke is going on?"

Kesida took the seat beside him.

"I showed your Great Work to the Maestri, Chide, your Lightbox. I was hoping they would give you an Electrum Guild Mark so that you could take the twins as your apprentices. The thing is, Telchide, it *should* have been accepted. There was no reason for it not to be. But they refused."

"Oh," Telchide said softly. He took off his hat and started playing with the rim. "Would it have made a difference if we waited until I tested it more – found a way to stop the automation after a certain amount of time rather than letting it run its course?"

Kesida smiled sadly and patted his arm.

"No, Chide. It wouldn't. They don't want your Lightbox on display. At least not right now. There's too much tension with the Inter-Guild Edict. The Authorities can't prove that you collaborated with Eduardo to create this, but they're suspicious enough of everything to make both your lives difficult. We'd be forced to punish you – possibly strip you of your Silver Guild Mark."

Telchide stared at her uncomprehendingly. "But that's absurd! We can't be the only ones doing this. Aveline worked with the Sarta Guild to create her zipper and you have *that* on display."

"True." Kesida nodded. "But Aveline created that before the ban. We have the paperwork to prove it."

"I see."

Telchide stared at his knees. Not only had Eduardo ruined his family, but their partnership had almost ruined their Guild status.

"Now, I *do* still have an apprentice for you. It's one of the twins. When the Maestri refused your Great Work, they ruined the hopes of these young men to stay together. My hope is that you'll take one of the twins and Eduardo takes the other. That way they'll live as close together as possible."

"But you've just told me I can't see Eduardo anymore. How will it help our situation if we share twin apprentices?"

Kesida shrugged. "It'll give you both a proper excuse to see each other or exchange messages without being noticed."

"We already have a method for that," Telchide said numbly.

Kesida leaned forward, a look of intense interest on her face. "What do you mean you already have a method?"

Telchide explained about the message box he'd invented so that he and Eduardo could communicate when the Inter-Guild Edict started.

"Why didn't you ever submit *that* as a great work?" Kesida asked incredulously. "I'm certain it would be considered."

"I always assumed the Authorities would find the one going between my house and Eduardo's." He sighed heavily. "I doubt it'll be used much anymore."

"Why's that?"

"I don't want to talk about it," Telchide said firmly. "If you think it'll be considered as a Great Work, then I'll disassemble it from our houses and submit it. If I don't get the Electrum Guild Mark, I don't want to take one of the twins. It would be unfair of me when I never want to talk to Eduardo again. I wouldn't want my apprentice to feel awkward visiting his brother or the other way around."

"Chide, what in Caldera's smoke happened?" Kesida studied him closely. "Eduardo's your best friend. Everyone knows that. Why would you never want to speak with him again?"

Telchide pursed his lips. He couldn't tell her. Not when he was still so angry. Kesida sighed.

"Very well, I'll pick it up when I come tonight," she told him. "We'll submit it as a Great Work. Even if it isn't quite enough to earn you an Electrum Guild Mark on its own, I'm certain I can persuade the Maestri to grant you one because the Lightbox should've earned it for you."

Telchide smiled gratefully. "So, if they agree, the twins will come along at some point in the next week or two?"

Kesida laughed. "No, Chide. I'll pick them up and bring them to your place tonight. Serenita showed me the room she prepared. Florio and Gaspare won't mind sharing a bed for now."

"But, but, but, what if the Maestri don't agree to the Electrum Guild Mark? I don't want them to get their hopes up."

Kesida waved a hand. "Never you mind about that. You *will* earn your Electrum Guild Mark. I'll make sure of that. Just don't start their training until it's all official. Agreed?"

"Agreed," Telchide said automatically.

An Electrum Guild Mark! He could barely fathom it. It would put him at the same level as Aveline. He'd be able to charge an even higher premium for his work. His family would never need to worry about money again, even with two extra mouths to feed.

"Kesida, what do I pay them? What are the standard fees? How does this work?"

Kesida laughed. "Oh Chide! You never pay attention at Guild meetings, do you? Apprentices don't get paid. You feed, clothe, and house them for seven years while you teach them your trade. They only start to earn a wage if you hire them after they earn their Copper Guild Mark."

"That's not fair at all!" he cried out indignantly.

"Did *you* get paid as an apprentice?" she asked him.

Telchide paused and thought about it. Eventually, he shook his head.

"If you'd like to give them a copper a week as a token gesture, that's entirely up to you. But don't feel obliged. These boys won't be expecting anything. After all, you don't pay your daughter, do you?"

"Well, of course not ... she's my *daughter*."

"Exactly, and you should treat these boys as your sons – your almost grown-up sons. At least until their apprenticeship is over."

Kesida got to her feet. "I can't be absent from my desk too much longer. Let's go."

"So, about the Lightbox," Telchide said as he got to his feet. "Can I patent it without it being a Great Work? Do I have permission to reproduce it for sale?"

Kesida paused, halfway to the door.

"I know it would bring you a small fortune, Chide, but is that money worth your status and freedom?"

Telchide sighed. "No, no it isn't."

Kesida walked to the door and paused with her hand on the lock. "Chide, this Edict won't last forever. When it ends, you can bring your Lightbox back to us and you might even earn your Gold Guild Mark from it. You'll be set for life. Just have patience."

Telchide sighed. "I didn't think the Edict would last as long as it has already. Three years is a long time! How can the authorities not see that the only Guild profiting out of this arrangement is the very Guild which pushed for the Edict to be introduced?"

"The Mercantili Guild is rich," Kesida replied in a matter-of-fact tone. "Everyone knows they brought in the Trading Edict because their profits were dwindling. Who knows how they managed to convince Ministro Ercolano to agree to the Inter-Guild Edict? But with their profits increasing due to all their smoking edicts, they can afford to keep paying to ensure they continue."

"It's not fair," Telchide muttered, sulkily.

"No, it isn't, but it won't last forever. Things like this never do."

Telchide sighed. He'd never understand how money corrupted people so thoroughly.

***

Telchide limped home slowly. He blamed the progress on his broken leg and learning the most efficient way to move with the crutches, but he knew it was because his mind was a blur of activity. When he finally arrived, he'd come to a decision.

"Serenita, we need another bed. It appears I am to have twin apprentices."

Serenita stared at him in shock. "But Chide, you can't! You only have your Silver Guild Mark."

Telchide shrugged. "Kesida's handling things. The boys will arrive tonight, and I don't want them to feel unwelcome. I can make another bed; I just need the wood."

"No," Serenita told him. "You need to focus on the music box that stuffy lady commissioned. If we're to have two extra mouths to feed, we'll need that money as soon as possible."

Telchide looked at Serenita in confusion.

"I have a small sum stashed away, Serenita. You needn't concern yourself about money."

Serenita waved his reassurance aside. "You listen to me, Chide. If the boys eat as much as I think they will, you won't make money quickly enough to feed them. And if Teresina's nightmares continue, you won't be clear-headed enough to make your inventions in a timely manner. Not on your Silver Guild Mark."

"I won't be on a Silver Guild Mark much longer. Kesida made it clear she will ensure I have my Electrum within a week. Until then, the boys will stay here without beginning their apprenticeship."

Teresina came down the stairs and into the workshop.

"So ... I'll get two new brothers tonight then?" she asked in an odd tone.

Telchide nodded. "I suppose that's one way to see it. Their apprenticeship will last for seven years."

He handed her a slip of paper.

"Florio and Gaspare," she read their names aloud. "What if we don't like them? Can we send them back?"

"Teresina, I don't think that's how it works."

"But you haven't met them. *I* haven't met them," she said angrily. "What if they're horrible? What if they're mean to me?" She stopped and whispered, "What if you start to love them more than you love me?"

Telchide wanted nothing more than to quickly cross the workshop to sweep her up in his arms. But the smoking cast wouldn't let him. He held his arms out for her, but she stood still. Telchide was forced to limp his way over to her with his crutches. He tried to draw her in for a hug, but she resisted.

"I will *never* love my apprentices more than I love you. It simply isn't possible."

Teresina sniffed, tears starting to roll down her cheeks. "But you'll spend *all day* with them. You'll forget I even exist."

"My little Resi, if I didn't forget you, even for a single day, on the Caldera, what makes you think I'll forget you when we live in the same house?"

She wiped her teary face on her sleeve, then threw her arms around his waist. "I love you so much, papà. I'm so sorry that I'm ruined."

Telchide's chest hurt inexorably. He motioned for Serenita to bring over a chair. He sat down and pulled Teresina onto his lap.

"You're not *ruined*, Resi," he told her, voice thick with emotion.

"That's what you told Ardo," she said quietly. "I heard you."

Telchide held her close and kissed the top of her head. "I said it, that's true, but I didn't mean it the way you think I did. I was angry with him. He should never have given you those pills if he thought they might be unsafe. *Eduardo* is the one who is ruined. If we let word of this out, his business would dry up overnight."

Teresina pulled away from him. "You wouldn't do that, would you papà? He was only trying to help."

"Just like he was just trying to help with your mamma," Telchide said bitterly. "She lost her memory, and I didn't even realise. I sent her to her death."

Serenita lay a hand on his shoulder.

"Chide, you can't blame yourself for that. I know you're as angry with yourself as you are with me and Eduardo right now, but that's not helping anyone. You can't stay distant from him forever."

"Actually, I can, and I must," Telchide sighed. "The Authorities are suspicious that we're working together. We can't be seen together anymore. In fact, Teresina, I'm going to need your help. You need to ask Eduardo's apprentices to help you disassemble the message box and bring it back here. Kesida wants me to give it to her this evening."

Teresina hopped off his lap and stared at him.

"But papà, we *need* that box."

"We can't afford to have anything linking this house with Eduardo's – it's too dangerous right now," Telchide explained. "So, I need you to watch what I do with this one and then go through the back door to Eduardo's and do the same there. Do you think you can do that for me?"

Teresina nodded solemnly. He adored her so much. How many other six-year-olds would he be able to entrust with such an important task?

"Serenita, while we do this, could you please arrange for a message to be sent to Signora Loyola to inform her that I've returned. Did she send the sheet music in my absence?"

Serenita nodded and opened his workbench drawer to reveal it.

"Good, then I'll let her know that the music box will be ready in six weeks."

He wrote a note on a slip of paper. Serenita would need to take it to the Postal Service connected to the Inventrici Guild. It was the closest one and cost less for them because he was a Guild member. Serenita took the paper and the coins that he held out to her.

"If you give me enough money, I'll order you another bed. You don't have time to waste on making one."

Telchide sighed. He knew she was right, but that didn't make it any easier. He was a Falegname's son. He *knew* how to make a bed. Why should he have to pay someone else to make it for him?

"Go to the Falegname Guild Hall and ask for Maestro Filippo. Tell him the order is for me and I need his recommendation for a Falegname."

Serenita looked at him strangely. "Chide, I'm not going to bother a maestro over a bed. Why can't I just go to any Copper Falegname?"

A small smile flickered over Telchide's face. "Because Filippo's my friend and I trust his judgement. He knows how I work and what I like. If you won't let me build the bed myself, this is the only way around it."

He waited until she rolled her eyes at him and sighed heavily before handing over the extra coins for a deposit for a new beds.

***

True to her word, Kesida showed up that evening with Florio and Gaspare. The boys were short for their age, or so it seemed to Telchide. Both had chestnut hair, but while Florio had dark brown eyes, Gaspare's were a light hazel. Telchide was glad for the distinction. He would never be able to tell them apart otherwise.

"Come in, come in." Serenita ushered them in from the pouring rain. "I'll fetch a pot of tea. You boys like tea, yes?"

They both nodded, shivering in their threadbare clothes. Kesida deposited her umbrella by the coat rack, bundled the boys further into the room and nodded towards Telchide.

"Boys, meet Telchide Inventore," said Kesida. "You'll both be apprenticed to him but, as I've already explained, he won't be able to start training you until the paperwork for his Electrum Guild Mark is finalised. In the meantime, I expect you to help around the house."

Telchide coughed uncomfortably. He didn't like the way Kesida made it sound as though they needed to earn their keep. That wasn't the way he wanted them to feel.

"This is my daughter, Teresina," he said, hugging her tightly. "She'll be wonderful company for the two of you. I know she's young, but she's more well-read than most children I know."

Florio raised an eyebrow and looked at his brother.

"Papà, they might not be able to read," Teresina whispered, her eyes fixed firmly on the boys.

Telchide looked at her in surprise. "Nonsense. I'm sure they can read. Can't you, boys?"

The boys shook their heads.

"We know our numbers," Gaspare said quickly, his face bright red with embarrassment. "But they didn't teach us much at the orphanage. We..."

"...weren't worth the effort. That's what they told us." Florio finished his sentence. "If you don't want us because of that, we'll understand."

Telchide saw Kesida's panicked look contrast with the sad acceptance of the boys.

"Nonsense," Telchide said forcefully. "Just because no one bothered to teach you to read is no reason for me to discard you. You're part of this family now and that's final. Kesida, how long do you think it will take before the paperwork's finalised with the Guild? I have that message box ready for you here."

Kesida looked to the two machines and the bunch of cables connecting them.

"I'd say no more than a week. Less if I get my way."

Telchide waved his hand dismissively. "No, no. A week is fine. Boys, if you don't think it beneath you, I'll ask Teresina to begin teaching you to read this week. How does that sound? Once your apprenticeship begins, I'll need you to be able to take orders and follow written instructions."

Gaspare started. "You mean, you'll take us?"

"And teach us to read?" Florio added with excitement.

"Every child should be taught to read," Teresina said proudly. "I would love to teach you if you'll let me."

The twins looked at each other and grinned.

"That would make us very happy," Gaspare told her with an enthusiastic nod.

Serenita came down the stairs and retrieved a tray laden with a teapot and cups from the dumbwaiter. She placed it on the workbench closest to the stairs and began pouring the tea. Florio and Gaspare immediately went to help her. Serenita, flustered by the sudden attention, shooed them both away.

"For tonight, you're guests. Tomorrow you can start helping. Agreed?"

"Agreed," the boys said in unison.

"Kesida, sit down. Join us." Serenita didn't give the Guild Amministratrice a choice in the matter. She was shown to a chair and a cup of tea placed in her hands. The boys sat near her. Telchide mused that the three must have had a fair amount of interaction if the twins were so comfortable with her.

Telchide watched Teresina. He hoped she would accept the boys. If she taught them how to read, they should respect her as an equal – that was a good start.

"Teresina, do you remember the way to Aveline's house?" he asked her suddenly.

She nodded. He'd taken her there twice before the purple pills had affected her memory.

"Florio and Gaspare can accompany you there tomorrow morning after your first lesson with them. I need you to ask her to pick me up in her blazermobile on Orodi on her way to the Guild Hall. Can you do that for me?"

"Of course, papà." She smiled brightly. "And if you've finished Greta Sarta's music box, we could bring that to her and pick up my new sleeves."

"Indeed, I'll go over it again tonight to be certain," he said.

Gaspare smiled at Teresina. Telchide took that as a good sign. Florio didn't seem so interested. His eyes were wandering all around the workshop.

"Inventore, what inventions do you usually make?" Florio asked in a very formal tone.

"Please, call me Chide. You're going to be here for seven years!"

Kesida held up her hand. "As your apprentices, Chide, they will address you as Maestro or Inventore."

Telchide wanted to argue, but she shook her head at him. He sighed. A lot of things were going to change around the house. He hoped the required formality wouldn't lead to disharmony in the household.

"I must be off." Kesida finished her tea, rose, and placed her cup on the workbench. "Chide, this message box is too cumbersome for me to bring back to the Guild Hall by myself. Bring it when you come with Aveline on Orodi. I'll have the paperwork ready for you to sign."

"Of course, Kesida," he replied, struggling to get to his feet.

Kesida waved him back down. "Very well. Then I bid you good night. Boys, don't give me a reason to regret the decision to go out of my way to help you. Be respectful to this family and try your best to learn as much as you can. Telchide is one of our best Inventrici. You can learn much from him."

The boys nodded and rose to farewell Kesida. Once she left, they both placed their empty teacups on the copper platter and stood awkwardly. Florio's eyes wandered around the workshop again.

Telchide hoped it was with interest.

"To answer your earlier question, Florio, I create many things for my clients. However, the items I prefer to work on are pocket watches and music boxes."

"Music boxes?" Florio asked incredulously. "Shouldn't that be a Musicisti Guild creation?"

"Ah, yes, well, they are brilliant at producing music from their instruments, but not from anything else. Come, have a look at this one."

Telchide motioned for Teresina to pass him his display music box. She brought it over promptly and stayed by his side as he wound up the key underneath then opened the lid. The music immediately played. It was a simple song, but perfectly timed and in tune. Florio and Gaspare leaned closer, pointing to the metal that had been cut into varying length strips so all the bumps could make the right sound.

"But that's amazing!" Gaspare gasped. "It looks so complicated!"

"This is one of my simpler ones in fact. I'll be creating one of my most elaborate ones this month. You'll be able to see it in action before the client comes to pick it up. She requested dancers atop the box. It will be a true work of art when I'm done."

When the music box had run its course, Telchide closed it up and passed it back to Teresina. He rose, with difficulty, to his feet.

"Time to close the workshop."

Serenita walked to the front door. "I'll do that. You get yourself upstairs and show the boys to their room. I ordered another bed today, but it won't be delivered until later this week. Until then, you'll have to share. I hope that's not a problem."

"No, signora," said Florio.

"No problem, signora," agreed Gaspare.

Serenita nodded and locked the door. Telchide took his crutches and looked hesitatingly at the stairs. He'd never minded them before, but the broken leg was making things difficult. He wished that Aveline had finished her chair lift invention. It would certainly come in handy now.

One slow step after another finally brought him to the upper level. The boys and Teresina were close behind him. Telchide pointed to the left.

"The kitchen's over there. Should you need a drink or something to eat at night, don't hesitate to help yourselves. The water closet is just here."

He pointed to a door almost opposite the staircase, just a little to the left. The boys poked their heads inside as Telchide walked down the right hallway.

"This is my room, and Teresina's is the next one." He pointed to the doors on the right-hand side, then pointed to the ones on the left. "This first door's yours and the next one is Serenita's."

Telchide smiled at Teresina fondly as she raced past him to her room. "I'm going to get ready for bed."

The boys didn't move. Both were staring at their bedroom door. It was closed. Telchide opened it and lit a lantern on the bedside. They didn't follow him in.

"You don't like it?" he asked, scratching behind his neck. "I know there's only one bed, but we're fixing that. You won't have to share for long."

The boys stayed still and continued to stare.

"Is something the matter?" he asked them anxiously.

"No, Inventore," Gaspare said in a soft voice. "We've just ... we've never had a room to ourselves before."

Telchide stared at them blankly. "What? Never?"

"Never," Florio replied.

"Well, then this should do quite well for you for the next seven years."

Gaspare walked over so determinedly that Telchide felt a wave of concern. The feeling was quickly washed away when the young man shook his hand heartily. Telchide smiled and patted the boy's arm.

"Well then, I'll leave you to get settled. If you need anything, I'm just across the hall."

With that, he left the room and walked across to his own room. He lit a lamp and closed the door. It had been a long day. How his household had grown to include an extra two people still confused him. He was certain Kesida would sort it all out. He hadn't been expecting two apprentices. He didn't even know how he was meant to teach just one. Teaching two at the same time could prove difficult. What would happen if they were competitive, but one showed more skill as an Inventore than the other? Would there be a friendly sibling rivalry, like with his brothers and sisters, or would it turn nasty? There were so many questions that couldn't possibly be answered until their apprenticeship began. It was certainly going to be interesting.

***

A scream ripped through the air. Telchide startled awake. For a terrifying moment, he thought one of the boys was hurting Teresina. He struggled with his blankets and was just reaching for his crutches when he saw a light in the hallway through his open door. Not knowing what was happening, Telchide limped out of his room and down to Teresina's room.

One of the twins was sitting by her bedside, his hand stroking her hair and whispering soothing sounds to her. He turned when Telchide stepped in and put a finger to his lips. Telchide watched in fascination as the young man soothed his daughter back to sleep. None of them – not him, not Serenita, not even Sebetine – had ever been able to do that. Every time he went to her after a bad dream, she'd ended up in his bed the rest of the night or he'd ended up in hers. Serenita had resorted to giving her an extra pill.

He stood quietly and waited for the boy to come out of Teresina's room. By lantern light, he could now tell it was Gaspare. The boy waved him back up the hall.

"There were a lot of children in our orphanage who had nightmares," he whispered. "We used to take it in turns to soothe them back to sleep. I hope you don't mind."

Telchide smiled faintly. "No, I don't mind. Thank you. I ... thought the worst for a moment. I'm sorry."

Gaspare looked at him carefully. "You're a good papà, Inventore. She's lucky to have someone like you looking out for her."

The boy walked back into his room and closed the door. Telchide was left alone in the dark hallway. He felt his way back to his room with his crutches. For a long while, he lay awake in bed.

He shouldn't have said that to Gaspare – about thinking the worst. What must the poor boy have thought? He wondered, if Roque hadn't attacked Aveline on the Caldera, would he still have thought that?

It seemed like impossibly good fortune that Gaspare had managed to soothe Teresina back to sleep. Did that mean the household would have fewer nights of interrupted sleep? He fell asleep faster than usual with these thoughts running around in his head.

Chapter 31 – Legaramedi 5 Alchimisti 230 Years After Implosion

Telchide woke to the sound of his clockwork alarm. He did not remember setting it himself – it must have been Serenita. He tried to change his clothes, but quickly realised he couldn't pull on new pants himself.

"Serenita!" he called out from his bed. "I need help!"

Florio knocked on the door before poking his head in. Telchide tried to pull the sheet up to cover his bare legs.

"Serenita sent me. She said to tell you she's making breakfast for five now and doesn't have time to wait on you."

"But, but, I can't get dressed by myself," Telchide sputtered.

Florio entered the room. "I can help with that. Are these the fresh pants?" he asked, pointing to the pair of trousers on the bed.

Telchide nodded. Florio proceeded to carefully pull the trouser legs up, and carefully over the cast, to Telchide's thighs. With practised ease, he ducked his head under Telchide's arm, lifted him off the bed and slid the pants up to the waist. In a matter of minutes, Telchide was fully dressed in fresh clothes.

"Thank you, Florio," he said at a loss for anything else to say. These boys were going to be more helpful around the house than he'd thought possible. "How did you know how to do that?"

Florio shrugged. "We took turns doing it at the orphanage."

Telchide tried to figure out what he wasn't saying. "Gaspare said you took turns soothing children to sleep after nightmares. You say you took turns dressing people. What kind of orphanage was this?"

Florio looked uncomfortable. "Have you ever been inside an orphanage, Inventore?"

Telchide shook his head.

"Most of the children who live there are ... disabled in some capacity. That's why their parents leave them there. There are very few of us who are truly orphans. The crying happens because most of us know we'll never be adopted and will be extremely lucky to be apprenticed out to anyone. Gaspare and I never thought we'd be apprenticed because we refuse to be separated. We can't believe our luck."

Telchide smiled at the boy's easy manner. "That makes three of us. I thought the two of you would complain about Teresina's nightmares and find it difficult to deal with me and my, erm, bad social etiquette."

Florio laughed. "Inventore, you'd have to be the worst kind of monster to scare us away. Now, do you need help with your grooming, or shall I return to my breakfast?"

"Breakfast for you," Telchide said, waving the boy away.

He made a quick visit to the water closet then joined the others in the kitchen. He was surprised to hear Teresina joking with Gaspare. For all her fears that they would be mean to her, she was getting along with them amazingly well.

"Papà, do I recall correctly?" Teresina asked as he sat beside her. "I think Gaspare and Florio are lying. Am I teaching them to read today?"

Telchide smiled. "You do indeed recall correctly. Mind you aren't too harsh a teacher or they mightn't want to continue their lessons. You can begin after breakfast and go to Aveline's house afterwards."

Teresina waggled her eyebrows up and down conspiratorially which only served to make the twins laugh.

"Serenita, do you mind if they use the kitchen for their lesson? I'm not meant to have two apprentices until the Guild officially grants me my Electrum Guild Mark and it would be unfair to allow either one of them to begin before the other."

Serenita sighed but nodded. "I noticed the boys only have two sets of clothes. I was thinking of measuring them up to sew new clothes for them."

"Oh signora, don't waste your time and money on us," Gaspare said.

"Two pairs of clothes are plenty," Florio quickly agreed. "We can wear one set while the other is being cleaned."

"No. That will absolutely not do," Serenita asserted. "I've seen the way Chide works – you'll have oil stains on all your clothes before long. You'll need one set to remain presentable."

The boys looked imploringly at Telchide.

"Actually boys, much as I hate to admit it, Serenita's right. There will be customer deliveries, Guild functions and Mercatodi stalls. I've learnt the hard way that one cannot wear oil-stained clothes to these things."

Telchide saw the smiles they were trying to hide as he left them grumbling and went down to open his workshop.

He worked on the mechanisms of the music box for most of the day. The internal workings of it should have been the most enjoyable for him as an Inventore, but Telchide was also an artist. He left the decorations, his favourite part, to last every time.

He studied the sheet music Signora Loyola had left for him in his absence. Certain phrases had been marked as favourites. Telchide cut a strip of copper about a pollice wide and ten pollici long. It was longer than he usually made his strips for music, but this was to be a larger box and he hoped to be able to make a decent length song for it.

Signora Loyola had been quite clear – the music box would be presented to all her acquaintances at her next dinner party. If they liked what they saw, they would ask where she'd found such a delightful music box and would order one themselves.

Telchide hoped he'd have his Electrum Guild Mark by then. He'd be able to charge them a premium and have his initial customer feel the pleasure of having "discovered" him before he became popular and expensive.

Her dinner party would be in six weeks from yesterday. That gave Telchide a little less than that to finish and test it. He wouldn't need that extra time, but it was nice to have a buffer for any other jobs that came in or for any difficulties that might arise.

He lined up the sheet music beside him and placed the strip of copper over a punch board. The punch board had been modified so that he could create bumps without punching a hole through the metal, if he was careful. He laughed at the memory of Aveline punching it so hard that her bump became a hole! It was those bumps that would help create the music. Of course, Aveline had been so heavy handed when she tried it that she'd still managed to punch actual holes. The thought of working side by side with her made him smile.

Telchide spent the rest of the day punching out different sections of the song. He never knew which bits would sound best in his music boxes until he tried them out. All his anger with Eduardo and Serenita, his longing for Aveline, Teresina's memory loss, the upheaval of his way of life with the arrival of two apprentices – it all faded away as he lost himself in the methodical nature of the work.

Chapter 32 – Orodi 6 Alchimisti 230 Years After Implosion

By the time Aveline arrived to pick him up on Orodi, Telchide had three sections of the new music for Signora Loyola's music box punched out in different strips. He nodded to her in greeting and picked up the first strip to place it on his test drum.

"Put it down," Aveline said.

"This won't take but a moment," Telchide insisted.

"Chide, put it down *now*. I know the way you work. If I let you keep at it, we'll miss our appointment with Kesida."

Aveline put her hand over his, gently forcing him to release the copper strip. His stomach flipped suddenly. He twined his fingers around hers and smiled. It felt like an age since he'd last touched her. Their eyes locked and his chest swelled with happiness. She looked as tired as he usually felt – he knew Nevio had taken a lot of orders for her in their absence.

"Let's be off then," she told him, quickly disentangling her fingers from his.

Telchide deflated a little but tried not to let it show. "Florio, Gaspare, in the workshop please!"

Aveline frowned. "Who are Florio and Gaspare?"

Telchide looked at her in confusion. "Didn't you meet them yesterday morning with Teresina?"

Aveline shook her head.

"But they escorted her to your workshop."

"Then they must've waited for her outside," Aveline replied. "Teresina came in by herself to ask me to stop by for you this evening."

The twins rushed down the steps together and almost tripped over one another's feet as they tried to avoid the box of music strips in the middle of the floor. They justifiably gawked at Aveline in her favourite green coat with silver trimmings.

Aveline stared at them in surprise. "Who are these lavalumps?"

Florio and Gaspare blushed a deep shade of red, both instantly smoothing down their hair and shirts. Telchide stared at Aveline in shock.

"They're to be my new apprentices."

"Your ... new apprentices? *Apprentices!*" Aveline's frosty politeness confused him. "Chide, you're only on your Silver Guild Mark. You can't have two apprentices."

"Boys, could you please put the message box in Aveline Inventrice's blazermobile? You should find it just outside."

He waited for them to leave the workshop before confronting Aveline.

"I'm surprised at you, Veli. The boys have done nothing to you, yet you speak of them so impolitely. And I didn't say they *are* my new apprentices.

I said they're *to be*. Kesida is finalising the paperwork. I should have my Electrum Guild Mark within a week."

"I see," she replied slowly.

Telchide searched her face for any sign of emotion. He often had difficulty reading people, especially when they were trying to hide their feelings. But Aveline definitely looked angry.

"You're unhappy?"

She gave him a quick smile. "No, no of course not. You're a brilliant Inventore. You deserve the Electrum Guild Mark. I just didn't expect you to get two apprentices so quickly."

"Quickly? It's been three *years* since I was entitled to one and *you* were the one pushing me to apply for one."

"I pushed you to get *one*, Chide," Aveline said, returning to her usual calm and polite manner. "Even I don't have two apprentices yet, and my first has been with me a few years now."

The boys re-entered the workshop. Aveline glanced at them then back at Telchide.

"Are you sure you can handle two right now?" Aveline said quietly.

"I'm excited to start working with them. I'd hoped you'd be happy for me," Telchide said coldly. He turned away from Aveline. "Boys, I may be gone a few hours. Please ask Serenita to close the shop for me and don't wait for me for dinner. I'll eat when I return."

"Yes, Inventore," they mumbled, nodding.

He wanted to say something to them, to apologise for Aveline's coolness towards them, but he couldn't find the words. Not now. Instead, he walked towards the coat stand and attempted to take his coat off to dress himself. He failed.

Gaspare immediately stepped over to help him. Telchide suffered the indignity of not being able to dress himself in front of Aveline.

"Thank you, Gaspare. Will you be so kind as to help Serenita with Teresina tonight? I think my daughter's taken quite a liking to you."

Gaspare smiled brightly. Telchide realised he'd unintentionally praised the young man, raising his esteem once more. He only wished he'd been able to do the same for Florio.

Telchide made to open the door, but Gaspare beat him to it. He held the door open and waited patiently for them to leave. When Aveline passed him, Gaspare stared straight ahead. Telchide saw Aveline pause and wondered if she was about to apologise, but the moment passed, and she walked out of the workshop. Telchide followed her out and got into her blazermobile in silence.

Before she took off, Telchide popped a ginger tablet into his mouth. The sharp taste reminded him of Eduardo. He almost spat it out but reasoned that he'd need it to survive the evening without emptying the contents of his stomach in the street or the blazermobile itself.

They didn't speak on the way to the Guild Hall. It was too short a trip and there was too much to say. Telchide was incredibly hurt by Aveline's reaction. He thought she'd be proud of him, not dubious of his ability to handle his new responsibilities.

He waited in the blazermobile as Aveline walked briskly inside to find Kesida. The two of them appeared with Kesida's lackey, Zeno. The boy handed Telchide some paperwork to sign, then took possession of both the paperwork and the message box.

Kesida shuffled into the blazermobile, squashing Telchide to the side of the converted carriage. Much as he didn't want to be squashed next to anyone, he was at least glad that it wasn't Aveline he was next to for the longer drive to the workshop.

Kesida handed Aveline a map and pointed to a street on the other side of town, near the rubber factory. Aveline screeched off in that general direction. It was a tense trip with infrequent instructions given by Kesida.

When they finally arrived, Telchide stood on the pavement, his eyes firmly averted from Aveline's.

"What's in your bonnet?" Kesida asked Aveline before handing her a copper key. "You're in an awfully sour mood today considering the enormous favour I'm affording you."

Aveline took the key, angrily. Telchide could hold his tongue no longer.

"She's out of sorts because of my soon-to-be apprentices. She doesn't think I can handle them."

"That's not like you, Aveline. Is anything the matter?" Kesida raised an eyebrow. "I know he's a bit of a burbler, but Telchide a brilliant Inventore and will make a fine maestro. "

"Of course, he will. I just wasn't expecting *two* apprentices," Aveline replied, shaking her head. "This makes things come complicated."

"More complicated how?" Telchide asked, his temper rising with the added insult of being accused of burbling.

Aveline shook her head, opened the door and ushered them both inside. Only when the door was firmly closed behind them did she look at Telchide. The anger was gone. Now there was only exasperation.

"I can't do this!" she cried out. "I can't work with you."

"What? Why not?" Telchide asked, baffled by her behaviour this evening.

Kesida stood in front of Aveline, hands on hips.

"You tell me the problem and you tell me now. Chide is one of the best Inventrici in Tor'Esint. The two of you could make a fortune working together, so what's the problem?"

Aveline shook her head and refused to answer.

"If Aveline does not wish to work with me, we'll find a way to do this. We'll split the time we spend in this workshop. Or I'll give up my rights to the sparking plant."

Aveline gasped sharply. Kesida looked from Aveline to Telchide. She huffed to herself and raised an eyebrow.

"I don't mean to pry, but if the two of you got up to something on the Caldera, it's not going to disappear just because you're home. Chide, you can't give up your rights to the sparking plant – I won't let you."

"I wouldn't let him either," Aveline protested, rubbing her arms distractedly. She looked on the verge of tears. "I'm not trying to take this project away from him."

Kesida paused and eyed her carefully. "Are you in love with him, then? Really, not just for a laugh."

Aveline looked at Telchide. His heart was in his throat. He could barely breathe, waiting for her to answer.

"Yes," Aveline whispered.

"Then you have nothing to worry about. He's a good papà and a good man."

"And he's *committed!*"

Telchide coughed, unimpressed by being left out of the conversation.

"I've been thinking," Telchide said hesitantly, "if what Eduardo told me is true, it's most likely Sebetine is dead."

"What difference does that make if you can't find her body?" Aveline asked. Telchide ignored her bluntness.

"I was thinking to go to the Authorities and explain the situation – that I think she's dead. That may end the commitment," he said in an unsteady voice. "I would then be free to ask you if you'll have me."

"What?" Aveline whispered in an impossibly soft voice.

"Will you allow me to court you, Aveline?" Telchide asked with half a smile. "Perhaps even commit to you one day?"

"But ... I have a workshop, and *you* have a workshop. And Serenita. And Teresina."

"Yes, Florio and Gaspare too," Telchide added. "And you have Nevio."

"Exactly!" she cried out. "It's impossible."

"No, it's not." Kesida said earnestly, taking Aveline's hand and patting it. "This sort of thing happens more than you might imagine. Granted, not the part about another companion, but two established Inventrici or other Guild members committing to each other. It *does* happen."

"But how?" Aveline asked, bursting into tears. "We can't possibly make this work."

"You keep both workshops," Kesida said firmly. "That's the important part. Your independence and space are necessary. But, at the end of the day, you live in the same house. Your apprentices bunk together and share their experiences from the day. You'd be amazed at the friendly competition it fosters amongst them. Quite good for their progress."

Telchide took Aveline in his arms and kissed her forehead, despite Kesida standing right there.

"I can't do it. I *can't*. I won't live with Serenita and I didn't make the best impression on the twins. And what about Teresina? She may not appreciate me coming in to be a mamma for her."

Telchide hugged her tightly. "Never mind about the twins. I'll explain it all to them in the morning. As for Teresina and Serenita, it may have escaped your attention, but they're both rather fond of you.

"Teresina's been mimicking your clothes since the day she met you. And after you did her hair and pierced her ears, you became her friend for life.

"And, as you pointed out yourself, Serenita suspected something would happen between us sooner or later. She just doesn't want to be left out of the picture when you come into it. If you're happy to come and live with us, with Nevio, I'm sure we'd be happy to have you."

"There, see, it's all sorted," Kesida said chirpily. "Now if you'll turn your attention back to the workshop. We keep most of them furnished with workbenches and stools, but I thought, with your particular needs, you might appreciate one of the empty ones."

Aveline shrugged her way out of Telchide's embrace and went quiet. Telchide was in too much of a happy daze to consider why – no matter what, she loved him. Kesida clapped her hands in front of his face, snapping him back to the present moment. He looked around the room. It was stone with a wooden framework, like most buildings in Tor'Esint. The windows were up high, so the sparking plants shouldn't do any damage there.

"This will be perfect, Kesida," he replied with a smile so wide, it hurt his cheeks. "We can do without workbenches for a short time, and we'll bring in any equipment we need ourselves. May we line the walls with rubber?"

"Line the walls with rubber? Whatever for?" asked Kesida.

Telchide shrugged. "The sparking plants don't seem to react badly to rubber. And I don't want to damage the building."

Kesida stared at him. "In that case I think you'd better line the walls with rubber. Now, for the rent. It will be five silvers a week. Will you be splitting it evenly?"

Telchide nodded, his head reeling from the extra expense on top of two new apprentices.

"I'll bill your Guild Accounts accordingly until you hand back the keys. Will you be requiring anything else?"

Telchide looked over at Aveline.

"No, I think that's everything," she said, her voice coolly impassive. "Let's go."

Aveline locked up behind them. Telchide watched her carefully. She silently hopped into the blazermobile, not looking anyone in the eye, looking almost sick.

"You can drop me off home," Kesida said as she sidled into the blazermobile. "It's only a little out of your way."

"Chide, get in! This wind is chilling me to the bone," Kesida grumbled at him.

Telchide lumbered in after her with his crutches and shut the door. Aveline barely waited for him to be seated before setting off. Telchide would never get used to the way Aveline drove. He was alternately pressed up against the side of the blazermobile or attempting to hold himself off Kesida around corners. The rough movements made his stomach lurch, but the ginger tablet was still doing its work. Telchide tried to keep his eyes on the streets, but the lanternlight did not reach far enough through the incoming fog to make it easy for him. Instead, he focused on his breaths, counting them in and out, just to focus on something.

Eventually, they arrived at the Inventrici Guild Hall. Once again, Aveline alighted from the blazermobile to avoid Telchide having to hop in and out with his crutches for Kesida. Before Kesida left the blazermobile, the Guild Amministratrice turned to him.

"I'll give your paperwork to the Maestri first thing in the morning with your explanation of how the message box works, but it's Mercatodi tomorrow and I know they won't look at it until Gildadi. I'll bring your Electrum Guild Mark to you as soon as it's ready."

Telchide smiled proudly. "Thank you, Kesida. It's more than I dreamed possible."

"You deserve it, Chide."

Aveline said nothing as she settled back into the driver's seat of the blazermobile. Telchide averted his gaze every time he noticed her glance at him. Within a few minutes, they were back outside his workshop.

Telchide sat in awkward silence. He did not get out of the blazermobile. As the silence continued, he began to play with his buttons.

"Would you like to come in?" he asked nervously.

"No." The answer was immediate and forceful. Telchide cringed.

"Aveline, I meant what I said," he said, turning to her. "I'd be happy to have you live with me, with or without a commitment ceremony."

"But you're not the only one who lives here," Aveline pointed out. "There are *five* of you now to contend with. This is not the way I ever imagined starting my life with a companion. There were never children involved at such an early stage – most certainly none that weren't mine. When you think of our three apprentices combined, when would there be any time for us? To really get to know each other, to find our place in a household together? Please try to understand."

"I know it's not an ideal situation." Telchide agreed. He opened the door to the blazermobile and positioned his crutches so that he wouldn't fall upon getting out. He half expected Aveline to stop him, but she didn't. Telchide got out but did not close the door behind him.

"May I ... can I tell them?" Telchide asked hopefully.

"About the workshop?" Aveline asked, frowning. "I suppose so."

"No, about you, and me. At least that we're courting?"

Aveline shook her head. "Chide, no. You're still committed. We agreed, on the Caldera, that it isn't a good idea for you to court me. Especially not before the matter of Sebetine is resolved."

Telchide sighed heavily. He understood her reasons, but it didn't make him feel any better. He closed the door to the blazermobile and watched as Aveline drove off. He decided there and then that he would not wait any longer. He would go down to the Authorities on Gildadi and tell them what he suspected about Sebetine. The rest would be up to them.

Chapter 33 – Mercatodi 7 Alchimisti 230 Years After Implosion

There was a soft knock at his door. Telchide opened his eyes to the early morning light streaming through the cracks in his curtain. The knock came again after a short pause.

"Papà?" Teresina called out softly as she cracked his door open. "Papà, it's Mercatodi. Are we setting up a stall today? Or are you still too sore?"

Telchide turned to look at her. Teresina looked so much like her mamma.

"Papà, why are you crying?" she asked, running to his bed.

She flung her tiny arms around his neck. Telchide sat up as much as he could with his leg in the cast and hugged her tightly, quietly crying into her shoulder.

"Did something bad happen with Kesida and Aveline last night?" she asked.

He pulled back from her. "No, Resi. I just didn't realise it would hurt so much to admit to myself that your mamma is dead."

Teresina stroked his face. "I know you're sad, papà, but I can barely remember her."

"You look more like her each day, you know. You have her lovely, round, brown eyes and her soft, wavy hair. How she moaned about not being able to follow hair fashion without great trouble." He laughed through his tears. "You know, she didn't fool me. She moaned mostly so that I would tell her how beautiful she was, and I always did."

Teresina gave him a small smile. "She'd have looked lovely in Aveline's trinzale then, wouldn't she?"

Telchide couldn't answer. The idea of Aveline and Sebetine together brought such a torturous mixture of guilt and pain that he could barely breathe.

"Did I say something wrong?" Teresina asked. "Don't you think mamma would've looked nice in a trinzale?"

Telchide let out a deep trembling breath. "I'm sure she would have, Resi," he reassured her. "Now, why did you come in so early?"

"It's Mercatodi, papà," she reminded him. "Do you want me to reserve your spot with Gaspare? And Florio can help you bring your wares down? That way Serenita can stay home and rest."

Life crashed back down on Telchide. No matter what else was happening – with Aveline, the sparking plant, his apprentices to be – there was still his everyday life to go on with.

"Yes, Resi. That's a good idea. Take Gaspare and show him our favourite spot."

Teresina grinned. "I'll show him *my* favourite spot, if it's still available."

Before he had a chance to ask her *not* to set up next to Aveline, Teresina was out the door and calling to Gaspare. Telchide closed his eyes tightly. Much as he'd tried to reassure Aveline that Teresina adored her, he could not reassure himself that his daughter would *still* adore the Inventrice when she realised he wanted Aveline to be his companion, to merge their families, to take even more of his attention away from her.

And how long could he hide his affection for Aveline from Teresina? If they set up next to each other again, there were only two options, awkward silence of which he was well familiar with, or more familiar conversation and touches. If their time on the Caldera had proven anything, it was that there was little in-between ground for them. It was pointless to hope no one would notice the difference between them.

***

"Inventore, I can pack that myself," Florio insisted, as Telchide tried to secure the Mercatodi box to the Spiderseat.

He gave up and sat on his chair. "Very well. I need those copper strips there, my notebook, my order book, those spare parts over there and my tool belt."

Florio dashed around the workshop getting all the requested items with very little direction and depositing them in the Mercatodi box. Telchide couldn't help the rising happiness over his new apprentices-to-be. He'd felt so insecure about passing on his skills, but Florio, in particular, seemed to have already found his way around the entire workshop. It was making things easier, *much* easier.

"Thank you, Florio! You're going to make a fine apprentice."

Florio beamed at the compliment as he finished the preparations.

Serenita came down the stairs as they were walking out the door, the Spiderseat following them one step behind.

"Chide, don't forget your little spat with Aveline about the list of available songs." She waggled her eyebrows at him. "You know, when she told that customer each new song would be fifteen silvers and template songs would be ten?"

Telchide *had* forgotten. So much had transpired since that day. At least now he could almost legally afford to charge them an Electrum price.

Florio, perceptive as ever, passed Telchide his notebook and a pencil. Telchide quickly scribbled away, listing all the currently available tunes.

***

They walked slowly to Piazza Mercantile, Telchide in front with his crutches, Florio behind, leading the Spiderseat.

"You know, Inventore, if you have something for it to follow, you could always use this around your workshop instead of your crutches."

Telchide beamed at the way Florio's mind worked. "That's just what my maestro invented it for, Florio. I've just never needed to use it that way before. Perhaps you can help me work on that modification tomorrow."

Florio's eyes went so wide, Telchide thought they might pop out of his head.

He huffed a laugh and continued to stumble his way forward with his crutches.

By the time they reached the piazza, Telchide's good humour with Florio had melted away and his stomach was in a ball of knots. He saw Teresina talking animatedly with Aveline and Nevio, grinning and playfully patting Gaspare's arm.

Teresina's easy manner with the three apprentices should have signified to him that everything would be fine, but it didn't. He couldn't help but think that she would feel betrayed by him – that he'd let her make friends with them so easily in the hopes that she wouldn't mind at all when he upheaved their household.

"Ah, here he is," Aveline said brightly as they approached her corner. "We were beginning to think you wouldn't show up before the Mercatodi stalls open."

Florio led the Spiderseat to its final position and placed the Mercatodi box next to it. "Maestro Telchide was writing out a list of tunes, as you suggested."

Telchide ignored the startled look that Aveline threw him. There was already too much noise here today. He was trying hard to block it out.

"I see," she said quietly. "Nevio, why don't you take Gaspare to bring some chairs out here. I doubt Telchide will be able to stand all day with that leg."

"Aveline, do we have time before the stalls open for you to do my hair?"

"No, sweet thing. Not right now. You can come over tomorrow morning if you like, and I'll do it then."

Telchide's heart ached at the sight of the two of them getting along so well, even if he and Aveline still had things to work through themselves. He sat heavily on the box, landing awkwardly because of the cast and ended up in the gutter.

"Inventore!" Florio was immediately by his side, helping him to his feet. "Are you feeling unwell?"

"I slipped. That's all," he replied quickly.

He unintentionally caught Aveline's eye and wished he hadn't. She looked like he'd punched her in the stomach – there was no hiding his feelings from her.

"Florio, why don't you let Aveline help you set up the stall. I don't think my leg will permit me."

"And she makes it look so much nicer than you do," Teresina added with a giggle. Telchide raised an eyebrow at her. "Well, it's *true* papà, she does!"

Telchide nodded. "Indeed, she does. Aveline, would you mind?"

Aveline stared at him a moment longer then plastered a brittle smile to her face. "Of course. Florio, why don't you take out that inner box there, and turn over the larger one. That's right, place it here, next to mine."

Telchide watched silently as they worked to put his stall together. By the time they were done, Nevio and Gaspare had returned with chairs and forced him to sit on one of them. The Guild Hall clocks struck nine o'clock and the street flooded with people.

Before he had time to position himself as comfortably as possible, he was accosted by two ladies, vying to be his first customer.

"Signora, *please*, you can see I was here first. Kindly *wait your turn*." The thin faced, thin-lipped lady looked down her narrow nose at a rather plumper lady jostling her from the side.

Telchide watched in fascination. He'd never had people fighting over his stall before.

"Erm, yes, what can I help you with, signora?" he asked the lady who had so firmly claimed her position as his first customer.

"My *darling* Serafina was at Angelo's birthday party a few weeks ago and simply will *not* stop bothering me for one of your music boxes. I must insist on ordering one as quickly as you can possibly make it. My poor ears cannot withstand another *moment* of her whining. I believe ten silvers is the going price for a tune you already have prepared?"

Telchide nodded dumbly as she held out ten silvers. If it weren't for Florio handing the lady the list of available songs, he'd have remained motionless. He took the proffered silvers and placed them in his money pouch as Gaspare passed him his order pad and pencil.

He wrote down her name, Signora Isabella, and the selected tune, Adalgisa's Sonata Number One. *Paid ten silvers. Due Legaramedi.*

Signora Isabella smiled at Telchide as he thanked her for her order. She looked down her nose at the plumper lady, sniffed and moved aside to Aveline's stall. Telchide saw her glancing over as the second lady began her order.

"My adorable little Adamo is willing to wait a few extra days for his music box. His papà and I have agreed to let him spend the required *fifteen* silvers to have his favourite tune rather than whatever else is available."

Telchide's eyes fairly bulged out of his head at this statement. He wrote down her details on the next order pad. *Signora Pina, Tune to be delivered, Paid fifteen silvers, Due five days after tune delivered.*

He took her silvers and quickly placed them in his money pouch along with Signora Isabella's coins. It was so unusual for customers to pay him before their orders were ready that Telchide felt fairly faint at the thought of all that money on him all day.

He'd barely had time to put away the order pad before Signora Isabella stepped back over. Her eyes followed the quickly retreating figure of Signora Pina. When she was out of sight, the thin-lipped lady turned her attention back to Telchide.

"I've changed my mind. If her *adorable* Adamo can have a tune of his choice, so can my Serafina." She placed another five silvers on Telchide's makeshift table. "I'll bring her favourite tune on Gildadi."

"Very good, signora," Telchide said, not quite believing his luck at already having two new orders for simple music boxes.

Signora Isabella smiled, her lips spreading so thinly they were barely visible lines. Telchide returned her smile and waited until she'd walked away before letting out a deep breath.

"Inventore, is it always so busy?" asked Gaspare, handing Telchide a glass of water.

Telchide took the glass, noticing that it was from Aveline's house, and drank deeply. "No, Gaspare, it most certainly is *not* always this busy."

"What changed?" Florio asked, with about as much tact as an exploding volcano.

"I know, I know!" Teresina jumped up and down and raised her hand. "This spot next to Aveline's is the *best* spot. We're always busier here."

The twins looked at Aveline with renewed interest. She raised an eyebrow at their attention but quickly turned back to her own customers.

"Papà, can Gaspare take me to Greta Sarta's stall? I want to have a look at her pretty dresses."

Telchide looked up at Gaspare who nodded amiably.

"Very well. Here's six coppers. Why don't the two of you find something nice for everyone at one of the pasticcerie on your walk. I'm certain Aveline and Nevio will appreciate a treat as well. Florio and I will tend the stall."

They left in a flurry of activity. Telchide felt tired just watching them and was thankful that his stall was devoid of customers for the next little while. It didn't remain quiet for long. Soon enough, there was a string of customers passing by for quick repairs to music boxes that had been dropped, adjustments to pocket watches which had been overwound too many times and the now expected increase in orders of both those items.

Telchide began to wonder if customers were aware he could create other items as well. Not that he minded, of course. Pocket watches and music boxes were both intricate enough to hold his attention but not overtax him.

***

Towards the end of the day's trading, Teresina dragged Florio back to the stall. She'd taken the twins away in turns to explore the market and visit Serenita.

"Aveline! Aveline!" she cried out from halfway across the piazza.

Aveline looked around her last customer and held up a hand to Teresina. To Telchide's surprise, his daughter closed her mouth and waited, foot tapping impatiently, until Aveline's sale was complete.

"Aveline, Serenita told me to invite you and Nevio for dinner to thank you for all the help you've been to papà. Will you come?"

Aveline went pale and held out a hand to steady herself on her table. Telchide went to step forward to help her, but a tiny shake of her head warned him off.

"That's very kind, Teresina, but we wouldn't want to be an imposition," she replied easily. "Besides, I don't think we've been as great a help as you may imagine."

Telchide saw his daughter's eyes fill with tears and waited for the inevitable explosion. It didn't come. Instead, Teresina walked over to his stall, picked up his order book and took it to Aveline.

"Look at this," she said, flipping through the day's orders. "Papà never had so many orders in *one* Mercatodi before you two started working together and you allowed us to set up next to you. Serenita said to tell you, she won't take no for an answer."

Telchide risked a glance at Aveline. She bit her lip and looked to Nevio who was nodding so forcefully she thought the poor boy's head might fall off.

"I suppose we have no choice then," Aveline threw her hands up in defeat. "We'll just pack up and then come along."

"Inventrice, leave the packing up to us," Gaspare said quickly. "We'll help Nevio put your things inside, and we'll take Maestro Telchide's things back with us. The two of you can proceed at your own pace. Don't worry about Teresina – she can keep us company."

Aveline looked between the three apprentices and Teresina, all of whom were grinning from ear to ear.

"Very well, then, I'll just be a moment, Chide. Let me freshen up a little," Aveline said before walking up the steps to her home.

Telchide waited on the street, at a loss of what to do. Gaspare helped Nevio bring Aveline's goods back into her house while Florio and Teresina packed up Telchide's own wares in his Mercatodi box and secured it to the Spiderseat.

"We'll see you back at the house, Inventore," Florio called out as he took Teresina by the hand. Gaspare and Nevio followed close behind them, leading the Spiderseat, as all four walked down the quickly emptying piazza.

Telchide checked his pocket watch. It had already been ten minutes – what in Caldera's smoke was taking so long? Instead of loitering on the street, Telchide lumbered his way up the stairs with his crutches and let himself into Aveline's workshop. It was empty, the absence of noise denoting she was not downstairs.

He took the opportunity to take a peek at her workstation. In one corner was a more detailed mock-up of the chair lift they'd worked on together. He was just playing with it when Aveline entered the room.

His breath stuck in his throat when he saw her. Gone was her amply pocketed and well-worn work dress. In its place was a rusty toned dress with sunset-coloured sleeves. The effect with her chestnut hair and hazel eyes was delightful – it put Telchide in mind of autumn.

"You look stunning," he finally stammered out.

Aveline blushed and looked down at herself, smoothing out imagined creases on the skirt.

"Well, I was taught one must dress nicely when invited to dine. I'm certain Serenita would not expect me to come in my work clothes."

Telchide frowned. "But you've come in your work clothes every other time."

"True," Aveline conceded, "however, I've always come over to work, not to dine."

He knew it was true, but Telchide was hesitant to point out that her dress was finer than any garment in his entire household. Serenita would certainly *not* be expecting this, and Teresina would positively fawn over the finery.

Instead, he swallowed and held out his arm to her. She only hesitated a moment before pointing to his crutches. Telchide rolled his eyes and grimaced.

"You'll have to be a gentleman some other time. Let me get the door for you."

Aveline slung her green and silver coat over her arm. It would be much cooler when she and Nevio returned home. She opened the door and waited patiently until he was on the street before locking up behind herself.

Telchide walked slowly beside Aveline. The winter sun was already low in the sky, highlighting the colours on Aveline's dress. It really was quite stunning.

"Did Greta Sarta make that dress for you as a present?" he asked.

Aveline looked at him in surprise, then down at her dress. "No, Chide, this isn't something a Gold Sarta would trade for an invention, no matter how great that invention was. I did, however, buy it from her."

Telchide nodded silently. It would be terribly inappropriate for him to ask how rich she really was, but every time she mentioned some expensive item or wore such expensive clothing, it made him wonder. And then a horrible thought occurred to him.

"Aveline?"

"Mmm." She glanced sideways; eyebrows raised.

Telchide felt terribly awkward as he tried to phrase his question into something appropriate. "Aveline, is your wealth one of the reasons you hesitate to agree to let me court you?"

Aveline's features froze. She stared straight ahead and walked so quickly Telchide had to take long hops with his crutches to catch up to her.

"Aveline, please, I didn't mean to upset you," he called out to her from behind.

She stopped and turned on him with such fury he wished he could hide. "Should *I* be concerned that my wealth is the reason you asked to court me?"

Telchide frowned in confusion. "Of course not. I ... thought you might not want me because I'm not as wealthy as you."

Aveline's eyebrows shot up and she started laughing. Telchide couldn't understand what was happening.

"Chide, I don't care about your wealth, or mine for that matter. It's something I was born into. Of course, my papà gave me a helping hand to purchase a workshop when I earned my Copper Guild Mark, but I worked hard to maintain myself after that with no further assistance. If anything, I admire the fact that you've managed to build a life for yourself in a new city with no financial assistance from your family."

Telchide said nothing. Her quick temper and sudden laughter left a queer feeling in his stomach. He didn't know what else to say. So, he began to walk again, Aveline keeping pace with him once more. The silence lasted an entire street.

"I see you wrote out a list of available tunes," Aveline said suddenly.

Telchide nodded. "Serenita made me take your suggestion before I left this morning. That's why Florio and I took so long to arrive."

Aveline smiled shortly. "It seems Serenita can get you to do almost anything. She's ... a very important part of your household."

"Of course," Telchide replied easily. "Especially now with the twins. I don't know how I'd manage to work with them and feed the four of us at the same time. We'd likely have bread and cold meats most days otherwise."

He stopped talking as he realised something. "Those times I came to help in your workshop ... is that how you eat every night?"

Aveline shrugged. "It's hard work having an apprentice and an extra mouth to cook for. Most of the time, I'm so busy with intricate orders that I can't leave Nevio to finish work while I cook, so he's usually the one preparing meals. Only, he isn't very good at it. I don't think he had much practice growing up."

"Don't tell Serenita. She won't ever let you have another meal like that if she hears about it."

Telchide didn't mean to say it aloud, but he was talking before he realised it. Aveline pulled herself up to her full height.

"I'm a perfectly good cook," she said firmly. "I just don't have the time."

Telchide cursed under his breath and caught her hand, pulling until she stopped walking. They were almost at his house.

"Veli, I'm sorry. I seem to have my foot in my mouth today and can't say anything right. Please forgive me. I'll try my hardest not to blunder again this evening."

Aveline looked down at their hands with a sad smile. She gently, but forcefully disentangled her fingers from his.

"Yes, well, we'll both have to do our best. Your situation hasn't changed and neither has my stance on the matter." She sighed heavily. "Let's just make the best of the evening and enjoy Serenita's food."

The door opened ahead of them – Teresina had been playing lookout for them. Telchide was not surprised to see that she'd changed into her best green tunic with her new cream sleeves. He now suspected that even Serenita had dressed up for the occasion. At least the twins and Nevio would not have had a chance to change and outclass him.

"Oh Aveline, your dress is *gorgeous*!" Teresina gasped as she took Aveline's coat and hung it up on the coat stand. "You have the loveliest clothes."

Teresina folded her hands behind her back and twisted side to side, her skirt swaying around her, seemingly hoping for a compliment. Aveline did not leave her waiting.

"And I see you're wearing your new sleeves today. Greta did a lovely job for you. It's not every day she embroiders patterns along the length."

Teresina blushed brightly. "They're lovely, aren't they?"

Before Telchide could stop her, Teresina took Aveline by the hand and led her up the stairs. He was left to lock the door behind them and follow up the stairs much more slowly with his crutches. Gaspare came to help when he was halfway up, but there was no easy way with his leg in a cast.

They took so long that Aveline came back to check on their progress.

"Chide, would you mind terribly if we set up the first trial chair lift here? You'd be able to keep it, of course, but it will mean the Guild might need to come here to inspect it if we submit it as a great work."

"We?" he asked.

"Inventore, that would be marvellous!" Gaspare exclaimed at the same time.

Aveline looked between them. Gaspare helped Telchide up the last few steps, noticed the silence and fled to the kitchen. Telchide was left standing alone with Aveline.

"Veli, I'm not certain that's such a good idea. I'm not certain I could afford to purchase the material. And the chair lift was *your* idea. I cannot submit it alongside you. It would not be proper."

Aveline crossed her arms and stared hard at him. "So, I suppose you'd want to submit the fuel cell by yourself if we ever manage to make it work then? After all, that was *your* idea."

"Well, of course not!" Telchide replied indignantly. "That's an entirely different matter. I may have come up with the idea of a fuel cell, but without your expedition to the Caldera, it would never have amounted to anything. We're in that project together."

Aveline opened her mouth to argue but was forestalled by Serenita's strong voice calling from the kitchen.

"No shop talk after hours! Aveline, I invited you here for dinner, not to argue with Chide over technicalities. Come in before the food gets cold."

It was perfect timing – had Serenita waited a moment longer to call them in, it was likely he and Aveline would've fought over nothing just because tensions were running high. Telchide drew a calming breath and laughed it out when he realised Aveline was doing the same thing. He was still laughing as he hobbled into the kitchen.

Dinner was a delight. Serenita had outdone herself. There was a pot of Telchide's favourite pasta with basil pesto, accompanied by freshly baked bread, roast carrots and cauliflower, and a whole grilled branzino with sliced lemons covering it. The scents were mouth-watering.

Serenita led him to a free seat at the edge of the table next to Aveline and began ladling pasta into bowls. The youngsters took it upon themselves to pass the bowls around until everyone had one. Only then was Serenita satisfied to sit down herself. She took her favourite seat, nearest the stove. Everyone looked to her before beginning their meal. As Telchide often told people, it might be *his* house, but it was Serenita's kitchen.

"Aveline, we find ourselves indebted to you for helping Telchide increase his business and convincing him to join you on such a beneficial expedition. I hope this meal can begin to repay those debts. Enjoy."

Aveline made to protest, but Telchide covered her hand with his under the table. There was no use arguing with Serenita.

She grasped his fingers tightly – he wasn't sure whether from affection or some sort of fear. It didn't matter, either way, he was thankful to be able to hold her hand just that little bit longer.

Everyone started eating and the room instantly filled with compliments over every dish. Aveline and Nevio exclaiming more ardently than the others how lovely it was. Telchide's stomach tightened at the thought they did not eat so well very often.

Towards the end of the meal, Telchide tapped his fork against his wooden cup until everyone was silent.

"I have an announcement to make."

Aveline stiffened by his side, so he quickly ploughed on before she could react badly before he got out his perfectly respectable announcement.

"As you know, Aveline and I went on an expedition to Sentigura Caldera. We found what we were looking for and have hired an extra workshop to conduct our experiments. This will mean that we may need to leave our workshops in the hands of our apprentices some days or have quite late evenings other days."

Teresina and the apprentices groaned while Serenita nodded knowingly. Telchide tilted his head to one side and rolled his eyes.

"I promise it will be worthwhile. Once we perfect this invention, it will ... well, it will be good," he finished lamely.

Aveline rolled her eyes at him. "It will increase our reputations and, if we don't already have our Gold Guild Marks by then, it will guarantee that rank."

There was silence around the table. The apprentices exchanged curious glances but Teresina and Serenita eyed them both carefully.

"But papà, you already have so much work and not enough time. How will you manage it?"

Telchide saw her eyes fill with tears, but she was bravely holding them back.

"We'll find a way, Resi," he told her.

Aveline held out her hand across the table to Teresina who placed her tiny hand within hers.

"Teresina, I promise not to allow your papà to spend too much time away from you. If I need to work in our shared workshop more to ensure that, then I will."

"No, you won't," Serenita said sharply. Everyone turned to her in surprise.

"This has been a combined project from the start. If it's so very important that you could *both* gain a Gold Guild Mark from it, then you both need to work on it in equal amounts. I won't have you annoyed with Chide for spending less time on it even though you offered that option.

"As Teresina pointed out, Chide is too busy to put aside other orders to work on this and I'm certain it's the same for you. So, I'll insist that the two of you work on this project after hours every day until it's done. Nevio can come here for dinner and the two of you can eat when you return."

Telchide cringed. Though it was exactly the working arrangement he'd wanted because they could spend every evening together, even if it was working on a project rather than getting to know one another better, Serenita had no right to demand it.

"No," Aveline said quietly. "I don't think that will work. If we need to share the load equally, we can take it in turns, I'll do one evening, Telchide can do another."

"But how will I get there?" Telchide asked, annoyed with himself for taking Serenita's side in the argument. Even if his leg wasn't in a cast, it was too far to walk, and he would hardly be able to drive her blazermobile himself to get there.

Aveline hesitated for only a moment. "Nevio can drive you in my blazermobile. He's becoming quite a good driver now."

Telchide stared dejectedly at Aveline. The room went very quiet.

"Teresina, why don't you show the boys all the tunes your papà has made for the music boxes," Serenita said in a level voice. "You can use his test one for all the templates. I'm sure they'd like that."

Telchide paid little attention as the four of them left the room. He turned away from Aveline and pushed around the few stray carrots on his plate with his fork.

"There was no need for that," Aveline said quietly, but firmly when the kitchen was empty of all but the three of them.

She shifted ever so slightly away from Telchide, then rose to begin clearing the table in complete lack of proper etiquette for a guest. Serenita stood across from her, hands splayed on the table. Telchide could barely meet her fiery eyes.

"Put that plate down and take a seat," Serenita said forcefully.

Aveline narrowed her eyes and sat.

"Now, you listen to me, Aveline. I'm not a blind vecchietta. I know exactly what the two of you got up to on the Caldera – it's written all over your faces. I don't know what it was for you, but I know for Chide it was nothing but love. He would not put himself through such torture for anything else.

"How dare you now punish him for that? How dare you deny him the opportunity to work *together* with you on this just because you feel uncomfortable about this situation? Do you not think *he* feels uncomfortable? Look at him!"

Telchide couldn't look up. His stomach had squeezed into such a tight ball, he felt it would rupture if he moved. From the side of his vision, he saw Aveline clasp her hands together under the table.

"I have proposed a perfectly reasonable alternative to working together every night," Aveline said calmly. "That will do for now."

Serenita tapped her foot on the floor.

"If it was such a bad arrangement, why did you ask to work together so many nights before you left on your expedition? Why did you even invite Chide to join you? It's not fair for you to only work with him on your terms and when it suits you."

"We can share our notes," Aveline pointed out. "It wouldn't be so very difficult. It would be like working together, just not at the same time."

"For Caldera's sake, girl, why are you fighting this?" Serenita shouted.

Telchide jumped in his chair and stared at her. Serenita almost never lost her temper. She was the most mild-mannered person he knew.

Aveline remained silent for a long time. Telchide finally gathered the courage to look at her only to see cold, emotionless eyes.

"Serenita, you may think you have Telchide's best interests at heart, but you certainly don't have mine, otherwise you would never have suggested this.

"Thank you for dinner. It was lovely but I'm afraid I must leave now. As you pointed out, we Inventrici are both extremely busy." She rose to leave. "Telchide, I'll have the workshop fitted out with rubber and will send Nevio with a message when we can start experimenting. In the meantime, I'll go to the warehouse periodically to ensure the plants are still alive. Good evening."

Telchide didn't get a chance to reply before she left. The situation had reversed so completely that he didn't know what to do. He excused himself and closed himself in his room. He did not want to see anyone after that debacle.

Chapter 34 – Riposidi 8 Alchimisti 230 Years After Implosion

Telchide opened his eyes. It was still dark, but he couldn't sleep. He wound his friction light to see it was only four in the morning. The sun would not be up for a few hours yet, but he couldn't stay in bed a moment longer.

Trying to make as little noise as possible with his crutches, he made his way down the stairs in the clothes he'd fallen asleep in the night before. It took him a few tries to light the fireplace, but eventually he managed a nice roaring fire. It provided him enough light to work with if he turned towards it.

He tried not to think of Aveline's mirror idea to reflect the firelight all over the room – he didn't want to think about her. Try as he might, he couldn't understand what had transpired the night before. Serenita had thoroughly ruined everything.

Music boxes. That's what was important right now. Not a working arrangement with a fellow Inventrice, no matter how much he wished she were more than that.

Telchide had five new orders for simple music boxes, but he knew they wouldn't distract him enough for his thoughts to stop bothering him. Instead, he pulled out the music that Signora Loyola had sent him and began to work on that. He'd already tested a few sections but this time, instead of cutting a strip of copper, Telchide unwound a decent length from the coil of flat copper and began punching away from the beginning of the song. It was probably a waste of time – he had no idea how he was ever going to fit an entire song in a music box, but he didn't care. It was something to work on that would keep him well occupied and that's all he needed right now.

Tap. He punched the first dent. Tap. The second took only a little more concentration. Tap. Tap. Tap.

"Inventore?"

Telchide jumped and cursed as he punched an error. He looked up to see Gaspare standing in front of him.

"What is it, Gaspare? I'm busy."

Gaspare clenched and unclenched his fists. "Inventore, how long have you been here?"

Telchide rubbed his gritty eyes and looked at the wall clock. It was a quarter to nine.

"Almost five hours," he replied with some surprise.

It hadn't felt like five hours. He was mere bars away from finishing the piece, so he turned his attention back to it.

Gaspare coughed. "I'll bring you down some breakfast."

Telchide nodded absently but did not stop his work. By the time Gaspare sent down a tray of honeyed cinnamon porridge and tea in the dumbwaiter, he was almost finished. Gaspare went to put the tray in front of him, but Telchide waved him angrily aside. He kept his attention firmly on the task at hand. Just two more notes. Tap. Tap.

"There!"

Telchide sat back in satisfaction. "Gaspare, hand me the trial music box over there."

"Inventore, you need to eat something," the young man replied firmly. "I promise to bring it over for you if you just eat something."

With a loud sigh, Telchide motioned for Gaspare to bring his breakfast tray. He was surprised to see the room was not yet flooded with light but then realised he still hadn't opened the blinds. Gaspare understood and immediately set about opening the blinds around the workshop. Telchide dutifully ate, his stomach now rumbling at him in a belated reprimand that it needed to be fed.

"It's a longer strip than usual," Telchide said between mouthfuls. "You may need to do it on the floor or I'm not certain you'll have space for it. And don't cut the copper just yet. I'm not certain about this length."

Gaspare nodded and dutifully set the long copper strip and its attached coil on the ground then went to find the trial music box. Telchide held his breath in anticipation. Had he managed to hold the tune over such a long strip or had the increased length diminished the accuracy of his dents?

He watched impatiently as Gaspare fed the beginning of the copper strip into the trial music box. The poor boy fumbled a few times. Telchide clutched at his spoon and porridge bowl in an effort not to yell at him to hurry. After what felt like an age, the first note sounded and then the next.

Telchide sat, frozen, as he listened to the song all the way to the end.

"It worked!" he exclaimed triumphantly. "It really worked!"

Gaspare grinned up at him. "You're a genius, Inventore!"

Telchide brushed aside his comment. His mind was awhirl with ideas. Somehow, he needed to figure out how to fit such a long strip of copper into a music box and have a key with long enough mechanisms to make the entire song play without having to wind it up multiple times.

A larger drum wouldn't work. He'd need one so large as to make the music box unwieldly. Unless ... what if he made it a hollow drum?

"Gaspare, can you very carefully cut the copper strip off a piede from the end of the dents and bring it here?"

The boy stood up straight. "Certainly, Inventore. As soon as you've finished your breakfast."

"For Caldera's sake, boy! This is important. Pass me the copper strip."

"No, Inventore," he said quietly. "You need your strength. You said yourself you've been working for five hours already. I won't help you until you've eaten something."

Telchide opened his mouth to protest but thought better of it. He just wanted to get on with his work. Without another word, he shovelled the porridge into his mouth, barely taking the time to chew.

Victorious, he held out his empty bowl to Gaspare in exchange for the copper strip. The boy did not have the courage to cut the strip himself and brought the entire coil to Telchide. A little snip, and the strip was free of the coil. Carefully, Telchide placed it sideways on his workbench and touched the two ends together. The circle it made was as large as a dinner plate. Telchide stared at it a long while, thinking of and discarding a dozen ideas.

"Gaspare, pass me that sheet of wood," he said, pointing to a corner of the room where he kept his wood stores.

When the wood didn't appear on his workbench, Telchide turned to find the workshop empty. He frowned and looked over at the wall clock. Half past nine. He shrugged. The boy must have become bored watching him and left the workshop. Telchide used a single crutch to walk over to get the wood himself. He picked up a piece about the right size and tried to walk back to his workbench. He'd not taken two steps before the wood slipped from his grip, landing on his good foot. The world went sideways as he fell, yelping in pain as his ribs smashed into the floorboards.

He drew in painful breaths as three pairs of feet came into view down the stairs.

"Papà, are you hurt?" Teresina's face was close to his, as he lay in an ungainly heap on the floor.

"Inventore!" Florio and Gaspare were there, one on either side of him, helping him to his feet.

"What were you thinking?" Florio reprimanded him.

"You should've called us," Gaspare chimed in.

They worked seamlessly to bring him back to his workbench and retrieve the wood he'd taken such trouble to collect.

Teresina walked up to him and stared sternly. "Papà, Lucrezia Alchimista will not be pleased if she has to come out here to heal you again. Besides, what are you doing working on this? It's Riposidi and you need to bring me to Aveline's house to get my hair done."

Aveline's house? Telchide froze. He'd completely forgotten about that. He reached out and caressed Teresina's cheek.

"I'm sorry, Resi, but I don't think we're welcome at her house right now."

Teresina frowned. "Why not?"

Telchide glanced at Florio and Gaspare, both of whom avoided his eyes.

"She's, erm, very busy right now."

Teresina crossed her arms and raised her eyebrows. "Papà, just because *you* had an argument with her last night, doesn't mean *I'm* not welcome there anymore. Besides, if you apologise, I'm certain she'll forgive you."

Telchide's shoulders sagged. How could he possibly explain it all to her?

"I'm sorry, Resi."

"But she'll be expecting me!" Teresina stamped her foot.

"I can take her," Gaspare suggested. "And Florio can stay to help you. Would that be acceptable, Inventore?"

Telchide weighed his options. "Indeed. Only let me write a note to Aveline first."

He tore a page from his notebook and began to write.

Aveline,

Forgive my daughter's intrusion but she couldn't understand why we are no longer welcome in your home. If you wish to send her away before doing her hair, you are more than justified in doing so. I have warned her you might, to spare you any difficulties.

I apologise for Serenita talking out of turn. She had no right and I'm sorry it means we won't be working together anymore.

Please know that I release you from your kind offer to install the chair lift in my house. I do not wish to cause you to feel unduly awkward.

If you would do me the kindness of not offering any extra visits to my daughter, that would probably be best for all involved.

If a time comes when you feel comfortable working with me again, I will welcome that with no other expectations.

Your friend,

Chide

With a heavy heart, Telchide sealed the letter with his Inventrici Guild seal and silver wax and handed it to Gaspare.

"Please make sure Aveline reads this before you enter the house. Teresina, if Aveline declines to do your hair, I do not want to hear that you pleaded or argued. Is that understood?"

Teresina frowned. "But papà..."

Telchide held up a hand. "Teresina, I won't even allow you to go if you do not promise me this."

He stared at her until she nodded. "I promise, papà."

She slipped her hand into Gaspare's and led him to the door. Telchide turned back to his workbench as soon as they'd left. He would return to his work, but while it had helped him survive Sebetine's disappearance, this time he would *not* let it consume him. It would just be one of the ways he survived Aveline's choice to be rid of him. This time, he wouldn't let himself fall into the same pit of despair. He would spend more time with his daughter, not forgetting to laugh and smile for years on end. He would train his two new apprentices to the best of his ability so that perhaps they could all work together one day on exciting new inventions.

"Erm, Inventore?" Florio stood beside him. "We were going to modify the Spiderseat for you today, remember?"

Telchide's nodded automatically. One project or another, it wouldn't matter what it was, as long as it took his mind off Aveline and the fact that she wouldn't have him.

"Yes, let's do that first then."

He instructed Florio about which items they would need and worked together with the boy to create a directional arm for the Spiderseat's sensor to follow and reinstalled the back of the seat so he wouldn't fall off it as the Spiderseat moved around.

Within an hour, Telchide was comfortably settled in the Spiderseat and navigating himself all around the workshop. He knew the Spiderseat could manage the few stairs down to the street without toppling, but it was not designed to go up an entire flight of stairs. The crutches would still be necessary for that, but this was a vast improvement.

Florio stayed by his side the rest of the day, fetching whatever was required for him, asking questions in an unobtrusive way. Telchide barely noticed when the boy disappeared, but every now and then he would reappear with tea, or a tray of food. He didn't know if Serenita was purposely making herself scarce because of her smoking interference with Aveline the evening before, but he was selfishly glad not to have to deal with her today.

When Gaspare escorted Teresina back home a few hours later, he bore a letter sealed with Electrum wax and the Inventrici Guild Mark. The boy held out the envelope, but Telchide only looked at it until the boy set it on his workbench and walked away. He desperately wanted to know what was inside but was too scared to open it. So, he ignored it, or tried to, all day.

Eventually, when the entire household was asleep and Telchide was secluded in his room, he finally opened the letter.

Telchide,

Your daughter was no trouble whatsoever. I hope you don't mind, but I allowed her to keep the very simple, and not at all expensive, lace trinzale and leather lenza. I taught Gaspare to secure it properly so Teresina can wear it whenever she likes without visiting me.

Serenita's forceful opinions were difficult to listen to, however, her words made it very clear to me that I cannot allow you to court me. I'm sorry. It may be selfish of me, but I cannot agree to a life involving your first companion's mamma. Nor could I bear to be the reason you send her away.

I stand by my desire to work on the fuel cell with you. It would be unfair for either of us to work on it entirely alone. My idea of working one night each with Nevio driving you may not be the best solution for the main part. Perhaps I could

*agree to work together with you one full day a week, to share and compare notes,
but I cannot promise to commit to that arrangement.*

*If you could find a suitable time, when Serenita will not be present, I would
still like to install the chair lift at your house. Your current situation is one of the
many reasons I wanted to create it in the first place. It seems foolish not to install
it because of a little discomfort on my behalf. Please send one of the twins with
enough notice for me to make the arrangements to come.*

Your colleague,
Aveline

Telchide read the letter over and over again. His anger with Serenita grew
stronger with every minute. Aveline had worked easily beside him, the three
apprentices and Teresina all got along marvellously well. But Serenita seemed
to be ruining everything she had a hand in. Why hadn't she just kept her
thoughts to herself? She wasn't *his* mamma. She'd had no right to interfere
so disastrously. How could she so thoroughly destroy any hope he had of a
life with Aveline?

He lay down, angrily, sleep evading him for hours as he seethed with anger.
Tomorrow was Gildadi. He would have Sebetine declared dead and effectively
end his companionship. No matter what Aveline's decision was, that was still
an important step.

Chapter 35 – Gildadi 9 Alchimisti 230 Years After Implosion

Telchide woke with his alarm, tired from the few hours of sleep. A wave of guilt swept over him, but he brushed it aside angrily. He'd felt guilty about Sebetine for too long. He knew it wasn't entirely Eduardo's fault, but he'd been blaming himself entirely for three years and was happy to shift some of the blame. With new apprentices in his life, and his beloved daughter to think of, he would try not to let his work entirely consume him again.

There was a soft knock on his door.

"Yes?" Telchide called out.

The door opened and Florio poked his head in. "Inventore, do you need help getting dressed?"

Telchide swallowed down his anger. Florio had done nothing wrong. Only Serenita and Eduardo had.

"Thank you, Florio. That would be appreciated."

Telchide tried to stand and reach for his crutches for the hobble to the water closet, but Florio would not let him until he'd pulled a sock and shoe onto Telchide's good foot, tying the laces securely.

"Is there anything else you need, Inventore?"

Telchide shook his head and waited until the boy had left his room before reaching out for his crutches and lumbering upright. He felt odd allowing the boys to call him "Inventore", but Kesida had insisted. It was how he'd addressed his own maestro so hopefully he would get used to it soon.

By the time he was finished with the water closet, he could hear loud voices in the kitchen. Not quite in argument but definitely raised.

"Gaspare, I won't tell you again, keep your hands away from my stove," Serenita waved a wooden spoon at him. "You can earn your keep some other way if you're determined to do so."

"Sorry, Serenita," mumbled Gaspare. "I was only trying to help."

"*I* need help today," Telchide said, purposely avoiding Serenita's look.

Teresina ran over and flung her arms around his waist. Telchide stifled a groan. His broken ribs did not enjoy this kind of abuse.

"I can help you, papà!"

Telchide thought quickly and bent down towards her. "I believe Serenita will need your help choosing a Copper Sarta to make some new clothes for the boys. You can make sure the Sarta doesn't try to cheat her."

Teresina jumped up in excitement, almost butting heads with him. Telchide reeled back just in time but lost his balance. The world spun as he fell. In a matter of moments, the twins were by his side, picking him up off the floor.

"I'm so sorry, papà!" Teresina cried out.

She looked ready to burst into tears. Telchide forced a smile and stroked her cheek with his finger.

"My little Resi, I know it was an accident. You're just so excited. Try not to be so excited at the Sarta's. We wouldn't want Serenita to fall."

Serenita scowled at him. "Out! Out of my kitchen. No breakfast for you today."

Telchide shrugged coldly. "Never mind, I have errands to run. Florio, Gaspare, finish your breakfast and then come meet me in the workshop."

He walked out of the kitchen and laboured down the stairs, ignoring Serenita's shouted complaints. It was remarkable how liberated he felt. The guilt swept over him in a wave, almost knocking the wind out of him. Telchide brushed it away. He would not let guilt stop him.

He paused at his workbench.

But he was the one who was glad he could finally request that Sebetine be declared deceased. All so he could court a woman who now refused to have him. Telchide felt dizzy. He reached for his Spiderseat and sat heavily.

He was still sitting, staring at nothing, when Gaspare ran down the stairs, chased by a shouted protest from Serenita. Telchide looked up at the sound. Gaspare stood before him, holding out a slice of buttered bread.

"Breakfast, Inventore. Can't be running errands on an empty stomach."

Telchide took the bread gratefully and nibbled at it. Gaspare stood for a moment, then pulled up a seat beside him.

"Inventore, if you don't mind me asking, what errands are we running today?"

Telchide took out his notebook. It was always easier for him to order his thoughts on paper. He spoke as he wrote.

"I need to go to the Authorities; and organise for Aveline to fit the chair lift to our stairs. We'll need to work out a schedule between our regular work and our joint efforts."

"We know the way to Aveline Inventrice's workshop," Florio said, as he came down the stairs. "Would you like me to organise a time on your behalf after trading hours?"

Telchide shook his head slowly. "Actually, if you could let her know that Serenita will be going out this morning, should she wish to come then, that would probably be best."

The boys glanced at each other uneasily but neither commented on the arrangement.

"Er ... which Authorities are we going to?" Gaspare asked after an awkward pause.

Telchide stared at him. "Which Authorities indeed. I don't know."

Gaspare and Florio exchanged glances.

"What do you need the Authorities for?" Gaspare asked. "Is it a Guild matter?"

"No. I need to have my companion declared dead," Telchide said.

The boys looked at each other with uncertainty. Telchide couldn't decipher their expressions.

"Inventore, you don't have a companion."

Telchide frowned. "Well, of course I do. How do you suppose Teresina was born?"

They did not answer.

"Oh, I see. Kesida did not mention her to you."

They shook their heads. Telchide sighed. With any luck, he wouldn't have to deal with such difficulties soon.

"My companion, Teresina's mamma, has been missing for three years. Until recently, we didn't know what could have happened to her. But I now have reason to believe that she is, in fact, dead. I need to alert the authorities to this."

"Inventore!" cried Gaspare.

"That's terrible!" gasped Florio.

The brothers looked at each other and agreed something by unspoken communication. Telchide wondered how they did that.

"I'll go to Aveline Inventrice's workshop," Florio told him. "Gaspare will go to the Tor'Esint Authorities, they're the ones you need, and ask them to come here. After all, they might need to question more than just yourself about the matter."

Gaspare nodded his consent. "Yes, that will give you all day to work on your music box and take any other orders."

Telchide began to protest.

"Please, Inventore," Florio pleaded. "Let us do this for you. If we can't begin our apprenticeships yet, we want to do everything we can to be helpful. Your music box looks complicated and will take a long time to finish. Don't waste a day's work on something we can help you with."

Telchide didn't know what to say. They were right, of course. He should utilise them in any way possible until they could start their apprenticeship.

"Very well," he relented. "Florio, ask Aveline if this morning suits her. If not, find a time that she prefers, and I will ensure Serenita makes herself scarce."

Florio nodded, but still looked slightly uncertain. Telchide frowned and tried to think why.

"I'm certain you heard the tone if not the words last night. Aveline and Serenita had ... a difference of opinions. After Aveline installs the chair lift, it's quite possible she won't be a guest in our house for ... quite some time." He paused, distracted by the sudden tightness in his chest. "I'm certain we can arrange for you to visit Nevio. It would be good for you to have a fellow Inventore apprentice as a friend."

The twins nodded but said nothing further. They unlocked the door and closed it gently behind them. Telchide stared after them a while. He wished his maestro had encouraged him to make friends with the other apprentices around Tor'Esint while he was young. If nothing else, at least he was doing this one thing right by the boys.

***

Serenita left the house with Teresina in tow not a half hour after the twins had departed. If Aveline was going to come today, it would be soon. Telchide couldn't concentrate on anything too complicated. He busied himself with the smaller music boxes. He could complete the template orders and set up the new ones in preparation for the sheet music to arrive.

Every time a person walked past his workshop window, Telchide looked up in anticipation, hoping to see Aveline. When she finally arrived, he was caught unawares as he'd led the Spiderseat over to his spare workbench to test another copper music strip.

The bell above the door tinkled as she walked in alone with a large wicker basket. His mouth went dry, his heart raced. He'd not expected her to come alone.

"Where's Florio?" he asked, inwardly cursing himself for not greeting her properly.

Aveline set down the heavy basket and raised an eyebrow at him. "He and Nevio were getting along like lava down a mountain. I thought it unfair to drag him back here when his apprenticeship hasn't begun yet."

She took a pulley out of the basket and walked over to the stairs.

"Will you need one of my chairs?" Telchide asked, as she began working.

"No, something rudimentary will do for now. Do you have a square of wood strong enough to take your sitting weight? If you could bolt it to a thicker, but smaller piece of wood, I can attach the magnet to it."

Telchide led the Spiderseat over to his wood stores, careful to maintain his distance from Aveline. He found two suitable pieces of wood and secured them together with a handful of bolts. When he was done, he tried to bring it over to her, but almost toppled out of the Spiderseat as the wood fell from his grip and clattered to the floor.

Aveline glanced over. "Leave it there. I'll get it when I'm ready. Could you just come over here and keep this section of the pulley in place as I take the other end up the stairs?"

Telchide led the Spiderseat over to the stairs and almost fell when it bumped into the wall. All that stopped him falling sideways was Aveline catching hold of him. Her hair tickled his nose as she propped him back up again. He couldn't avoid taking her arms to steady himself.

Smoking Caldera but it felt good to touch her!

"I think perhaps I should've asked Florio to come back to help me after all." Aveline's voice with thick with emotion as she moved away from him. He let go of her reluctantly. "Hold the pulley steady over the banister."

Before Telchide could reply, she was off up the stairs, carrying the rest of the pulley system with her. It didn't take her long to attach it at the top of the stairs and tighten it to her desired tension. Telchide kept his end steady until she descended the stairs to take it from him.

Not wanting any further awkwardness, he released it to her and moved all the way back to his workbench. Aveline did not complain. She fetched the supercharged magnet out of her wicker basket. He couldn't see exactly what she'd used to insulate it, but this time it didn't fly out of her hand when she went to attach it to the pulley system.

Before she connected the seat to the contraption, she hammered a thin sheet of metal to the thicker wooden block. It was a marvellous idea. Instead of needing two supercharged magnets, this ensured she only needed one, drastically reducing the cost she'd have to pass on to her customers. From his angle, he couldn't quite see what else she was doing.

"There. Let's try it," she said. "Come and sit here."

Telchide led his Spiderseat over and very carefully stood. He did *not* want another incident. Aveline made way for him. He manoeuvred himself from the Spiderseat to the chair lift. The seat was rather hard and uncomfortable, but he wouldn't complain if this worked.

"I've attached the hand crank above the chair, as you can see, so you don't have to wait for someone to help you." She paused and looked straight into his eyes. "I thought that might be best."

"Indeed." Telchide forced a smile. "Very thoughtful of you."

She stepped back and gestured at the pulley. "Well, try it."

The hand crank was surprisingly easy to use, not requiring nearly so much force as Telchide had anticipated. With only a little effort, he began to inch his way up the stairs. Halfway up, he re-evaluated his stance on the ease of use.

"It's a bit of a strain," he puffed. "Though that might just be the broken ribs talking."

Aveline's eyes went wide. "Oh, I forgot about that. Let me help you!"

She raced up the stairs, skirts swishing his legs as she went past him, and took over the hand crank. With exaggerated ease, she began to turn it, walking up just a step ahead of him as the chair moved.

It took all his strength not to reach out to touch her skirt, her arm – Sweet Caldera –*anything!* At the top of the stairs, she held her hand out to him, then quickly clenched her fist and withdrew it. Her emotions appeared to mirror his own, both of them struggling.

"Well, it works," she said with a smile that looked forced. "It won't really be useful if someone isn't home to fetch your crutches up or down the stairs, but otherwise, it should be some help."

Telchide nodded. "It will be a great help. And if we attach a wind-up key, here, it could automate the hand crank so I can hold the crutches on the way up or down."

Aveline took a step closer to see where he was pointing. It was obvious that she was trying to stay as far from him as possible, but her scent wafted over him as she leaned over to inspect the hand crank.

"Yes, that would make it much easier for more elderly customers as well." She retreated down to the workshop. "Have you any materials to make that now or shall I come back later to fit one?"

It was difficult to have a conversation with her from the top of the stairs. Telchide reversed the direction of the hand crank and began turning. Two turns were all it took for the crank to flick out of his hand and spin wildly, letting the chair slide down unfettered. Telchide held onto the seat of the chair so tightly his knuckles went white.

To his surprise, he didn't fall. The chair slowed towards the bottom. It was only when he reached the bottom that he noticed an extra device at this end of the pulley system.

"Aveline, what's this?"

He pointed to the odd metallic cylinder that had prevented a catastrophic landing. Aveline leaned in to see where he was pointing.

"Oh, that's my hydraulic preventer."

Telchide raised his eyebrows. "Your what?"

"My hydraulic preventer," she repeated, smiling broadly. "I picked it up at the Inventrici Convention in Tor'Dumere last year. They were the ones who developed the mechanism to force a speeding blazermobile to stop before it runs out of blazer fluid. Isn't it marvellous?"

Telchide transferred himself to the Spiderseat to inspect it. It looked like two metal cylinders, one inside the other.

"What's inside it?"

"The hydraulic fluid," Aveline told him. "The Inventore in Tor'Dumere had his Alchimista develop it specifically for this purpose. The Mercantili Guild doesn't have such a stranglehold on them there."

Not for the first time, Telchide wished this smoking Edict could be revoked. Not that it would solve his problems with Aveline, or Eduardo for that matter, but perhaps he could then start working with Lucrezia instead. Perhaps, in fact, she just might work with him anyway. He could ask her at their next meeting.

"I'll be off then," Aveline said suddenly. Telchide only belatedly realised the yawning silence between them. "I'll try to rig up a way to automate it, but at least you have a rudimentary working chair lift for the time being."

"Thank you, Veli. Aveline." He lengthened her name when she flinched. "Forgive me. I ... did not mean to be so familiar with you."

She tilted her head and pursed her lips. "Yes, well. I might send Nevio around with the automation once it's ready. The two of you will be able to fit it together and he can report back to me on how it works."

Telchide swallowed. This was it – the last time they would spend any time together aside from the sparking plants project, without even the intimacy of friendship to comfort them. He wanted to say so much to her. He held out his hand to her. Pleadingly. She looked down at his hand, eyes glazed over with tears.

"I ... can't Chide. I'm sorry."

In a flurry of activity, she collected her belongings and left, leaving Telchide alone and wondering what it would take to bring her back into his life in a meaningful way.

***

Serenita and Teresina returned soon after Aveline's departure, closely followed by Florio. Telchide largely ignored Serenita but led his Spiderseat over to Teresina and scooped her into a warm embrace. She laughed and hugged him gently, thankfully remembering his ribs! Determined not to let Aveline's abrupt departure ruin his entire day, Telchide led the Spiderseat, with Teresina in his lap, over to the new chair lift.

"Oh papà, is this what you were working with Aveline on? Can I try it?"

She jumped off his lap and onto the seat without waiting for his permission and immediately began turning the crank. Her delighted squeals brought a smile to Telchide's face. She made it halfway up the stairs before giving up and turning the crank the other way. With a whoop of joy, she held on tight as the chair lift glided back down to the bottom of the stairs, with Florio waiting to catch her in case she fell.

"Papà it's wonderful! Just imagine what you'll come up with for your special project together!"

Telchide could only nod in response, glancing at Serenita who squared her shoulders and did not flinch. Somehow, that only served to increase his anger with her. Before either of them had the chance to make the situation worse, Gaspare returned from his errand, followed by a Tor'Esint Amministratore, dressed in his navy uniform with the Tor'Esint Crest on his left breast pocket.

Serenita frowned. "What's the meaning of this?"

"Signora, we're here about the request to declare the death of Sebetine di Serenita," the Amministratore told her.

"What?" she asked in a whisper, turning to Telchide. "You're declaring my Sebetine dead?"

He shook himself free of her wounded eyes, suddenly ashamed he hadn't already mentioned this to her. "In light of recent events, I thought it appropriate."

The Amministratore looked between them uncertainly. "Which of you is the next of kin?"

"Papà, what's happening?" Teresina asked, slipping her hand into his and squeezing tightly. Telchide pressed her hand to his cheek, not knowing how to explain it to her.

"Gaspare, Florio, will you take Teresina upstairs? I'll explain everything later, Resi." He handed her over to the young men and waited until he heard her bedroom door close before turning back to the Amministratore. "As her companion, I'm her next of kin. This is Serenita."

"Ah, Sebetine's mamma, yes? We'll need you at the hearing. For now, I have a few questions to ask Telchide before we progress to that stage. Shall we take a seat?"

The Amministratore sat in a chair by the door and waited expectantly. Serenita shot Telchide an injured look as she brushed past him and up the stairs.

"I didn't realise a hearing would be necessary," Telchide said, finally leading his

Spiderseat to the other side of the workshop. "I'm ... not a good public speaker."

The Amministratore shook his head. "It will be a discreet hearing at the Tor'Esint Town Hall in the private chambers of Ministro Ercolano. We can even hold it tomorrow if we can get everyone together in time. Now, first thing, explain to me the circumstances surrounding this request."

Telchide related the story by rote, he'd repeated it so many times now. The Amministratore asked clarifying questions here and there, but mostly just listened. As he was finishing, the workshop door burst open and Filippo Falgename walked in, directing his workers to bring in the new bed, his Electrum arm shining in the sunlight.

"Chide, you finally did it! You applied for an apprentice. I'm so proud of you!" He paused and looked around when Telchide didn't greet him, his eyes losing their spark as they landed on the Tor'Esint Amministratore. "What's going on?"

"Maestro Filippo!" The Amministratore jumped to his feet. "I'm here at Telchide Inventore's request."

"It's Sebetine," Telchide explained.

"You found her?" Filippo sat down hard on the spare chair. "After all these years, you finally found her?"

Telchide shook his head. "No, I'm..." He turned to the Amministratore who cleared his throat.

"He wants to declare her death."

"Oh Chide, I'm so sorry we never found her."

The Amministratore startled at that. "*You* had a hand in all of this?"

"Of course! I helped Chide as much as I could in those first weeks. Even Carlotta did what she could."

"I see," the Amministratore said slowly. "We may need you both for the hearing tomorrow then. Is there anyone else we need?"

At a cough from Filippo's workers, he turned and remembered himself.

"Take it upstairs and then you're done for the day. Thank you, signori."

The workers nodded and got to work, leaving Filippo to devote all his attention to the task at hand.

"Who's on the list so far?"

The Amministratore consulted his notebook.

"Telchide Inventore, Serenita di Albertina, Teresina di Sebetine, yourself and Maestra Carlotta," he said.

Filippo clicked his fingers, repeatedly, a look of concentration on his face. "What's the name of that Corallino who drew the likeness of Sebetine for you?"

"Ciro," Telchide said automatically. "Ciro Corallino."

The Amministratore scribbled down his name and looked up. "I suppose we'll need the Alchimista, what was his name again?"

"Alchimista?" Filippo asked, putting his hand on Telchide's arm to prevent him from answering.

"Yes, the Alchimista with the pills?" He looked expectantly at Telchide.

"I see." Filippo smiled carefully. "You must have a lot of work to do to prepare this hearing by tomorrow. Why don't we let you get on with it and I'll organise the people to come along tomorrow with Chide. Will ten o'clock be suitable for you?"

The Amministratore looked surprised, but then shrugged. "Yes, fine. I'll clear Ministro Ercolano's schedule for ten o'clock. Mind you bring everyone necessary and don't be late."

Filippo smiled politely and ushered him out of the workshop along with the two Falegname workers who happened down the stairs at that moment. Telchide was left wondering what had just happened.

"Chide, what's this about the Alchimista?" Filippo asked him as soon as the Amministratore was gone.

Telchide explained about Eduardo's purple pills and watched as Filippo's eyes grew larger.

"Oh Chide, what have you done?" Filippo asked, rubbing his temples between his fingers. "I'll try to make excuses for Carlotta so that she doesn't come. The last thing you need is to give a Maestra of the Mercantili Guild reason to accuse anyone from the Alchimisti Guild of wrongdoing. We'll have to keep this as quiet as we can. Now, is there anyone you can think of who will be a good character witness for both you and Eduardo?"

"I didn't mean to get him in trouble. I just wanted to put this all behind me." Telchide twisted his fingers anxiously. "Maybe Aveline and Kesida can help, Lucrezia too if it comes to it."

Filippo rose to go. "Send messages to them all asking to meet here tomorrow morning. Eduardo and Ciro too. We'll need to go over what we can and can't say, especially if I can't stop Carlotta from coming."

Telchide covered his mouth, nodding, suddenly feeling ill. What had he done?

Chapter 36 – Ramedi 10 Alchimisti 230 Years After Implosion

As the Tor'Esint Guild Halls clanged out nine bells, Telchide's workshop flooded with people from four Guilds. He sat to one side in his Spiderseat as they made polite introductions to each other, Teresina on his lap unusually silent. Earlier that morning, he'd sorted through the boxes Serenita had set aside with Sebetine's personal items to find the cameo Ciro had made for her. If there was only one thing that Teresina could have to remind her of her mamma, that should be it. Kissing the top of her head, Telchide held his daughter close as she traced her finger over the carving of Sebetine on the cameo brooch pinned to her bodice.

"Thank you all for coming," Filippo said in a loud voice. Everyone quieted down and turned their attention to him. "As you all know, we're here to support Chide at the hearing to declare Sebetine's death. Unfortunately, the circumstances are less than ideal."

"You can say it's my fault. I know everyone's thinking it," Eduardo said bitterly.

"It *is* your smoking fault!" Lucrezia spat. "Why didn't you do more testing before you gave those pills to Sebetine? And poor Teresina! She's slept fine using my sleeping pills and I didn't damage her memory."

"Alchimisti, *please*!" Filippo shouted. "This is exactly why we're meeting here beforehand. I tried to keep my companion out of it, but she was determined to ensure the Mercantili aren't found at fault through anything to do with the funicolare. For those who don't know, my companion is Carlotta Mercantessa, Maestra of the Mercantili Guild. If you continue your bickering at the hearing, she'll ensure the Alchimisti Guild are thoroughly investigated for any wrongdoing."

"How can you stay committed to a person like that?" Lucrezia muttered, none too softly.

Filippo shot her a withering look but did not respond.

"I've already mentioned Eduardo's pills to the Amministratore," Telchide pointed out. "We can't keep that out of the hearing."

"True, but if we stick to Eduardo's story that they were not used as prescribed, he might not be prosecuted himself," Filippo explained. "Lucrezia, you may need to back him up with your anecdotes of customers overusing certain medicines if it comes to it. Can you do that?"

Lucrezia sniffed and lifted her chin. "Of course. Customers are all idiots. Every Alchimista know that! If you don't explain things to them three times and write it down, they come back to complain their medicine isn't working properly."

Teresina giggled suddenly. Telchide covered her mouth in embarrassment as Lucrezia glared at her.

"Right then, let's go together down to the Tor'Esint Town Hall. Chide, you've got everything you need, yes? Sebetine's letter, the newssheets with her likeness?"

Telchide patted his breast pocket and nodded, leaving instructions for Florio and Gaspare not to touch anything while he was out.

***

They made a strange procession, the eight of them walking together. Teresina walked hand in hand with Aveline just in front of him – their easy intimacy a painful sight for Telchide to see. Lucrezia and Eduardo ahead of them, heads bent together discussing something in voices too low for anyone else to hear. Ciro and Serenita led the way, arm in arm, setting the pace for everyone else. Beside him, Filippo walked in a broody silence.

"I did not mean to cause trouble between you and Carlotta," Telchide told him softly.

Filippo huffed. "Chide, *everything* causes trouble between us these days. One more problem won't make a difference."

At the stairs of the Tor'Esint Guild Hall, Telchide hobbled up with Filippo's help, while Aveline, Lucrezia and Eduardo carried the Spiderseat up to the landing. They entered just as the Guild Hall clocks struck ten o'clock. Carlotta Mercantessa was already inside waiting for them, her foot tapping impatiently. Just the sight of her made Telchide angry, masking the nervousness which had settled in his stomach. *She* was the person responsible for the Trading Edict and the Inter-Guild Edict.

"Filippo, where have you been?" she snapped. "I've been waiting here a quarter of an hour already."

"Amore, the hearing was scheduled for ten o'clock," he replied with strained politeness. "I *told* you that. It's not my fault if you arrived early. Your Guild Hall is right next door. I'm sure it won't inconvenience you too much. Don't forget, Sebetine went missing on *your* precious funicolare."

Carlotta pursed her lips, her tapping foot stilled. Telchide had never been able to find anything in common with Carlotta. His visits to their household had been spent entirely with Filippo, until the day Sebetine disappeared. He hadn't understood Carlotta's interest and compassion then, but it all made sense now. If Sebetine's disappearance was due to a problem with the funicolare, the Mercantili Guild would be found at fault.

A door opened off to the side and Ministro Ercolano himself stepped out. Telchide, throat suddenly dry, still couldn't believe the Ministro of Tor'Esint himself would preside over the hearing.

"Telchide Inventore in the case of the disappearance of Sebetine di Serenita" he read from his ledger before looking around at all their faces in some surprise. "I didn't realise we were expecting so many people. Come in then. Adriano, we'll need a few more chairs. And coffee. Lots of coffee."

The Amministratore by his side motioned to two of his colleagues who instantly scurried out to fetch more chairs.

Within minutes, their entire party was seated comfortably in Ercolano's private chambers. Telchide was uncomfortably aware the Aveline had settled next to him. He hoped there was some way to get through this proceeding without bringing their tenuous relationship to light. Ercolano looked down at his ledger again and leafed through a notebook Telchide recognised from the day before where the Amministratore had written all the details of the case.

Eventually, Ercolano looked up and around the room until he found Telchide.

"Telchide Inventore, I'll keep this as brief as possible. I understand how painful this hearing must be for you, for everyone involved, but we must follow certain procedures." The Ministro looked at him with the same pitying eyes Telchide had come to expect from everyone when it came to Sebetine. "Now, I assume you have some proof that Sebetine was on her way to visit her mamma?"

Telchide nodded and pulled Sebetine's letter from his breast pocket. Teresina took it from his trembling hands with a small smile and walked it over to Ministro Ercolano. The Ministro took the letter and read it silently, then looked back over at Teresina.

"Do you still have dreams?" he asked kindly.

"Yes, Ministro," Teresina said in a quiet voice. "Papà and Nonna tell me I take after mamma because she dreamed a lot too."

"I see. And do you remember anything else about your mamma?"

Teresina shook her head. "I don't remember her at all. Papà remembers her for me, don't you papà?"

Telchide gave her a sad smile and nodded. He knew Ministro Ercolano's eyes were on him, but he couldn't bring himself to meet them. This was already so much more difficult than he thought it would be.

There were a few minutes of silence as Ministro Ercolano read further through the notes. Cups of coffee were brought in on a large tray, everyone taking a cup, even Serenita who, Telchide knew, hated the taste.

"I must ask, before we proceed, why you have you chosen not to wait the obligatory seven years for Sebetine to be declared dead rather than missing. It's highly unusual to hasten the process and could raise uncomfortable questions for everyone involved."

Telchide tugged at his collar, as everyone in the room stared at him.

"Well, you see, it's difficult," he faltered. "Living with the uncertainty. It's ... difficult."

Ministro Ercolano coughed. "I do understand, Inventore, but I need a more concrete reason than that."

Telchide's crumpled into himself as Aveline stiffened beside him. How could he possibly explain? The last thing he wanted to do was make things more difficult for Aveline.

"It's because of me," Aveline said in a calm voice, though Telchide could see her knuckles were white, her fists shaking slightly. "Telchide and I have recently grown close, working together on numerous projects the past few months. I think our feelings have taken us both by surprise. He wishes to court me, but he can't bring himself to while still committed to another woman."

Telchide couldn't help but stare at her. She'd lied. She'd outright *lied*. To set him free.

"Papà is that true?" Teresina asked, climbing up into his lap, her eyes going back and forth between him and Aveline.

"Yes, Resi. It's true," Telchide admitted. "I ... didn't know how to tell you. I don't want you to think I'm trying to replace your mamma."

Teresina glanced down at her mamma's cameo now clutched in her hand and rested her head against his chest. Telchide risked a glance at Aveline and caught her eye before she turned away.

"I believe that's reason enough," Aveline said. "Let's just get this over with. He's been through three years of scrutiny already. What more do you need of him?"

Ministro Ercolano ran a pen down his ledger, reading the list.

"Statements from friends regarding the relationship between Telchide and Sebetine before her disappearance. What was done to find Sebetine after her disappearance. Evidence to prove she didn't run away. Evidence for why you think she's dead be it by suicide or misadventure."

The formal proceedings began. Telchide sat there without contributing much himself. It seemed his words were the least useful or sought after in this matter. With something to gain from her death, it appeared Ministro Ercolano could not rely on his statements much at all.

Try as he might not to pay attention, not to let himself drown in the past again, Telchide couldn't help it. He was reliving those early days in agonising detail. His own guilt at not noticing the problems with Sebetine's memories was only mitigated by the fact that Eduardo had given her the pills in the first place.

"Now, this memory loss, tell me more about it," Ercolano said. "There was Alchimista involvement as I understand it."

Telchide saw Carlotta sit up straighter and Lucrezia bristle.

"Now you listen here," Lucrezia said, wagging a finger at the Ministro. "I'll not have blame laid at an Alchimista's feet for a customer's disregard of instructions. We've seen it twice in the same family now. Sebetine overdosed on the medicine, causing side effects that would never have occurred had it been used as prescribed.

"True, Telchide *should* have noticed the change in his companion but, by his own admission, he was also suffering *three years* of sleep deprivation alongside working towards his Silver Guild Mark. He didn't even know Sebetine sought medication to help her sleep. It's a wonder he had the presence of mind to mount as widespread a search for her as he did when she disappeared."

A deafening silence followed her words. Even Carlotta Mercantessa didn't dare say anything. Telchide was surprised to find Aveline was squeezing his hand. He looked over in surprise to see her smile of encouragement. It filled him with hope, despite the dreadful circumstances.

Ministro Ercolano closed his ledger and rose from his desk.

"Well, I think that's about everything I need. My decision will be published in the "Public Notices" section of the newssheets here and in Tor'Dumere, and you will receive notification of the decision before publication. In due time, both the formal record of my decision and copies of the certification of the dissolution of your union with Sebetine and her death certificate will be delivered to you. If you have a further case to answer, you will be summoned to court. Thank you for your time."

Telchide's fingers reached out reflexively as Aveline let go of his hand, but he clenched his fists, trying not to let anyone else notice. Teresina climbed out of his lap and took Aveline's hand once more as everyone filed out of the room.

"Inventore?" Ministro Ercolano stopped him before he left. "I'm sorry about your companion. It sounds like you were quite devoted to one another. It's a shame that it came to this."

Telchide didn't know what to say, so he nodded in thanks and left, guiltily hoping that this would finally be the end.

***

Out on Corso delle Gilde, the hearing party helped Telchide back down the stairs with his Spiderseat. Carlotta shook his hand and disappeared back into the Mercantili Guild Hall. Filippo watched her departure with narrow eyes.

"You two, watch your backs," Filippo told Lucrezia and Eduardo. "There's no telling what she'll do with this new information. The rest of you, just keep your heads down for a while. I don't know what's going on in there, but Carlotta's worried about something and that's usually bad news for every other Guild."

Telchide glanced at the Mercantili Guild Hall and shook his head. There was nothing else they could do to him – not if he stayed away from Eduardo, which was exactly what he intended to do.

"Thank you everyone, for your support today," Telchide said, voice thick with emotion. "I don't know what I'd have done without each and every one of you. Now, please, return to your workshops."

It was true. Even Eduardo and Serenita. Both, in their way, had helped him even if they had also been responsible for many of his difficulties. But he couldn't bring himself to look at them. His anger was still too raw.

Ciro and Filippo made their farewells and walked together down Corso delle Gilde back to continue their workday.

"Come, Teresina, come with me," Serenita said suddenly. "Let's walk the docks and find some nice fish for dinner."

Teresina turned to Telchide with raised eyebrows, but he nodded his assent and she happily skipped beside her nonna towards the docks.

"Chide, I'm going to Eduardo's to trade supplies. I'll pass by your place when I'm done to check you over."

And then there was just himself and Aveline, standing on the street, and he was too afraid to look her in the eye. They set off in silence, well behind the Alchimisti, walking in silence all the way to his workshop. He was surprised when Aveline followed him in, and more surprised when she asked Florio and Gaspare to give them a moment alone.

"I'm sorry I forced our situation into the open," he told her, when it appeared she didn't know how to begin. "I don't expect anything to change between us whether they approve my request or not. I've had time to think about it and it was wrong of me to ever expect you could be happy with our situations both so complicated as they are. But I do hope we can find a way to work together – on the sparking plant project at the very least. If nothing else, I do not want to lose your friendship. It means so much to me."

He watched her carefully as he spoke, the emotions flickering across her face too fast for him to read until she came to a decision.

"Perhaps..." She faltered. "Perhaps we can work on the sparking plant together, as we always meant to, but I will not – I *cannot* – be under the same roof as Serenita. Your boys, and Teresina, are free to visit me and Nevio as they please around trading hours and even while the two of us are at our new workshop, but I will *not* concede to Serenita's plan that we dine here after our working nights."

"Of course!" Telchide instantly agreed, holding out his hand to shake on it. "We can begin as soon as I have my Electrum Guild Mark so Florio and Gaspare can manage the workshop in my absence."

Aveline hesitated, but shook his hand firmly, her touch, as always, sending tingling sparks up his arm. The moment was broken by Lucrezia bustling into the workshop.

"Right, Chide, let's take a look at you." Lucrezia paused, and Aveline dropped Telchide's hand. "Come to an understanding, have you? Good! Now, Veli, out of my way. I'll see you at the Exploding Beakers in a few weeks."

Telchide felt Aveline's gaze lingering on him before she left the workshop. Friends might be all he could expect for now, but that didn't mean there was no hope for the future.

Chapter 37 – Legaramedi 12 Alchimisti 230 Years After Implosion

That morning, Telchide rode the chair lift down to the workshop and made himself comfortable in the Spiderseat with the morning's mail before noticing Teresina sitting under his workbench, reading a newssheet.

"Resi, what are you doing under there?" he asked with a laugh.

"Reading," she said quietly.

He nodded absently and opened the first letter.

Argentodi 11 Alchimisti
230 Years After Implosion
To Telchide Inventore, 6 Via Corallo, Tor'Esint
From Ministro Ercolano, Tor'Esint Town Hall, Corso delle Gilde

Dear Telchide,
After careful deliberation, it has been decided that Sebetine di Serenita will be declared dead. The paperwork will take some time to organise, but the decision will be published in tomorrow's newssheet for public notification.
I hope this brings some closure to your family.
Ministro Ercolano

Telchide read it twice, his eyes blurring suddenly. He blinked away the tears, folded the letter and peered under the workbench at Teresina. She looked up, almost guiltily, and handed the newssheet to him. Telchide spread it out over his workbench to read the "Public Notices" article.

This Legaramedi 12 Alchimisti, Sebetine di Serenita has been declared dead. Three years after her disappearance, new evidence came to light this week, extinguishing all hopes of finding her alive. The deceased is survived by her companion, Telchide Inventore, and daughter, Teresina di Sebetine. By order of Ministro Ercolano, charges will not be made for wrongful death.

"Did you understand all of that?" he asked her gently, holding her small hands.

Teresina chewed her lip. "Enough of it. They've agreed mamma is dead now."

"Yes, they have," he agreed. "Do you ... want to talk about it?"

She shook her head. "Do you?"

"No, my little one. I think we've said everything there is to say." He drew her close and kissed the top of her head. "If you can send nonna down though, I think I should tell her myself."

Teresina nodded and walked slowly up the stairs. She may not remember her mamma, but Telchide could see the news had still affected her.

A few minutes later, Serenita descended the stairs, drying her hands on the dishcloth tucked into her skirt.

"What is it, Telchide?" she huffed. "I was cleaning the breakfast dishes."

Telchide opened the newssheet again and read out the article to her. Serenita stilled, tears spilling down her cheeks. Try as he might, Telchide had no words of comfort for her. He was still furious over her carelessness with Teresina and her forceful demands of Aveline.

"It's done then." Serenita dried her eyes with her dishcloth. "You and Aveline are free."

"Don't talk to me of Aveline!" Telchide snapped. "If it weren't for you, none of this would be as difficult as it is. Just ... go upstairs."

He turned his back on her, not wanting to lash out further. There was work to be done, and that's what he would focus on.

***

The door opened with a chime from the bell. Telchide did not look up from his work. Florio and Gaspare had proven themselves quite handy during the previous days. They'd taken care of the front of the shop, while Telchide secluded himself away at his workbench. He took his meals downstairs now – all of them. In fact, he spent so much time downstairs that he'd barely seen Serenita since the hearing other than that very morning. The two of them weren't the only ones suffering through this situation. Something would need to be done to resolve it one way or the other.

"Kesida!"

The boys jumped to their feet and raced over to be the first to help her out of her coat. Telchide grumbled at the commotion. Glad as he always was to see Kesida, she was interrupting his work. He didn't bother looking up until she was standing by his side.

"Good morning, Kesida."

Kesida raised an eyebrow. "Good *afternoon*, Chide."

He looked over to the wall clock. Quarter past three. Where did the time go?

"It would seem so. I've been working on this music box, you see, and time gets away from me."

Telchide motioned to the modified version of a music box he was making for Signora Loyola. He hadn't asked his customer's permission to change it so dramatically, but he doubted she'd mind if it meant she got a whole song out of it rather than a fragment. Kesida looked at it closely.

"Curious. Doesn't look a thing like your others," she pointed out.

"No, I'm making a few modifications. I think this will work better for longer pieces of music. Perhaps I could submit the change when I'm done?"

Kesida raised an eyebrow at him. He'd chosen his wording very carefully not to ask, in company, about a patent. Even apprentices did not know about them until they applied for their Copper Guild Mark.

"We can discuss that when you've finished it," she replied evasively. "That's not the reason I'm here."

"Oh." Telchide rubbed his cheek. "Are you here to ensure I'm not mistreating the boys? I can assure you I'm not."

Kesida rolled her eyes. "Oh, for Caldera's sake, Chide. I *know* you're not mistreating them. I'm here to give you your Electrum Guild Mark. The boys are now officially your apprentices. Congratulations!"

She smiled proudly and reached out to undo his Silver Guild Mark pin, carefully replacing it with a brand new, shiny Electrum Guild Mark pin.

"Now, if you have a screwdriver handy, we can swap over the Guild Mark on your door."

Telchide wasn't really listening. He was staring down at the new Guild Mark on the collar of his shirt. He'd done it. He'd really done it. An Electrum Guild Mark! His chest swelled with pride. He heard Florio and Gaspare whoop, and the sound of Teresina running down the stairs. She peered at his new Guild Mark and hugged him as tightly as her little arms could manage.

Kesida laughed at the jubilation. "A screwdriver, Chide. I can't stay here forever."

"A screwdriver, of course."

Telchide put a screwdriver in his tool belt and led the Spiderseat over to the door. Gaspare opened the door for him and held it steady with Florio as Telchide got to his feet and took down the Silver Guild Mark from the door. Kesida took it and passed him the large Electrum Guild Mark. His hands trembled as he screwed it onto the door. An Electrum Guild Mark for all Tor'Esint to see!

"Oh papà, it's wonderful!" Teresina squealed, dancing around them happily.

Telchide stood back and admired his new rank. He could now rightfully charge more for his work and people would be forced to pay it if they wanted his wares. How much would Signora Loyola have paid him if he were already an Electrum Inventore when she'd ordered? And what of the simpler music boxes? Now he could charge an electrum for each one rather than ten or fifteen silvers.

"How about that," Kesida said softly by his side, "You're Aveline's equal now and you can work towards your Gold Guild Mark together."

A blush rose to his cheeks at the mention of her name. Kesida laughed lightly.

"Don't get any ideas, Kesida," Telchide chided her quietly. "Aveline still won't have me, but at least we have a plan to work together."

"Well, that's a start." Kesida admitted. "Good luck with it all, Chide. I'll see you at the next Inventrici meeting."

Telchide waved her farewell and then turned to the boys.

"Florio, Gaspare!" he announced happily. "Time to begin your apprenticeship."

They fought each other to be the first into the workshop.

"I want you to build a set of display shelves to go along this window. The wood is over there, the tools are here. My only rule is that you try before you ask for help. Understood?"

Telchide almost smiled. Training them would be quite the challenge.

Even if his life hadn't quite worked out the way he'd hoped, Aveline had promised they could work together. Perhaps, if they focused on their joint Guild Mark project, and made that work then the rest of their lives would fall into place.

Perhaps.

Whatever happened next, he refused to let himself fade away again.